... romance stories St...   ...re set
...against the backdrop of Regency Eng... ...ntinue
to exert a special attraction for her. As an escape from the
...y world of professional science, Stephanie started writing
Regency romances, and she is now a *New York Times*, *USA Today* and *Publishers Weekly* bestselling author.

Stephanie lives in a leafy suburb of Melbourne, Australia, with her husband and two daughters, along with two cats, Shakespeare and Marlowe.

Learn more about Stephanie's books from her website at www.stephanielaurens.com

Praise for Stephanie Laurens:

'This sensual tale of lust and seduction in 19th century
England will leave you weak at the knees'
Now

'Stephanie Laurens' heroines are marvellous tributes to
Georgette Heyer: feisty and strong'
Cathy Kelly

'Sinfully sexy and deliciously irresistible'
Booklist

The Reckless Bride

The Black Cobra Quartet

Stephanie
Laurens

piatkus

PIATKUS

First published in the US in 2010 by Avon Books,
An imprint of HarperCollins Publishers, New York
First published in Great Britain as a paperback original in 2010 by Piatkus
By arrangement with Avon

Copyright © 2010 by Savdek Management Proprietory Ltd

A CIP catalogue record for this book
is available from the British Library.

ISBN 978-0-349-40005-1

Printed in the UK by CPI Mackays, Chatham ME5 8TD

Papers used by Piatkus are natural, renewable and
recyclable products sourced from well-managed forests and certified
in accordance with the rules of the Forest Stewardship Council.

 Mixed Sources
Product group from well-managed
forests and other controlled sources
www.fsc.org Cert no. SGS-COC-004081
© 1996 Forest Stewardship Council
FSC

Piatkus
An imprint of
Little, Brown Book Group
100 Victoria Embankment
London EC4Y 0DY

An Hachette UK Company
www.hachette.co.uk

www.piatkus.co.uk

The Reckless Bride

She tried to suck in a breath, but her lungs had constricted. By sheer force of will she kept her feet moving and managed to climb the steps into the carriage. He released her hand and her senses snapped back into focus.

A second later, the carriage tipped as Carstairs climbed in. He hesitated, then sat alongside her, leaving the place beside Rose for Hassan.

Carstairs's shoulder brushed hers as he settled.

She couldn't breathe again. Worse, her wits had scattered. As for her senses, they were flickering and flaring, not in alarm but in a most peculiar way.

Fixing her gaze forward, she forced her lungs to work. It was preferable that Carstairs sat beside her rather than opposite; at least she didn't have him constantly before her. Bad enough that she could somehow *feel* him alongside her; his warmth, his solidly muscled strength, impinged on her consciousness as if every nerve she possessed had come alive and locked on him.

She was irritated and utterly mortified.

Prologue

September 15, 1822
North of Bombay, India

The incessant tattoo of his horse's hooves thundered through his skull. Rafe Carstairs, erstwhile captain in the British Army serving with the Honorable East India Company under the direct command of the Governor-General of India, glanced over his shoulder back along the trail, then urged his mount up the first in a series of low hills that spread across their path.

Riding alongside him, Hassan, his man, more companion than batman, kept pace. The long, lanky, frighteningly fierce Pathan warrior had fought at Rafe's side for the past five years; without hesitation, he'd accepted Rafe's invitation to join him in this dangerous flight across half the world.

Rafe's mission was simple. Ferry the original of a damning letter—evidence enough to hang the Englishman who had spawned and now controlled the Black Cobra cult and who, through the cult's vicious tyranny, was draining the life from too many Indian villages—back to England and into the hands of a man powerful enough to bring the Black Cobra down.

Simultaneously, Rafe's three closest friends and colleagues, Colonel Derek Delborough, Major Gareth Hamilton, and Major Logan Monteith, were also heading for England via separate routes carrying inadmissible copies of the vital evidence—decoys to distract the Black Cobra from the one man who had to get through.

Rafe.

Like Rafe, Hassan had seen too much of the Black Cobra's villany not to seize the chance they now had to bring the fiend to justice.

Drawing rein on the crest of the hill, Rafe wheeled his mount and, through narrowed eyes, searched the wide, flat plain they'd crossed through the morning.

Hassan looked, too. "No pursuers."

Rafe nodded. "It's too dusty down there to miss racing horses." Nerves that had been taut since they'd left Bombay the day before eased a fraction.

"Leaving immediately after your meeting with the other three was wise." Hassan wheeled his mount and walked on.

Rafe followed suit, then they nudged their horses back into a canter, heading nor'northwest. "If they didn't pick up our trail yesterday, soon after we left Bombay, it'll be difficult for them to guess our route."

"They will expect you to go by water—they will look to the harbor and ships. Even if they think to look inland, there will be no one to point a finger this way. We are just two tribal warriors, after all."

Rafe grinned and glanced at Hassan, unremarkable in his tribal robes. Rafe was similarly garbed. With his more European build swathed in loose fabric, his blond hair hidden beneath the headdress and attached scarves, and with all visible skin well tanned by years of campaigning, only his blue eyes gave him away.

And one had to get close to see the color of his eyes.

He looked ahead. "Given the cult aren't hot on our heels, it's possible we'll have an uneventful journey, at least until we near the Channel. I just hope the others got away as cleanly."

Hassan grunted. They picked up the pace and rode on, the rich lands of the Rajputana their immediate goal, with the more dangerous, desolate reaches of the Afghan Supremacy beyond. There was a lot of Asia Minor to be crossed before they reached Europe, let alone the English Channel. They had a long journey before them, and a schedule to meet.

Rafe still felt a sense of deep satisfaction that he'd been the one to draw the scroll-holder containing the original document from the four identical scroll-holders; the other three had contained the decoy missions. His friend and colleague Captain James MacFarlane had given his life to secure the incriminating letter. Rafe had seen James's body, twisted and tortured by the Black Cobra's minions. To his soul, Rafe thirsted for vengeance.

The only acceptable vengeance was to ensure the Black Cobra hanged.

Rafe tapped his heels to his mount's sides. "Onward. With luck and St. George, we'll win through."

They would, or Rafe would die trying.

September 18, 1822
The Michelmarsh Residence
Connaught Square, London

"I deeply regret being so disobliging, but I simply cannot accept Lord Eggles's offer." Loretta Violet Mary Michelmarsh surveyed her siblings and their spouses disposed on chairs and chaises about the library. She wasn't entirely sure why her rejection of Lord Eggles's suit was causing so much more consternation than the seven rejections that had gone before.

"But . . . why?" Catherine, Loretta's sister-in-law, her elder brother Robert's wife, spread her hands, her expression one of complete bafflement. "Lord Eggles is everything that could be hoped for—so very eligible in every way."

Except that he's a dead bore. And a pompous ass. "I believe I've mentioned," Loretta said, her tone one of the utmost reasonableness, "that I have no wish to marry—well, not at this juncture." Not until she met the man of her dreams.

"But Lord Eggles was the *eighth*—the eighth perfectly eligible suitor you've rejected!" Catherine's voice rose to a more penetrating note. "You cannot just keep rejecting suitors—everyone will start wondering why!"

"Will they?" Loretta raised her brows. "I can't imagine why they would waste the time."

"Because you're a Michelmarsh, of course." Margaret, Loretta's elder sister, glanced at Annabelle, their middle sister, then with a sigh met Loretta's gaze. "I hesitate to press you, but in this Catherine's right—your continuing dismissal of all suitors is bordering on the scandalous."

"You're a Michelmarsh female," Annabelle said, "so it's expected that you will wed. And while all would grant you've affected a quieter style than Margaret or I, or indeed any Michelmarsh young lady in recent memory, that in no way excludes you from that generally held expectation. All Michelmarsh females marry, usually well. Add to that the significant inheritances that will pass to your husband on your marriage and the question of who you will accept as said husband is one a sizeable portion of the ton is in constant expectation of hearing answered."

Loretta hadn't missed the subtle emphasis Annabelle had placed on the word "affected." The look in Annabelle's blue eyes assured Loretta that Annabelle, two years older than Loretta's twenty-four and closest to her in age, understood very well that Loretta's reserved demeanor was indeed an affectation, an adopted façade. And if Annabelle knew, Margaret did, too.

"What your sisters are attempting to explain," John, Margaret's husband, said from his position propped against the back of the chaise, "is that your peremptory and immediate dismissal of all suitors brave enough to approach is raising speculation as to whether, rather than the individual suitors, it is the institution of marriage you reject."

Loretta frowned. She knew precisely what she wanted in a suitor. She just hadn't found him yet.

Robert, her elder brother and guardian, seated behind the desk to the left of the straight-backed chair Loretta occupied, cleared his throat. Looking his way, Loretta saw color tingeing his cheeks. Embarrassment, she knew, not anger. Anger, after all, was a strong emotion, and Robert, aided and abetted by Catherine, had made a point of being the only Michelmarsh in history to be reserved, staid, prim and proper, as close to emotionless as made no odds.

In his case, that demeanor was no affectation.

Robert was the white sheep in a family of, perhaps not black sheep but at least distinctly brindled. Michelmarshes were, and always had been, the very souls of outrageous vivacity, extroverts to their very toes.

All except for Robert.

Orphaned at the age of twelve and left to Robert's guardianship, taken into his family and placed under Catherine's well-meaning but smothering wing, Loretta had quickly realized that affecting a prim and proper façade was the easiest path.

Over the years, following the easiest path had become a habit, one she'd discovered had pertinent benefits, namely shielding her from a social round she found largely unnecessary. Keeping her gaze downcast and her voice at a whisper meant she could stand by the side of a ballroom, or sit in a drawing room or dining room, and think of other things. Of things she'd read, of matters a great deal more stimulating than the company around her.

She'd come to appreciate that there was a great deal to be said for prim and proper behavior. It could be used to avoid all sorts of interactions she didn't want to be bothered with.

Like paying attention to gentlemen she had no interest in.

Her façade usually worked.

Sadly, some had been attracted to the façade and, given the many years' practise she'd put into perfecting it, she'd found it well nigh impossible to make them understand that the prim and proper, highly reserved young lady they thought would be perfect as their wife did not exist. At least not in her.

Hence the peremptory and immediate dismissals.

"My dear." Robert clasped his hands, lowered his chin to his cravat, and regarded her gravely from beneath his thickening brows. "I greatly fear that your current attitude to all suitors who approach cannot continue. You appear, as all here would agree, to be an exemplary paragon of delicate ladyhood and as such are viewed as the perfect match for gentlemen who seek such a wife. Lord Eggles would make you a fine husband. Having given my permission for him to address you—as indeed I have for the previous seven gentlemen—I feel I must press you to reconsider."

Loretta fixed her eyes on Robert's. "No." Irritation and anger swirled; she tamped both down, drew breath, and added in a steady, collected tone, "I cannot believe you would wish me to marry a gentleman for whom I feel nothing."

Catherine frowned. "But—"

"I am convinced, " Loretta continued, "that ultimately a suitable gentleman will appear and make an offer for my hand. Until then, I shall, of course, refuse all offers from gentlemen who do not . . ." She hesitated.

"Measure up to your expectations?" her younger brother Chester suggested.

He'd taken the words out of her mouth.

His blue eyes trained on her face, Chester went on, "Your problem, dear sister, is that you—prim, proper, exemplary paragon that you appear to be—attract the wrong sort of gentleman."

"Nonsense!" Catherine fluffed her shawl, an offended hen. "Lord Eggles is a paragon, too."

"Precisely my point," Chester replied.

"I have no notion what you mean," Catherine said.

She didn't, but Loretta did. The possibility had occurred to her, but it was a shock to discover that even twenty-one-year-old Chester saw through her façade—and saw the same problem she'd started to suspect.

"Perhaps"—Margaret looked at Robert—"in the interests of giving Loretta a chance to clarify what she wants in a husband, she might stay with us for a few months. The Little Season is about to start, and—"

"Oh, no." Catherine laid a hand on Robert's arm; she captured his gaze. "That wouldn't do at all." She glanced at Margaret and smiled placatingly. "Besides, I daresay you'll be atrociously busy entertaining all of John's political acquaintance. Hardly fair to ask you to chaperone Loretta as well."

While her sisters tried tactfully to ease her out from under Catherine's determined wing—a lost cause; Catherine would view Loretta transferring to Margaret's chaperonage as an admission of failure—Loretta wondered if political circles might indeed hold better prospects for her. She felt certain the man of her dreams existed somewhere—she was a Michelmarsh female, after all—but she had assumed he'd have the good sense to find her, present himself, woo her, and then make an offer which she would then accept.

It was all very clear in her mind.

Sadly, her theory had yet to translate into reality.

And she was increasingly concerned that Chester might be right. She might have to change her tack.

Even if only to avoid more suitors of the likes of Lord Eggles.

But change in what way? To what? And how?

"I'm sure—"

"Truly, it would be no great trouble. Why—"

"I really feel it wouldn't be right to—"

Focused on defining her direction, letting the arguments—futile—wash over her, Loretta was the only member of the company to hear the sounds of an arrival in the hall. She glanced at the double doors.

Just as they were flung wide, allowing a lady of striking magnificence to sail through.

She was tall, slender, her startlingly white hair superbly coiffed and finished with fine feathers, her gown the very latest Parisian fashion in ecru silk and lace, her jewelry classic pieces of ivory and jet. She wore long gloves and carried a filigree reticule while a velvet mantle in rich dark brown draped from her shoulders.

All conversation died.

The apparition halted, poised in the space midway between the open doors and the chaises, calmly considered the stunned expressions turned her way, then smiled. Delightedly.

Esme, Lady Congreve, spread her elegant arms and declared, "Darlings, I've come to steal Loretta away."

"You knew, didn't you?" Finally alone in the private parlor of the Castle Inn at Dover, Loretta sat, her back poker straight, in one of the twin armchairs before the hearth and fixed her gaze on her outrageous relative, elegantly disposed in the other armchair.

Until then, Loretta hadn't had a chance to ask the questions piling up in her head. From the instant of her declaration in Robert's library, Esme had taken charge. Like an unstoppable force, she'd rolled over all objections, explained in imperious fashion that she had need of a companion to accompany her on her imminent travels and that she'd determined Loretta would suit.

She'd given Robert and Catherine little time to mount any effective defense. Margaret, Annabelle, Loretta, and Chester had exchanged glances, then sat back to await developments.

Esme—she'd always insisted they call her Esme, rather than "Great-Aunt"—was their late father's oldest aunt, their late grandmother's elder sister. She was the last of her generation still alive, and therefore entitled to act as matriarch of the family.

A right she'd unexpectedly decided to exercise to the full.

Her husband, Richard, Lord Congreve, a Scotsman and

senior diplomat, had passed away fourteen months ago; matters pertaining to the settlement of his considerable estate had kept Esme in Scotland until now. In search of a change of scenery, she'd decided on a form of the Grand Tour—one in which she revisited all the European cities in which she and Richard had held court during his extensive career.

An unusually long and entirely literal trip down memory lane.

When Esme had let fall that she'd already sent orders to Loretta's maid to pack her mistress's belongings for a few months' travel, Loretta had not just seen but read the writing on the wall. She'd slipped out of the room to direct Rose, and take care of a number of other matters made suddenly urgent by the prospect of leaving London forthwith.

As she'd closed the library door behind her, she'd had very little doubt who would win the ongoing argument.

Less than half an hour later, she'd been summoned downstairs—and had left Robert's house in Esme's train.

In response to Loretta's question, Esme arched her finely drawn brows. "If you mean had I heard about the looming scandal your rejection of Eggles is about to cause, then yes, of course. Therese Osbaldestone wrote to me. That aside, however, I was heading your way regardless."

Loretta frowned. "To see Robert and Catherine?"

"No. To kidnap you."

"Why?"

"Because I promised Elsie that I would take you under my wing and do what she ran out of time to."

Elsie was Loretta's late grandmother. Esme and Elsie had been close. "She asked you to . . . take charge of me?"

"She asked me to ensure that you turned into the young lady you're supposed to be—a proper Michelmarsh young lady. To make sure you sloughed off this ridiculous reserve you've acquired under Robert and Catherine's tutelage. As well-meaning as they are—and please note I give them due credit for that—they were entirely the wrong people to have been given charge of you. Sadly, with your sisters and Chester too young and Robert so serious about taking on the responsibility of the head of the house, there wasn't any alternative at the time." Esme considered Loretta. "Now, however, matters have changed, as I made clear to Robert and Catherine. This entire near-scandal, and it is indeed that as Lord Eggles and his family are not at all amused at the implied insult of your abrupt rejection, is a direct and entirely predictable outcome of attempting to impose on a Michelmarsh young lady such an alien regimen as a prim and proper reserve."

Loretta eyed Esme with inner disquiet and welling resistance. "I often find a proper reserve very useful."

"Has it gained you the husband you wish for?"

"No."

"I rest my case. So now, if you please, you will travel with me and learn to live as a true Michelmarsh. And then . . ." Esme's words trailed away. A martial light gleamed in her eyes. "And then we'll see."

Loretta wasn't at all sure she liked the gleam in Esme's eyes. "You've never done this before, have you—acted as chaperone for a young lady?"

Esme, her gaze still dwelling assessingly on Loretta, shook her head. "No. No children, no grandchildren. I have to admit that until now I hadn't seen the attraction, but I do believe Therese Osbaldestone might be right—this will indeed be very like the *facilitating* one does as a diplomat's wife." Esme suddenly smiled. She met Loretta's eyes. "I do believe I'm going to enjoy transforming you into a fitting testament to your heritage, then parading you temptingly beneath the right gentleman's nose."

Loretta frowned.

Undeterred, Esme flicked her fingers at Loretta's skirts. "Apropos of which, I can only give thanks that our first stop will be Paris."

October 10, 1822
Caravanseri outside Herat, Afghan Supremacy

Rafe crossed his forearms on the weathered earthen wall and looked out across the desolate landscape eerily lit by the waning moon. Behind him, in the rectangular compound protected by the walls, a large trading caravan lay sleeping, the camels picketed to one side, the wagons staggered across the open gap that provided entry into the caravanseri. Tents and rude shelters lay deeper in the compound, protecting the caravan's people from the intensifying chill.

Out across the flat plain, nothing moved. Not robber, not cultist.

Standing on the narrow walkway hugging the inner face of the walls, Rafe stared out at the emptiness, at the rock-strewn plain unbroken by trees, with barely a stick of brush to soften the stark lines.

A zephyr whispered past, then faded. Died.

Rafe heard soft footsteps approaching. Hassan. They'd taken positions as guards with the trader who owned the caravan. It was the best camouflage they'd been able to find for crossing this too open, too uninhabited land.

"Still no sign of pursuit," Rafe murmured as Hassan halted beside him.

"There is no way the cult could trace us in such barren territory."

"No. So the next time we see them, they'll be ahead of us, waiting for us to come along. I wonder where?"

Hassan said nothing. A moment later, he walked on, circling the compound in the achingly cold silence.

Rafe drew his long cloak closer, and wondered where his friends, his three brothers-in-arms, slept tonight. Wherever they were, he suspected they'd be warmer than he, but were they safer?

He and Hassan had been lost to the cultists from the moment they'd ridden out of Bombay's northern gate. He doubted the other couriers had been so lucky.

Nearly a month into his mission, yet it had yet to truly start. Impatience niggled; he was a man of action—of facing enemies he could see, meet, and defeat.

Around him lay nothing. Not even a hint of a threat on the wind.

How long would it be before this hiatus ended and his final battle at last began?

November 3, 1822
Villa in Trieste, Italy

"We need to start for home—for England—now." Loretta folded her arms, her gaze on Esme's face. "You said you'd promised we'd be home for Christmas. If we don't start now, we'll never make it, and the weather will assuredly turn against us, too."

Reclining on a daybed before the windows of the drawing room of the villa she'd hired for their extended stay, Esme arched her brows. Consideration seeped into her otherwise relaxed expression, then she wrinkled her nose. "You're right. I do so hate traveling in slush."

Relief shot through Loretta; her trial was nearing an end. "So we'll head back to Venice, then via Marseilles to Paris?"

Frowning, Esme studied her, as she often did, assessingly. "Hmm . . . I'm not quite finished with you. You've learned to be more forthright, and we've rectified your wardrobe, thank heavens."

By "losing" all the demure and decorous clothes she'd brought from London. Loretta didn't bother glancing down at the periwinkle blue gown she wore, the color matching her eyes, the delicate fabric clinging lovingly to curves she would prefer remained hidden.

"And you can now laugh, converse, and dance with the best of them—not that I ever doubted you could." Esme wagged a finger at her. "But your flirting needs work, and you've declined to indulge in even one small fling. Your overall attitude still leaves much to be desired."

"Nonsense. There's nothing wrong with my attitude. If I happen to meet a man I find interesting, you may be sure I'll pay him due attention."

"Yes, well, therein lies the rub. You need to be interesting first, enough to make him draw near. Gentlemen—certainly those of the sort you'll find interesting—are like elusive game. They have to be tempted to draw close, so they can fall into the pit."

"You make it sound like hunting."

"Good gracious, girl, that's precisely what it is. You can't expect them to know what's best for them—they need to be persuaded to take the bit. But before we start bandying further metaphors, the fact remains that my work with you is not yet done. I have, therefore, decided that we will return to England by a different route. We'll head to Buda—Richard and I spent a pleasant few months there before the Treaty of Vienna. From there, we can take the rivers back to the Channel—much less chance of our plans being disrupted by the weather."

The latter consideration stilled any protest Loretta might have made.

Esme sat up and swung her feet to the floor. "Different cities—fresh fields."

That was what Loretta feared. However. . . . "If we're traveling to Buda, now that we've lost Phillipe we'll need to hire outriders as well as a coach ourselves." The courier-guide Esme had hired in Paris to see to their party's needs through the journey had fallen victim to a local contessa. The contessa had captured him and whisked him off to her isolated castle; Esme had confirmed that Phillipe would not be traveling on with them. Loretta frowned. "Or should we try to find another courier-guide?"

Esme considered, then shook her head. "If we're to go by boat from Buda on, we'll have no need of one."

"In that case"—Loretta straightened—"I'll go into town now and make the arrangements."

And send off another *Window on Europe* vignette to her agent. The readers of the *London Enquirer* had, apparently, become quite addicted to her latest reports.

November 20, 1822
Hillside above Drobeta-turnu-Severin,
*   at the southwestern tip of the Transylvanian Alps*

Rafe blew on his hands, stamped his feet, then crouched to hold his hands to the tiny blaze of their campfire. "I still can't believe the Black Cobra stationed men in Constanta."

He didn't expect a reply to his grumble; Hassan had heard it before. After seeing not so much as a hair of a cultist all the way through Persia and Turkey, they'd taken a ship from Samsun across the Black Sea to Constanta—and found cultists waiting for them in the first narrow street they'd tramped down.

They'd fought their way out of that ambush, but only just. Both he and Hassan were sporting fresh scars. They'd immediately hired horses and raced out of town, but in this much different landscape, with its mud, slush, and snow, it was impossible to hide their trail, and the cultists were, by and large, excellent trackers.

"They are still following," Hassan eventually said.

Rafe nodded. Huddling in the thick woollen coat he'd bought in Turkey, he stared into the fire. "Our mission is to avoid being taken at all costs, which sadly means we shouldn't engage, not if we can avoid it."

The necessity bit at him. He'd much rather turn and savage their pursuers, but the scroll-holder he carried, the one containing the crucial evidence that had to get to the Duke of Wolverstone in England, put paid to that. He was having second thoughts over how pleased he was to have drawn the critical mission.

But duty was duty, and he knew where his lay. If running and hiding was the price he had to pay to see the Black Cobra hang, he'd pay it.

Anything to avenge James MacFarlane.

Moving slowly, careful not to let the wind, knife-edged with ice, slice through his outer wrappings, he drew out the map he'd bought in Constanta and unfolded it. Hassan shifted to look over his shoulder.

"We're here." Rafe pointed. "Just ahead is the pass they call the Iron Gate, where the Danube flows through a gap in the mountains. We'll reach there tomorrow, and if the snow holds off we should be able to pass through and out into the plain beyond." He shifted the map the better to examine the area beyond the pass. After long moments of silent considering, he exhaled. "It's as I thought. Once we get onto the plain, we have to make a decision. Do we keep heading directly east, cutting through the Slavic lands to northern Italy, then into southern France, and from there turn north for Rotterdam, or do we take the other route and head north on the plain, then follow the rivers—the Danube and then the Rhine—east to Rotterdam, and so to Felixstowe?"

"It is Rotterdam that we must reach to get a boat to Felixstowe?"

"That's the Channel crossing we're supposed to take. There'll be guards waiting for us at Felixstowe, to escort us on from there."

They studied the map, then fell to discussing the cities, the roads. There seemed little real difference between the two routes. "Either should see us to Felixstowe by the date Wolverstone stipulated. We're earlier than expected thus far, so we'll have to go slowly, or pause at some point, but other than that . . ." Rafe shrugged. The routes seemed much of a muchness.

Until Hassan asked, "As we cannot risk standing and fighting, which way will be better for us to avoid notice?"

Brows rising, Rafe stared at the map. "With that in mind, there's only one choice."

One

November 24, 1822
Danube Embankment, Buda

afe walked out of the office of the Excelsior Shipping Company, tickets for two passenger cabins on the *Uray Princep*, a riverboat due to start up the Danube two days hence, in his pocket.

He glanced up and down the street, then strolled to where Hassan waited outside a nearby shop.

Rafe tapped the pocket of the well-tailored, distinctly European-style winter coat he now wore. "The last two tickets. No chance of an assassin getting on as a passenger, and the boat's too small for them to stow away or join the crew at the last minute."

Hassan nodded. Rafe was still getting used to the sight of his friend without his headdress.

They'd reached Buda two nights before. The first thing they'd done yesterday had been to visit a tailor and exchange their Turkish shirts, loose trousers, and coats for European garb. Throughout their journey they'd constantly changed clothes to better blend with the natives. Now, in the well-cut topcoat over a stylish coat, waistcoat, and trousers, a cravat once more neatly knotted about his neck, with his blond hair trimmed, washed, and brushed, Rafe was indistinguishable from the many German, Austrian, and Prussian merchants traveling through Buda, while Hassan's hawklike features, with his black hair and beard neatly trimmed, combined with a plain coat, breeches, and boots, fitted the part of a guard from Georgia or one of the more dangerous principalities. They were one with the crowd jostling on the docks and strolling the embankment. No heads had turned as they'd passed; no one paid them any heed.

The chance of merging into the stream of travelers, of taking effective cover among the multitude, had been the principal attraction that had made Rafe decide on the northerly route. With his distinctive height and blond hair, he, especially, would have had difficulty passing unnoticed through Italy and France.

The second place they'd visited yesterday had been a gunsmith's. Rafe had laid in a stock of pistols, powder, and shot. The cultists' one true weakness was a superstitious fear of firearms; Rafe intended to be prepared to exploit it. He and Hassan now carried loaded pistols.

They still wore their swords and carried the knives they'd feel naked without. Although the wars in Europe were over, pockets of military unrest still lingered and brigands remained an occasional threat, so swords on intrepid travelers raised no eyebrows; no one could see their knives.

Rafe had also found a cartographer's studio; he'd bought the best maps available of the areas through which they planned to pass. He and Hassan had spent yesterday afternoon studying their prospective route, then had sought advice from their innkeeper and the patrons of the inn's bar on which shipping company to approach.

Hassan looked at the quays lining the opposite side of the street. "Going by river is a good strategy. The cult will likely not think of it."

Rafe nodded. "At least not immediately." In India, rivers were not much used for long-distance travel, not like the

Danube and Rhine. And as the majority of cultists couldn't swim, staying on a riverboat was a better option than hotels and inns on land. "According to the shipping clerk, our journey via the rivers should land us in Rotterdam with a day to spare—no need to schedule any other halts to align us with Wolverstone's timetable."

"We have seen no cultists here yet," Hassan said. "None around the docks. If any are in the city, they must be watching the coaching inns and the roads leading east."

Following Hassan's gaze to the wide river buzzing with craft large and small, then lifting his gaze to the stone bridge linking Buda with the city of Pest, clustered on the opposite bank, Rafe murmured, "If they had cultists in Constanta, there'll be cultists here. We need to remain on guard."

He started strolling along the embankment. Hassan fell in beside him. They headed toward the small inn in which they'd taken rooms.

"The Black Cobra will have stationed cultists in every major town along the highways," Rafe said. "Here, Vienna, Munich, Stuttgart, Frankfurt, Essen, among others. By taking the rivers, we'll avoid most of those. On our first leg along the Danube, Vienna is the one city we can't avoid, but for the rest it's as we thought—the river towns are smaller, and most lie away from the major highways." That had been the reason they'd decided to travel by riverboat up the Danube and then down the Rhine. "Nevertheless, we should put some effort into shoring up our disguise. We need a believable story to account for who we appear to be—an occupation, a purpose, a reason for us traveling."

They'd reached an intersection where a narrow cobbled street rolled down from the fashionable older quarter to join the embankment.

"No!"

The shrill female protest jerked them to a halt. They looked up the street.

In the shadows cast by tall buildings, an older woman—a lady by her dress—flailed at two louts who had backed her against a wall and were reaching for her arms, presumably to seize her reticule, bangles, and rings.

There was no one else in the street.

Rafe and Hassan were racing up the cobbles before the woman's next cry.

Her attackers, wrestling with her as, breathlessly protesting, she fought to beat them off, knew nothing until Rafe grabbed one man by his collar, shook him until he released his hold on the woman, then flung him across the street. The man landed with a crunch against a wall.

A second later, courtesy of Hassan, his accomplice joined him.

Rafe turned to the woman. "Are you all right?"

He'd spoken in German, deeming that language more likely to be understood by any local or traveler. He clasped the gloved hand the woman weakly held out to him, took in her ageing, yet delicately boned, face. She was old enough to be his grandmother.

Beside him, Hassan kept an eye on the pair of louts.

The lady—Rafe might have been away from society for more than a decade, but he recognized the poker-straight spine, the head rising high, the haughty features—considered him, then said in perfect upper-class English, "Thank you, dear boy. I'm a trifle rattled, but if you'll help me to that bench there, I daresay I'll be right as rain in two minutes."

Rafe hesitated, wondering if he should admit to understanding her.

Her lips quirked. Drawing her hand from his, she patted his arm. "Your accent's straight from Eton, dear boy. And you look vaguely familiar, too—no doubt I'll place you in a few minutes. Now give me your arm."

Momentarily bemused, he did. As they neared the bench outside a small patisserie a few paces away, the chef appeared in the doorway, a rolling pin in one hand. He rushed to assist the lady, exclaiming at the dastardliness of the attack. Others emerged from neighboring shops, equally incensed.

"They're recovering," Hassan said.

Everyone turned to see the two attackers groggily stagger to their feet.

The locals yelled and waved their impromptu weapons.

The attackers exchanged a glance, then fled.

"Do you want us to catch them?" one of the locals asked.

The lady waved. "No, no—they were doubtless some layabouts who thought to seize some coins from a defenseless old woman. No harm done, thanks to these two gentlemen, and I really do not have time to become entangled with the authorities here."

Rafe surreptitiously breathed a sigh of relief. Becoming entangled with the local authorities was the last thing he needed, too.

He listened while the patisserie owner pressed the lady to take a sample of his wares to wipe out the memory of the so-cowardly attack in their lovely city. The lady demurred, but when the chef and his neighbors pressed, she graciously accepted—in German that was significantly more fluent and colloquial than Rafe's.

When the locals eventually retreated, returning to their businesses, Rafe met the lady's gray eyes—eyes decidedly too shrewd for his liking. He gave an abbreviated bow. "Rafe Carstairs, ma'am." He would have preferred to decamp—to run away from any lady who called him "dear boy"—but ingrained manners forced him to ask, "Are you staying nearby?"

The lady smiled approvingly and gave him her hand. "Lady Congreve. I believe I knew your parents, and I know your brother, Viscount Henley. I'm putting up at the Imperial Hotel, just along from the top of this street."

Suppressing a grimace—of course she would know his family—Rafe bowed over her hand, with the other gestured to Hassan. "We'll escort you back once you're ready."

Lady Congreve's smile widened. "Thank you, dear boy. I'm feeling quite recovered already, but"—she gripped his hand and Rafe helped her to her feet—"before I return to the hotel, I must complete the errand that brought me this way. I have to collect tickets from an office on the embankment."

Rafe gave her his arm and they turned down the street. "Which company?"

"The Excelsior Shipping Company." Lady Congreve gestured with her cane. "I believe they're just around the corner."

Half an hour later, Rafe and Hassan found themselves taking tea in the premier suite of the Imperial Hotel in the fashionable castle quarter of Buda. Lady Congreve had insisted. Rafe had discovered that his grande-dame-avoiding skills were rusty. There hadn't seemed any way to refuse the invitation without giving offense, and as he'd learned, to his horror, that Lady Congreve and her party were among the passengers due to depart on the *Uray Princep* the following morning, trying to avoid closer acquaintance seemed pointless.

He had to admit the array of cakes that arrived on the tea tray were the best he'd tasted in a decade.

"So you and Mr. Hassan were with the army in India." Lady Congreve settled back on the chaise and regarded him. "Did you ever meet Enslow?"

"Hastings's aide?" Rafe nodded. "Poor chap's usually run ragged. Hastings has a finger in so many pies."

"So I've heard. So you were based in Calcutta?"

"For the most part. In the months before I resigned and departed, a group of us were operating out of Bombay." Rafe understood she was checking his bona fides, but he wasn't sure why.

"So you've been soldiering for all these years, and have been a captain for how long?"

"Since before Toulouse."

"And you fought at Waterloo?"

He nodded. "I was part of a compound troop—part experienced regulars, part ton volunteers. Heavy cavalry."

"Who of the ton fought alongside you?"

"Mostly Cynsters—the six cousins—plus a smattering of other houses. Two Nevilles, a Percy, and one Farquar."

"Ah, yes, I remember hearing about the exploits of that troop. And now you've resigned and are heading back to England?"

Rafe shrugged. "It was time."

"Excellent!" Lady Congreve beamed.

Every instinct Rafe possessed went on high alert.

"It seems, sir, almost as if fate has sent you to me." Lady Congreve glanced at Hassan, including him in the comment. "I wonder if I might impose upon you—you and Mr. Hassan—to act as my party's courier-guide and guard? We left Paris with an experienced guide, but sadly had to part with him in Trieste. Knowing we would be traveling on by riverboat once we reached here, I didn't see any point in securing a replacement, but today's events have demonstrated my error. It simply isn't safe for ladies to walk these foreign streets unprotected." Lady Congreve held Rafe's gaze. "And as you are going the same way and, indeed, have already secured passage on the same boat, I do hope you can see your way to joining my party."

By sheer force of will, Rafe managed to keep all reaction from his face.

When he didn't immediately reply, Lady Congreve continued, "Our meeting does seem fortuitous, especially as you've taken the last tickets on the boat, so even if I could find any men as suitable, I wouldn't be able to secure passage for them."

Rafe inwardly cursed the clerk at the shipping office, who, of course, had recognized him and commented. Racking his brains for the right form of words with which to decline, aware of Hassan looking at him, waiting for him to get them out of this trap, Rafe opened his mouth . . . then shut it.

He and Hassan needed some reason that would explain their traveling on the river, some purpose that would make people accept their presence and not look too closely.

"And of course," Lady Congreve went on, "I'm sure your brother will be pleased to know you've been able to extend me this small service. I will, of course, take care of all the expenses involved and reimburse you for the tickets you've already purchased."

Rafe recognized that she'd rolled out her heavy guns—his brother, no less. His gaze abstracted, distracted by a prospect he was still trying to define, he waved her last words aside. "No need for recompense. If we do as you ask . . ."

Refocusing on Lady Congreve, he wondered at the wisdom—and the morality—of involving her, however much at arm's length, in his mission. The cultists throughout Europe would be watching for him and Hassan. As a pair of men traveling together, they were easy to spot—both over six feet tall, one distinctly fair, the other distinctly dark, both with military bearing.

But the cultists most likely would not look closely at two men traveling as part of a larger party.

Rafe glanced briefly at Hassan. "It *might* be possible for us to act as your guide and guard. We'll be on the same boat regardless, and as you noted, you won't be able to add more passengers to the list. . . ."

Lady Congreve was clever enough to keep her lips shut and watch him vacillate.

Rafe remembered James MacFarlane's body.

Remembered the scroll-holder presently strapped to his side.

Remembered that the closer they drew to England, the more cultists they would need to slip past.

And Lady Congreve was the sort of lady who, if she knew the details, would wholeheartedly support his mission.

He focused on her face. Should he tell her of his mission?

He opened his mouth, the revelation on his tongue, then remembered the other tickets she'd picked up. "Who else is traveling with you? You have four tickets."

"As well as myself, there's my maid, Gibson, whom you've met."

The maid had been waiting in the suite, and had taken her mistress's coat and cane, then gone to order the tea. Rafe judged it likely that Gibson, a woman of mature years, had served Lady Congreve for decades; there was an unspoken degree of empathy and loyalty between maid and mistress that suggested Gibson would fully support any decision her mistress made. No threat to his mission there. "And the other two tickets?"

"Another lady and her maid." Lady Congreve tilted her head, regarding him curiously. "They would be included among the people you would guide and guard, if that makes any difference."

Rafe knew that ladies of her ladyship's generation often traveled in pairs, providing company for each other on the journey, someone to share the sights with, to converse with of an evening. He imagined that any lady Lady Congreve chose to travel with would be much like her. Which meant there was really no reason he shouldn't explain his mission and, if subsequently Lady Congreve stood by her offer of making them her courier-guide and guard, accept.

He drew breath, met Lady Congreve's gray eyes. "I'm inclined to accept your offer, ma'am, but first I must tell you what has brought Hassan and me this way." He glanced at Hassan, who raised his brows a fraction, but didn't seem disapproving, then looked back at her ladyship. "If once you've heard our story you still wish us to take up the positions of your courier-guide and guard, then I believe we can accommodate you."

Lady Congreve's smile was triumphant. "Excellent! Now what's this secret—"

She broke off as the knob on the corridor door turned. An instant later, the door opened, and a vision in a vibrant dark blue pelisse, with a fur hat with a jaunty feather perched atop swirls of lustrous dark hair, swept in.

"Esme—" The vision broke off, stared at Rafe, then glanced at Hassan. But her gaze returned to Rafe as he came to his feet, and she simply stared.

He stared back. He was only vaguely aware of another female—presumably the other maid—slipping into the room and closing the door; his entire attention, all his senses, had fixed, unswervingly, on the lady in blue.

The *young* lady in blue.

She was tallish, slender, and intensely feminine; an aura of suppressed—or was it controlled?—vibrancy all but charged the air around her. Her eyes, large and just faintly tip-tilted, were of an arresting shade of periwinkle blue made only more striking by her royal blue pelisse. Her curves were sleek, yet definite. He'd heard women with such figures likened to Greek or Roman deities; he now understood why. She was Athena, Diana, Persephone, Artemis— she seemed to be those constructs given life, just with sable hair and blue, blue eyes.

He felt like he'd taken a clout to the head. Just as in battles when he was staring down Death, time stood still.

It took effort to restart his mind, to return to the real world.

To the here and now.

"Esme" she'd said, and meant Lady Congreve. She was the other lady, Lady Congreve's traveling companion. A young lady her ladyship had taken under her wing.

The goddess had halted at the back of the chaise on which her laydship sat. Lady Congreve raised a hand, gracefully waved. "Allow me to present Miss Loretta Michelmarsh, my great-niece. The Honorable Mr. Rafe Carstairs, and his companion, Mr. Hassan."

Rafe inclined his head. Stiffly. The goddess was a relative; that made matters worse.

Miss Michelmarsh, her gaze still locked on him, her expression oddly blank, bestowed the barest bob that would pass for civility.

"You're just in time, Loretta dear, to hear the latest news." Lady Congreve twisted around to smile at her great-niece. "Mr. Carstairs and Mr. Hassan saved me from two attackers in the street near the shipping office, and at my request they've agreed to fill the positions of our courier-guide and guard."

Rafe now understood the reason behind Lady Congreve's triumphant expression, realized that the trap he'd fallen into was of quite a different nature than he'd foreseen. He'd forgotten the principal entertainment grandes dames such as Lady Congreve delighted in. Matchmaking. Preferably with those of their acquaintance.

Her ladyship knew his family. She knew her great-niece. But he'd be damned if he allowed her to matchmake him— even with a vision that brought to mind a pantheon of goddesses.

Aside from all else . . . dragging in a deeper breath, he forced his gaze from its distraction, and looked down at her ladyship, who was clearly waiting to gauge his response. "Lady Congreve, I regret it will not be possible for me and Hassan to act as courier-guide and guard for you during your upcoming journey."

Lady Congreve regarded him, a frown forming in her eyes. "I understood, dear boy, that you had already agreed to fill the positions subject to informing me of the reason behind your current journey and my confirmation of the appointments subsequent to that." She opened her eyes wide. "What on earth happened in the space of just a moment to change your mind?"

She knew. Rafe held her gaze, felt his jaw firm. "Regardless, my lady, on further consideration it will be impossible for me and Hassan to join your party."

Lady Congreve's eyes narrowed on him, something her niece couldn't see. "Surely you aren't reneging on our agreement because of Loretta?"

Yes, he was. While he'd entertained the possibility of joining forces with Lady Congreve, a lady in the latter years of her life and, he judged, with significant life experience, and had been prepared to court the risk that through him she might be exposed to the Black Cobra's minions, he would not, could not even in his most reckless mood, countenance putting a young lady like Loretta Michelmarsh in any danger whatever.

He held Lady Congreve's gaze. "There's a certain degree of risk involved in being associated with me and Hassan, and while I would have considered, should you have been agreeable once you were fully informed of that risk, accepting the positions you offered in your train, it would be unconscionable of me to continue with that arrangement while you have a young lady such as Miss Michelmarsh traveling with you."

Loretta frowned. What was going on? Her first thought on sighting the tall, blond-haired man, clearly a military man—she could tell by his stance, the way he held his broad shoulders—was a simple, albeit dazed: *Who is he?*

Her mind had stalled at that point, her senses scrambling to fill in details, none of them pertinent to answering that question.

How bright the golden streaks in his sandy blond hair, how unexpectedly soft his eyes of summer blue, how absurdly long his brown lashes seemed, how deliciously evocative the subtle curve of his distinctly masculine lips, how square his jaw, how imposingly tall, how strong and powerful his long body seemed to be . . . all those observations flashed through her mind, and none helped in the least.

Adrift, her gaze locked on him, her senses . . . somewhere else, all thought had suspended, and had remained beyond her reach, until he'd spoken.

His deep voice, its timbre, the reverberation that seemed to slide down her spine and resonate within her, shook her—enough to shock her out of her mesmerized state.

Bad enough. But apparently Esme had invited him and his friend to act as their courier-guide and guard.

Her immediate thought—the first rational one after her wits had returned to her—was that Carstairs and his friend were charlatans out to rob Esme . . . but then he'd refused the position.

Because of her. Why?

She listened as Esme artfully twisted Carstairs's words, then invoked his honor as an officer and a gentleman, intent on browbeating him into acquiescing to being their courier-guide, apparently all the way back to England. She could have told Carstairs that he didn't stand a chance of wriggling out of Esme's talons, but . . . the notion of having him squiring her around in the guise of their courier-guide filled her with an odd mix of anticipation and trepidation.

If just the sight of him could make her temporarily lose her grip on her wits, what would prolonged exposure—and closer exposure at that—do?

She couldn't afford to be distracted, especially not now. She needed to get another vignette off to her agent tomorrow; her editor was waiting on it, holding column space for it.

Over the past six years, writing as *A Young Lady About London*, she'd steadily developed a following with her little pieces published in the *London Enquirer*, three or four paragraphs of philosophical social commentary, a mix of observation and political satire all delivered with a highly sharpened pen. The public had taken to her writings, but her abrupt departure from England had put paid to that endeavor; she couldn't observe London society from abroad. But then she'd had the notion to continue in similar vein with her *Window on Europe* vignettes, and her public had happily followed her through her brief sojourns in France, Spain, and Italy.

She'd known Esme would halt at Trieste, so had warned her agent, and a letter from her editor had been waiting for her there. Apparently the publisher of the *Enquirer* was an admirer of her work, and the paper was eager to publish whatever she could send them.

Her agent had also written informing her of the sizeable increase in remuneration the publisher was providing for each witty installment.

She'd thought her departure with Esme would spell the end of her secret career; instead, it had brought her work more forcefully to the attention of both her publisher and the public.

Her secret endeavor had taken a highly encouraging turn, but close acquaintance with Rafe Carstairs might well endanger that—in more ways than he imagined.

Yet she couldn't help but be curious over what, exactly, he was so set on keeping her away from.

"Perhaps," she suggested, taking advantage of a temporary silence, "Mr. Carstairs might explain what this unprecedented danger inherent on being associated with him and Mr. Hassan is?"

Carstairs, who, she had to admit, was giving Esme a run for her money in the stubborn stakes and was presently giving every indication of being as immovable as a monolith, lifted his sky blue eyes to her. He studied her for a fraught moment, then looked down at Esme. "There is no point continuing this discussion. We cannot—"

"Captain."

The quiet word came from Hassan, who had retreated to stand by the window; turning, Rafe saw him looking outside.

Glancing up from whatever he'd seen, Hassan met his eyes. "Before you make your decision you should consider this."

Rafe inclined his head to Esme and her great-niece. "A moment, if you would."

He crossed to Hassan. Halting alongside, Rafe looked down through the lace curtains to the street below.

To where two Black Cobra cultists were ambling along, looking this way and that.

"They are looking, watching, not searching specifically," Hassan said.

"Which means they don't yet know we're here."

"True, but . . ." Hassan waited until Rafe raised his gaze to his before continuing, "What will happen if they learn we have been here, not just in Buda but here in this room, speaking with these ladies?"

Rafe's heart sank.

"The cult will not have forgotten that it was a young English lady, Miss Ensworth, who brought you and the others the Cobra's letter. Even if we part from the ladies now, that will not save them—the cultists will reason that they have to be stopped and they and their baggage searched, just in case."

"Damn!" Rafe all but ground his teeth. After a moment, he murmured, "We shouldn't go on with them and expose them to danger, but not being their guards might be even more dangerous for them."

"So I think."

Rafe sighed and turned—and discovered Lady Congreve just behind him. She'd been peering around his shoulder.

Raising her eyes to his face, she arched her brows. "I think, dear boy, that you had better tell us all." Swinging around, she led the way back to the chaise. "And as we are, apparently, to be traveling companions all the way to England, you may call me Esme."

Elegantly sitting, beckoning her great-niece to sit alongside her, she lifted openly curious eyes to his face.

Rafe stifled a groan, but, accepting the inevitable, walked to the chair he'd earlier occupied. Once Loretta Michelmarsh sat, he sat, too.

Drawing in a long breath, he started at the beginning. "Several years ago, a man—an English gentleman of noble family—went out to India and, exploiting his position in the Governor of Bombay's office, devised and created a native cult. The cult of the Black Cobra."

He had them call in their maids, then related the story in its most abbreviated version, alluding only where necessary and in general terms to the atrocities committed by the cult; those he deemed too ghastly to be described in polite company he left out.

By the time he finished, the sky outside was darkening and evening was closing in.

Esme had listened intently, putting shrewd questions here and there. She hadn't been all that surprised to learn that the man Rafe and his friends were working to expose as the

Black Cobra was Roderick Ferrar, the Earl of Shrewton's younger son.

Esme's lips had tightened, her features growing severe. "I never did like that boy—or his father, come to that. Vicious blackguards, the Shrewtons, except for the heir, Kilworth. He's altogether a different sort."

Rafe took her word for that. All he cared about was bringing Roderick Ferrar to justice.

"So let me see if I have this correct." Somewhat to Rafe's surprise, Loretta Michelmarsh had seemed as fascinated with his mission as her great-aunt. "You are one of four . . . for want of a better term, couriers, who left Bombay on the same day, all heading for England by different routes. All four are carrying identical scroll-holders, but only one contains the original letter—and that original letter must reach the Duke of Wolverstone in order for the Black Cobra to be stopped."

When she paused and opened her blue eyes wide at him, he nodded. "In a nutshell, that's it."

"So which do you have—one of the decoys, or the vital original?"

Rafe shook his head. "The four of us decided that information shouldn't be revealed to anyone, not even shared among us."

"In case this fiend of a snake seizes one of you and tries to coerce the information from them in order to concentrate solely on the one who carries the original?" Esme nodded. "Excellent idea. Don't tell us. We don't need to know that you're carrying the original."

Expression blank, Rafe stared at her, but Esme only smiled.

"The Duke of Wolverstone." Loretta glanced at Esme. "Isn't he something of a secret war hero? A spymaster or some such?"

"At one time. He retired some years ago, then assumed the title, but I seriously doubt he'll have lost his lauded skills." Esme met Rafe's eyes. "If you're working for Royce,

Dalziel—Wolverstone—whatever name he goes by these days, then as loyal Englishwomen it clearly behooves us to do whatever we can to aid your quest."

Rafe inwardly blinked. If he'd known Wolverstone's name would have such an effect, he'd have used it sooner.

"Regardless, however, now that we know about your mission and have been seen with you by people the serpent's minions might question, then there's clearly no option other than to join forces." Esme smiled with satisfaction. "So no more muttering—you, dear boy, henceforth will be our courier-guide, and Hassan will be our guard."

Esme glanced at Loretta, then looked back at Rafe. "Which makes us your charges." Her smile was triumph incarnate.

Lips thin, Rafe nodded, then with a glance at Loretta, added, "Until we reach England."

Two

onsense, dear boy! You can't seriously expect us to spend the day hiding like frightened rabbits. Besides, the point of you and Hassan joining us is to disguise you—even if some of these heathens spot you, as you said yourself, as long as you're with us they're unlikely to recognize you."

It was the next morning, and Rafe had been summoned to join Esme and Loretta at the breakfast table in the sitting room of Esme's suite. Meeting Esme's animated eyes, he drew breath to reiterate that the principal imperative behind him and Hassan joining her party was to keep her, Loretta, and their maids safe.

"It's also most unlikely," Loretta said, speaking before he could, "that the cult people will be watching the places tourists visit—they'd never imagine you would amble out to take in the sights."

"Just so." Esme nodded decisively. "So you and Hassan can accompany Loretta and Rose on their expedition to Buda Castle and wherever else she has in mind."

"The Matthias Church and the fisherman's town," Loretta supplied, glancing down at a sheet of notes.

"Meanwhile," Esme continued, "Gibson and I will spend the day at the Rudas Baths, and you may fetch us in the afternoon on your way back to the hotel." She smiled and reached for her teacup. "That sounds an excellent disposition of our day."

Rafe glanced at Loretta Michelmarsh. Her glossy dark head nodded absentmindedly; she was busy studying her list.

Reaching for his coffee cup—he was in need of the fortification—he searched for some argument strong enough to trump Esme's and her great-niece's oh-so-rational intransigence, and found none.

That was rapidly becoming the story of his mission. Esme, and more quietly but equally effectively Loretta, had taken charge, and while their party continued more or less in the direction he needed to go, he had little grounds on which to deny them. They weren't soldiers under his command. He couldn't order them about.

All he could do was grit his teeth and bear it, as he had the previous night.

After learning of his mission, Esme—deftly supported by Loretta—had insisted he and Hassan, as their newly hired courier-guide and guard, should relocate to the hotel, to rooms just along the corridor from Esme's suite. He'd been in two minds over the wisdom of such a move, but had been overridden. With a smile and a wave, Esme had secured the extra rooms and had dispatched hotel staff to fetch his and Hassan's bags from their inn.

So he'd found himself sharing a dinner table with Esme and Loretta, and had had to quickly buff his rusty manners to an acceptable shine.

Then, as now, Esme had largely carried the conversation. He was still observing, feeling his way with the pair, yet last night Loretta had been strangely quiet, at least in his opinion. She'd been absentminded, distracted, her mind elsewhere, much as if she'd been composing something in her head and hadn't wanted to be bothered by his and Esme's chatter.

This morning, she still seemed distant, but more in the manner of planning something. Given Esme's insistence on adhering to their day's schedule, it was possible he might learn what.

Half an hour later, he was waiting in the hotel foyer when Esme and Loretta, with Gibson and Loretta's maid, Rose, trailing behind, came down the stairs. Hassan followed, playing shepherd.

Rafe realized he was staring, inwardly quashed the compulsion. He'd seen fetching young ladies before. No reason one in a vibrant blue pelisse should so command his attention.

Going forward, he offered Esme his arm. "I've organized carriages—we'll see you off first."

"Excellent, dear boy." Clearly pleased he was actively playing his assigned role, Esme allowed him to conduct her out of the hotel's doors onto the pavement, to the carriage that waited, door open, footman at the ready.

Rafe handed her up, stepped back to let the footman hand Gibson in, then looked up at the driver. "The Rudas Baths."

He'd learned that the baths, dating from antiquity, were renowned for their medicinal properties, and as such were a magnet for wealthy ladies from all over Europe; within such hallowed portals, Esme and Gibson would be safe.

As soon as the footman had climbed up behind, the driver cracked his whip and the carriage rolled away.

Another replaced it at the curb. The others emerged from the hotel. Rafe glanced at Loretta, then, as the hotel's footman rushed to open the carriage door, offered her his hand.

Head high, determined to keep a rigidly proper and therefore safe distance between herself and the too-handsome captain Esme had drawn into their circle, Loretta laid her gloved hand across his palm, felt his fingers, long and strong, close around hers—and even through the fine leather felt searing awareness flash up her arm, streak along her nerves, surge down her veins.

She tried to suck in a breath, but her lungs had constricted. By sheer force of will she kept her feet moving and managed to climb the steps into the carriage. He released her hand and her senses snapped back into focus.

Battling a dire frown—*what the devil was that*?—she sank onto the seat, looking down, arranging her skirts as Rose followed her into the carriage and sat opposite.

A second later, the carriage tipped as Carstairs climbed in. He hesitated, then sat alongside her, leaving the place beside Rose for Hassan.

Carstairs's shoulder brushed hers as he settled.

She couldn't breathe again. Worse, her wits had scattered. As for her senses, they were flickering and flaring, not in alarm but in a most peculiar way.

Fixing her gaze forward, she forced her lungs to work. It was preferable that Carstairs sat beside her rather than opposite; at least she didn't have him constantly before her. Bad enough that she could somehow *feel* him alongside her; his warmth, his solidly muscled strength, impinged on her consciousness as if every nerve she possessed had come alive and locked on him.

She was irritated and utterly mortified.

"Where to?"

The question from alongside was a rumble of thunder, a warning of impending storm.

Increasingly worried that was indeed the case, she wracked her brains, recalled. "The Matthias Church."

Carstairs relayed the destination to their driver through the trapdoor in the roof, then the carriage rocked and started rolling.

It was perfectly acceptable for her to remain silent, to say nothing at all. She should spend the time bringing her unruly senses to heel, shoring up her defenses against the unexpected, persistent, and annoyingly strong physical attraction Carstairs evoked, and not allowing her fascination with his history, his mission—with him—to lead her into courting danger . . .

"I would have thought"—the words were on her lips, placed there by curiosity before she could censor them—"that the cultists sent to keep watch would have been provided with detailed descriptions of the four couriers." She cast a frowning glance at her nemesis. "From what you told us, that doesn't seem to be the case."

He met her eyes, then looked forward. "We left Bombay unexpectedly. The Black Cobra had to rush to get his troops into the field—to spread them across Europe before we had a chance to pass through. The Black Cobra himself and presumably his closest henchmen might know the four of us by sight, but the majority of cultists won't. Even assuming the Cobra has put men who can recognize us in charge of the various watching groups, there must be many towns—and I would wager Buda is one—where the cultists are relying on a description sent to them, not personal knowledge."

"At Constanta," Hassan put in, glancing at Rose, then looking at Loretta, "they did not so much recognize us, ourselves, as that we were two men of the right size and style traveling together, coming from and heading on in the expected directions. They were not sure when they approached us. It was only when we fought them off and ran that they were sure."

"Sure that we were one of the courier groups they'd been told to intercept." Carstairs nodded. "The cultists sent to keep watch, at least this side of the Channel, will in my case be looking for two tall men, one fair and blond, the other dark, an English cavalry officer and his Pathan companion. The descriptions they'll have for the other three might be more specific. They spent more time than I in Bombay. Delborough and Hamilton especially were known to the Black Cobra, Monteith less so, but even he spent more time in areas where the cult was strong. Hassan and I spent most of the time we were investigating the Cobra out in the field at the edge of the cult's territory."

He shrugged. "The truth is that the cultists watching will most likely expect me to be wearing my uniform and Hassan his robes and turban. Without those distinguishing marks, and also not traveling alone, there's no reason for their attention to fix on us."

"Especially if you're squiring ladies about." Loretta felt a certain relief—except that it was relief for him and therefore not entirely reassuring. "So you've traveled through areas of India far from the major towns?" When he nodded, she asked, "What was it like—the country, the villages, the people?"

His brows rose, but after a moment apparently gathering his thoughts, he replied.

Somewhat to her surprise, the carriage drew up outside the Matthias Church before she'd grown bored.

But then she had to allow him to hand her down. With his hand hovering at the back of her waist, he perfectly correctly guided her up the steps. She was aware of him looking around, his blue eyes surveying their surroundings; she was grateful his concern over potentially watching cultists kept his attention from her.

Rallying her wits, stiffening her spine, she hauled in a breath, dragged her notes out of her reticule, and swept into the church, determined to keep her mind, and his, on the notable features of the ancient building that, despite its history of frequent and violent change, yet remained.

After one rather sharp look at her, he fell in with her lead and, hands clasped safely behind his back, dutifully followed in her wake as, with Rose by her side, she examined monuments, sculptures, and wonderful stained glass, then, under the pretext of spending a moment in prayer, sat in a pew and quickly scribbled notes to jog her memory when she later came to write her next *Window on Europe* vignette.

Buda Castle was their next stop—after another two incidents of Carstairs gripping her hand, another ten minutes of sitting beside him in the carriage trying to suppress her senses' witless awareness. Yet when she stood on the pavement outside the gates, she suspected the castle would be worth the ordeal. She eagerly followed the young scholar-monk who the custodian deputed to be their guide; informed of her specific interests, constantly pushing heavy spectacles up his nose, he led them through the massive building, showing her examples of the changes the centuries had wrought.

As an illustration of the damage so often visited upon art by politics, the castle was close to perfect.

At the last, hoping her enthusiasm had paved the way, she smiled at the young man. "I had heard that there are catacombs."

His gaze flickered; he glanced nervously about. "You mean the labyrinth."

"Indeed." She caught his gaze, tried to impress him with her earnestness. "I'm really very keen to see the tunnels."

She was sure her readers would be equally keen to hear of them, perhaps in a vignette on otherworldly, atmospheric sights. Anything that hinted at ghosts always did well in the popular press.

The young scholar hesitated, but then nodded. "This way."

Turning to follow, she met Carstairs's eye, saw an intent expression sharpening the soft blue, but let the look slide past as she hurried after their guide.

He led them through increasingly narrow corridors, then pushed open a heavy, iron-studded door and walked into a small antechamber. He glanced again at her eager expression, then he lit an oil lamp, turned to an archway in the wall, beckoned, and led them on.

Down. Down a stone stairway that spiraled ever deeper into the rock on which the castle sat.

"Ah . . . Miss Loretta?"

Rose's disembodied voice had Loretta pausing and glancing back, not that she could see anything past Carstairs's shoulders.

"If it's all right with you, miss, me and Hassan will wait in the chamber at the top."

Guessing from her nervous tone that Rose didn't appreciate the close atmosphere, Loretta called back, "Yes, of course."

Avoiding Carstairs's eyes, she turned and followed their guide on.

The stairway led down and down. Then the light from the guide's lamp was suddenly swallowed by a vast blackness. He slowed, and stepped away from the stair. Following, Loretta stepped down onto dust-covered rock. The air about them smelled of damp stone, although all she could see seemed dry.

The guide hoisted the lamp high, letting light sweep the walls of a large oval chamber. "This is the main entrance to the labyrinth—there are others, but some distance away." He pointed to the black holes in the walls; Loretta counted eight. "Those are the tunnels. It is said those foolish enough to venture into the labyrinth are never seen again." The young man shrugged. Walking forward, he shone the lamp into one tunnel. "So it is said, but we do not truly know, for no one has tried to learn the labyrinth's secrets in recent times."

Loretta quelled a shiver. The chamber was wonderfully gothic. She looked around, impressing as much as she could on her memory—the sense of great age, the rough-hewn walls, the eerie stillness of the air. The almost palpable temptation to walk forward and enter one of the tunnels—just a little way, just to see . . .

"I think we've seen enough."

The low words brushed her ear. Startled, she glanced around—and found Carstairs close.

So close, she stopped breathing. In the dimness, she couldn't read his eyes, but she could feel the heat of him down her back, feel prickling sensation wash beneath her skin, leaving warmth in its wake.

Beyond her control, her gaze locked on his lips. For an instant all she heard was her heart thudding as a wave of giddiness washed over her. . . .

Dragging in a breath, she raised her gaze to his eyes, then stiffened and stepped away.

Recalling his words, she nodded curtly. "Indeed." Strengthening her voice, she spoke to the guide. "Thank you. I've seen all I need."

The guide returned and led the way up the stairs. Loretta followed; Rafe brought up the rear. He was grateful that with the guide carrying the only lamp, he couldn't truly see Loretta Michelmarsh's hips shifting this way and that before his face.

It was a long stairway. Going up took longer than coming down; he had plenty of time to think about his current obsession.

Last night, having accepted that he would have to play the part of courier-guide to Loretta as well as Esme all the way to England, he'd lain in bed and lectured himself on the folly of being distracted by a pretty face, a pair of fine eyes, and a lushly tempting body. He'd reaffirmed the importance of his mission, then had closed his eyes and slept—and dreamed of making very slow love to a goddess with lustrous dark hair and periwinkle eyes.

This morning he'd assured himself, dreams notwithstanding, that he was strong enough to deal with Miss Michelmarsh in the flesh; she was just another young lady after all. The strength of his attraction to her was merely a reflection of how long it had been since he'd seen any young lady worth lusting after; it would fade with time.

It hadn't faded yet.

If anything, it had grown. And not because of anything physical—like glimpsing her bare ankle or more of her breasts. No. It was a combination of her reaction to him— that subtle leap of her senses, of her pulse and her awareness, that occurred every time he, however innocently, touched her.

He knew it, felt it, every time, and the knowledge pricked his awareness of her—the intensity of his senses' focus on her—to new heights.

And as if that weren't enough, she was proving something of a puzzle. A mystery. There was something behind her choice of sights, something that drove her strangely intent interests.

Some mystery cause that lit a fire of enthusiasm inside her. That fire drew him.

It transformed her from a merely interesting young woman to a vibrant young woman of mysterious allure.

Back in the antechamber, they collected Rose and Hassan, and strolled back to the castle gates. Rafe paid off the guide, tipping him generously. Falling in behind Loretta as they walked to their carriage, he heard her tell Rose of the labyrinth. Even though he'd seen it himself, Loretta's words brought it alive, casting it in a gothicly fanciful light that wasn't entirely fictitious.

Once back in the carriage, they rolled on up Castle Hill to Loretta's next halt—the fisherman's town. Or, more precisely, the spot that gave an extraordinary view of Buda, Pest, and the Danube between. Descending from the carriage, they strolled the path that curved along the ridge high on the hill, watching various folk from the fishing community pointing to this boat or that, bandying views on the likely catch.

The views both up and down the river were spectacular. Although chilly, the day was clear, with only a few slate gray clouds hovering on the horizon. River breezes kept the air fresh, sweeping away the sulfurous taint of coal smoke from the town below. Rafe noticed the latter only because he saw Loretta, strolling beside him, lift her head and sniff. She seemed to be concentrating on every little thing, as if taking an inventory so she could describe the scene accurately.

Perhaps she kept a travel journal.

Regardless, it was time to return to the hotel for luncheon. He gathered Hassan with a look, and Hassan brought Rose. Rafe reached for Loretta's elbow—felt her start when his fingers closed about her arm. When she shot him a narrow-eyed look, he merely said, "We should get back to the hotel."

He steered her to their carriage, released her, but offered his hand as he opened the door with the other.

She considered his hand for an instant before steeling herself and placing her fingers in his.

Pretending he didn't notice the leap of her pulse, the hitch in her breathing, he helped her into the carriage. Moments later, they were all inside and the carriage started its lumbering journey down the hill.

Head back against the squabs, eyes apparently closed, through the fringe of his lashes he watched Loretta, this time sitting opposite him. For half the journey back, she peered out at the steetscapes, concentrating as if fixing the various styles of architecture in her mind.

Her observational intensity impressed him, and tickled his curiosity. It was too acute to be innate, yet looked to be something of a habit.

When the carriage reached the Castle quarter, an area with which she was already familiar, she turned to him. He opened his eyes, met hers.

"You mentioned before, when speaking of the villages in India, that they often had no council to run them. How do they manage community decisions, then?"

It wasn't the sort of question he would expect a young lady to ask, yet it fitted with the thrust of her earlier interest in his observations of India. So he answered, and let her interest lead her to ask further questions.

When the carriage drew up outside the hotel, he stepped down. After a survey of the street revealed no cultists lurking, he handed her down and escorted her inside. Climbing the stairs in her wake, he debated asking why she was so interested in social customs, but decided the time was not yet.

She wouldn't tell him yet.

Lengthening his stride, he closed the distance between them. As she neared the door to the suite, he reached around her and opened it.

She gave the smallest of jumps. From close quarters she met his eyes, her own a touch wide, then she raised her chin, haughtily inclined her head, and swanned in.

Lips curving fractionally, he followed.

He bided his time through luncheon, then, leaving Hassan with Rose at the hotel, he and Loretta set off once more in the carriage. This time, she asked to be driven into Pest. As they rolled off the bridge over the Danube, he glimpsed two cultists idly watching the carriages rumbling onto the bridge, heading toward Buda. Neither cultist saw him.

He looked at Loretta. "What are you planning on seeing this afternoon?"

She glanced at the notes in her lap. "According to the guidebook, if we stay on this road, we'll see many of the mansions of the local aristocracy."

"Do you intend making calls, or just looking?"

"Just looking." She glanced out of the window, but at the moment the street was lined with shops. "Ah—there's the museum."

She peered at the structure as the carriage slowly rolled past.

"Are you a student of architecture, then?"

She blinked at him, then sat back. "No, I'm"—she waved a vague hand—"merely interested in such things."

"Museums or buildings?"

"Both." After a moment, she amended, "I'm interested in buildings that are museums, churches, castles, and the like."

"And the houses of aristocrats?"

She nodded.

"Why?"

She glanced at him, then looked out of the window again. "I just am."

And he would eat his busby, fur and all, if that were the truth.

She sat forward when the carriage obligingly slowed as a succession of large mansions came into view. Set well back from the road behind iron fences, the houses were of much the same ilk as those lining Park Lane.

When he said so, she nodded. "Very true." But she was absorbed again, distracted again.

He seized the moment to study her face, drank in the fine

features, the delicacy of her brows, the luscious curve of her lips. Looking wasn't dangerous; it might even dull the growing compulsion to taste those lips. . . .

The carriage rumbled on, turned, then rumbled back. As they neared the bridge and the spot where he'd seen the cultists, he shifted deeper into the shadows. Tensed as the paving leading to the bridge rang beneath the horses' hooves. The end of the bridge came into view, then receded as the horses trotted on.

The cultists had gone, leaving the question of whether they would recognize him or not untested.

Once back in Buda, the carriage turned away from Castle Hill and the embankment below it onto a road that followed the river.

The Rudas Baths sat in a strip of land between the next hill along and the Danube. Esme and Gibson were waiting in the foyer; they came out when Rafe descended from the carriage in the portico. He helped both in, then followed, sitting beside Gibson, facing Esme.

As the carriage headed back toward the hotel, Esme heaved a richly satisfied sigh. "I had a lovely day, my dears—how was yours?"

After a moment, Loretta said, "We covered all the sights I wished to see. An uneventful, but successful day."

She glanced at Rafe, as did Esme.

He briefly met Loretta's eyes, then transferred his gaze to Esme. "My day was . . . surprisingly entertaining."

Surprisingly intriguing. He now had more questions than he'd had that morning, and an even greater desire to learn the answers.

The next morning their party boarded the *Uray Princep*.

With the big riverboat tied up at the wharf directly down the hill from the hotel, transferring Esme, Loretta, the two maids, and their collective baggage to the docks in safety wasn't all that difficult; getting them on board was another matter.

At that hour the docks were a hive of activity; with crowds of thronging passengers, and sailors and porters swarming everywhere, onto boats and off, with this trunk, then that, ferried on or ferried off, the confusion was close to absolute. Rafe felt as if he were trying to look everywhere at once.

"I haven't seen any cultists." Hassan paused by Rafe's side.

Loretta, standing before him, her way blocked by passengers milling before the gangplank, glanced over her shoulder. "I haven't seen any either."

Rafe looked down, met her eyes. "If you do, tell one of us. Immediately."

She merely arched her brows and faced forward again.

He grimly shifted his weight. Far from easing his obsession, dwelling on her lips the previous afternoon had only resulted in even more salacious dreams. And even greater resulting tension.

Especially given she was making it plain that although she was as attracted to him as he was to her, she had no interest in encouraging him.

He wasn't conceited, yet he wondered why.

Yet another question he had no chance of answering. At least, not yet.

Finally losing patience—they were at a dead halt—with no imminent danger looming he deserted his post guarding the ladies' rear, and leaving Hassan to hold that position, shouldered his way past the gaggle of porters bearing their luggage, then, exploiting his height and the width of his shoulders, cleaved a path through the melee to the gangplank. Once there, he stood like a bulwark and waved their porters past him, then followed the last up onto the boat.

Crewmen materialized to relieve the porters of their loads. As Rafe stepped on board, the purser came hurrying up, a board with various lists attached in his hands.

"Lady Congreve's party," Rafe announced. He glanced at the first list as the man scanned it. "And Jordan and Rivers— the last two names. We're her ladyship's guide and guard."

"Ah—yes, sir." The purser lifted the top sheet and looked at the one beneath—a plan of the cabins.

"In the circumstances, we'll need to be as close to her ladyship's rooms as possible." Rafe's tone brooked no argument. His hand passed over the purser's board; a large-denomination gold coin fell onto the top list.

After a second's hesitation, the board tipped. The coin slid off and disappeared; the purser glanced up, met Rafe's gaze, then studied the cabin plan again. "Lady Congreve has booked the main stateroom. We can place you in the next cabin along on one side, and her guard in the cabin opposite. Getting to her ladyship's cabin will mean passing both your doors. Will that suit?"

Rafe smiled charmingly. "Admirably." He flicked the man another coin, which he deftly caught. Turning to the gangplank, Rafe saw Esme being assisted up it. "That's her ladyship now."

The instant Esme set foot on deck, cabin boys appeared and she, Loretta, and their maids were escorted below with all due ceremony. Leaving Hassan on watch, Rafe followed, but as soon as he'd confirmed the women were safely ensconced in their stateroom, he climbed up, not to the main deck where they'd boarded and Hassan stood on guard, but further up to the observation deck at the prow of the ship.

All the other passengers were still below, settling into their cabins. Rafe found a wooden chair, pulled it to the rail, and sat. He could see out between the wooden rails, but the high side of the boat largely hid him from view, and while he was seated it was difficult to tell that he was tall.

The sights and sounds of the river embraced him. He watched, but saw no sign of cultists near the ship, or anywhere on the docks, not even keeping watch over the docks and the boats putting in and out. Sloppy picket work on the cultists' part; the Black Cobra wouldn't be pleased.

He, on the other hand, was quietly delighted.

A heavy bell clanged, and with a flurry of activity from the crew, the *Uray Princep*'s gangplank rattled aboard, the anchor chain clanked and groaned, then a rear sail was hoisted, and oars extended from the embankment side and pushed the heavy boat out into the current.

Rafe felt the river take hold. He scanned the shores as under the steady thrust of oars, the *Uray Princep* pushed steadily on, and the roofs of Buda slowly fell behind.

When the river mist obscured the town, he stood, stretched, then ambled around the upper deck, taking note of the various ladders and doors, then headed down the wooden stairs he'd come up.

The *Uray Princep* carried both passengers and goods. The boat had three decks above the waterline. The upper deck contained the passengers' observation deck, which extended from the prow to the front of the centrally located raised bridge; other than the bridge which overlooked it, the observation deck was the highest part of the boat.

The next deck down was the main deck, half of which was given over to the passengers; Rafe found an elegantly appointed salon in the prow, with a narrow bar between it and the dining salon beyond, where cabin boys were setting tables with white cloths and cutlery.

From the clatter of pans and the smells issuing forth, the galley lay beyond the dining salon. Opposite the bar, the staircase, a solid, well-polished wooden stair, not a narrow ladder, led up to the observation deck and down to the passengers' cabins.

Only the main deck had an outer walkway on which one could circle the ship. After chatting to the purser and confirming that the rear half of the main deck was the domain of the crew and out of bounds to passengers, Rafe returned to the stairs and went down to the cabin deck.

There, a single corridor ran down the boat's center, from the main stateroom in the prow, the one Esme's party now inhabited, to a door toward the rear of the vessel. Rafe strode down the dim corridor, hearing voices behind most doors he passed. Reaching the end door, he tried it, and found it locked and bolted. Most likely the captain's cabin and crew's quarters lay beyond, reached from a stern companionway.

Satisfied he'd established the general layout of the vessel, Rafe strolled back up the corridor to the first single cabin on the starboard side, immediately alongside the stateroom door. His bags sat on the narrow berth inside.

According to the purser, the passengers' first event was a gathering in the salon in half an hour to meet with the captain and their fellow travelers.

The captain, a jovial man, welcomed them with a toast to a pleasant voyage, then remained to chat as in a soireelike atmosphere, the passengers exchanged names, home cities, and destinations. All the other passengers, four couples, were German or Austrian, and all were making for Vienna to enjoy the festive season there.

Their various attendants hung back, chatting among themselves near the stairs. Rafe exchanged a glance with Hassan, but doubted there was any danger lurking among either the passengers or their staffs. Leaving Esme chatting avidly to a German couple from Frankfurt, with Loretta supporting her, he made his way to the captain's side.

After introducing himself as Esme's courier-guide and exchanging various innocuous comments, he asked, "Your crew—have they been with you long? Or do they change frequently, take work on different boats to see different countries?"

The captain laughed. "Not my crew. We've been together for years."

"No newcomers?"

"I haven't had to find a new hand in years, for which I thank the gods. It can be difficult when one has a solid team used to each other's ways."

The captain turned as another passenger approached. After shaking hands and exchanging names, Rafe excused himself and moved on.

From the corner of her eye, Loretta watched him. Realizing the captain had been his goal, she'd followed him across the room and stopped to chat to another group of passengers nearby—near enough to overhear his conversation with the captain.

On the one hand she was relieved to know he was taking guarding against the cult so seriously, while on the other she was insatiably curious over what he did and why. Curious about his mission, its mechanics and logistics.

She told herself it was her investigative streak—that she was gathering information that might, at some later date, prove useful for her writings. An excuse she refused to examine too closely.

Biding her time, she eventually spoke with the captain, finding him a sane and sensible man, then continued her examination of the other passengers.

It was nearing time for luncheon when she paused in the prow, where the salon narrowed to a point. To her surprise, Rafe joined her. She had until then kept a sensible distance, continuing to tell herself that her reaction to him would eventually fade and die.

Clearly that eventuality had yet to occur; as the space between them shrank, her lungs seized and her nerves flickered, then sparked.

Thankfully oblivious, he halted beside her, glanced over the other guests, then turned to her. "Do you sense any threat from any of the other passengers or their staffs?"

She blinked. "No." She frowned. "Why do you think I would?"

"Because you observe everyone and everything so closely. If there were anything amiss, you'd sense it."

An unaccustomed feeling blossomed inside her; she felt chuffed that he'd noticed and considered her observations useful. She glanced at the other passengers. "They are what they purport to be—just travelers looking forward to enjoying a short cruise." Then she frowned. "Do you think it possible—"

"No. I don't think anyone here is a cult hireling. I just thought to get another opinion." He inclined his head. "Thank you."

With that he wandered off, leaving her staring after him. Telling herself there was no need to feel so thrilled.

He stopped to chat with one of the Austrian couples. Loretta's gaze shifted to Esme. She was pleased to see her great-aunt deep in conversation with two of the other ladies. With any luck, the other couples would distract Esme from her latest scheme. Her certain-to-be-doomed latest scheme.

Rafe Carstairs was too dashing, too handsome, too daring, altogether too adventurous for Loretta's taste.

Or, more to the point, for her to suit his.

She was determined to do nothing to further Esme's purpose, but when Loretta entered the dining salon that evening she was woefully aware that her attire did not support her aim.

Between them, Esme, Gibson, and Rose had managed to "lose" every demure gown Loretta had brought with her. If she didn't want to appear in her chemise, she had to wear one of the gowns Esme had delighted in purchasing for her in Paris and Rome. Each a unique creation, the gowns showcased her figure, highlighted her eyes, and made the most of every asset she possessed.

Accepting the inevitable, she'd chosen the most severe of the evening gowns, a creation in midnight blue silk that by its very severity made her, in it, appear more softly feminine. As she stepped into the salon, she hoped Rafe and everyone else would see only the severe style and ignore the overall effect.

He was seated with Esme at a table across the room. He glanced up before she was even halfway there.

If his reaction was any indication, her hopes were doomed. He stared, his gaze locked on her; he was patently no longer listening to Esme.

Who had noticed, and looked smug.

As she neared the table, Loretta started to frown. At him. She didn't appreciate the effect of his attention. It sent warmth stealing through her; not a blush, but something that reached deeper.

She halted at the table as he rose. Slowly, his gaze very slowly rising to her face.

She inclined her head curtly. "Sir." She looked across the table vase at Esme. "Ma'am."

Feeling as if his head had been struck by a mallet, Rafe pulled out the chair opposite Esme's, held it while Loretta sat.

The captain chose that moment to join them, taking the last seat at the table, opposite Rafe.

Resuming his seat, Rafe felt torn by contradictory reactions—annoyed to have the captain vying for Loretta's attention, while simultaneously immeasurably glad that he was.

He needed to exorcise his feelings for Loretta Michelmarsh. This was neither the time nor place to be overcome with lust.

Ruthlessly suppressing his inclinations, he gave his attention to Esme, and strove to keep it there, sadly with mixed results.

Next time, he vowed, he'd seat Loretta opposite him. That way, their hands would have no chance to brush, to touch—however inadvertently, however innocently—as they passed this and that.

By the end of the meal, his nerves felt rubbed raw.

It was little consolation that, he suspected, she felt the same.

At last the company rose and headed into the salon for digestifs and wider conversation. After drawing back Loretta's chair, then following her into the salon, he thereafter strove to keep at least six feet between them.

Loretta circled the room, every nerve tight. If he touched her again, just tapped her arm, she was sure she would jump like a startled hare. She'd never felt the like, not ever, and could have done without feeling it now.

And the affliction was only growing worse. She'd been sure it would fade, but no. Even though he stood at the far end of the room and she was fighting to pay attention to Herr Gruber's story about his and his wife's excursion to Godollo Castle—a place she was actually interested in hearing about—she, her nerves, her senses, were much more acutely aware of Rafe Carstairs.

How she was going to deal with it—with him—she had no clue.

As matters stood, it was shaping up to be a very long journey home.

Shortly after dawn the next morning, Rafe climbed to the observation deck to relieve Hassan, who had kept watch through the small hours. After reporting no activity of any kind, Hassan retreated to his cabin to get some sleep.

Alone, Rafe paced the open deck, welcoming the chill breeze off the river, eyes scanning the largely flat fields rolling back from the banks to meet the foothills of the distant mountains. Snowcaps gleamed as the sun touched the peaks. The sky was a tapestry of shifting clouds, thick enough to block the sun. Waterbirds wheeled overhead, disturbed by the passage of the boat.

He fought to keep his attention on his surroundings, to engage his mind with evaluating the potential for ambush, likely hiding places, the chances of cultists getting close enough to board.

Anything to keep his mind from his dreams, from the increasingly explicit images that had taken root in his imagination.

To keep his thoughts from the woman of said dreams who he'd learned was sleeping in the cabin next to his.

"It is a fine morning, is it not?"

Rafe swung to see the captain coming toward him from the bridge. Rafe inclined his head, politely said, "I imagine the weather can turn nasty at this time of year."

"Indeed, indeed." The captain nodded sagely, halting two paces away. "However, Herr Jordan, I wished to ask why you and your friend are so watchful—even to standing guard through the night." Shrewd eyes fixed on Rafe's face. "Is there something I should know?"

Rafe considered, then said, "Two days before we left Buda, before she hired myself and Rivers, Lady Congreve was attacked in the street. We assumed it was merely street thieves, but . . . it seemed wise to keep watch. Lady Congreve has been a party to many diplomatic missions over the years. No telling who might decide they hold a grudge."

The captain's brows had risen; concern filled his eyes. "I would be very sorry were any harm to befall Lady Congreve while she was on my boat."

Rafe said nothing.

The captain regarded him for several moments, then said, "If there is anything I or my crew might do to assist, you have but to ask."

"Thank you." Rafe half bowed. "I don't expect anything to come of it, but should anything happen, that's good to know."

Late that afternoon, Loretta was forced to escape the salon to avoid responding too sharply to the pointed comments of the other ladies, artfully orchestrated by Esme, on the subject of one too-handsome ex-captain.

Exasperated, she climbed to the observation deck, certain that, with the brisk wind currently strafing across the river, it would be deserted.

It was. Except for the subject of the conversations she'd just fled.

She hesitated at the top of the stairs, wondering where else she could go, but then he glanced back and saw her dithering. Lifting her chin, she calmly—much more calmly than she felt—stalked forward to join him at the forward rail.

This couldn't go on; she was going to have to get over her reaction to him. Perhaps heightened exposure would deaden her senses.

He was leaning on the rail. She was grateful that, as she halted beside him, he didn't straighten, leaving his head level with hers.

He didn't say anything, either, simply watched her for a

moment, then, when she kept her gaze locked on the river before them, faced forward, too.

Irritation, frustration, a certain level of anger; she felt those emotions well and churn. A good foot separated them, yet her senses were rioting; she felt an insane, irrational, nearly overwhelming desire to shift to her right, close the distance between them and snuggle into his warmth, the warmth she could feel reaching for her, a seductive lure, protection against the wind, and something more.

Gripping the rail, she stood straight and tall, head high. "Given your mission, shouldn't you be riding hard for England?"

She made no effort to disguise the waspishness of her tone.

He turned his head and looked at her; his gaze lingered on her face for long enough to have her desperate to breathe, then he looked at the river once more. "I can't."

Rafe heard his temper in the clipped words. If she had any sensitivity, she would hear it, too.

The swift glance she threw him, frowning, puzzled, suggested she had.

"I have a timetable." He hadn't mentioned it earlier, but saw no reason he couldn't tell her; she already knew so much. "There's four couriers, so four threads to this mission. I'm supposed to land in England on December twenty-first, not before, not later. I don't know when the others will get there—before? On the same day? Regardless, having others involved means I can't rush. As things stand, traveling up the Danube, then crossing to the Rhine and taking another boat downriver will get me to the Channel at about the right time."

After a moment, she asked, "So if you get to the Channel coast too early, you'll have to wait before you cross?"

He nodded. "And there's sure to be cultists thronging that shore." He sighed. "We got to Constanta earlier than I, or indeed Wolverstone, anticipated. We had a quick and undisturbed journey from Bombay until there, something I certainly hadn't expected."

"You expected the cult to pursue you out of Bombay?"

"Yes. But they missed us entirely." He shifted, a familiar restlessness building, frustration over having to consistently take evasive action rather than stand and fight. "If we'd gone on by road from Buda and weren't stopped along the way, we'd be on the Channel coast weeks too early. That's one reason why, as much as the pace irks, we opted to go via the rivers."

After a moment she asked, "Were there other reasons for your choice?"

"A number. If we traveled by road, we'd need to be constantly on guard. On land, no matter where we stopped the chance of a cult attack would be very real. Worse, when they attack they don't care who else gets hurt—they have a penchant for using fire to flush their quarry out, and if innocents die as well . . . they simply don't care. They'll happily set fire to a crowded inn with no thought for who else might be killed."

He straightened. "Against that, the riverboats are too small and their crews too few for the cult to easily slip anyone on board, either as a stowaway or a last minute addition to the crew, so the boat itself is safe. Setting fire to a boat on the river in this weather is also as close to impossible as makes no odds, so we don't have to fear that. We still need to keep watch for anyone sneaking aboard, but the crew and passengers help with that—if anyone sees someone who isn't crew or passenger, they'll sound an alarm, and that person will be caught. On top of that, most cultists can't swim, most can't even row worth a damn, which further decreases the chance of them sneaking onto the boat while it's on the river. Those cultists who can swim or row have most likely been sent to the Mediterranean, to the Channel, or to other ports."

"So while crossing Europe, you're safer on the river than on the roads, staying at inns."

"I know there are cultists keeping watch for us—for

me—all through Europe. I'm running a gauntlet of sorts. But I'm wagering on the chance—and I think it's a real chance—that the cult won't think to watch the rivers at all. The Black Cobra, Ferrar, would, but it's entirely possible he's sent his men to watch and not thought to specifically name each and every route. Why would he? So there were cultists in Constanta and Buda, but they were watching the roads, not the river. I expect there'll be cultists stationed in every city, in every large town. But the cultists themselves won't think of the rivers as highways. With any luck, they won't have any inkling we're traveling this way."

He fell silent. As a commander he was happy with the choice he'd made; it was the right one, he had no doubt of that.

As a soldier, he'd rather face action than flee.

But he knew his duty, and that wasn't to be. This time he was the rabbit and he had to run.

She'd fallen silent, too. But, oddly, it felt comfortable; he didn't feel obliged to make conversation simply to fill the quiet.

Nor, apparently, did she. As the silence lingered, he glanced at her face. She'd lifted it to the breeze; errant tendrils of dark hair streamed back from the porcelain oval of her face.

Although her eyes had been closed, she must have sensed him looking; her lids rose and she slanted him a glance. It lingered, too, then she looked forward. "The cultists in Buda didn't notice you leaving, so they—the cult—don't know you're on the river, don't know you're on this boat."

It occurred to him that she might feel threatened. "No. And until one of them sees and identifies me, this boat and all who sail on her are under no threat at all."

From his tone, Loretta realized that he'd thought she was worried. She didn't correct him, but that hadn't been the reason for her questions, her interest.

Straightening from the rail, she murmured, "It'll be time to dress for dinner soon. I'll see you at table."

She left him by the rail and headed for her cabin. Every time she spoke with him, every morsel more about his mission she teased from him, only gave her more to think about.

Only enthralled her more.

Three

November 27, 1822
The Uray Princep *on the Danube*

L oretta tossed and turned. It was night, and all the passengers had retired to their beds long ago. Doubtless all were snoring.

Lifting her head, she thumped her pillow, laid her head back down, and closed her eyes. She willed herself to sleep.

Within a minute, her mind had drifted . . . to cultists. To what one might look like. To what weapons they would carry.

To how many Rafe Carstairs had fought and dispatched.

To Rafe Carstairs.

"Arrgh!" Sitting up, she hesitated, then, hearing nothing from the stateroom's sitting room beyond her door, she threw back the covers and climbed out of the berth.

Enough moonlight washed in through the porthole for her to find her boots and pelisse. Pulling them on, she fastened the pelisse tight to her neck, wrapped a shawl about her head and shoulders, then eased open her cabin door.

The sitting room was deserted. Moonlight washed through the wide windows on either side of the prow. Quietly closing her door, she walked silently to the stateroom door, opened it, and slipped out into the corridor.

Moments later she pushed through the swinging doors near the bar and trudged up the stairs to the observation deck. A turn about the deck in the cold, damp air would, she hoped, settle her enough for sleep.

She had to get her mind off Rafe Carstairs.

Just because she was now involved in his mission didn't mean she had to draw close to him. She didn't need to understand him to play her part.

Stepping onto the deck, she straightened, and looked toward the prow.

And saw him standing there, watching her.

"Wonderful!" she muttered. Then again, she should have guessed. He had mentioned keeping watch to ensure no cultist slipped on board.

She debated simply waving and going downstairs again, but she wasn't that cowardly.

Drawing her shawl close, she walked across the deck. As she neared, she stated in an even tone, "I couldn't sleep, so came to get some air."

His brows arched, but when she marched to the rail and stood looking out, a good yard and more between them, he obligingly turned back to his own staring out at the night.

He didn't say anything.

As the silence stretched, she again felt an almost physical compulsion to sidle closer, to ease nearer to his heat. She wasn't all that cold, yet the urge only grew.

She focused on the river, the scenery. "I hadn't realized the view at night would be so . . . poetic." The change was striking. "The moon makes everything look ethereal, as if its light reveals some things and hides others, and the river mist softens and screens like a veil, all mystery and illusion." She raised her gaze. "I didn't notice earlier that we can see all the way to the mountains." The moonlight glimmered on the distant peaks, turning the snowcaps pearlescent. "They look so fantastical in this light, as if they guard some magical faraway place that only intrepid travelers will ever see."

He'd turned his head to look at the mountains. From the corner of her eye, she saw his lips quirk.

Eventually, he spoke. "Those are among the highest mountains in Europe, but after seeing the Himalayas, these look like mere hills."

"You visited the Himalayas?" She didn't have to fabricate her interest. "What were they like? Are they as majestic as people say?"

Rafe smiled. "More. They're . . . intensely impressive. The sort of sight that literally leaves you breathless."

"Did you see them in winter or summer? Are they ever without snow?"

Shifting to face her, he answered her questions—letting his eyes drink in her face, her expressive features just visible in the moonlight. He kept his tone even, his answers factual, and resisted the building, welling urge to reach out and draw her near. Nearer. Much closer. Until he could feel her warmth, her curves, against him.

But as that couldn't be, he could at least distract her. He knew all about not being able to sleep.

So he talked and she listened. She was good at that, at giving her complete attention to something—in this case, him. Or at least his memories. Her fixed attention was some consolation.

Eventually, she sighed. She glanced around. Contrary to how he was feeling, she seemed more at peace.

After a moment, she looked at him and smiled. "Thank you for talking with me. I believe I can sleep now." Her smile deepened a fraction as she turned away. "Good night."

"Good night." If she noticed his farewell was a trifle gravelly, she gave no sign. He watched until she disappeared down the stairs, then, regretfully accepting that he couldn't follow her, turned back to stare at the river.

Regaining her cabin without incident, Loretta stripped off her pelisse, then sat on her berth and unbuttoned her boots. Falling into her bed, she dragged the covers over her shoulders. She lay on her back staring at the ceiling, wondering why she felt so . . . light.

So at ease.

All they'd done was talk about scenery.

Closing her eyes, she saw him in her mind's eye, standing against the rail in the moonlight. She felt her lips curve. . . .

And fell asleep.

The next afternoon, Loretta was sitting in a deck chair on the observation deck embroidering in the weak sunshine when Rafe drew another chair up alongside and dropped into it.

After a moment, she glanced at him. He'd stretched out his long legs, leaned back, and closed his eyes. But she caught a glimmer of blue beneath his lashes.

"Strange," he murmured, "but I hadn't taken you for the embroidering type."

She smiled and looked back at her work. "I don't embroider much usually, but during this trip I've frequently given thanks I remembered to pack my embroidery bag. When she's not actively doing, Esme is relatively quiet—she's not a big talker."

"How do you come to be traveling with her? Is she your only relative?"

"Oh, no. In fact, until she came and whisked me away on this adventure, I hadn't seen Esme in years."

"But she's your great-aunt."

"Yes, but she's led a very active life. Her husband was a high-ranking diplomat and he was sent all over Europe to represent our government at this court or that, and of course Esme went with him. He passed away last year, and Esme was stuck in Scotland sorting out his estate until recently. To celebrate the end of that, she decided to visit many of the cities where she and Richard had spent time—hence this trip."

"And she chose you to accompany her? You must be her favorite great-niece."

"No—just the one who could leave London at a moment's

notice. My sisters are both married, and we're all the family Esme has, at least on her side."

Rafe searched for a question that would get her to reveal more about herself and her family. He couldn't ask directly, but asking about Esme had got him some tidbits.

After a moment, he ventured, "Where had you visited before Buda?"

She named a string of cities from Paris, through France, then Spain and Italy. "From Trieste, we came to Buda."

He knew Spain and France well, enough to guess how long they'd been away. "So you left London . . . when? In September?"

"The eighteenth. Esme descended and whisked me up and we were in Dover that night."

He'd been away for decades, but some things he hadn't forgotten—like his older sisters' excitement over the Little Season. "So you left just before the Little Season started?"

She nodded.

He cast again, a little more directly. "Unless things have changed dramatically since I was last in town, I'm surprised Esme was able to inveigle you away from the balls and parties. Your mother must be a lot more accommodating than mine."

Her lips curved, but from this angle he wasn't sure it was in a smile. "My parents are dead—it was my eldest brother Esme had to convince, and I assure you when she has the bit between her teeth, it takes someone a great deal more resolute than Robert to deny her."

"But what about you?" The crucial question. "Weren't you looking forward to whirling giddily around Almack's floor?"

She gave a little snort—of derision?

"I assure you Esme didn't have to argue her case with me." She set a stitch, then added, "I have little real passion for ballrooms—my interests lie elsewhere."

"Indeed?"

He waited, hoping, but all she gave by way of answer was a "Hmm."

He wanted to know more. Why he wasn't sure, but when did Reckless ever stop to work out the reasons behind his impulsive acts? That would make them "not reckless."

If he couldn't be his usual self with respect to his mission, then he needed an outlet, and he'd decided she was it. That was answer enough.

So how to tease more information from her?

The sun, although weak, was pleasantly warm. He closed his eyes, and gave the matter his undivided attention.

Loretta waited for his next question, carefully setting stitch after tiny stitch, quite willing to give him time to think . . . she heard a soft snore.

Turning her head, she studied his face, saw his broad chest rhythmically rise and fall, saw that this time his eyes truly were closed.

A soft smile spread across her face. There was no one else on the deck to see it, so she allowed it full rein. She remembered the previous night, remembered him standing guard in the moonlight.

Watching over them all.

He deserved to sleep, to catch up, in safety.

Returning to her embroidery, she continued stitching, content to watch over him while he did.

Some hours later, after taking tea with Esme and the other ladies in the salon, Loretta swung her shawl about her shoulders and went up on the deck, feeling the need for a brisk walk before dinner, not least to clear the clamor of ladies gossiping from her head.

Not only did they gossip, but their dearest topic was Rafe Carstairs-Jordan. The Honorable Rafe Carstairs-Jordan, brother of the current Viscount Henley of Oxfordshire, late of His Majesty's Army in India. Etcetera, etcetera.

She didn't need to hear more on that subject, the very one she was trying, without notable success, to steer her too frequently avid curiosity from.

She'd completed one circuit of the deserted observation

deck when she heard laughing and cheering. The sound drew her toward the stern.

At the rear of the observation deck, a small gate barred the walkway that ran along the side of the elevated bridge. She paused, debating, but the captain saw her through the bridge's window, smiled, bowed, and waved her on. Too curious to resist, she pushed open the gate and walked through.

The walkway ended at the rear of the bridge, where a sloping ladder led down to the open rear main deck. She hadn't previously been that far into the crew's territory. Pausing at the head of the ladder, she looked down, past the various masts, spars, and sails that helped propel the boat along, to the stern deck. The shouts and laughs were coming from there.

Numerous men were congregated at the stern, hanging over the rails, laughing, talking, clapping each other on the back and generally having a good time. Various crew members and most of the male passengers were there, including Rafe and Hassan.

Her eyes locked on Rafe's blond head. She strained her ears, trying to make out what he was saying, what was going on.

Then his head came up; he turned and looked at her.

One of the German passengers followed his gaze and beamed genially. "Fräulein! Come and join us." He waved. "We need a lady's eye—a lady's wisdom to judge our contest."

Others heard, saw her and beckoned her to join them. One of the crew came hurrying to help her down the ladder. Rafe prowled in the man's wake.

He was there to take her hand as she stepped off the ladder. His eyes danced. "Fishing contest."

"Ah." Of necessity gripping his hand, she let him steady her around the coils of rope and various impedimentia strewn over the deck.

The men were on a slightly raised platform at the stern. Drawing in a breath, fixing a smile on her lips, she dragged her senses from the strong clasp of Rafe's fingers about hers, from their warmth and the strange conviction of comfort, of safety, she now experienced whenever he was close, and focused on the group.

On the interesting way the passengers had mingled with the crew. Was it the fact they were traveling and so were out of their customary society that allowed them to ignore the usual social barriers and speak man to man? She knew that come dinnertime, the barriers would be back up and functioning. The concept would make an interesting vignette. She really should concentrate on that.

As they neared the group, Rafe said, "This curve of the river is apparently an excellent fishing spot, and the cook"— with a wave he indicated that individual, who grinned and bowed—"has declared that if the passengers catch fish enough for the purpose, he'll prepare a special fish dish for dinner."

"Of course," Herr Gruber said, "we must have a contest to see who catches the biggest fish."

Loretta couldn't help but smile. "Of course."

Herr Gruber pointed into a large wooden barrel. "See? We have caught three so far, but we need many more."

Loretta looked at the three gray-scaled fish flopping in the bucket. They were of decent size, much of a muchness.

"There are much bigger ones than that to be caught," the purser informed her. "The rules of our contest are that if a passenger catches the biggest fish, then the crew clean all the fish, but if the crew catch the biggest, then the passengers— the men, anyway—have to help."

Loretta glanced at Rafe, then at the other passengers. "That sounds like an excellent incentive to win."

As one, they grinned—boys all as soon as a contest was in the wind.

"We need an impartial judge," the purser continued. "If we could impose on you, miss?"

She smiled. "I'll be your judge on one condition—that you give me a rod and line, too."

Rafe's brows rose, along with those of all the other men. But they were happy to indulge her whim, and quickly found her a rod with a wooden reel. One sailor helpfully baited her hook. Then they all went back to their own rods. Silence descended. Only when a fish was hauled aboard did they break out with exclamations and laughter.

Loretta eyed the group lining the stern rail, then went to the side rail closer to the bank and looked over. The boat was sliding slowly through the water under a single, large, high sail. It had been years since she'd fished, but she rather thought the river side of the boat would yield better pickings.

Rafe, standing with the group with their rods hanging over the stern, watched her as she crossed to the river-side rail. She smiled as she passed him, paused at the rail, checked her hook, then expertly flicked her line out over the water.

She watched it sink, then the line drew taut with the current. She played it out lazily, then let the line drift and settled against the rail.

Ten minutes later, she had her first bite. Her line bowed as she reeled in the fish. Rafe appeared by her shoulder. "Do you need help with that?"

"No, no." She flashed him a smile. "I can manage."

One of the sailors leaned over the side and scooped her catch up in a net. With it flopping on the deck, everyone gathered around to compare it to the others in the bucket. "It's much the same size," she declared, although in fact her fish was fractionally larger.

All the men smiled, laughed, and congratulated her. She accepted their accolades with a bright smile, and thanked the sailor who rebaited her hook.

Of course, they all thought it was beginner's luck.

Their attitude changed somewhat with her next catch—a fish distinctly larger than her earlier one. Some shifted their rods to the river-side rail.

She smiled and sent her line snaking further out into the river.

Her next catch was simply enormous.

And then the contest truly was on. Every man shifted to the river-side rail and tried to get their hooks as far out as hers.

She couldn't rein in her smile. As she sent her line whizzing out over the water again, she felt carefree, truly happy. Rafe stood beside her, his technique almost, but not quite as good as hers. The comments he mumbled under his breath nearly had her in stitches.

It was all good-natured—everyone laughed and joked and she encouraged them—yet there was no doubt whatever that both passengers and crew were exerting themselves to trump her monster catch.

None of them managed it, but they caught a lot of fish, enough to have the cook eventually declare the contest at an end—and her the winner.

They all cheered, and she laughed and accepted their applause. Then the passengers turned and made their way back to their side of the boat, and the mingling was at an end.

She was thinking of that—of the activities that welded men into a single group beyond the boundaries of class—as she climbed back up the ladder, at the top taking Rafe's hand to step onto the walkway.

The other passengers had gone ahead; she and Rafe were the last of the group heading onto the observation deck.

Rafe fell in behind Loretta as she strolled the walkway. And wondered. Eventually, he said, "We'd never have switched to the river-side rail if you hadn't shown us."

She glanced at him over her shoulder. An elementally female gleam lit her eyes. "I appreciate fish."

With that, she faced forward and walked on.

Leaving him even more intrigued than before.

That evening, Loretta found herself blushing. Constantly.

First in the dining salon, where the sumptuous fish course was introduced with a toast to her, accompanied by a great deal of enthusiasm, laughter, and general merriment, and then later in the main salon to which the passengers retreated, when the gentlemen decided to relive the Great Fishing Contest, and her role as winner, for the edification of their wives.

Even more than the fulsome compliments the gentlemen paid her, the knowing looks and open encouragement from the ladies made her squirm. Especially those from Esme. Her great-aunt lived to see the day she, in Esme's words, "emerged from her chrysalis and unfurled her wings as a true Michelmarsh."

Her behavior at the fishing contest had definitely been a Michelmarsh moment. A moment when her true self, the one she normally kept well-reined, had stepped forward and taken charge.

And while she didn't exactly regret relaxing just for that time, the outcome only emphasized the wisdom in keeping her Michelmarsh self well hidden, allowing only the assumed façade of the prim, proper, demure young lady to show.

As a prim and proper young lady, she could avoid notice she didn't want, and temptation she didn't want, too.

Like that of Rafe Carstairs. Despite her senses' preoccupation with him, she didn't have room in her life to deal with him, with the attraction he evoked. She had matters to observe, thoughts to think, vignettes to write, and her own rather different path to follow.

That no one but she knew of her secret career was neither here nor there. She was as devoted to it as, she judged, he was to his mission.

"Do not say a word." She growled the warning as, a distinctly teasing smile on his lips, he joined her in the narrow prow end of the salon. "I am not some witch or harpy or siren who magically lures fish to her hook."

His brows rose, but his eyes gleamed. Raising the glass of brandy he carried, he took a sip while surveying the others in the room. "If you say so."

She shot him a sharp glance. "I do. There is no need to say anything more about that blasted contest."

He faced her; the disturbing light in his eyes had grown

even more pronounced. "The contest, while amusing, was not the principal element of the afternoon's activities that caught my interest."

She blinked, conscious of an impulse to take a step back. The look in his eyes, the intentness in his expression, made her nervous—made her pulse kick and her instincts come alive. But she had to ask . . . "What did catch your—I'm sure peripatetic—attention?"

He smiled. "You."

Her senses skittered, but she arched a brow back, infusing the gesture with world-weary boredom. "Why? Because I can fish?"

"No. But incidentally, where did you learn?"

"At home in the local river—my sisters, younger brother, and I always ran our own competitions."

"Did you win those, too?"

"Generally." She lifted her chin. "I watched and learned better than they did."

"I've noticed you're very observant."

The way he said the words made her nerves jangle. She fixed her eyes on his, felt her pulse leap as he shifted a fraction closer. "So?" She shrugged. "Many people are naturally observant."

"Not like you." He held her gaze. "Or me."

She let her eyes fly wide. "You?" She could see in his eyes that he was playing with her, but it was a game to which she'd refused to learn the rules.

"Indeed." He smiled again. "For instance, I've observed that you are not quite the young lady you pretend to be, but the why of that is a mystery. A puzzle, a conundrum. And if there's one thing guaranteed to fix my interest, it's a mystery. I enjoy unraveling them."

She narrowed her eyes. "You are not going to unravel me. So just forget whatever revelation you think you've had, and put the entire notion from your mind."

His eyes held hers while he took another sip. Then his lips curved. "Too late."

"Nonsense!" She was flustered, and she'd never been that before; she didn't appreciate the sensation. She only just stopped herself from wagging a finger beneath his nose. "Listen—"

"Loretta, dear?"

Swinging around, she saw Esme gliding up.

Smiling, her great-aunt laid a hand on her arm. "I forgot my shawl, dear. Could you fetch it from my cabin?" Still smiling, she glanced at Rafe. "I'm sure Rafe will excuse you. You know the one I want—the black silk."

"Yes, of course." Delighted to escape any further verbal clash with her nemesis, she nodded his way. "Sir. If you'll excuse me?"

She didn't wait for any reply but quit the scene, heading for the stairs and the stateroom below.

Esme transferred her gaze to Rafe.

He met it, arched a brow. Waited.

She considered him, then, still smiling, patted his arm. "Do be careful, dear boy. I know dear Loretta is something of a prize, and a definite challenge even though she doesn't mean to be, but while I have no doubt you'll be able to prevail, I have to warn you it'll be an uphill battle." She lifted a finely drawn brow. "Are you sure you want to engage?"

He made no attempt to answer. He had no intention of giving her any more ammunition to use against him.

A tactic Esme understood. Her smile deepened and, with another pat, she turned away. "Good luck, dear boy. I'll be watching your progress with interest."

With that she swanned away—to the stairs so that when Loretta came up with Esme's shawl in her hands, she could deliver it while keeping her distance from him.

Rafe sipped his brandy as he digested what he'd heard, what he'd learned, then considered what it meant.

He was starting to figure it out. He'd correctly identified Esme's intention from the first; all she'd done and said since had only confirmed it.

Loretta, however, he'd only just started to see clearly.

He fully intended to see a lot more.

Fully intended to uncover her secrets.

Even without Esme's calculated prod he didn't think he could resist.

Esme had engineered the situation; regardless of her manner of showing it, he was certain she'd be thrilled when he picked up the gauntlet her dear Loretta, however unintentionally, had just flung at his feet.

Hours later, hip propped against the starboard rail just forward of the bridge, Rafe stood on the observation deck idly scanning the river sliding slowly past. Along this stretch, forests of fir reached down to the banks, dark sentries lining the gently rippling stretch of moon-silvered blackness.

He stared, but didn't really see. In the silence, he could hear every little sound—an owl hooting in the forest, the creak of a rope from the stern; he would hear if any cultist tried to swim up and climb on board.

It was just after midnight. Hassan wouldn't relieve him for several hours yet. Time enough to decide his tack with respect to one Loretta Michelmarsh.

The passionate female who hid behind a façade of demureness for no reason that he, or apparently even her great-aunt, could discern.

He'd suspected the existence of that façade before today, but this afternoon he'd seen the passion. Not completely unleashed and in full flight, but during the contest she'd been unrestrained, direct, fearless, and bold.

She'd been herself—and he'd been ensorcelled, enthralled.

He had to learn more, but how? Especially now she knew he knew, and was determined to deny it.

How did one get a woman to be herself when she didn't want to be?

He was still wrestling with that when he heard the squeak as the swing doors on the stairs opened, followed by the sound of footsteps climbing the treads. He held still in the shadows, waiting, watching.

A dark head emerged, followed by a graceful, willowy figure, clad once more in her pelisse with a shawl slung about her shoulders.

She halted at the top of the stairs and looked around. Then she spotted him and strode swiftly and purposefully across the deck.

He straightened as she neared. "Couldn't sleep?"

"No." She halted before him. Stared up into his face. "And it's all your fault. I'll sleep like a baby once I've got this . . . you"—wildly she waved one hand—"sorted out."

He suppressed a grin. "How do you plan to do that?" She'd worked herself into a state.

"By making it very clear that I will not play your games, that contrary to what Esme may have led you to believe, I have no interest in . . . in . . . in exploring anything—not anything involving me." Loretta let her temper color her eyes, but in the poor light he probably couldn't see.

Folding her arms, she glared at him. She had to put an end to this before it truly began. Before it could go any further, and undermine her carefully constructed life. "I realize I might appear in some respects to be a challenge, especially because I have no interest in gentlemen. But as that is the case, and I assure you it is, then I'm sure you're too much the gentleman to keep pursuing me, Esme's encouragement or not."

There! Let him argue that.

She waited—waited for him to incline his head and agree to stop teasing her.

After a long moment of studying her face, his face in unhelpful shadow, he reached out and ran the back of one finger down her cheek.

Her nerves literally leapt. So did she. "Stop that!"

"Why?"

"I just told you why!"

"No. You told me that you had no interest in gentlemen— which group I take it is supposed to include me." His shadowed gaze held hers. "That"—he pointed to her cheek—"or more specifically your reaction, says otherwise."

"It does not!" She felt her cheeks heat, and was suddenly grateful for the weak light.

He tilted his head. "So you're not attracted to me?"

She lifted her chin. "No."

He pushed away from the rail and swung around her; instinctively she pivoted to keep facing him—facing the danger—then he stepped forward and she backed against the rail.

Locking a hand about the rail on either side of her, caging her, he lowered his head and looked into her eyes. "Prove it."

She blinked. Her eyes were as wide as they could get. "What?" The word came out perilously close to a squeak.

"Prove it." His tone didn't grow any less uncompromising with the repetition.

Her mouth felt dry. Her heart thudded. But . . . "How?" Perhaps if she could. . . .

"Kiss me."

"No!" She wanted to push him away, but didn't dare touch him. Didn't dare risk any further damning reactions.

He sighed as if she were a difficult child. "If you're truly not attracted to me, then if you kiss me, and I kiss you in return, nothing will happen. Definitely not for you, and certainly not for me. I'm not in the habit of kissing ladies who aren't attracted to me—I imagine the experience will be quite off-putting."

"Off-putting?"

"Indubitably. So if you want to put an end to all speculation over what might or might not come to be between us, then kissing me should spell an end to any suggestion of a mutual attraction."

She held his gaze, then glanced at his face, briefly studied his expression. He was serious. Serious about calling her bluff. The thing was . . . it wasn't exactly a bluff. More like a calculated decision.

What would happen if she kissed him? Was her will strong enough to keep her senses in line—for the space of just one kiss?

Looking at things another way, could she get out of this trap she'd backed herself into without kissing him?

Staring into his eyes, sensing the implacability in him—in the battle-hardened commander he actually was—she inwardly cursed. She had, she suspected, just thrown down a gauntlet she hadn't meant to toss.

Clearly she was going to have to learn the rules of this game sometime—and that time appeared to be now.

She tipped up her chin, narrowed her eyes on his. "So if I kiss you and feel nothing, you'll agree to treat me as you would a younger Esme?"

"If I kiss you and you feel nothing, I'll agree to whatever you want."

That sounded fair. "In that case—"

In a rush, she raised her hands, framed his face, and pressed her lips to his. She didn't give him a chance to kiss her. She wasn't going to let him overwhelm her; she intended to remain in control. . . .

Firm, resilient, mobile. His lips moved under hers, and captured her awareness.

Her world stopped. Her senses focused, fixated.

She pressed her lips against his, wanting to see . . .

And he did it again. Shifted his lips beneath hers again, more this time, and she had to follow.

Had to see where the path led—had to know . . .

Then he was kissing her and she was kissing him, and the exchange seemed to have no beginning and no end. It drew her in, effortlessly held her senses, then he parted her lips, and her senses spun.

Whirled as his tongue slipped between her lips and stroked, touched, caressed.

Waltzed as he found her tongue and tempted, and she returned the pleasure, followed, and tasted him as he tasted her.

Never had Rafe walked an edge so fine, so fraught with the danger of taking too much, moving too fast, and sending her running.

By sheer force of will he kept his hands locked on the rail, denying the almost overpowering urge to seize her instead, to wrap his arms around her and lock her against him, her soft feminine warmth to his much harder heat.

Not yet.

But soon.

That much was now written in stone.

Even with only her hands on his cheeks and their lips and tongues touching, he could sense her curiosity welling, flaring out of control. Could taste it like honeyed wine on the slicked surface of her luscious lips. Could sense it grow to a steady flame as he pressed further, deeper, slowly but subtly claiming her mouth . . .

She pulled back on a gasp, eyes wide. She stared at him for an instant, and he couldn't read her thoughts.

"Good God!" She breathed the words more than said them.

For an instant her hands remained cradling his cheeks, then they dropped to his shoulders, she pushed and he stepped back.

Still she stared, then she abruptly shook her head, looked away. "No."

Without another glance or utterance of any sort, she stepped around him, walked to the stairs and quickly went down.

Rafe stood where he was and watched her. Only after she'd disappeared did he let his lips curve.

Her "Good God!" hadn't been uttered with heat, with horror, not even with shock. Her fascination, her enthrallment, had rung clearly.

Discovery. Revelation.

Unbounded interest.

All had resonated in her stunned voice.

As for her "no" . . .

Smile deepening, he turned to lean on the rail and look out at the night.

Her "no" hadn't been directed at him, but at herself.

Four

November 29, 1822
The Uray Princep *on the Danube*

The following morning, Rafe joined Esme and Loretta at the breakfast table in the dining salon. Esme greeted him warmly. Loretta barely glanced his way.

Although he tried to catch her eye, she refused to meet his. The predictable exchanges between him and Esme about the weather—chilly—and the scenery—increasingly dominated by dark forests—failed to elicit any response from Loretta.

After that kiss that, contrary to her intention, had demonstrated conclusively that there was indeed a powerful attraction between them—an attraction he was determined to pursue—she appeared to have grown even more repressive, not less.

Eventually, driven to prod, he asked, "I do hope your walk on the deck last night didn't leave you with an unexpected chill."

Brows rising, Esme glanced at Loretta.

Meeting Esme's gaze, Loretta stated, "I couldn't sleep, so I took a quick turn about the deck." Without looking at him, she continued, "It was quite mild. The outing didn't affect me in the least."

Too irritated to gawp, he narrowed his eyes at her—at her

profile, since she still refused to look his way. "I had thought the change in temperature during the time you spent on deck would have registered—indeed, would have made some impression."

She cast him a sharp glance. "Clearly it did not."

He trapped her gaze. "You seemed very aware of the change when you left the deck so precipitously."

"I can't recall anything noteworthy."

"You can't be that forgetful." He arched a brow. "Or is it intentionally forgetful?"

Her eyes had narrowed to bright blue slits. Setting down her teacup, she pushed back from the table. "If you'll excuse me, I'm sure there's something else I should be doing." She rose; annoyed, he got to his feet, too. To Esme, she said, "I'll be in the stateroom if you need me."

With that, she turned and marched away, around to the stairs; he heard her slippers pattering as she went down to the cabins.

Irritated and not above showing it, he frowned and re-sumed his seat. Glancing across the table, he took in the smile wreathing Esme's face. She was utterly delighted.

"What game are you playing?" His growled question only made her smile more brightly.

"I'm not playing at all, dear boy. In this, I'm merely an observer."

He humphed. "You could at least help."

"You know, I don't think I can. This is one of those chal-lenges one has to manage without assistance. I did tell you it wouldn't be easy."

His response was a distinctly unencouraging look.

She grinned, laid down her napkin, and rose. "Admit it, if it were easy, there would be no thrill in the chase—you'd grow bored."

Rising again, he just grunted.

She was right, on all counts. But he didn't have to like it.

It was afternoon, and the boat was slowing to come along-side the docks in Pressburg; Rafe was on his way up from the cabins to join the rest of the passengers on the observation deck when the captain hailed him.

"We have cargo to put ashore here, and some to take on. It is likely we will remain at dock for the next twenty-four hours."

Rafe inclined his head. "Thank you for the warning."

The captain wryly smiled. "It is not only that we will be tied up, you understand, but that the ladies will wish to go sightseeing." He tipped his head toward the observation deck. "I have heard them talking."

Rafe inwardly groaned. "Again, thank you for the warning."

With a salute the captain went on his way. Rafe paused, marshaling the arguments most likely to succeed in keeping Esme and her great-niece safely on board, then continued up the stairs.

Emerging onto the observation deck, he located Esme and Loretta, their maids behind them, standing with all the other passengers at the starboard rail, all pointing and exclaiming at the sights as the boat angled to come alongside the wharf.

He hadn't spoken to Loretta since she'd left him at the breakfast table. He was fairly sure she was avoiding him. Given how he felt over her attempt to dismiss the kiss they'd shared the previous night, that wasn't perhaps surprising. He felt like glowering at her; in response, she seemed determined to keep her nose in the air whenever their paths crossed.

They were doomed to cross now. Steeling himself for the anticipated battle, he walked over to join her and Esme.

"I can't believe it's in such a sad state." Loretta stared at the ruins of the castle that, according to the guidebooks, stood proud and tall on a plateau above the river, dominating the town at the plateau's base. "There's nothing but rubble left."

"It used to be magnificent." Frau Gruber, wrapped in shawls, nodded at the ruins. "Queen Maria Theresa used to hold court there. When I was a girl, I was lucky enough to see inside. So much gilt and enamel, and wonderful carving! It was a beautiful palace."

"What happened to it?" Esme asked. "Napoleon?"

"No. It was a fire. An accident, I heard." Frau Gruber shrugged. "These things happen."

Loretta stared at all that was left of such magnificence; she felt so deflated it was difficult not to sag. "I was so looking forward to seeing it."

"Never mind." Esme patted her arm. "There's still a great deal to see here. The town has a wonderfully rich history."

"I suppose there's still the Grassalkovich Palace, and the Archiepiscopal Palace as well as the cathedral." Loretta continued to stare at the ruins above the town. "But I was so set on seeing a castle of such longevity, one that still functioned."

She'd hoped to use it as the centerpiece for a vignette. She'd managed to send three installments off to her agent from Buda, but her editor wanted more; she would need to send at least two more from Vienna, their next stop.

Re-sorting the various topics that had occurred to her, looking for another that might resonate with what remained in Pressburg, she was nevertheless aware of their courier-guide hovering behind her and Esme.

She was doing her best not to think of him by name in the hope that stressing his position would help her remember to keep him at arm's length, more particularly to keep herself at arm's length from him. Yet even though she kept her gaze fixed on the town, she was aware of him studying her, then looking at Esme, then back at her.

Esme, too, was pretending not to have noticed him, although Loretta was quite sure she had. "I know it's a great disappointment that the castle is in ruins, dear, but I suspect the Primate's Palace will be even more richly decorated. As I recall, Napoleon and King Francis signed the Peace of Pressburg there. As the Corsican upstart was ever one to insist on the highest degree of pomp and circumstance, that suggests that the Primate's Palace was, at least at that time, the most significant palace in the town."

As if just noticing Rafe, Esme turned. "Ah—there you are, dear boy. I was about to suggest that we visit the Primate's Palace this afternoon. There's plenty of other sights worthy of our attention, but we can leave them for tomorrow when we will have the whole day, yet poor Loretta here is so cast down with discovering the castle has been reduced to blackened rubble that we really should do something to distract her."

If Loretta had been one of his sisters, Rafe would have scoffed, but she truly was, as Esme said, cast down, her expression lacking the animated eagerness he was accustomed to seeing; the spark of intelligent enthusiasm usually lighting her eyes was doused, absent.

Even as, inwardly frowning, he studied her, Hassan came up from the stern. When Rafe looked at him, he murmured, "No sign of cultists anywhere."

"There—see?" Esme smiled at Rafe. "No reason whatever we shouldn't indulge in an afternoon's excursion."

Eagerness lit her gray eyes, but Rafe couldn't tell which she was most set on seeing—the architectural sights, or the sight of her great-niece tormenting him.

"I suppose you're right." Loretta turned to join the discussion, animation reinfusing her features to a small degree. "The Primate's Palace is sure to be interesting." She'd spoken to Esme, but then looked at Rafe. "And a short excursion off this boat will do us all good."

He met her eyes, was peripherally aware of the others—Gibson, Rose, and Hassan, as well as Esme—waiting on his decision.

At least she was acknowledging his existence again.

"All right." He glanced at Hassan, then at Esme. "Just the Primate's Palace, then back."

"Of course, dear boy." Esme beamed. "Whatever you decree."

A strong commander would not have been swayed by such frivolous arguments. On the other hand, the wisest commanders rescripted their plans to gain the most out of every situation.

Rafe told himself he'd been wise. He fully intended to put his foot down and ensure Esme, Loretta, and the two maids remained safely aboard whenever danger threatened. As it happened, there didn't appear to be any overt danger in Pressburg.

Strolling behind Esme and Loretta as their party was conducted through the Primate's Palace by a helpful custodian, Rafe was glad he'd chosen the course of wisdom. Not only was Loretta fully reengaged, energized and eagerly putting shrewd and insightful questions to the custodian, but contrary to every expectation he'd had, he, too, found the palace's history of interest.

"And this," the custodian pushed open a pair of doors, their intricate carving heavily gilded, "is the room where Napoleon and King Francis the Second met. It was after Napoleon's victory at Austerlitz. King Francis had little choice." Preceding them into the chamber, the custodian waved at an ornate table and two chairs. "They sat there, Napoleon on one side with his generals arrayed behind him, and behind them the standard-bearers with many of their legions' eagles, and on this side, King Francis with his three advisors."

The custodian knew his history. Either that, or he had an excellent imagination. His descriptions of the signing, in vivid and exact detail, brought the moment to life.

When the custodian came to the end of his recitation, Rafe blinked back to the present, then glanced at Esme. She seemed interested, but unmoved. Beyond Esme, however, Loretta looked as enthralled as he'd felt.

With the high point of the tour behind them, they walked back through the long corridors to the door through which they'd entered.

Loretta chatted and exclaimed, her imagination fired by all she'd seen and felt. Esme, however, was clearly thinking of other things, and appeared to respond to her comments at random.

Exasperated, Loretta finally turned to their courier-guide. "You fought against Napoleon. Did you not feel a lingering sense that matters of great import had occurred in that room?"

For a moment, she thought he would scoff and dismiss the idea as a fanciful feminine notion, but after studying her face, he said, "Not ghosts of the people involved but a shade, a lingering shadow of destiny?"

"Yes! That's it." *A lingering shadow of destiny.* She could use those words. They perfectly encapsulated what she'd sensed.

Feeling thoroughly vindicated, she walked on. If a male like Rafe Carstairs could sense the echoes in that room, then she was hardly imagining things. She was sure she could fashion a truly engaging vignette on the importance to history of maintaining places that had hosted great change—like the Primate's Palace—and not letting them decay or fall victim to lack of care, like the castle.

"Did you ever see Napoleon?" She glanced at Rafe.

"Not close—only in the distance in the wake of Waterloo."

"How did he appear—like an all-powerful emperor or a petty tyrant?"

"I only saw him that once, after the battle. He looked . . . lost." After a moment he went on, "The edifice he'd fought all his life to build had come tumbling down about his ears—for good and all, that time. He was a smallish man, and when I saw him he was on foot, with Wellington, Blücher, and the other generals around him. Napoleon looked like a tradesman who found himself in the company of kings."

They reached the door and took leave of the custodian. Loretta was especially effusive. Rafe smiled and gave the man a respectable donation toward the palace's upkeep. Giving Esme his arm, he assisted her down the steps to where the carriage they'd hired waited to return them to the wharves. Hassan materialized and opened the door.

Rafe helped Esme in, then turned and offered Loretta his hand.

She looked at it, hesitated, then set her fingers in his.

They both felt the connection—the sensual spark—when he closed his fingers about hers.

She raised her eyes to his; her chin firmed, but then she inclined her head and allowed him to help her up the carriage steps.

The two maids were already inside. Rafe turned to Hassan.

"I'll travel with the driver and keep watch," Hassan said.

Rafe nodded and followed Loretta into the carriage.

They spotted no cultists on the way back to the boat. However, because they were so alert, Rafe and Hassan noticed two men, locals by their dress, loitering in the shadow of one of the warehouses lining the wharf.

Their party had descended from the hired carriage at the top of the wharf, and walked the fifty yards to where the *Uray Princep* bobbed on the gentle river swell. The men's attention had fixed on their group the instant they'd set foot on the wharf. While there were many men of all types going in and out of the nearby warehouses and back and forth along the wooden wharf, all except the two loiterers had a clear purpose.

Hassan remained on guard at the bottom of the gangplank while Rafe helped Esme, then Loretta, aboard, then Hassan watched over the two maids as they followed their mistresses onto the boat.

Neither Rafe nor Hassan had given any sign that they had seen the two men hovering in the shadows. With a tip of his head, Rafe summoned Hassan on board. As the big Pathan joined him, he murmured, "The observation deck."

They went up. Hunkering down by the boat's side, they watched the men through the rails; the pair gave no sign of noticing them. While the ladies took tea in the salon below, they watched the two men talk and grin—waited to see if the pair paid as much attention to the other passengers returning to the *Uray Princep* as they had to their party.

But the men appeared disinterested in anyone else.

"Not good," Rafe said as, with the light fading to an early winter's dusk, the two watchers stood, stretched, and with one last look at the *Uray Princep*, disappeared down an alley between two warehouses.

"Could the cult have hired locals to act for them?" Hassan asked.

Rafe grimaced. "It's possible. We'll have to remain on guard."

They divided the remaining hours of the day as well as the night; one of them would always be on watch, armed and alert. While Hassan went downstairs to nap, Rafe walked to the other side of the deck and looked out at the river, at the forests stretching away as far as he could see.

He looked east, toward England.

He had a mission to complete. That was his priority. Pursuing Loretta Michelmarsh was less urgent.

Seeing the men sent to watch their party had reinforced that fact, had readjusted his focus.

Had reminded him of his goal.

Despite the slowness of his journey, he didn't have time to indulge his fascination with a young lady who, it seemed, didn't actually want him to be interested in her.

Loretta noticed the change. Finally alone in her cabin with the boat silent around her, she paced, and wondered.

During dinner and the gathering in the salon afterward, Rafe's attention had appeared tightly focused elsewhere.

Outward. Outside the boat.

The deflection of his attention was similar to when he and Hassan had been expecting attack from cultists in Buda, but the intensity was heightened, honed, more controlled and absolute.

Added to that, Hassan had not been present at dinner. When she'd remarked on his absence, Rafe had merely said that Hassan had eaten earlier.

Esme had noticed the shifting currents, too. When she'd asked if anything were amiss, Rafe had denied it, passing off his increased watchfulness as merely being on guard.

"Huh!" Loretta swung around. "Something must have happened, but what?"

She hadn't seen anything; neither had Rose or Gibson. She was sure Esme hadn't either. So what had caused the change?

"I should be glad of it. At least he's no longer watching me." She kicked her skirts out of her way. "And it's reassuring to know he's paying attention to his mission and its attendant dangers—as he should."

She knew she should mean that, yet. . . . "Damn it! What a time to revert to being just a guard."

After their afternoon's excursion, she'd wanted to re-engage. To learn more. Not just about that astonishing kiss and what it might mean, but more about him—the man who'd understood what she'd meant enough to label it the *shadow of destiny*.

Instead, he'd drawn back, shifted focus, and if she were honest, she missed his attention. Missed the warmth of his gaze resting on her, missed looking up and finding him watching her as if he wanted to know all her secrets.

She missed the teasing exchanges. Even though she hadn't appreciated them at the time, she'd found them stimulating in an intellectual way.

She missed looking up and meeting his gaze, seeing warmth and laughter in the soft blue.

Halting, she frowned at the wall. Yes, she'd been less than encouraging—positively discouraging—that morning. He was entirely justified in drawing back from her.

She'd never engaged in any such interactions before, but she suspected that if she wanted his attention back, enough at least so she could learn what the unexpected connection between them—a connection she could hardly deny after that scorching, mind-scrambling kiss—portended, it might be up to her to make the next move.

Whatever that might be.

She felt a tad ridiculous—twenty-four years old and with less experience than a giddy girl of seventeen—but if she wanted to learn more, then it behooved her to make some attempt to reinstigate their . . . connection.

It was full dark; by now the rest of the ship's company would have retired to their berths. Pulling on her pelisse, she opened her door, then slipped through and out of the stateroom and headed for the observation deck.

She needed her customary stroll, and she felt certain Rafe would be up on the deck.

Reaching the top of the stairs, she emerged into the darkness, turned, and saw him by the rail. The moon was hidden by heavy clouds; he was no more than a denser shadow against the fluid ink of the river beyond, yet she knew it was him.

But he wasn't alone.

From the other shadow's height, she guessed it was Hassan standing alongside him.

They'd heard her and turned.

She hesitated.

Rafe left the rail and silently crossed to her.

In the dim light, she could barely make out his features.

"In the circumstances, while we're tied up in a town, you shouldn't come up on deck at night. I suggest you return below."

She wanted to ask what circumstances, but his tone was that of an officer used to command; he might have couched it as a request but it was indeed an order. "I just wanted to take my usual constitutional," she replied.

"You'll have to pace below."

Her eyes had adjusted; just as there was no give in his voice, there was none in his features. She felt rebellious, considered refusing.

"Neither Hassan nor I need the distraction of you strolling the deck while we're on guard and there's a possibility of attack. Please—go below."

The "please" worked. She swallowed a sigh, inclined her head, then turned and went back down the stairs.

It wasn't fair to make guarding them more difficult. He and Hassan weren't out there because they wanted to be up all night.

She was slipping back into her room when she registered what he'd said.

The more she considered it, she was perfectly certain her strolling the deck wouldn't distract Hassan.

The following morning, somewhat to Loretta's surprise Rafe made no attempt to dissuade her and Esme from their proposed excursion to take in more of the town's sights.

A number of riverboats had tied up at the main wharf. Their party passed numerous other visitors as they strolled the town's streets. Despite Rafe's and Hassan's increased tension, no threat seemed likely with so many others around.

They ambled through the Grassalkovich Palace and the Archiepiscopal Palace, admiring the architecture and ornate furnishings, then stopped at a picturesque inn for lunch.

While Loretta, Esme, Rose, and Gibson chatted about what they'd seen, Rafe and Hassan continued grimly silent, constantly surveying their surroundings. But all remained calm and serene.

When they emerged into the pale light of the winter's afternoon, Esme halted and glanced around. "Just the cathedral, I think, then we can return to the boat for afternoon tea." With her cane, she waved at the tall spire of St. Martin's Cathedral.

The cathedral was only five minutes' gentle stroll away. One half of the cathedral's double doors stood open; they passed into the quiet, reverential gloom of a wood-paneled foyer, then walked along beside a heavily carved screen to the entrance to the nave.

Soaring arches and massive beams framed the cathedral's roof and led the eye to the stained-glass window behind the altar. With Esme beside her, Loretta slowly walked down the nave, taking note of the richly appointed pews, the jewel-toned runners and crimson prayer cushions. The altar was draped with a fabulous altarpiece of fine linen embroidered with gold thread. Atop it sat two massive candlesticks flanked by two chalices.

She and Esme went straight to the altar to examine the gold-thread embroidery more closely. Rose and Gibson followed at their heels.

Rafe hung back in the foyer, but after one last glance at the open door, he motioned Hassan on, and reluctantly started down the aisle. The church was solid stone; while footsteps were easy to hear inside, it was well nigh impossible to hear anyone approaching the church door, and that door appeared to be their only exit to the street. He wasn't entirely comfortable with the situation, but was even less comfortable allowing too much distance between him and Hassan and their charges. Inwardly grimacing, he walked slowly down the aisle.

He and Hassan were scanning the choir stalls behind the altar when a sound drew their attention to a chapel to the right of the nave.

Four men emerged from the shadows.

Two were the loiterers from the wharf the day before.

Rafe swore and started down the nave at a run.

None of the four men brandished weapons, yet their threat was clear as they rushed toward the women, presumably to seize them as hostages.

Even as the thought formed, Rafe saw Loretta and Esme whisk themselves around the altar, pulling Rose and Gibson with them.

He had time to offer one word of thanks for quick-thinking women before the four men, now in a loose line in front of the altar, swung to face him and Hassan.

Neither he nor Hassan slowed. Leading with one shoulder, elbow braced, they allowed their momentum to carry them into the men.

The man Rafe collided with slammed back against the

altar. His head snapped back, hitting solid marble, then his legs buckled and he slid down to the floor. The man Hassan collided with fared similarly.

One of the two attackers left standing snarled, and swung a hamlike fist at Rafe's head. Rafe blocked the blow, and struck hard at the man's stomach.

They traded blow for blow. Rafe managed to avoid the worst of the wild punches. From the corner of his eye, he glimpsed the man he'd knocked into the altar struggling to his feet, presumably to join the fray. Rafe spotted an opening in his opponent's defense, stepped in, and landed a solid blow to the man's jaw. The man went down like a felled fir.

Rafe swung to face the man's revived friend just as Loretta, leaning across the altar, brought a chalice down on the man's head.

The man's eyes rolled up and he slid down to the floor again.

Rafe turned to help Hassan, who was battling one groggy opponent and one very intent one. Rafe made short work of the groggy man, and by then Hassan had knocked the other unconscious.

The chalice Esme had thrust at her still in her hand, Loretta went around the altar to stare at the man she'd downed. She couldn't quite believe she'd struck a man and rendered him unconscious, yet there he lay, slumped as if drunkenly asleep.

She expected to feel shocked, or at least overcome with some form of sensibility, yet all she felt coursing her veins was excitement and an exhilaration akin to triumph.

Before she could dwell further on the unexpected feeling, Rafe grabbed her hand, tugged the chalice from her fingers, and set it back on the altar. He waved Esme and the maids forward. "Quickly—out!"

Esme, Gibson, and Rose hurried out from behind the altar, past Loretta and Rafe to where Hassan was waiting to usher them quickly up the nave.

Rafe thrust Loretta before him. "Into the foyer."

She hurried after the others, Rafe on her heels. He glanced back as they went. She glanced back, too, felt his hand graze her back as if he needed to be sure she was there, close, even when he was looking the other way.

The others were waiting in the foyer.

"Shouldn't we report this to someone?" Esme asked.

Rafe met her eye. "Do you want to leave the *Uray Princep* and spend the next weeks explaining things to the authorities here?"

Esme blinked. "No."

"Nor do I." Rafe looked at the others, then at Loretta. "Luckily, no one got hurt bar a few bruises, and we were the only ones in the cathedral. I suggest we leave those four where they are, and walk calmly and sedately back to the wharf."

"As if nothing happened?" Loretta asked, and received a grim nod in reply.

By general consensus that was what they did, which gave her time to relive the experience and examine her feelings.

Her surprise at the attack. Her surprise of a different sort as she'd watched Rafe come racing to their rescue, then trade violent blows with one of their attackers.

Her shock as she'd realized the first man he'd hit had recovered and intended to join his fellow-thug in attacking Rafe, two on one. She'd frantically looked around for something with which to hit the man; as usual all the men had dismissed the women and weren't even looking their way. Esme had grabbed the chalice and handed it to her. Hefting it, she hadn't even hesitated, but had grimly raised it and determinedly brought it down on the cowardly thug's head.

It had felt *so* good, so satisfying to be able to do something, to contribute to their party's relief in however small a way.

To save Rafe from sustaining any unnecessary injuries.

She was fairly sure that a prim and proper young lady was supposed to swoon on witnessing physical violence of that nature. Yet no matter how hard she searched within, she simply didn't have a swoon in her. Not with excitement still bubbling through her veins.

No. If anything she felt proud—proud to have done her bit and assisted Rafe and Hassan in defending their party.

They reached the wharf without further incident, and, under Rafe's and Hassan's watchful eyes, trooped back on board for what she considered a well-deserved afternoon tea.

Rafe didn't breathe easily until he had the women back on board the *Uray Princep.* His first thought had been that the men had been cult hirelings sent to seize the scroll-holder. Now he wasn't so sure.

Joining Hassan on the observation deck, he scanned the wharf. "Other than those men, I've seen nothing that even hints of the cult here."

"Nor I." Hassan stared at the town. "Could they have been local thieves looking to steal from travelers?"

"Possible, I suppose. In the aftermath of war, there's often trouble with disbanded soldiers who no longer have homes or jobs . . . but I would have thought the wars too long over for that to still be a problem." Rafe grimaced. "I wish now that I'd stopped to inquire whether they'd been hired, or if they'd acted on their own."

"It matters not now." Hassan straightened from the rail. "We are safe and we'll keep watch, and the crew will help if we need them."

"True." Rafe looked at the bridge. "I'll have a word to the captain, mention that we were accosted in the town and suggest he pulls out onto the river as soon as possible. It looks like they've finished loading."

Pushing away from the rail, Rafe headed for the bridge.

Once apprised of the situation, the captain expressed his outrage at the attack, and with his cargo fully loaded and all passengers back on board, readily gave orders for the boat to quit the wharf.

Half an hour later, they were sailing slowly upriver once more.

Late that night, Loretta lay in her bed, and tried logically to examine the changes within herself.

She'd understood from the first that Esme had intended to, indeed had designed their trip to, shake her, Loretta, from her habitual and determined adherence to Robert and Catherine's straitlaced ideals.

With the exception of Robert, Michelmarshes were not straitlaced. She knew she was not, but had long ago discovered that life was much easier to live, to maintain complete control of, when people believed she was demure, decorous, timid, and quiet.

At least life *had* been easier to control until one too many suitors had begged for her hand.

She had—somewhere about Madrid—accepted that she couldn't return to London and continue to live as she had been, continue to live a convenient lie. What she hadn't had any real sense of, and still didn't, was what sort of life she wanted, what sort of person she wanted to be instead.

Her own person, of course. In dispensing with her prim and proper façade, she wasn't proposing to replace it with some other misleading persona. No. What she now needed to define was who Loretta Michelmarsh truly was.

Not until she knew that would she be sure how to behave from now on.

Throughout the trip, Esme had been assiduous in challenging her, in this manner or that, to question who she was so she would discover the necessary answer. The greatest challenge Esme had thus far flung in her path was Rafe Carstairs.

He'd already challenged her—pulled her out of her usual patterns of behavior—enough to make her kiss him.

And he'd kissed her back, which had raised her curiosity to a level where the impulse to badger him for more kisses bedeviled her every time she set eyes on him.

But more than anything else, he made her *feel*.

In the short time she'd known him, she'd felt more emotions—excitement, exhilaration, anticipation, a lick or two of fear, irritation and anger, as well as something she suspected was desire—and she'd felt those emotions more intensely than she'd ever imagined she could.

Just being in his company left her alive and enthused to live in a dangerous, reckless, throw-her-heart-over-every-hurdle way. He was a potent temptation to live as a Michelmarsh—with giddy abandon.

She didn't need to look to know Esme was preening.

Yet for herself, she wasn't so sure. She could have understood her reactions, the changes within, if Rafe had been the man of her dreams. Yet she couldn't see how he could be.

Heaven knew he was handsome enough, yet he was also high-handedly arrogant, superior and dictatorial when it suited him, charming when that seemed the better course to getting whatever he wanted. He was autocratic, brusque when crossed, and growled like a bear when he didn't get his way.

Most telling of all, she was fairly certain that she'd never be able to control him—he was simply too strong a character. Like recognized like in that regard, and as he would never be able to control her, that didn't auger well for a peaceful married life.

An *interesting* married life, perhaps.

But she wasn't some witless ninny to plunge into anything without due consideration. Until she'd determined what sort of lady she truly was, she should follow the course of wisdom and keep him at arm's length.

Meanwhile . . . sleep drew her lids down. She sighed and relaxed.

On the border of sleep she relived again those thrilling moments in the cathedral.

She had to admit she liked feeling alive. Feeling fiercely engaged with life.

Esme would be happy; her sisters would be, too.

Whatever her path forward proved to be, prim and proper Loretta Michelmarsh had died.

Five

December 1, 1822
The Uray Princep *anchored off Vienna*

I cannot wait to see the shops!" Frau Hemleich beamed. "Spending Christmas here is going to be wonderful!"

Frau Gruber agreed. "I'm so glad Wilhelm suggested we break our journey here."

Loretta smiled and strolled on, moving through the salon, stopping to chat here and there. All the other passengers were leaving the boat in Vienna, either to spend time there or travel on by land. The boat was currently anchored off the city's wharves, but would tie up the following morning and remain at dock until the next day.

She wondered if Rafe was behind the captain's decision to remain in the river, and to tie up for, as she understood it, only the minimum time.

Through the crowd she glimpsed their courier-guide speaking with Herr Gruber. It had been that way all day; aside from meals, taken in the dining room with everyone else about, she'd only seen Rafe from a distance. Even when they'd shared a table, he'd appeared focused on other things, contributing little to the conversation.

That was, she'd reminded herself, a good thing, given she'd determined to keep him at arm's length, at least for the moment.

Pausing beside Esme's chair, she wasn't surprised to hear her great-aunt discussing her sightseeing plans for the following day with the captain. What did surprise her was the restricted nature of those plans.

Even the captain remarked on it, to which Esme replied, "Oh, I've been to Vienna many times. There's really not that much here I need to see again."

Somewhat puzzled, Loretta smiled at the captain and moved on. Halting in the narrow forward end of the salon, she glanced at the scene outside, the black silk of the river sliding past with the brilliant lights of the city beyond.

A sudden ripple of awareness had her turning. Had her senses leaping, her heart thudding, then settling to a steady, but faster, beat.

Rafe halted beside her, also looking out. With his head he indicated the buildings of Vienna. "Has Esme decided what she wants to see tomorrow?"

He sounded grim, as if anticipating a battle over a busy, varied, and potentially dangerous schedule.

"I just heard her telling the captain. Apparently she wishes to walk the city walls to see if the views are as she remembers them, and to visit St. Stephen's Cathedral."

He frowned, met her eyes. "That's all?"

"All she admits to wishing to see."

"It sounds, for her, remarkably restrained."

She shrugged lightly. "Perhaps the incident in Pressburg unsettled her."

He humphed. "I could hope."

There wasn't anything she could say to that, yet . . . even though he stood perfectly still, she sensed he was restless.

He shifted. "No doubt we'll learn the truth of it tomorrow." With a nod, he moved away.

Loretta stayed where she was, looking out at the night,

and wondered at the feeling sliding insidiously through her. Disappointment?

She didn't like it—didn't approve of feeling it. Briskly turning, she strolled on, fetching up at Frau Gruber's side. "Where do you plan to go after Vienna?"

The next morning, Rafe left the boat immediately it docked. He returned at ten o'clock with the tickets to all the recently vacated passenger berths in his pocket.

He found Esme and Loretta in the salon, seated in the wide window bays. They'd been looking out at the city and plainly waiting on him; both had their hats and pelisses on. They turned to face him as he entered.

"I've just come from the Excelsior Shipping Company office here. We'll be the only passengers until Ulm."

"Ulm?" Esme frowned, then her face cleared. "Ah, I see. That's where we'll leave the Danube and go overland to Strasbourg to join the Rhine."

He nodded. "In the circumstances, I thought it wise to eliminate the distraction of other passengers—in the event of any attack, neither Hassan and I nor the captain and crew will have to concern ourselves with protecting others."

In eliminating that distraction, he'd simultaneously removed all social diversion for Esme and Loretta, but he hoped they wouldn't argue. The chance to improve their defensive position had been there, and he'd seized it.

To his relief, after a moment of consideration, Esme smiled. "It'll make things much quieter, but also more private." She glanced at Loretta. "We'll have the entire passenger half of the boat to ourselves."

He hadn't thought of that; he glanced at Loretta, then quickly refocused on Esme. "Are you ready to venture forth?"

At least during their excursion he wouldn't be tormented by being private with Loretta Michelmarsh.

While they waited by the gangplank for Rose and Gibson

to join them, Hassan ambled up, ready to assist in guarding the women. He'd been keeping watch on the observation deck while Rafe was in the town.

When Hassan halted beside him, Rafe tapped his pocket. "I bought all the free berths. It'll be just us from here to Ulm."

Hassan nodded. "That will make life easier."

So Rafe hoped. He glanced at Esme and Loretta, chatting a few feet away, and lowered his voice. "I saw cultists in town—not on the embankment, but further in. They seemed to be patrolling the major squares. They didn't see me, and they weren't actively searching."

"That suggests they do not yet know we are heading this way, nor that we are using the river." Hassan glanced at the women as Rose and Gibson joined them, then met Rafe's eyes. "Do you think the cult members will recognize us?"

"If we're with four women?" Rafe pulled a face. "I can't say."

He went forward to help Esme down the gangplank, then returned to give Loretta his hand. As usual, when he grasped her hand he sensed that indefinable spark, sensed her reaction, but steadfastly ignored it.

When he released her, she glanced sharply at him.

"I don't do it on purpose, you know." Frustration edged his mumble.

She frowned, but then turned away as Esme gestured with her cane and they started into the town.

They went first to the cathedral as at that hour it was between services. Loretta ambled in Esme's wake, examining the richly decorated finishes, drinking in the ornate, somewhat overwrought ambience, and wondering if there was anything she might make of it. She'd completed an excellent vignette based on her experiences at Pressburg, but then her mind had stalled. She needed some subject to inspire her.

Sadly, the cathedral, while undoubtedly noteworthy, didn't light any spark.

Not like Rafe Carstairs, but she wasn't going to think of him.

Then again . . . was there any way she could use his mission, or even him, his attributes, as the cornerstone of a commentary? The more she thought of it, the more inspired she felt, but such a piece would have to wait until she was back in England and resumed her usual column. For now . . . she was stumped.

After half an hour of wide-eyed wandering under Rafe's and Hassan's watchful eyes, Esme declared she was ready to quit the cathedral. They proceeded in good order to the city walls. The wide bulwarks had become fashionable promenades along which visitors and locals both strolled, the former taking in the views from the elevated battlements, while the latter used the wide walks as an impromptu meeting place.

Although the wind was chilly, the sun had won a battle with the clouds and in triumph cast a weak glow upon the stone walks. As they were all well rugged up against the wind, it was pleasant to stroll and observe, both the views and the others ambling past.

When Rafe ranged alongside her, Loretta commented, "Vienna must be one of those cities on everyone's itinerary. I've seen foreigners from a larger variety of countries here than anywhere else on our travels—even in Paris."

Eyes scanning the crowds, he nodded. "Useful for us— we're indistinguishable from any number of visiting parties out to see the sights."

So he can relax his vigilance a trifle, and perhaps look at me when he speaks to me. Loretta bit the words back, not entirely sure where they sprang from.

Just ahead, Esme had halted by a section of the battlements. They joined her and she pointed. "When Richard and I were last here, we stayed in a lovely little auberge off that square."

The square she'd indicated was in the center of what, from

the roofs and what they could see of the houses, was one of the wealthier districts.

"Many from the embassies stay in that area." Esme smiled. "It was a whirl of social activity from morn 'til night."

From their vantage point, they could see into the square, about half of it visible from that angle. Loretta caught sight of two men in long plain coats walking steadily down one side of the square. They were wearing turbans of a sort with what looked to be thin black scarves wound about, the ends left to flap in the breeze.

Eyes locked on the figures, she reached out and grasped Rafe's arm. Tightened her grip. "Are those cultists down there?"

She knew the answer—felt steel infuse the muscles beneath his sleeve—before he murmured, "Yes." After a moment, he went on, "I saw them this morning, but then, as now, they seem to be patrolling."

"There are more over there," Rose whispered.

They looked where she pointed, and saw another pair, similarly garbed, walking along one of the fashionable avenues.

"There's another spot a little way along that gives a good view into the fashionable streets," Esme said. "Shall we head on?"

They did, and from that other position sighted four more cultists; like those before, they were simply walking along.

"They seem to be only in the better areas," Loretta said.

"Actually," Esme said, "if memory serves, those are the streets and squares where there are major hotels catering to the carriage trade."

Rafe nodded. "They're watching and waiting for us to arrive."

"Which means they don't know we're already here." Loretta glanced at his face.

It was unreservedly grim as he replied, "Yet." He looked at Esme. "Is there anywhere else you wish to go?"

Her gaze on the cultists, Esme shook her head. "I believe I've seen all I need to."

It took some time to retrace their steps.

Once they were back in the streets not far from the embankment, Rafe felt forced to ask if Esme wished to stop at one of the comfortable inns they were passing for lunch.

To his relief, she shook her head. "No, no. We can have a late luncheon when we get back on board. I rather think I'll rest this afternoon."

It was the first he'd heard of Esme resting during the day, but although sprightly, she was definitely not young. Yet he noted the surprised look Loretta directed at her relative, as if the concept of Esme resting was novel to her, too.

But he wasn't about to argue.

He'd been torn over whether to hope they passed some cultists; he wanted to know if their disguises would hold. But having sighted eight, with Loretta, Esme, Rose, and Gibson with them, the principal imperative dominating his mind was to get the women safely on the boat.

He wasn't about to argue with his instincts.

They'd entered the narrower streets leading to the wharves, and were two blocks from the embankment when six men walking up the street in the opposite direction suddenly fanned out, blocking their way.

Rafe grabbed the women and thrust them into a recessed doorway. With the lunch hour upon them, the street was temporarily deserted.

Eyes on the six men, locals by the look of them—bruisers from dockside taverns was his guess—he caught the glint of a knife in one meaty fist. The next instant his saber was in his hand.

Beside him, Hassan already had his sword unsheathed.

"I'd prefer not to kill any," Rafe murmured.

Eyes on their opponents, Hassan merely said, "We'll see."

The men rushed them.

The clash was swift and brutal. Their attackers had thought to overwhelm them by sheer weight, but both Rafe and Hassan stepped aside at the last moment and two of the locals were immediately on the cobbles—deftly knocked unconscious with their sword hilts as they'd passed.

That left Rafe and Hassan facing two large attackers each.

Wide-eyed, Loretta watched the ensuing fight—tried to follow the moves, the clash of blades, tried to anticipate the shifting bodies, the slashes. The attackers fought with two knives each, one in each hand, against Rafe's and Hassan's long swords. Time and again, her heart leapt to her mouth—she heard Rose and Gibson, too, suck in fearful breaths—but time and again Rafe and Hassan would duck and weave . . . they were truly good at this.

So absorbed were the four of them in watching the fight, none of them noticed that one of the men knocked unconscious at the start had regained his wits and crawled away from the melee.

They weren't aware of him until he loomed beside them where they huddled in the doorway. With a knife in one hand, with the other he reached across Rose and Gibson. "Come here, you, and it'll all be over."

Startled, Loretta backed away from that grasping hand, felt Esme beside and a little behind her. Loretta's hand touched Esme's where it gripped the head of her cane.

Setting her jaw, Loretta seized the cane—Esme released it as she did. Lifting it, sliding her hand down its length, she stepped out of the doorway and swung the cane at their attacker.

The heavy silver-mounted head connected with the man's elbow with a satisfying *crack*! With a yelp he dropped the knife, then snarled a curse.

As she drew the cane back again, Rose and Gibson both kicked hard at the man's shins, distracting him.

Loretta raised the cane high and brought it down over his head.

He howled, then cowered as she swung it again, from the side this time, clipping him over the ear.

"Excellent, my dear," Esme called. "But don't break my cane."

Loretta doubted she could; the cane had a silver-plated casing. Regardless, she swung again. The man turned away, trying to protect his head with his arms.

Gibson and Rose hit him with their fists, kicked him with their boots.

With a strangled cry the man lurched away, paused to glance back at his companions, then fled.

Once again in the grip of euphoric victory, cane in hand Loretta whirled to see Rafe knock the last of the attackers out with his sword hilt. Even as the man slumped to join his mates on the cobbles, Rafe looked at her, then at the other three, then beckoned urgently. "Come on. Let's go."

Loretta handed Esme her cane, then took her great-aunt's arm and helped her hurry on down the street. As they did, she glanced at the shops lining the pavements, wondering why no one had come to their aid.

Then she realized. The men had chosen well. The street was filled with businesses that closed for the midday break, the shopkeepers returning to homes elsewhere for luncheon.

Rafe had noticed the same thing. He wanted to stop and question the men, but with the women present and multiple cultists in the town, he couldn't risk dallying there and then.

But the wharf was close. In less than ten minutes, he and Hassan had the women safely aboard.

He turned to Hassan. "Stay here, keep watch, and if you get a chance warn the captain. I'm going back to see if I can learn who hired those thugs."

Hassan merely nodded.

Rafe went quickly down the gangplank, then strode off down the wharf, breaking into a run as he turned up the street they'd come down minutes before.

Loretta watched him go. She'd heard his orders to Hassan, but . . .

Walking to stand beside Hassan, she said, "You should go with him. We're perfectly safe here—the captain's on board and the crew will see off any would-be attackers."

Hassan looked at her, then gently shook his head.

She frowned and pressed. "Those men might have all woken up by now. If they set on him all at once, who's to say what might happen?"

Hassan smiled. "Do not worry. He will be all right."

Folding her arms, she narrowed her eyes at him, but he only held to that gentle smile . . . he was probably as stubborn as his master.

She humphed, swung around, and headed for the salon. "He'd better be all right," she muttered. As for her not worrying . . . pigs would fly first.

Rafe returned to the boat in no good mood.

It was midafternoon when he trudged up the gangplank, then climbed the stairs to the observation deck. He joined Hassan at the rail. "No luck."

"They were gone?"

"Long gone by the time I got back there. But I couldn't have been far behind them, so I searched the surrounding streets, then trawled through the local taverns." He shook his head. "Not a sight. They've gone to ground, or slunk away to some lair further afield."

"They have to be locals—they'd picked their ambush site too well."

He nodded. "So they're in hiding. Given I couldn't ask if they were hired by indians with black scarves, I went further into town, to one of the squares the cultists are patrolling. They're still there, calmly walking the streets, watching—they clearly hadn't heard that we'd been located and attacked near the wharves. Sadly, that doesn't mean they won't hear about it later tonight, once their hirelings report in."

"If they report their failure, and if they were indeed cult hirelings."

"Indeed. But while we don't know whether those men were cult hirelings, we have to assume that by this evening, the cult will know we're in town."

Hassan nodded. "But they still will not know where we are—that we are on this boat and traveling by river."

"True. No one followed us when we came back with the ladies, and no one followed me back just now. We're still safe on that count." After a moment, Rafe added, "I wonder when the captain intends to cast off tomorrow?"

"I do not know." Hassan glanced at him. "But you had better go and reassure the ladies that you have returned and are safe."

Puzzled, he looked at Hassan.

Who grinned. "Miss Loretta was worried."

He raised his brows. "Was she?" After a moment, he said, "Then I suppose I had better go down and report."

Leaving Hassan on watch, he went down the stairs. The murmur of feminine voices led him to the salon. Esme and Loretta were there, seated in two armchairs facing the door. Now that they were the only passengers aboard, the salon was both spacious and private.

He ducked through the doorway. Even as he straightened and across the salon met Loretta's eyes, he knew something was wrong.

Her blue eyes raced over him, as if assuring herself he was unhurt, but when her gaze returned to his face, her expression was carefully, rather rigidly, blank. The way she held herself, sitting very upright in the chair, her body angled toward Esme, suggested that she was unhappy with whatever her outrageous relative was planning.

In contrast, the instant she set eyes on him, Esme beamed. "There you are, dear boy. Just in time to rejoice in my wonderful news! Loretta and I, and of course you, too, will be attending the Winter Ball at the Hofburg Palace tonight."

Halting before the chairs, he simply stared at her, convinced he couldn't have heard aright. "The Winter Ball?" He glanced at Loretta; her grimace told him the outing hadn't been her idea, that she'd argued against it, but hadn't succeeded in dissuading Esme.

"Indeed!" that incorrigible grande dame continued. "I lived in Vienna for some years and, if I do say so myself, have a great many friends here." Esme continued to smile delightedly at him. "Naturally, I sent my card to a few of the dearest, explaining that it would be dificult to call and see everyone given we were not long in town." She arched a brow at him. "I knew you wouldn't wish us to be scurrying all over town paying visits. However, one of my dearest friends had the brilliant notion of securing invitations for us for the ball tonight. Every one of my old friends will be there, so I can see them all at once." She lifted three gilt-edged ivory cards from her lap and waved them. "The invitations arrived while you were out."

She was honestly delighted, sincerely thrilled.

All he could see was disaster. "There are cultists in town."

"But we'll be going by carriage, dear boy—they'll never see you. I've already organized to have a coach call here at nine o'clock to take us up."

"The entry to the Palace . . ." Even as he said it, he knew that excuse would never fly.

Sure enough, Esme laughed. "The cultists won't be looking for you at a local ball. And they certainly won't be able to get into the grounds of the palace, much less inside. If there's one place you can be sure we'll be safe from the serpent's minions, it's surrounded by the cream of Austrian society."

He desperately searched for some reason to veto the outing.

Esme caught his eye. "And of course, regardless of whether you join us or not, I will have to attend." She waved the gilt-edged cards. "These are not easy to come by at short notice. Now they've been secured, I'll have to appear." She glanced at Loretta. "And Loretta, too, of course."

Meeting Esme's eyes, he recognized that this was one battle he could not win. There was nothing he could say to dissuade her, and ultimately he couldn't command her.

Now he understood the look in Loretta's eyes. Resignation.

He narrowed his eyes, all but growled, "Very well." Turning, he headed for the door. "I'll have to go into town and find a tailor. I forgot to pack my evening clothes."

"Excellent, dear boy. You won't regret it."

In the doorway, he glanced back at Esme, then briefly at Loretta. At least he would get to see her in a ballgown.

As he headed up the stairs to tell Hassan the news, it occurred to him that, given his current state vis-à-vis her, seeing Loretta Michelmarsh in a ballgown might not advance his cause.

Half an hour later, Loretta sat at the desk in the stateroom's sitting room, scribbling frantically. "Wonderful!" she muttered. "A damn ball. Just what I need."

Esme was resting in her cabin. Gibson and Rose were in Loretta's cabin, fussing over her ballgown and the necessary accoutrements.

Finally setting down her pen, she blotted the page, then reread her piece. "Mountains near and far." She'd recalled the night on the observation deck, the sight of the distant snowcapped peaks, and had been struck by the idea of using the vision as an analogy for life's challenges. Mountains as barriers, as hurdles to be overcome.

Much like Rafe Carstairs—or, more correctly, her reaction to him. She still wasn't sure what to do about it. What she could do about it, what her options were. Ignoring the phenomenon hadn't made it go away. And as he was clearly aware of the effect he had on her, and couldn't control it any more than she could . . .

Minutes later, she blinked, and realized she'd been far away, and not on any mountain. She'd been daydreaming. She couldn't recall daydreaming about a man before.

Shaking off the unsettling occurrence, she decided she was satisfied with her piece. Sealing it together with the one inspired by Pressburg—"Preserving the Shadows of Destiny"—she penned the direction of her agent on the letter's face, then rose and headed for her cabin. Rose knew of her secret career; she would ensure the letter was posted.

While her mistress waltzed around the Hofburg Palace ballroom and tried not to yawn.

* * *

It was nearly ten o'clock by the time Rafe, with Loretta beside him and Esme on his arm, reached the top of the main stairs in the Hofburg Palace. The reception line snaked across the tiled landing to the grand doors of the ballroom, where their hosts, the Grand Duke and Duchess, stood waiting to greet their guests. Glancing down the stairs, at the crowd still waiting to ascend, Rafe gave thanks they'd arrived when they had. He'd forgotten what major balls were like—the long wait on the stairs, the crush in the ballroom.

He'd never been a fan of such so-called entertainments; avoiding them and similar ton social requirements had in part helped steer him into the army.

"You look extremely impressive, dear boy." Esme tapped his arm with her furled fan. Leaning back, she eyed his shoulders, encased in black superfine. "And I'm even more impressed that you managed to find a tailor who could cater to your requirements at such short notice."

He met her gaze. "Prussian Hussars. There are some stationed at the Prussian consulate here—I asked for their recommendation."

Esme laughed. "Clever. Permit me to tell you the effort was worth it."

He frowned. "I feel . . . odd." He glanced at his sleeve. "I keep expecting my coat to be red."

"Ah, well, you've sold out now, so there's no more dashing red coats for you. Only black if you follow Brummel's line, although as I recall the dear boy did allow that a deep midnight blue was also acceptable for a gentleman's evening coat."

He couldn't tell if she was baiting him or not, so he humphed and left it at that.

But the notion of midnight blue suiting had him slanting a glance to his right. Loretta stood beside him, resplendent in a gown of periwinkle blue satin that matched her eyes. Under the light from the chandeliers, her dark hair gleamed, spilling in a fanciful froth of curls from a knot on the top of her head; the uppermost curls were level with his eyes.

The expanse of creamy, satiny skin revealed by the scooped neckline of her gown made his mouth water. Her eyes, however, said she was absorbed, thinking of something far away, almost as if she were debating with herself. Whatever the subject, her lips were lightly pursed.

An impulse to kiss them shook him.

He looked ahead, and inwardly frowned. He'd seen that absorbed look before, but given their present location, he had to wonder what subject was strong enough to draw a young lady's interest from all the fashions and jewelry so abundantly on display all around them.

Then again, Loretta Michelmarsh was a very far cry from the average young miss.

They advanced in the reception line, then finally he was bowing before the Duke and Duchess. Esme was greeted as a long-lost friend. Loretta came back from wherever she'd been to smile and touch fingers with their hosts, then Esme drew them on—into the glittering throng.

For an instant, Rafe knew fear. It had been over a decade since he'd been in a ton crush. It wasn't the press of humanity that made him nervous but the open avidity in so many feminine eyes as their owners noticed him, and started to plan.

He'd forgotten about that aspect of ton life.

Esme released his arm and led the way, forging a path through the crowd. Instinct had him seizing Loretta's wrist and winding her arm in his. "Don't you dare desert me."

She turned her head and looked at him.

He glanced at her, and realized he'd managed to drag her from her inward contemplation.

Jolted from considering a potential vignette on the glamor of the Hofburg Palace, Loretta studied him, surprised by the vehemence in his tone. She'd made a point of not noticing him, of not allowing her mind or her senses to dwell on him; with his bright golden hair freshly washed and shining, his clean-shaven aristocratic features, his patriarchal nose, arresting blue eyes, and thoroughly sinful lips, all atop a body that was long, tall, and exuded sensual danger, wide in the shoulders, narrow of hip, and long of leg, he was assuredly the embodiment of many a lady's dream.

She tilted her head, her eyes on his. "I thought you were supposed to be guarding us—me in this instance, as Esme clearly needs no help."

He glanced ahead to where Esme had claimed a seat beside a lady whose ample bosom was terrifyingly overburdened with gems. "I'll make a bargain with you. A pact." Looking back, he caught her eyes. "I'll guard you if you'll guard me."

She was tempted to scoff, but he sounded deadly serious. She nudged him toward the end of the sofa on which Esme had come to rest. Once they'd taken up station there, backs to the wall, looking out at the other revelers, she caught his gaze. "Who am I supposed to guard you fr . . . oh."

Her "oh" was occasioned by the sight of an extremely well-endowed lady—not young, but a matron perhaps a few years Loretta's senior—who was, quite openly, trying to attract his attention.

He moved closer to Loretta. Lifting her hand, carrying it to his lips, he shifted to face her. "Precisely. Oh. That oh."

She glanced again at the lady. Noticed she was but one of several, all of whom appeared to have their eye on him. "There seem to be an abundance of ohs around."

"They're circling. You can't abandon me to them."

There was that hint of panic again. The man had faced down God only knew what dangers; she was fairly certain he would have looked Death in the face at least once in his career—at Waterloo, if nowhere else. Yet fashionable matrons on the hunt sent him running.

She was inexpressibly curious. "Don't you have any interest in . . . ?" She gestured.

"Dalliance? No. Well . . ." Rafe took a moment to consider his position. "I have no interest whatever in any lady here. Any other lady here. You are a different matter."

She arched her brows haughtily. "Indeed?"

He nodded. "You are not about to whisk me off to some secluded alcove and have your wicked way with me." He liked women—always had—but he preferred to be the hunter, not the hunted. One thing he would never be was some predatory female's prey. "You're my shield, and I'm not letting go of you."

She struggled to keep her lips straight, but failed. Miserably. She laughed.

The look he cast her had frozen subalterns in sheer terror; it had no discernible effect on her. The musicians saved her—or was it him? The opening chords of a waltz rose over the sea of heads.

"Hell's bells—you do waltz, don't you?" If he didn't lead her onto the floor, some harpy would approach and jockey for him to partner her instead.

Periwinkle blue eyes considered him. "Not well."

"Never mind. You'll do." Covering her hand on his sleeve, he led her into the crowd in the direction of a clearing he assumed was the dance floor.

He couldn't recall ever having uttered such a graceless invitation to a young lady to dance, but now he thought of it, he suspected she might have resisted a more conventional approach. As it was, she went with him readily enough, allowed him to turn her onto the floor.

He bowed extravagantly. She swept him a faintly mocking curtsy in response, then he drew her near and she came into his arms.

Even as he stepped out, whirling them into the revolving circle, he felt the difference—how could he not?

He looked into her face, saw her arrested expression, the interest, the fascination, flaring in her eyes, and knew she'd never felt the like, experienced the like, either.

As if they were physically two halves of the one whole.

Loretta felt it to her toes. Lost in his eyes, she lost all awareness of them being separate entities—of her being her and him being him, two separate, disparate people.

She told herself to breathe, to battle the constriction

banding her lungs. She managed it, yet she would swear he breathed as she did, that his pulse echoed the steady yet heated pounding of hers.

She'd steeled herself against the sensation of his fingers closing about hers, yet his hand clasping hers somehow balanced the pressure of his palm on her back, the heat of both contacts oddly pleasant, even welcome.

His arms seemed to cradle her, to hold her so safely. His assured steps, the brush of his powerful thighs against hers as he whirled them, spoke of ineffable control.

For once, she gave herself up to it. Without thought or reservation.

Lost in his eyes, ensnared in the moment created by the music, the waltz, and the man, she couldn't explain or excuse the effect—the outcome of a host of unexpected sensations.

She wasn't a gifted dancer—or so she'd thought—yet in his arms she whirled light as thistledown on the breeze. He was an expert exponent of the art, yet why his masterful, powerful lead should so draw her in, so capture her that she transformed into the perfect partner for him, she couldn't fathom.

Dancing, even waltzing, had never held her interest—had never held the power to capture and hold her thoughts. But this was quite different, something outside the norm. Intriguing, fascinating, tempting.

Rafe couldn't tear his attention from her. His wits only grudgingly spared the awareness necessary to guide them through the sea of whirling couples.

He should have guessed. He'd known she was different, that his interest in her was different in nature to how he'd viewed women in the past. He'd known that she captured his attention, his awareness, as no other lady ever had.

He'd known, but had determined to put her and all she evoked in him to one side until his mission was complete.

Clearly, on a dance floor engaged in a waltz, that determination wasn't going to hold.

Yet the intensity of his interest in her puzzled him. Why

her, or was it why now? Was it simply that she was the first passable lady he'd met after resigning his commission and leaving his bachelor army life behind? Was it simply an aspect of his age that he now appreciated independence, a dry wit, and a dash of acerbity along with soft curves and silken skin?

He didn't know, but the physical and mental attraction he felt for her was undeniable.

The waltz drew to a close. He whirled her to a halt, bowed, then raised her from her curtsy and wound her arm in his. "You waltz perfectly well—why did you imagine you didn't?"

She studied him; he could see her mind focusing behind her lovely eyes. "I hesitate to further stroke your ego, but I suspect I haven't previously had the opportunity of waltzing with a gentleman as accomplished as you. I hadn't realized soldiers were so well-drilled in the dance."

He grinned. "Wellington was a hard taskmaster, at least when it came to the social skills he expected his officers to master."

"Really?"

"Oh, yes." He steered them into the ambling crowd. They were some distance from where Esme still sat, but as long as they kept strolling, the feminine vultures were unlikely to descend. "Under his rule, we had to waltz, had to know the proper observances for all the noble ranks, had to instantly know the correct title to use for anyone we might meet. In his view, officers had to be able to hold their own in ballrooms as well as on the battlefield."

"What a fascinating concept." Loretta stored it away for later use, once she returned to England and her commentaries. "The Duke is quite active in politics now."

"So I'd heard, but it's difficult to imagine old Hooknose toeing anybody's line."

Loretta made a mental note to learn more about Wellington. Esme might be a valuable source.

A gentleman hailed Rafe. They detoured to join the gentleman's circle; he proved to be an old schoolfriend of Rafe's, currently with the embassy. He introduced them to others. Loretta found herself chatting with other ladies in a way she rarely did in London. Of course, most of these ladies were married, and Vienna was a fascinating city; they were happy to tell her of their experiences there, of what they found most different and most similar to London.

All excellent fodder for further vignettes. Loretta happily pursued her purpose, while beside her Rafe seemed equally relaxed as he renewed old acquaintance.

The next waltz started up, and one of Rafe's friend's acquaintances asked her to dance. In the interests of determining whether her transformation on the floor was restricted to dancing with Rafe, she accepted. In short order she learned that if with Rafe she was thistledown, with any other, she was considerably heavier.

The music didn't move her; the dance did not sweep her away. As for her partner . . . he was just another boring man.

At the end of the dance, she returned to Rafe's side, satisfied she now knew what was what.

They chatted some more. More old acquaintances, including some friends of Rafe's father, materialized from the crowd. Esme had warned that it would be a long night. As a matter of tradition, the Hofburg Palace Winter Balls lasted until five o'clock in the morning. Loretta decided she needed confirmation of her earlier result with the waltz, so she accepted several further invitations, yet each time returned to Rafe's side with the same degree of disillusion.

She didn't like waltzing with any other gentleman. That was the only conclusion she could reach. In no other man's arms did she find the same magic.

He'd been aware of her excursions; she'd felt his gaze on her every minute she was away from his side. When the next waltz started up and he solicited her hand, she accepted readily.

By the time they returned to the circle they'd been chatting with, there was no longer any doubt in her mind.

With him, the waltz was magic. With others, it touched her not at all. So what did that mean? What was she supposed to conclude from what was now a very thorough examination?

She wasn't at all sure.

But she wasn't averse to the suggestion he, through his attentions to her, the way he kept her by his side and deferred to her, endeavored to project—that he and she were a couple with some degree of understanding between them.

That façade protected him from the still-circling harpies, and gave her the option of declining any invitation she did not wish to accept.

She was tempted to refuse the young Austrian gentleman who bowed before her and invited her to dance the waltz just commencing, but he was Austrian. All the other gentlemen she'd danced and conversed with had been English. Hoping to gain some novel insight for her vignette on the ball, she accepted, and let the young man—he was, she judged, younger than she—lead her to the floor.

As a dancer he proved sadly wooden and stiff. She made an effort to engage him in conversation, yet unlike most men who were always happy to talk of themselves, young Herr Wittner seemed reticent and distracted.

She was more than ready to return to Rafe's side when the music ended. In this instance, that meant making her way up the full length of the immense ballroom. Stifling a sigh, laying her hand once more on Herr Wittner's arm, she swung in the right direction, but he didn't budge.

"Fräulein, I wonder if you would care to stroll the terrace. It is uncomfortably warm in here, is it not?"

She blinked at him. He sounded tense. It was December in Vienna; it would be bitterly cold outside. It wasn't that warm in the ballroom; she was certainly in no danger of swooning from the heat.

Glancing at the nearby terrace doors, she saw—thought she saw—a darker shadow hovering beyond the light thrown through the long glass panes. She looked more closely, but the shadow whisked back, out of her sight. A person, or a shadow cast by some tree? Regardless . . . "No, thank you." She refocused on Herr Wittner's face. "I'm quite comfortable."

"Ah, but the view from the terrace is quite remarkable, you know. I understand you are a visitor to our fair city." He shifted his arm. His fingers closed about her elbow. "You really must allow me to show you."

He'd propelled her two steps toward the terrace doors before she snapped out of her stunned amazement and dug in her heels. "Herr Wittner! Let me make myself perfectly clear—I do not wish to go out onto the terrace."

Instead of easing, his grip on her elbow tightened. "But the view—"

"Will do me no good if I catch my death!" She'd been keeping her voice down, but was growing increasingly worried.

Herr Wittner might be young, but he was more than strong enough to manhandle her outside. He'd already separated her from the crowd; if she wanted help, she would have to raise her voice—have to cause a scene—which was quite the last thing she wanted to do.

"Unhand me, sir!" She poured as much command into the order as she could.

Herr Wittner's mask of polite civility contorted in a snarl. "You don't understand—"

"There you are, my dear. I wondered where you'd got to."

Relief swamped her; she struggled not to slump. She turned as Rafe stepped free of the crowd. "Does my great-aunt want me?"

"Doubtful—it's still early. But we should perhaps wander that way." Rafe leveled his gaze at the hapless young gentleman who, from what Rafe had glimpsed through the crowd, had been attempting to inveigle Loretta away somewhere— apparently against her will.

What he felt about that wasn't at all civilized.

Then he noticed the man had hold of her elbow.

Something of his reaction must have shown in his face.

The young man paled and quickly released her. He hesitated for a second, then stiffly bowed. "Fräulein. I thank you for the waltz."

Coldly, Loretta inclined her head. "Herr Wittner."

She said nothing more.

With a wary nod to Rafe, Herr Wittner walked off, back into the crowd.

"What was that all about?" Rafe turned to keep the young man in sight.

"I have no idea. He seemed to have some bee in his bonnet about taking me out onto the terrace."

"The terrace?" Rafe turned to look at the doors nearby. "Why?"

"I'm sure I don't know." Loretta stared at the doors, then walked closer and peered out into the night. "The thing is, when he first mentioned it, I glanced this way and thought I saw someone lurking in the shadows."

Rafe stepped past her. Shading the glass with his hands, he looked right, then left. "There's no one there now—not that I can see."

"Never mind." Loretta resettled her silk shawl about her elbows. "Let's go and check on Esme."

He turned, offered her his arm, and together they headed toward the chaise Esme had made her throne. Without being obvious, he kept an eye on the main ballroom doors. On parting from them, Herr Wittner had cut a path directly to the doors and gone out. Even after they'd crossed the huge ballroom and reached Esme, he still hadn't returned. Which seemed odd.

After checking with Esme, who was still engaged catching up with her friends, he paused with Loretta by the side of the room.

Glancing down at her, he saw her eyes narrowed on his face.

"What is it?" she asked.

He debated, but couldn't see any reason not to tell her. So he did.

She frowned. "Could Herr Wittner be a—what do you call them? A cult hireling?" Her eyes widened and fixed on his. "Could the shadow on the terrace have been a cultist?"

He grimaced. "Theoretically, it's possible. Practically, however, I can't see how it could be. The cult couldn't have known we would attend this event. Even if they spotted us entering, that they just happened to have Herr Wittner in their pocket, ready to send in, seems too far-fetched a notion."

"But if not the cult, then what?"

He could have told her that although the cult were the obvious villains, there were other villains about, ones who might have thought to prey on an innocent lady unfamiliar with the city. Instead, he raised his head, then set his hand over hers where it rested on his sleeve. "That's another waltz starting up. Come and dance."

He set himself to distract her from the disturbing puzzle of Herr Wittner's intentions, and succeeded well enough to have the frown leave her eyes, to have her softly smiling in delight.

The sight made him feel better, less inclined to berate himself for having let her out of his reach.

He didn't for the rest of the ball.

They checked periodically with Esme. Eventually she declared it was time to depart even though it was barely three o'clock. "We'll be on our way tomorrow, and I've accomplished all I wished to here."

With that enigmatic statement, one Rafe—favored with a rather smug smile—suspected meant something other than the obvious, Esme rose and led the way from the ballroom. In short order they'd farewelled their hosts, reclaimed the ladies' cloaks, and climbed into their waiting carriage.

Ten minutes later they were climbing the gangplank onto the *Uray Princep*.

"I believe I will take a nightcap." Leaning on her cane, Esme glanced at Loretta. "Could you fetch it for me, dear—a brandy? You know the one I like."

"Yes, of course." Loretta diverted into the bar while Esme, with a goodnight wave to Rafe, went slowly down the stairs to the stateroom.

The night lay heavy on the boat. Only Hassan was awake, keeping watch on the observation deck. Rafe waited, watching as, in the faint glow from a nightlamp left on the bar Loretta poured a small measure of brandy into a tumbler, then restoppered the decanter and set it back in its rack.

Her cloak about her shoulders, her reticule dangling from one wrist, she picked up the glass and came around the bar.

He'd halted at the bar's end.

Reaching him, she paused.

Loretta looked up at him through the shadows. She couldn't put her finger on what had changed, but something had. Without questioning the impulse, without considering her reasons, she reached up, laid her free hand against one lean cheek, then stretched up and touched her lips to his.

Kissed him gently, in her own time, in her own way. Then she drew back, sank back. Let her lips curve. "Thank you for rescuing me."

His eyes held hers, then one brown brow arched. "What about for teaching you that you can dance like an expert?"

Her smile deepened. "I'd forgotten about that."

He reached for her and she met him halfway, met his lips with hers, then parted them and let him enter and taste.

Let him explore and claim. Set her own senses free to follow his lead, to seek and learn, to taste and savor.

The exchange lengthened, lingered, evolved.

Into one of muted hunger, of slowly burgeoning desire. Of controlled yet controlling need.

Rafe closed his hand about the wrist from which her reticule dangled, the hand that held the glass of brandy, and helped her to hold it steady.

While they played.

While with lips and tongues and the slick heat of their mouths they communed.

He knew well enough not to go too far, not to let a spark ignite the tinder of latent desire.

He drew back, reluctantly, yet knowing he must. Knowing that neither he nor she had yet made the choice, the decision to go further.

She sank back to her heels on a sigh, one redolent with sensual content. Her lids rose; she met his eyes, then her lips curved.

He caught the hand still cradling his cheek, turned his head. Eyes still locked with hers, he pressed his lips to her palm, watched her eyes widen. Releasing her, he forced himself to take a step back.

Letting her hand slowly fall, she stared at him for an instant, then, lips still curved, turned away. "Good night."

He didn't reply, just stood where he was and watched her descend the stairs.

When he heard the stateroom door snick shut, he finally dragged in a breath. He looked around, inwardly debated, then headed up the stairs to the observation deck.

As he wasn't going to get any sleep that night, he might as well relieve Hassan.

Six

December 3, 1822

Rafe remained on the observation deck until the *Uray Princep* slid out onto the river, and under oars and sail headed westward. To his relief, no cultists appeared on the wharf. He saw none on the riverbanks.

Once Vienna had been left behind, he headed downstairs. Even if they'd thought of it, he could understand that the cult might not have bothered watching the river. They'd assume that as a courier carrying a vital document he would make for his destination with all speed. Traveling by river was slower than traveling on land. That he might opt to drift along, might have a schedule that wasn't "get to England as soon as possible," wouldn't enter their heads.

So on the river they were, at the moment, safe. He fell into his berth and immediately fell asleep, and dreamed of an elusive, fascinating lady who loved to waltz.

He woke in time for luncheon, but approached the table—now one large table about which their party gathered—with due caution.

"There you are, dear boy!" Esme smiled. "Thank you for your escort to the ball—the event fulfilled all my expectations."

He wasn't sure he wanted to know what all her expectations encompassed. Inclining his head in enigmatic response, he reached for the chair beside her, across from Loretta.

Raising her gaze, she met his eyes, dipped her head. "Good afternoon, sir. I trust you slept well?" Her smile was a touch mysterious, as if she were thinking of other things. Pleasant things.

Letting out the breath he'd unknowingly held, he sat. "I did, thank you." *Eventually.* He bit back the urge to ask if she had; at least, this time after they'd shared a kiss, she wasn't trying to freeze him.

He deemed that progress.

Progress toward what, he wasn't sure, and wasn't, at that particular moment in time, all that keen and eager to find out.

There was a time and place for deeper cogitations, and the middle of a mission wasn't it. Whatever this was that had flared between them, whatever it was that had colored last night's kiss, whatever came of it, whatever might be, would have to wait until later. Now . . .

Now he had to keep his eyes peeled for cultists.

Luncheon passed in relaxed and uneventful fashion. After they all rose from the table, he spoke with the captain, then headed up to the observation deck and once again found Loretta embroidering there. He dropped into the deck chair beside her, exchanged an easy smile when she glanced his way, then he stretched out his legs, folded his hands on his chest, and stared out at the river unraveling like a steel-gray ribbon before them.

Gradually, his lids grew heavy, then fell shut.

Loretta heard the change in his breathing, then heard a soft snore.

She glanced at him. Then, softly smiling, she turned back to her embroidery.

Rafe was much more alert the next afternoon, tense and very much on guard as he and Hassan escorted Loretta, Esme, Rose, and Gibson on a short tour of Linz.

The *Uray Princep* had tied up at the wharf an hour before, the captain declaring they would cast off again early the following morning. So there were only a few hours to fill, and Esme was determined to see the sights and stretch her legs. After two days on board, Loretta was in wholehearted agreement. Between them, they'd given Rafe little choice; Loretta had pointed out that they were sensible females, for which he should be grateful.

The comment had made him blink, then grudgingly agree to their projected outing.

Following Esme down the aisle of St. Martin's Church, Loretta still wasn't sure what to do about Rafe, whether to reinstigate her arm's length policy—which had signally failed at the ball—or to readjust, to flow with the tide and see where it led her. Led them.

The latter impulse had moved her to use the excuse of thanking him for his rescue at the ball to kiss him again. Just to see what she might learn. As had happened previously, the exercise had only left her with more questions.

At Esme's heels, she dutifully examined the carvings, the ornamental altar, the chapels and the nave, but even though parts of the church were said to date from 799, she found little to inspire her muse. Leaving Esme to explore the choir, she strolled back to wait with Rafe at the head of the nave.

Nearing, she softly said, "I didn't seen any cultists in town. Did you?"

He shook his head.

Turning to watch Esme, she continued, "Linz isn't on any of the highways the cult would have expected you to take. They might not have sent any men here at all."

After a moment he replied, "I've learned the hard way never to take the cult for granted. The Black Cobra, Ferrar, has so many men at his disposal, there's no saying what out-of-the-way places he might have dispatched his minions to."

Esme had found a curate, and was engaged in earnest conversation. Watching the curate point, and Esme question,

Rafe had a sinking feeling they would shortly be on their way somewhere else.

Sure enough, parting from the curate with smiles and thanks, Esme walked briskly up the nave. "I've seen all I wish to here. Apparently the other major sight one must see is the pilgrimage church on the hill above town." She turned to Loretta. "The one whose tower you spotted from the boat."

Rafe frowned. "That hill looked steep."

"It is." Esme smiled her smug smile. "Which is why there are pony traps for hire in the main square."

Half an hour later, the two pony traps they'd hired halted before the Postlingberg church atop the Postlingberg mountain. Descending from the traps, they paused to admire the view of the river and the surrounding forests, then pushed open the church door and went inside.

They'd been assured by their drivers that the church was always open, but in this season, at this time of day, there were no other visitors, nor custodians to show them around.

As was often the case, a sign in the foyer requested all arms be left there, outside the nave. Grimacing, Rafe divested himself of his saber. Hassan followed suit, laying his scimitarlike blade on the sidetable alongside Rafe's sword.

The ladies had gone ahead. Rafe followed them in, pacing slowly down the nave while the four women examined the altar, then moved on to admire the ornate pulpit.

From beside him, Hassan murmured, "What is it about these churches that your English ladies find so fascinating? They look much alike to me."

Rafe thought about it. "It's the differences, I think—no two are alike—and the artwork. Throughout the ages, the church always had first call on the best artisans. Much of what's in churches can't be found anywhere else."

Noticing numerous side entrances, he lengthened his stride, closing the distance to come up with the women. Hassan halted at the end of the nave before the altar steps and settled to wait. Rafe followed the women around the altar, listened while they discussed the carved choir stalls, then trailed the group as they circled, eventually heading back toward the nave.

With the women just ahead, he stepped past the altar.

A door to his left flew open. Seven men—not cultists—stormed in.

The men had naked blades in their hands. They raced straight for their party.

Rafe had no weapon. He glanced around. Grabbed one of the two yard-long altar candlesticks.

The women fled across the front of the altar into a small chapel beyond. Hassan hurried them on, then grabbed the second candlestick.

Rafe had no time to see more. The first of their attackers was almost on him. Instead of backing away, Rafe stepped forward and swung the candlestick.

The first man went down like a rock.

Another heavy thump and courtesy of Hassan, another attacker was on the floor.

But that still left five. All very intent. They started circling.

Hassan was on Rafe's right. Rafe was facing the long aisle of the nave. Two attackers with blades stood between him and the foyer, and his and Hassan's swords.

They couldn't let the attackers circle enough to reach the women. From the corner of his eye Rafe saw that Loretta had pushed the other three into the chapel proper. They were arming themselves with anything they could find—prayer books, hymnals, altar cushions—whatever came to hand.

None of which would be much good against knives.

One of the men's eyes flicked to the women.

Abruptly straightening, Rafe let out a cavalry roar, swung the candlestick, and charged the two men facing him.

Surprised, they ducked back from the wildly swinging candlestick.

Rafe sprang past and raced up the nave.

The pair swore and gave chase.

The others cursed and leapt at Hassan.

Nearing the end of the long aisle, Rafe glanced back, then flung his candlestick at the nearest man. It struck the man across the face. He stumbled, then went down.

The second attacker had to leap over him.

Rafe raced into the foyer, seized his saber, turned and swung.

The slash made the oncoming attacker leap back, but Rafe followed up with a quick lunge and thrust, and the man crumpled and fell.

Rafe paused only to swipe up Hassan's sword, then raced back down the nave.

Hassan was desperately fending off two knife-wielding attackers with his candlestick.

The other attacker had gone for the women.

Faces like fury, Loretta and Esme were pelting him with books and cushions; the man had his arms up trying to weather the storm. Further back in the chapel, the two maids were tugging down a long curtain.

Rafe had to relieve them before they ran out of missiles, but first . . . he let his momentum carry him into one of the two men attacking Hassan.

At the last moment, the man heard him coming and turned. He got his long knife up—Rafe felt it slice across his upper arm as he mowed the man down.

Rafe tossed Hassan his blade, then whirled to face the man who had turned from attacking the women.

The man snarled, beady eyes assessing.

Leaving Hassan to deal with the other man still standing, Rafe beckoned to his opponent, raised his saber.

The man saw the long curved blade, hesitated.

A calvary saber beat a long knife. Always.

Eyes on the saber, the man eased back.

Rose and Gibson stepped silently up behind the man and dropped their appropriated curtain over his head.

Before he could react, Esme and Loretta whipped the curtain cords around him. By the time he started yelling and struggling, they were tying the knots off.

Gibson shoved and the man toppled, tied up like a parcel.

Mentally shaking his head, Rafe swung around. Saw the man he'd mowed down trying to struggle up, his long knife still in his hand.

Rafe stepped closer, kicked the knife away, and knocked the man out with his saber's hilt.

Looking up, he saw Hassan disarm his opponent, then knock him out, too.

Straightening, Rafe looked around. Seven bodies strewed the church, but not one of them was dead.

"We haven't killed anyone." He glanced at Esme and Loretta. "I suggest we leave. Now."

Both were shaken, yet showed no signs of hysteria. They'd taken in the situation, too. Both nodded.

But the four women paused to gather the fallen books.

Rather than argue, Rafe helped.

They quickly restacked the books and cushions, then the ladies smoothed down their skirts.

Rafe escorted Esme and Loretta up the aisle, steering them past the groaning men. Hassan followed, guiding Gibson and Rose.

In the foyer, the women straightened their coats and cloaks, then, spines straight, heads erect, walked out to where the two drivers waited with their traps, oblivious to the action inside the church.

Esme made a comment about the altar as Rafe helped her into one trap. Loretta responded, equally calmly.

Giving thanks once again for sensible females, Rafe joined them. A minute later, they were heading down the mountain and back to the boat.

Rafe didn't relax until they were back on the boat. He saw the ladies to their stateroom; although she'd borne up well, he suspected Esme needed to rest and compose herself.

Loretta seemed to agree. Her reserved façade had long slipped away; she was fiercely protective of her great-aunt as she helped her through the stateroom door.

Gibson and Rose had gone in ahead of Esme. Turning to shut the stateroom door, Loretta glanced at Rafe. "Thank you."

He nodded, appearing distracted, already turning away.

She started closing the door, then saw him look down at his left upper arm. Gripping the sleeve, he tried to shift the fabric, winced.

Frowning, she paused, peered . . .

"Good God!" She pushed the door open again. "You're wounded!"

The slash was on the back of his upper arm so she hadn't noticed the cut in the material, and the dark color of his coat hid the bloodstain.

Grasping his elbow, she angled his arm to look. Taking in the damage, she felt her face set. "That needs tending. Come inside and sit down."

She tugged, but he didn't shift.

"It's not that bad—I can manage."

She looked up, narrowed her eyes. "How? You can't even reach it properly, let alone see it."

Rafe hated, positively hated, being fussed over. He blamed his mother and elder sisters. He met Loretta's eyes, a flippant response on his tongue.

Her expression gave him pause.

Judging by her eyes and the set of her jaw, the fierce protectiveness she'd earlier displayed over Esme had transferred its focus to him.

As if to confirm that, she crisply ordered, "Don't argue." Her jaw firmed; her fingers tightened about his elbow. She tugged more forcefully. "Now come in!"

Rose, returning to the door, had overheard; concern in her face, she held the door wide.

Rafe found himself towed into the stateroom's sitting

room and pushed to sit on the window seat before the forward windows.

"A basin and some towels," Loretta directed. "We'll need to dampen the coat and shirt to get them free."

They set upon him, Rose rushing to get the required basin, Gibson coming to confer with Loretta, Esme reclining on her bed in her cabin observing from a distance and issuing instructions.

By the time they'd eased him out of his coat, he was ready to bolt. "Hassan and the crew can help—"

"Shut up." Loretta didn't even look up from where she was applying a damp towel to the dried blood plastering his sliced shirt sleeve to the wound. "You rescued us, so we get to tend your wound."

He glanced at Rose and Gibson, then without much hope at Esme, but they were all as grimly determined as Loretta.

So he had to sit and suffer their ministrations.

Hassan looked in. Rafe tried to claim his support in escaping, but the women would have none of it. His loyal henchman grinned, and left him to their mercies.

Once the material was freed from the wound, they unpicked the shirt shoulder seam and removed the sleeve, baring his arm. The slash, once fully revealed and thoroughly cleaned, was deep enough to need stitches. He couldn't see it well enough to argue, so he sat with teeth gritted, biting back his curses while Gibson neatly sewed him up.

Finally, Loretta and her handmaidens stood back.

She frowned. "We really should have some salve for that." She glanced at Gibson, who shook her head.

"Didn't bring any of that sort. And it should be properly bandaged, too."

"Indeed." Loretta turned away. "Wait there. I have something we can use."

He twisted and contorted, trying to see the wound.

Loretta returned from her cabin, a pile of soft material in her hands. "I cut up one of my petticoats."

He blinked. Sat perfectly still while she wound the soft white material around his arm, then briskly tied it off.

"There." She stood back with the others to admire her handiwork.

He seized the moment to get to his feet. He'd reached his limit; he had to escape.

Loretta's gaze tracked up to his face. She studied it for a moment, then nodded. "That's the best we can do for the moment." She stepped out of his way, turning to accompany him as, almost afraid to hope, he walked toward the door.

He paused as he reached it, then turned back and swept them all a deep bow. "Thank you, ladies."

Rose and Gibson smiled.

Loretta merely nodded and opened the stateroom door. "Now don't forget to bring us your shirt and coat. We'll have them washed and repair the damage."

He nodded obediently and stepped into the corridor. "Thank you."

Then he fled.

Loretta watched his retreating back, then humphed and shut the door.

Now that they were the only passengers on board, meals were much quieter, comfortable, and private. Even the crew seemed more relaxed.

Over dinner that evening, Loretta took stock. Esme, as always, kept the conversation flowing. After the excitement of the afternoon, she had plenty to exclaim over and relive.

Loretta did her share of reliving, too, but in her case the notable moments were not confined to the church. Admittedly, the shock that had lanced through her when she'd realized that—impossible though it seemed—they were being attacked in a pilgrimage church had left an indelible mark on her mind. Balancing that, however, was the knowledge of how they'd fought, of Rafe's and Hassan's unflinching bravery in their defense, and their own resourcefulness in assisting as they could. All straightforward enough.

It was Rafe's wound—her reaction on realizing he'd been wounded—that disturbed her. She was relieved they'd all survived the incident, but was simultaneously so . . . *exercised* that he'd been hurt.

She couldn't adequately identify the emotions she'd felt—still felt—over that.

Later, after she, Esme, Rose, and Gibson had retired to the stateroom, and subsequently each to their own cabins, the thought of Rafe's wound had her shrugging into her pelisse and heading up to the observation deck.

She should at least check that it was no longer bleeding.

As she'd expected, he was standing guard by the rail; he had heard her on the stairs and turned. He watched as she crossed the deck.

"I wanted to check your wound—how does it feel?" Halting beside him, she studied his face.

"It's . . ." He shrugged, moved his wounded arm slightly. "As to be expected."

Was the blue of his eyes a little brighter? "You're not running a fever, are you?" She was tempted to place a hand across his forehead, but restrained herself.

He smiled faintly and turned to look out at the night. "I'm all right."

She turned to look out as well, grasping the rail beside him. "Did you ask the captain to put out onto the river again?"

"After hearing what happened in the church he was happy to accede to my request."

"I still can't believe these men are attacking us in churches."

"The cult wouldn't recognize such prohibitions."

She frowned. "But those men were locals, weren't they?"

"Indeed." His voice took on a grim note. "It seems that the cult has hired locals to keep watch and attack in the smaller towns."

She considered that, after some moments asked, "Do the cultists always wear black head scarves?"

"It's their insignia. They wear it with pride, so are rarely seen without it."

"I didn't see any black head scarves, or even indian people, in Linz. Did you?"

"No. And no, I don't know what to make of that."

After several minutes of listening to the soft slap of the river against the boat's hull, she ventured, "What if these attacks aren't the work of cultists, but just locals who've taken to attacking travelers?"

Folding his arms, he leaned on the rail. "I find that difficult to believe, but I can't argue against it—it's possible. However, at this point my best guess is that the Black Cobra, seeking to cover as large an area of Europe as possible, sent his men through all the smaller towns recruiting locals to keep watch and act if any of the couriers were sighted, but had the cultists themselves draw back to concentrate on the major towns—those the couriers were more likely to pass through." He paused, staring out at the night. "The problem with that is that to date the Black Cobra has always left at least one cultist to watch over any locals, to give orders and bring back whatever the Cobra was after—in this case the scroll-holders. It also presupposes the cultists have an accurate description of me, enough for said locals to recognize me, which doesn't seem likely, although it is possible."

She shifted so she could study his face. "The Black Cobra—Ferrar. Have you met him?"

"No. Delborough and Hamilton have. The pair of them spent more time in the Governor of Bombay's office—the company's headquarters in Bombay—leaving the other three of us to scout in the field."

She frowned. "Three of you, plus Delborough and Hamilton, makes five. But you said there are four couriers. Did one of you remain behind?"

For a long moment, he said nothing—didn't reply, didn't move a muscle—then he murmured, "You could say that."

She guessed. "He died?"

Time passed; eventually, he nodded. "James—Captain James MacFarlane. He was the youngest—a few years younger than me. He joined our troop toward the end of the Spanish campaigns. He was an excellent soldier. He would have made a good commander. When the war was over, he went with us out to India. He was one of us by then."

He paused. She wanted to ask what had happened, was casting about for the right words, but then he continued without prompting, "It was he who found the letter I'm carrying."

There was pain in the words, so much she had to fight not to reach out and touch him—and risk breaking the spell of the past that had him in its grip. His eyes, darkened, remained fixed on the river, although she would swear it wasn't rippling darkness he saw.

"It was pure chance. We'd identified Ferrar as the Black Cobra within weeks of reaching Bombay, but then we'd spent months searching for proof—incontestable proof—to convict him. We'd seen too much by then, too much of the cult's atrocities, to stop. We were obsessed, all of us. But no matter how hard we looked, how far we pushed, nothing we unearthed was good enough." He drew in a breath and it shuddered. "Then James went on a duty mission to Poona—the hill capital—to escort a young lady, the governor's niece, back to Bombay. In Poona he stumbled across the letter, realized it was the proof we needed. He did the smart thing—pretended he was simply escorting the young lady back. But they realized and followed him."

He drew in another slow breath. For a moment she thought he wouldn't continue, but then, in a voice little more than a whisper, he went on, "They caught up with James's troop halfway down the mountain. The odds were hopeless. He sent the letter on with the governor's niece, along with most of the troop, while he and a handful of others stayed behind to delay the cultists."

She said nothing, could say nothing to ease the pain throbbing in his voice.

When next he spoke, his voice was lower still. "I was there when his men brought his body into the fort. I saw what the cultists had done to him—how they'd tortured him before they'd killed him. Of all the horrors I've seen in war, all the dead and the maimed and the gone, that sight is seared into my mind. For as long as I live, I will never forget."

She now understood something she'd sensed in him, a quality she hadn't been able to define. That element of his commitment to his misson that bordered on the fanatical.

Loyalty. Devotion. Those, she suspected, were his deepest, most ingrained traits.

She stood alongside him, silent and still, and stared out into the night. Simply remained there, an anchor to the present if he needed one.

Eventually, he breathed in deeply, eased his back. "I felt so damned chuffed when I realized I'd drawn the scroll-holder with the original document—that I would be the one to ferry the evidence James gave his life to secure back to England, to place it in Wolverstone's hands so he could ensure that the Black Cobra was brought to justice—and so James would be avenged. I was thrilled to have drawn the critical, most vital role in the mission."

She'd shifted her gaze to his face, so saw his lips quirk.

"But with that came responsibility." He glanced at her, met her gaze. "I'm not generally so careful, so cautious." He hesitated, then said, "You'd probably be surprised to hear that among the troop, my nickname was Reckless."

Holding his gaze, she nodded. "I am surprised. You've been anything but reckless in protecting us and in advancing your mission."

"It hasn't come naturally."

They'd edged back from the darkness. Enough for her to be able to say, "You're not alone, you know. I know we're not trained soldiers, but for what it's worth, whenever you need it you'll have Esme's, Rose's, Gibson's, and my support. We can and will keep our eyes open for any cultists—you can't look everywhere at once, and we're all involved in your mission now, whatever you may think."

He frowned.

She pretended not to notice and went on, "They've attacked us all and will keep attacking us all." Placing a hand on his arm, she gripped lightly. "We, us four women, are your weakness. Your enemies know it and so do we. So you and Hassan won't be alone in fighting back. We'll fight back, too."

"So I saw in the church." His lips curved, in appreciation, not disparagement. "I would never have thought of hymnals and cushions as missiles, let alone a curtain, but they worked."

"Women fight with what they have to hand—we're more accustomed to making do."

He smiled more definitely. Lifting her hand from his sleeve, he raised it as he said, "I forgot to thank you earlier for keeping your heads." Eyes on hers, he brushed her knuckles with his lips. "But I do most sincerely thank you."

She sensed he was thanking her for other things, too. He remained leaning on the rail, looking at her. He didn't let go of her hand; his fingers shifted lightly, caressingly, across the backs of hers.

Shifting closer, she lifted her face and kissed him. Not a light peck, not a mere brush of lips, but a definite, deliberate kiss. Drawing back a fraction, her lips all but brushing his, she whispered, "Thank you for protecting us. For defending us."

Time stood still. Desire and more simmered between them.

Then he closed the distance, closed his lips over hers, and kissed her.

He wasn't a green lad with no experience. He didn't rush her, overwhelm her; instead he took her mouth with a slow deliberation that curled her toes. There was no tentativeness, no hesitation, just an open desire to have, to taste, to know.

To take, to possess.

With lips and tongue he did, claiming her mouth as if he possessed some inalienable right.

Her hand rose, hovered, uncertain, but then she let it rest on his shoulder, gripping, steadying her.

Against the tide of unexpected yearning that swept through her.

A dim recollection of "keeping him at arm's length" briefly surfaced in her mind, then sank without trace.

She needed this, wanted this, wanted to follow and see where it led.

Without breaking from the kiss, he slowly straightened. She followed, moving closer, against him, into him, following his lips with hers, unwilling to surrender the contact, to break her fascination.

Rafe knew he should release her, that somehow a simple thank-you kiss had spun out of control and transformed into something else. But when she moved into him, all resolution fled. That he wanted her wasn't even a question in his mind. Hadn't been for some considerable time.

To be offered her mouth, freely, without guile, was too precious a delight to cut short.

He angled his head, his lips shifting over hers; closing his arms about her slender frame, he drew her in, locked her against him. Even through the thick pelisse, she was all warm softness and supple strength in his arms, all firm curves and tempting hollows. Graceful arms reaching up to twine about his neck, rounded hips pressing seductively against his thighs. Instinctively he turned so her back was to the rail, his body shielding her should anyone come up onto the deck and see them.

It might be late at night, but instincts were hard to ignore.

Because it was late at night, passion and desire were even harder to contain.

He kissed her again, feeding himself, feeding her, and she followed him gladly. Encouraged him with a touch of her hand against his cheek, with the clinging pressure of her lips beneath his.

Even if he had no idea where this was leading, neither of them seemed to care.

But he did care, and she would, too, once she could think again.

So he reluctantly drew back, pulled back, and supped at her lips, gently easing her back to the present. To the deck of the boat, to the rippling song of the river, to the night black and still all around them.

Finally lifting his head, he found he had to fight to step back and set her away from him, to lose her feminine warmth and put space between them.

She looked up at him through the dimness, for long moments studied his face. Then her lips gently curved and she inclined her head.

Whispered, "Good night."

Then she stepped back, out of his arms, and he clenched his jaw and let her go.

Turning, he watched her cross the deck, then disappear down the stairs.

He faced forward, stood for long moments battling the urge to follow her, then he let out a long sigh, leaned again on the rail, and went back to staring at the night.

The odd sound shook Loretta awake. She frowned, trying to place what she'd heard.

Then it came again—a harsh, choked cry.

She glanced at the wall beside her berth. The sound had come from beyond the wooden panels. She recognized the import from her nursery days when Chester had been prey to nightmares. From the tortured sound, it behooved her to wake the sufferer and release them from their torment.

Tossing back the covers, she grabbed her robe, shrugged

into it as she slid her feet into her slippers, then she opened the door into the stateroom's sitting room. Eyes adjusting to the dim light ghosting through the prow windows, she tiptoed to the door to the corridor. To her right lay the small cabin Rose and Gibson shared. She listened, wondering if the sound she'd heard might have come from there, but then another choked cry reached her.

Chin firming, she opened the stateroom door, stepped into the corridor. A few steps brought her to the first door on the left. Without much hope, she knocked lightly. "Rafe?"

A moment passed, then another tortured moan reached her. She eased open the door, heard the sussuration of a body threshing in sheets, along with harsh, strangled breathing.

In the weak light, she saw Rafe tossing and twisting, solidly in the grip of some painful nightmare. Even though he'd spared her the details, she could imagine what horrors he'd seen, what hideous details might haunt his dreams.

Without hesitation, she crossed to the berth. He twisted away from her, body taut as if in pain.

She reached out, grasped his shoulder. Tried to shake him. "Rafe? Wake up. You're having a—"

He seized her wrist and tumbled her across him.

Her eyes flew wide. "Wha—"

His hands clamped about her face, his lips crushed hers and he kissed her—devoured her—as if his life depended on it.

As if hers did, too. As if she and he were the last people on earth and their destruction could be held at bay only by that kiss.

Desperation and need drove him; she could taste it on his tongue, feel it in his hands, in the hard body that held her trapped against the wall. But even as her hand closed about the back of one of his, that realization was fading, pushed aside by a need and a desperation of her own, one that welled from within her and answered his.

To answer his. A potent need to sate his desperation, to ease the hunger behind it, to satisfy and soothe.

To be the port for his storm.

To draw him in.

Her hands fell to brace against his chest, then pushed wide across the muscled expanse, palms to naked skin; he felt hot, skin taut over rock-hard flesh, elementally masculine. Tantalizing. She pushed her hands up along the powerful column of his throat, then sank her fingers into the thick silk of his hair and gripped.

Held him steady as she returned his kiss with a fiery fervor the counterpart of his.

Their lips melded, fused, gave and took, and caressed. Their tongues tangled, stroked, then his probed and she moaned and urged him on.

The edge of his desperate need blunted, promised absolution and relief, he tightened his arms, locking her against him, and settled to kiss her as if she were a cornucopia of delights.

Pleasure bloomed and slid through her, welled and grew and flowed in warm waves to pool low in her belly, to throb between her thighs.

Her breasts swelled, ached with a yearning she'd never felt before.

Rafe could only give thanks for the sudden diversion, for whatever quirk of sleep had tipped him, ripped him, from nightmare straight into fantasy. From a nightmare soaked in blood and horror, to a dream steeped in passion and pleasure.

Gratefulness welled as he sank into the feminine warmth, the promise of bliss, the unalloyed delight offered so freely by the fantasy of Loretta that his mind had thrown up to shield him from his worst memories.

Would that nightmares always ended like this.

The thought made him inwardly smile, relax, let his senses surface and consciousness rise . . . enough to register the supple give of the lips beneath his.

Enough for him to realize that the warm, unmistakeably feminine weight against his chest was real.

Snapping his eyes open, he wrenched back from the kiss. Stared. Blinked, looked again, and still couldn't believe what he was seeing. "You're real."

His voice rang half an octave above its normal range.

He swallowed, eyes on hers tried again. "You're really real—really here, in my bed." He verified that by glancing around. His cabin. His bed. Loretta, en déshabillé, in his arms.

Returning his gaze to her face, he stared into her eyes— tried to ignore her lushly swollen lips. "What are you doing in my bed?"

That he had no idea made him nervous.

She blinked several times, as if bringing things into focus, studied his face, her expression unperturbed, a touch curious.

Dumbfounded, he saw a slow blush rise to her cheeks. As if feeling it, she cleared her throat, patted him on the chest. "You were having a nightmare. I heard and came to wake you, but you didn't wake up right away."

She wriggled, trying to sit up.

He gritted his teeth; he was entirely awake now. He clamped his hands about her waist. "Wait—hold still."

She froze.

Gripping, he lifted her up and over him, out from being wedged between him and the cabin wall, setting her down so she sat on the berth's outer edge.

He released her. She fussed with her nightgown, straightening it and her robe, cinching the latter tight.

He dragged in a breath. He was naked beneath the sheet. Sitting up might not be wise. He ran a hand through his hair. Opened his mouth.

"Don't you *dare* apologize."

His gaze snapped to hers. Even through the dimness he felt her glare.

"I came in here to wake you, to free you of your nightmare, and now you're awake and I have. What happened in between was no one's fault."

Her eyes dared him to contradict her. When he said nothing, she tensed to rise, but stopped. Her eyes remained locked on his face. "What were you dreaming about?"

He stared at her. A long moment ticked by, then he scrubbed both hands over his face. "You don't want to know."

"If I didn't, I wouldn't have asked." She just sat there, on the side of his bed in the middle of the night, and waited.

He exhaled through his teeth, looked away. "James. I see him."

"And?"

Something in him snapped. "I see his body. His body as it was the last time I saw it. Tortured and beaten in the back of a damned dray. There was nothing I could do—no way to make him come back. No way to save him."

The horror of his helplessness still ate at him; corrosive, it gave him no peace. "I see him—that—and then I see all the others I failed. All the innocents I never got to in time to save." He closed his eyes. Why the devil he was telling her this he didn't know, but now he'd started he couldn't seem to stop. Through the covers, he felt the warm weight of her hand on his knee. "There were so many in the villages the cult attacked. Women, children, old people, too. It was hell on earth—so often hell on earth." She didn't tell him to stop, didn't rise; her hand remained steady on his knee. He swallowed. "I remember—"

The worst came pouring out. The images he too often saw etched on the inside of his lids. The atrocities, the torture, the unmitigated horror.

Loretta listened. Sat still, her eyes, her attention locked on him, and let him speak. The images formed and flowed past her; they couldn't touch her, but they held him. Had sunk figurative claws deep in his mind.

He was a soldier, a defender; he saw himself as having a sacred duty to protect the weak and innocent and his specters were of those he believed he'd failed.

Even if he hadn't.

She listened, and if she hadn't guessed it, known it, before, had it confirmed with every word how deeply loyal, how committed, how selflessly devoted he was to his defender's role.

Only a man whose feelings ran deep could feel this degree of torment.

When his words finally slowed, then halted, she gently squeezed his knee, released him, and gave him the only words she could that might ease him. "Your nightmares will fade with the end of your mission." His lids lifted, his gaze found hers; she held it as she rose. "With its successful conclusion your debt will be erased."

One brown brow arched, his expression faintly skeptical.

For a moment, she looked down at him. "Thank you for telling me. Now I know why bringing the Black Cobra down is so important to you. God willing, you'll succeed."

With a brief nod, she turned away. "I'll leave you to get some sleep."

Rafe watched her go to the door, open it, and slip out. Watched the door close quietly behind her.

He stared at the panels, then relaxed back in the bed. That had been the strangest episode with a woman in his life.

Get some sleep, she'd ordered. As if he would. As if he could.

But for her, he would at least try.

He closed his eyes, drew in a deep breath, let his limbs relax, and slid into untroubled slumber.

Seven

December 7, 1822

wo mornings later, Rafe stood at the rail of the observation deck, Loretta on one side, Esme on the other, and watched two hefty bullock teams plod along the towpath that bordered the riverbank. Massive rope harnesses connected the beasts to the boat. Along that stretch, all boats relied on the brawn of the bullocks to get upriver; they'd been traveling at the plodding pace since dawn.

"The captain said there's an excellent apothecary in Regensburg." Loretta shaded her eyes, peering upriver in the direction of the town. "We should be able to get some salve for Rafe's wound there."

"It's not that bad," he muttered.

"We can't risk infection." Her tone was sharp. She cast him an equally sharp glance, which he pretended not to see. "I told you it's still inflamed."

She'd insisted on tending his wound morning and evening, had stood her ground and argued until he'd given in. He'd gritted his teeth and borne it, unable to find fault with her deft ministrations. He probably did need a salve for the stitches, and heaven knew he'd prefer bandages other than ones fashioned from her petticoats; the material was so soft, so unmistakably feminine it reminded him of her every time he felt the binding shift against his skin.

He didn't need that sort of torture.

Ever since she'd woken him from his nightmare in such a novel and effective way, and then wrung too many details of his past and of those nightmares from him, he'd been waiting for her to react—to do something, say something. But she hadn't tried to cut him off, to distance herself from him—either to deny the kiss or to back away from him and his harrowing memories.

She hadn't made any move to discourage him from thinking whatever he might think. Instead, she'd said nothing at all. All he'd sensed from her was . . . banked curiosity. She'd watched him as much as he'd watched her.

A sort of emotional circling, neither yet ready to make a move.

Quite possibly neither yet sure what their next move should be.

Esme, on his other side, thumped her cane lightly. "Regardless, dear boy, I intend to go ashore in Regensburg. Richard and I stayed there for a few weeks, long ago. There's a number of sights I want to show Loretta."

The bullocks came to the end of the towpath and halted. Rafe, Loretta, and Esme watched the captain speak with the bullock drivers, pay their fee, then the boat was pushed out from the bank, oars straining. With a rattle, a sail was hoisted at the stern. The sail filled and the boat slowly moved on, continuing upriver.

Heading back to the bridge, the captain saw them, detoured and joined them. He bowed deeply to Esme, then Loretta. "Ladies. We should be in Regensburg in half an hour, but as I have little cargo to unload there, and nothing to take on, I will be wanting to put out again by midafternoon."

"Perfect." Esme beamed. "That will give us just enough time to see all we wish to see."

"And to do what we need to do," Loretta added.

"We'll be back in plenty of time to sail on," Esme declared.

Smiling, the captain bowed and retreated.

Leaving Rafe debating whether there was any possible excuse he could conjure for keeping the ladies aboard.

Esme tipped up her head, regarded him shrewdly. "You're fighting a losing battle, you know."

So it proved. Half an hour later, the crew were making fast at the jetty at Regensburg.

"That"—Esme pointed to an ancient multiarched stone bridge spanning the river—"is the Steinerne Brücke. During the second and third crusades, the crusaders used it to cross the Danube on their way to the Holy Land."

That was the first installment of the guided tour on which she led them. Her enthusiasm was real, more definite than in other towns.

When, after being exposed to the high Gothic splendors of the Dom—the Regensburg cathedral—and having admired the singularly grotesque carvings decorating the principal doorway of the Schottenkirche, the Church of St. James, Rafe stood beside Loretta looking up at the remains of the Roman porta praetoria and murmured, "I take it Esme enjoyed her time here."

Loretta studied the ancient stonework. "From what she's let fall, I gathered she and Richard did not have all that much time to spend privately—Richard was always working in one fashion or another. I think their time in Regensburg was one of those rare times without distraction."

Rafe shifted, scanning their surroundings once again. He and Hassan remained alert and, true to Loretta's promise, all four women were keeping their eyes open, yet they'd detected no sign of any cultists, not even any locals lingering with intent.

They had passed areas of burned houses, damage dating from the Battle of Ratisbon in 1809 and still not repaired. For Rafe, the echo of the Black Cobra's methods, the reminder of the destruction wrought by man's ambition, kept his own mission in the forefront of his mind.

After taking luncheon in an inn not far from the cathedral, and at the last visiting the Adler-Apotheke nearby, they made their way back to the jetty and the boat. One glance at Loretta's face told Rafe she was pleased—appeased—by her discussion with the apothecary, who'd supplied her with bandages and a pot of salve, with strict instructions that it be applied twice daily for the next two weeks until the stitches could be pulled.

In two weeks, Rafe would be landing in England. That he would have to submit and endure Loretta's ministrations until then did nothing for his peace of mind. How he was going to survive without reacting—without taking advantage—he didn't know. After the incident in his cabin, having her close, her attention fixed on his arm, her fingers stroking his skin, was guaranteed to exacerbate his instinctive inclinations, making keeping his hands off her an escalating trial.

At least for the moment she was happy. He conducted her up the gangplank, then returned to help Esme, who'd lingered on the jetty looking back at the town.

She turned as he reached her. "Thank you, dear boy." Her voice was gruff. Looking down, she took his arm.

He helped her up the gangplank, secretly glad he'd given in and allowed her the time with her memories.

Her memories were so much more pleasant than his. At least to the present time. Catching sight of Loretta waiting to accompany Esme below, he found himself wondering if one day he, too, might have memories like Esme's, ones with the power to warm his heart.

The following morning, Rafe took refuge on the observation deck, ignoring the drizzle and the gray day, welcoming them as a guarantee of safety. Loretta had just finished resalving and rebandaging the stitched gash on his arm; the sensation of her cool fingers smoothing on the salve had proved even more debilitating than he'd expected.

Through gritted teeth he'd suggested Hassan should take

over, but had been rebuffed with crisp words and a glare. So she was going to keep tending him, flirting with danger and steadily draining his control.

Gripping the rail, he stared out at the dismal, dripping firs lining the riverbank. Impatience, restlessness, were living pulses throbbing beneath his skin. He wanted to be doing. His nature kicked and pricked, rebelling against his self-imposed restraint, both with respect to her and in regard to his mission.

He was accustomed to campaigning, to strategic planning, tactical maneuvers, feinting, and giving up ground in order to seize the greater prize of victory. He was used to action, to the heat and power of battle, to wielding both to win.

His instincts kept prodding him to precipitate the next clash. To do something to bring it on. To engage with the cult.

To engage with Loretta.

Neither were wise ideas.

His mission was fixed. He had to go slowly. Step by step, adhering to his preordained schedule.

He had to go slowly—no, more, he had to hold to his current line of stoic inaction—with Loretta. This was no time for advances on that front.

If she could distract him simply by smoothing cream on his arm, he couldn't afford closer acquaintance, not until his mission was complete.

He'd reached that conclusion days before; all that had happened since had only demonstrated its wisdom.

He had to concentrate on the cult, on avoiding their notice. Had to ensure that his party's defenses against attack remained sound and in place. He and Hassan continued to keep an unfailing watch on the river, but they'd yet to see any unequivocal evidence that the cult had divined his route.

Hearing a sound, he glanced around, watched as Hassan walked out to join him. The big Pathan leaned on the rail and, like him, stared out at the river.

"I was just thinking," Rafe said, "that perhaps the attack in Linz was just local thieves after all."

Hassan slowly nodded. "If those men had been cult hirelings, I cannot imagine that we would not have encountered a greater force by now. The boat is slow. They may not like the water, but they would have hired others to attack from other vessels, or on the docks. Yet we have seen no sign."

Still gripping the rail, Rafe exhaled. "For which, I suppose, we should be grateful. The next days look set to be uneventful."

Boredom was, quite possibly, his least favorite state. He'd rather be drenched to the skin, sitting on a horse hock-deep in mud doing picket duty than be bored.

By afternoon, he was prowling the deck, feeling a deep empathy with caged tigers. When Hassan, equally restless although he hid it better, insisted, strongly, on taking his turn on watch, Rafe descended to his cabin, looked around at the four walls, then stalked back upstairs to ransack the bar.

He found what he was searching for in a drawer. Extracting the pack of cards, he walked into the salon.

Loretta was seated on one of the window seats, embroidery hoop angled to catch the light. She glanced at him as he prowled near.

He lifted a small table from between two armchairs, set it in front of her, then swung one of the armchairs around to face the table, and dropped into the chair. "Do you play piquet?"

Expertly sorting the pack, discarding the cards not required for the game, then shuffling, he glanced up, met her eyes.

She stared at him for a moment, then nodded. "A little."

"In that case, pray indulge me with a game." He glanced at her embroidery. "Women always have something to do with their hands, to occupy their minds. Soldiers . . . play cards."

She smiled. "All right." Setting aside her embroidery, she shifted to face the table.

When he set the cards down and with a wave invited her to cut for the deal, she leaned forward and did. He followed, and lost, leaving her with the elder hand.

Swiping up the pack, he shuffled, then dealt.

Silence reigned as they picked up their cards, assessed their hands. She discarded and drew from the stock, then he did the same.

They settled to play.

Loretta made her declarations in a clear voice; eyes on his cards, he responded. She quickly amassed points, enough to claim the pic, then led for the first trick.

She won it, and the next three, and elicited a grunt.

He shifted, leaned forward, concerted concentration claiming his expression. Hiding a smile, she carefully kept track of his discards, determined to hold the lead.

The game quickly became a battle of sorts, a matching of wits and wills, of caution and fearless risk, of determination and focus.

In tactics and strategy, they seemed evenly matched.

"Who taught you?"

"My brother Chester. We were trapped indoors by heavy snows one Christmas and he found enforced inaction difficult, and there was no one else willing to play."

She took the first game. He claimed the second. The one after that was so close as to be a virtual draw.

They settled into the next game. After making their discards and declarations, she debated, then, acknowledging tricks would be difficult for her to win, led with a queen.

He glanced at her, appreciation in his eyes. "You take more risks than I'd expected."

"Not really."

"Yes, really—you're rather like Esme." He glanced at the card on the table. "You take calculated risks. Not wild forays, but you back your judgement—and your intuition."

She pulled a dismissive face. "I'm nothing like Esme—I don't have her courage."

When he didn't reply, she lifted her gaze from her cards to his face. Fell into the blue summer of his eyes.

"A lady who fights off a ruffian with prayer books, then helps tie him up in a curtain, doesn't lack courage."

"The others were there. I just helped." Rearranging her cards, she wrinkled her nose. "Besides, that was a necessity."

After a moment of studying his cards, he mumured, "Living is a necessity." He selected a card, laid the king over the queen. Met her gaze as he gathered the cards. "My trick, I believe."

She smothered a humph, and focused on her cards.

His comment about her taking risks—calculated though they might be—stayed in her mind. Circled. Nagged.

Late that evening, after she, Esme, Rose, and Gibson had retreated to the stateroom, Loretta sat on one of the window-seats, her legs curled beneath her skirts, and stared through the prow window opposite into the blackness of the night outside.

"I'm off to bed, dear." Esme paused at the door of her cabin. "I have to say I'm so very glad that we decided to go to Buda and take the river route to the Channel. What with the occasional excitement associated with Rafe's mission, and the contrasting peace while on the river, it's really been a most invigorating time."

Loretta couldn't help but smile. "Good night. I'm going to remain up for a little while longer. I might go for a stroll about the deck before heading for bed."

Although Esme only waved in acknowledgment and turned to enter her cabin, Loretta didn't miss the knowing twinkle in her incorrigible relative's eyes.

She'd already told Rose that she'd get herself to bed. Rose would help Gibson with Esme, then the maids would retire to their cabin.

But she wasn't sleepy enough for bed. Twisting around,

she rested her elbow on the windowsill, propped her chin in her palm, and stared unseeing at the inky dark.

Rafe's comment . . . had brought home to her a circumstance of which she'd been aware, but until then had largely ignored.

She'd changed. Irrevocably.

Over the journey, through the challenges she'd faced, the woman she truly was had come to the fore—and that woman was a Michelmarsh to her toes.

She hadn't foreseen how strong her true self, her wilder, more impulsive nature, would be. Could grow to be. She hadn't foreseen falling in with Rafe Carstairs.

Being around him, dealing with him, brought her true self to the fore increasingly strongly.

Her prim and proper façade was gone—or more accurately her disinclination to retreat behind said façade had grown to be absolute. She couldn't imagine going back to being that prim and proper young lady ever again, no matter how convenient. Not now she'd had such a definite taste of what being herself could be like.

Which, she acknowledged, had been Esme's goal.

She wasn't so foolish, so immature, as to battle the outcome merely because it had been Esme's goal, not hers. But letting go of her past had left her having to decide what manner of lady she would be from now on. The answer seemed increasingly clear.

"Good night, miss." Rose waved as she left Esme's cabin and headed to her own. "Shall I turn down the lamp?"

"Thank you." Loretta waited while the light dimmed, then faded. "Sleep well."

With a smile, Rose went off, followed by Gibson.

Loretta sat for a moment more, letting her thoughts roam, irritated when she realized their direction.

Before changing for dinner she'd tended Rafe's wound. Being that close to him, her fingers touching his warm skin, firm and resilient over muscle like rock, had played havoc with her senses, and even more with her control.

In his presence, she transformed into a wild, impetuous being wanting nothing more than to kiss him again, to pursue the desire she'd sensed in him when he'd kissed her in the night, after she'd attempted to wake him from his nightmare.

Just the memory of that kiss, of its heat before he'd woken up, curled her toes.

She didn't know what to do about him. Or about herself in relation to him.

That uncertainty hung in her mind. Taunted her with her indecisiveness.

"If I don't go up and walk the deck, I'll never get any sleep." That, at least, was certain. Rising, she picked up her cloak, swung it about her shoulders, then left the stateroom.

She was fairly certain she would encounter more than just fresh air up on deck.

Sure enough, she stepped onto the observation deck to find Rafe leaning on the rail in his usual spot, where the shadow cast by the bridge concealed him while he kept watch on the river and the banks sliding past.

She had no real plan for the encounter; she walked across the deck and halted alongside him.

He'd watched her approach, but had given no sign. The shadows cloaked his face, hiding his expression.

Placing her hands on the rail, she drew the night air deep into her lungs. Without looking at him, she asked, "What are you planning to do once you've completed your mission?"

Rafe blinked. One boot resting on a coiled rope, leaning on the rail, he turned from her to face the night once more. "I . . . haven't given the matter much thought."

"But you have family at home, waiting for you."

His lips twisted. "I have family, yes, but as for waiting for me, being in expectation of seeing me again and taking me to the familial bosom . . . no." He caught the glance she threw him, answered the question in her eyes. "I'm the youngest of four sons with two older sisters and one younger. I've been away campaigning for over a decade, and I haven't been home—back to Henley Grange—in all that time. I honestly doubt they'd recognize me, not at first."

He paused, imagined walking into Henley Grange at Christmas. Raised his brows. "As for all my nephews and nieces, I can barely name my oldest brother's heir, let alone all the rest. Regardless, given the inherent danger, I decided not to tell them I'd be back in England until I was."

She settled on the rail. "Aside from catching up with your family, what do you imagine doing with your life? Given you can't survive one afternoon of inactivity, living the idle life of a fashionable gentleman won't suit. You must have something in mind."

He grimaced. "Until you asked, I hadn't given it a thought. I haven't been thinking past completing my mission. However, you're right—although courtesy of my sojourn in India, I'm wealthy enough to rival Golden Ball, sitting back and counting my pennies—even wagering my gold on this or that—won't satisfy." He paused, then said, "A house, I suppose. Somewhere within easy reach of Henley Grange."

He met her eyes. "Once the prodigal brother returns, I'll be expected to remain within reach, at least for a while, and the country thereabouts suits me. Good riding, good hunting. Not so far from London that I can't dash down now and then."

"You'll need an estate—just a house won't be large enough to keep you busy."

"I have to be kept busy?"

"You need people to organize, to order about. Perhaps some estate that includes a small village or two might be best." She glanced at him. "A man like you needs people to watch over. To protect and defend, to encourage to grow and succeed."

He saw it—instantly saw himself in such a role, and knew she'd put her finger on the essence of what he needed. He'd gone into the army because as a fourth son there was no preordained role for him to play. But in the army he'd also missed place. Missed being settled, having roots.

That, too, was important to him.

The realization that she was right—that he would need to find both a place and a role for himself back in England—left him feeling vulnerable, knowing that even after his mission was complete, he would still have that challenge before him. That until he met it, he wouldn't have a life, not one he would enjoy living.

He glanced at her. "But what about you?" He shifted to watch her face. "What will you be doing with your life once we return?" Brazenly he asked, "A beau, a fiancé? Wedding bells and keeping house. Children?"

"None of the first two, ergo none of the third, fourth, or fifth." Loretta knew she should discourage such impertinence; gentlemen did not ask young ladies such questions, and proper young ladies certainly did not answer. Yet she'd already jettisoned the prim and proper creed. She lifted her face to the cool night breeze. "I'm here, traveling with Esme, precisely because I've rejected so many suitors."

A moment ticked by, then he asked, "How many?"

"Eight."

Even without looking, she knew he was struggling to keep a straight face.

"I've been out of society for over a decade, yet even I know that's not . . ."

"Normal? Customary? It's also not acceptable."

"Acceptable to whom?"

She waved. "The ton at large, or so I've been told."

"You don't know?"

"In England, I lead a rather quiet life."

She could feel his gaze on her face, sense him considering her.

"By choice. You live retired, out of society, because you prefer to."

"Not retired, not out of society." She glanced briefly at him. "I just avoid the glittering whirl, the balls and parties, the endless, all too often mindless, entertainments."

Rafe could understand that. "I'm not a great fan of mindless entertainments myself." After a moment, he asked, "So . . . why did you reject eight suitors? I assume they were eligible by the usual ton standards—weren't they quiet enough for you?"

She frowned. "Actually, they were quiet. Staid and strait-laced, rigid, conventional. They . . . wouldn't have suited me. They thought I was . . . someone I wasn't—prim, proper, demure, and decorous."

He thought of what he'd seen of her—the tigress flinging prayer books at an attacker, or beating one off with a cane or a chalice, the bossy female who insisted on tending his wound, the incisive and decisive card player who had challenged him at piquet—and smiled. "You're none of those things."

"I know." She sounded grim. "But in my rejected suitors' defense I have to admit that I used to pretend I was. It was excellent camouflage, and allowed me to avoid the worst of the social whirl."

"You used to pretend you were prim, proper, demure, and decorous?"

She nodded. "It worked, too. For years."

"But not now?"

She sighed. "No. Now my convenient façade has come tumbling down about my ears. Rejecting my eighth suitor caused a near-scandal, so when Esme came calling, I escaped with her. Presumably by the time I return the scandal will have blown over, or been superseded by something juicier."

Leaning on the rail, he searched for a way to ask what he most wanted to know. "In what way did your suitors not suit?"

"Because they thought I was someone I wasn't, their expectations of me as their wife didn't match the reality. If I'd accepted any of their offers, I would have been miserable, and I would definitely have made them miserable, too. So I declined."

Thank heaven. The thought came out of nowhere, but resonated strongly. He let it lie, and edged on. "So what sort of life do you want when you return? Different, more suitable suitors? Or do you envisage some other path?"

Was she against marriage? The notion seemed ridiculous; in his experience, all young ladies were brought up to imagine marriage as their sole acceptable goal in life, yet with her . . . he'd already learned not to make assumptions.

She straightened. Chin rising, she looked out at the night. "I don't actually know what I want. That's why I agreed to accompany Esme. I wasn't so concerned with the scandal, but saw the chance of traveling and seeing more of the world as an opportunity to consider my options and define what I want—what I want to do with the rest of my life."

He nodded. He, too, looked out into the blackness of the banks.

Impossible not to notice the similarities between them. They'd reached this place, this hour in time, by widely different routes, yet there they stood, facing the same challenges. Asking the same questions of themselves.

Seeking answers.

The same answers?

He wondered . . . glanced at her through the deepening shadows.

Just as she stirred. She drew in a deep breath. He struggled to ignore the swelling of her breasts, and the unsubtle effect the sight had on him.

Then she glanced his way, inclined her head. "Good night. I'll see you in the morning."

He murmured a quiet "Good night" in reply, and watched as she walked to the stairs and went down.

Eight

December 9, 1822

R afe had had plenty of time through the silent watches of the night to think and consider and ponder. His cogitations, however, constantly circled back to Loretta—to what she thought, what she wanted.

Finding out had become his latest challenge.

While the more sensible part of him still argued that he should leave all such exploration for later, another stronger, innate compulsion prodded him to pursue the subject.

They were, after all, stuck on a boat in the middle of a river, free of immediate threat and going nowhere fast.

As usual after breakfast, taken in the dining salon with the rest of their party, Loretta insisted on tending his wound. He dutifully followed her down to his cabin. Leaving the door open, he shrugged off his coat, dispensed with his waistcoat, then raised his shirt enough to draw his injured arm free. Sitting sideways on the edge of the bunk, he let her unpick the knot securing the bandage neatly tied about the stitched gash, then unwind the long strip.

Laying the bandage aside, she peered at the wound, then gently palpated the flesh on either side. "How does it feel? Does it still hurt?"

"No. It's just tight. The skin pulls."

"That will wear off." Stepping back, she crossed to the small washstand built onto the cabin wall. Picking up the towel he'd left there, she dampened a corner in the ewer, then returned to blot and gently clean the stitches.

Looking along his shoulder, he couldn't stop his eyes from dipping to the lush swells of her breasts, round and firm beneath her bodice, couldn't stop his gaze from lingering on the shadowed valley between.

Only when, frowning at his wound, she straightened, did he look away. Thankfully he was sitting, and had draped his waistcoat over his lap.

He cleared his throat. "How is it?"

"Healing quite well." She lifted her gaze to his. "The apothecary was right. Twice a day treatments are the trick."

She picked up the pot of salve from the stand beside the bed, opened it, and dipped her fingers in.

He steeled himself. Clenched his jaw, and his right fist, and fought to remain still while she delicately smeared the ointment across and around the wound.

He exhaled when she finally stepped back—and received a sharp glance in response.

Setting aside the salve, she picked up the long bandage, inspected it. Approved it. While she wound the long strip about his arm, he swiftly canvassed the field.

As Esme had pointed out, now their party were the only passengers on board, there was a far greater degree of privacy. The others had all remained on the salon deck. He would hear anyone coming down the stairs.

Until someone did, they were the only ones on the cabin deck.

Alone. Private.

"There." She patted the knot she'd put in the bandage and stepped back.

He rushed to push his arm back through the sleeve.

"If we keep on as we are, I doubt there'll be any further problem."

His hand slid through the cuff. He looked up, and found her heading for the door. Reaching out, sliding an arm around her waist, he reeled her back.

She staggered slightly, fetched up with her hips between his spread thighs, her hands spread on his shirt, the thin material no real barrier to the sensation of her touch.

Her eyes had widened. They locked on his. "What—"

"I realized I haven't thanked you." He raised a hand to cup her nape. "You've thanked me a number of times. I thought I should at least . . ." Her gaze had dropped to his lips. Slowly he lowered his head. "Return the sentiment."

He breathed the words across her lips, then, holding her head steady, still moving slowly, covered those luscious lips with his.

They'd kissed four times before, but this was the first time he'd initiated the caress.

The first time he'd admitted, to her or himself, that he wanted to kiss her.

He did.

Ravenously.

But he couldn't devour her—not yet. There were formalities to be observed, even in this arena. So he kissed her slowly, tempting her until she parted her lips. He slid his tongue slowly past the pliable curves, pressed inside, savoring the taste of her, tart and tantalizing, apples and brandywine.

She made his head spin.

Slowly, sensually. Made his heart beat faster, made it thud.

The long-drawn caress sent desire snaking insidiously through his veins, heating, then turning molten and racing.

Demand grew; desire kept pace.

Until he had at least one answer to the questions crowding his brain.

He wanted her.

He'd known she aroused him, but that might have simply been because she was a delectable female and he hadn't had a woman in more months than he wanted to count. But what she stirred in him was more than that.

Stronger than mere desire, more vivid than simple passion.

He felt need grow, unfurl, stretch. Like a powerful beast, it unsheathed its claws.

Scratched.

She shifted her hands, skating them, palms flat, up over his chest, to his shoulders, then further. He felt one small hand cover the sensitive skin at his nape, felt her other hand slide into his hair, and grip.

Another question answered: she wanted him.

He felt his muscles harden in response.

In reaction.

He recognized the signs well enough, but with her, his responses were stronger, the drive they fed more potent, more insistent.

Angling his head, he thrust deeper into her mouth, claimed, took, albeit with reined ferocity. He didn't want to frighten her, even though fear seemed far from her mind as she shifted closer.

Her breasts brushed his chest.

Loretta felt her breath hitch, then tangle in her throat. Felt her breasts swell, then ache. Her nipples tightened, heating, sensitive.

Her senses were alive, stretching, reaching . . . she wasn't sure for what.

Both his hands now clasped her waist; the long fingers of one flexed, eased . . . then his hand skated upward, palm to her gown.

Her senses focused, waited, teetered. . . .

Smoothly his hand rose and closed, gently, about her breast. About her heavy, aching flesh.

Sensation streaked through her, rich, warm, enticing.

He squeezed, still gentle, almost reverent, and excitement flashed.

Her breath hitched again, tighter, more constricted, then she was kissing him back, pressing her lips to his, sending her tongue to tangle with his.

The tenor of the kiss changed. Intensity flared, awareness closed in.

All she could think about was seizing more, tasting more, experiencing more, learning more. Recklessly demanding more.

Her hand at his nape tightened; she leaned closer, pressing her breast into his hand.

It closed more firmly, possessiveness riding the edge of his hunger. She tasted it on his tongue, sensed it in the increasing firmness of his lips as they pressed hers wider and he settled to plunder.

Her wits were waltzing, gloriously reeling—

Suddenly he wrenched his mouth from hers.

Lifted his head. Looked over hers.

Toward the door.

Suddenly she was standing two feet away from him. He'd picked her up and lifted her as if she weighed nothing and set her down, then retreated, leaning back against the bunk. His expression unreadable, he looked down, smoothed down his sleeve, tied the laces at the cuff.

She'd just caught her breath when Rose walked past the open door, then halted, stepped back and looked in.

"There you are, miss. Lady Congreve wondered where you were—she wants to speak with you if you've finished down here."

"Yes." Loretta swallowed, cleared her throat. Without turning, she spoke over her shoulder. "I've . . . done all I can for the moment."

Rafe raised his head, slanted her a glance, then his lips curved. He inclined his head. "Again, thank you."

She forced herself to nod briskly, bit her tongue against the urge to reply—God only knew what might come out of her mouth—then turned and made for the door.

Rafe watched her go.

Listened to her footsteps climb the stairs. Wondered some more.

He wanted her in his bed—not just as a woman, but specifically as her. Wanted her, her unusual, quirky, original self, beneath him.

Yet where they were heading—and they were definitely heading that way—then given she was a gently bred young lady, that destination customarily meant marriage.

In the past, just thinking that word had been enough to have him backpedaling. Running if necessary. Yet with her . . .

He frowned. Was it really her, herself, that he so craved? Or was this change in his wants, his needs, more a function of his situation? Or perhaps his age? Was their discussion the previous evening, his recognition that he needed to find a role and a place—marriage and a home—to be fulfilled, coloring his perception? She was, after all, the only potential bride currently in his orbit; if his inner yearnings were predisposing him to marriage, then she was the only candidate for his needs, his lusts, and his eyes to fix upon.

Leaning against his bunk, he picked up his waistcoat, shrugged it on. While doing up the buttons, he considered, weighed. He didn't believe his recent deliberations on his future had influenced him all that much, at least not with respect to his desire for her. That had been strong, unexpectedly strong, from the moment he'd first laid eyes on her.

"So." Standing, he reached for his coat, drew it on.

Frowned.

He needed to decide why he wanted her before he allowed matters to progress further. He liked her in a way he couldn't recall liking any other female; the last thing he wanted was to hurt her in any way.

He had to be sure. First.

Before he or she gave into their natures and precipitated the next engagement.

The morning continued overcast and rainy. Esme had taken up residence in the salon, reading a novel, then writing letters.

Loretta, Rafe noticed on one of his frequent passes, was

also writing, a frown tangling her brows, her concentration impressive. But the next time he crossed behind the bar, she'd set aside her correspondence and had picked up her embroidery.

He walked into the salon, nodded to Esme, then halted before Loretta. When she looked up, he said, "It's stopped raining for the moment. I wondered if you'd like to take a turn about the deck."

From the corner of his eye, he saw Esme grin and return to the novel she'd taken up again.

Loretta studied him, then to his relief she set aside her hoop. "I would like some air."

She rose, shook out her skirts, settled her warm shawl more definitely about her shoulders. He stood back and she preceded him out of the room, past the bar and up the stairs.

At the top, she paused, drew in a deep, deep breath, then stepped out onto the wet boards. He joined her. The air was cold and damp. Dismal gray mist cloaked the nearby mountains and hung eerily in the dark forests the boat was currently sliding past.

He waved her on, then fell into step beside her on a slow perambulation around the deck. Hassan was on watch, tucked away in a corner protected by the overhang of the bridge's roof.

Ignoring his friend, Rafe fixed his gaze on the slow-moving gray ribbon of the river. "I've been thinking of what we discussed last night. My putative future. As you know, I've been away from England and out of society for a decade and more, so I've lost touch with what's feasible. With what options are available to me. Especially in terms of"—he had to fight to get the words out—"marriageable young ladies." Baldfaced, he continued, "I wondered if you could help me better define my requirements."

He felt her sharp glance like a lancet against his skin.

"Your requirements? In a bride?"

Gaze still on the river, still slowly pacing, he nodded. "Exactly. As our discussion last night demonstrated, I'm sadly lacking in plans for my future. If I accept your suggestions of a house, an estate with a village or two to manage, then I strongly suspect my next requirement should be a wife." He risked a glance at her. "Am I right?"

She looked a trifle bemused. She glanced up and caught his gaze, studied him for a moment, then nodded. "My reading of your situation suggests your supposition is correct."

"So?" He arched his brows. "What sort of young lady should I seek as a wife? What criteria should I look for?"

Seeing her eyes start to narrow, he looked back at the river.

"I'm sure your sisters, and your sisters-in-law, too, will be delighted to assist you."

He ignored the false sweetness in her tone. "I'm sure they would be, which is why I'm asking you. They know nothing of me—of the man I now am, let alone what I might need in terms of wifely support—but they will think they know me better than I know myself, and will enthusiastically fling themselves into lining up candidates none of whom will bear the remotest resemblance to the young lady I need." *Her.* He glanced at her. "You can see my problem."

The look she cast him was suspicious, wary, but intrigued. She was, he felt certain, following him perfectly well. One of the reasons why he wondered if . . . "For instance, I don't believe a conventional young lady would suit me." He faced forward, ambled on. "After all I've seen and experienced, I find convention overrated."

"You reject adhering to convention for convention's sake," she said. "That's something those who live by convention find difficult to accept."

"Exactly my point. So we're agreed my lady needs to be unconventional."

"No—you want a lady who may or may not be unconventional herself, but who is not bound by convention, and therefore won't expect you to be, either."

He smiled. "See? That's why I asked for your advice. I

suppose I should also stipulate that she should not be too young."

"Define 'too young.'"

"Hmm . . . less than twenty-two? I mean that she shouldn't be of the wide-eyed-innocent-who-has-never-experienced-anything-beyond-the-ballrooms-and-drawing-rooms type." He glanced sidelong at her. "Perhaps a lady who has seen a little of the world. At least one with a wider experience."

"I believe that criterion can best be stated as 'possessing a certain degree of maturity.'"

He quashed a grin. "That sounds right. And no giddiness or giggling. She must be a lady I can have a sensible conversation with."

She glanced at him. "You're asking rather a lot."

"Nonsense. I'm sure there are ladies capable of conducting intelligent discussions. Of course, I would expect her to behave intelligently, too, and not get herself into idiotic scrapes or create unnecessary fusses."

"I hesitate to ask, but what about the physical? What are your preferences there?"

He frowned. "To be honest, I'm not all that set in my ways as to the specifics—as long as she's the epitome of beauty in my eyes, the details won't matter."

Her lips twitched; she inclined her head. "An estimable answer that adequately covers that aspect."

"So I think. So, what have we thus far? A lady unbound by convention, possessing a certain degree of maturity, intelligent, and of sufficient beauty to inspire my devotion." He arched his brows. "That seems to cover it."

"I suspect we should add 'with a temperament capable of dealing on a daily basis with you.'"

"Do you think so?" He opened his eyes wide. "I wouldn't have thought I was difficult to get on with."

"I'm beginning to suspect you have hidden depths and are by no means the charming, lackadaisical rogue you allow the world to see."

He hid a smile. A wolfish one that would have proved her point. He inclined his head. "Very well—we'll add a calm and unflappable temper."

"Plus a managing disposition and a backbone of steel."

"What the deuce will she need those for?"

"To manage you. Once back in England dealing with your house, your estate, and, as I understand it, your fortune, you're going to need managing on the social and practical fronts. You've admitted you're not socially adept. Being who you are, what you are, you won't be able to simply avoid society—your presence, or lack of it, needs to be managed in such a way as to appear unremarkable."

"Just as you've managed your social absence over recent years?"

"More or less."

He frowned. "I'll take that—the disposition and backbone—under advisement."

Loretta snorted and strolled on. The exchange had held her attention, held her absorbed. Although she knew it was cold, that the wind had a biting edge, she hadn't felt it. She felt energized, alert, her mind engaged, her nerves tense, tight, but pleasurably so. She felt challenged.

"So now we've dealt with me. What about you?"

She felt his gaze on her face.

"What sort of husband do you want? Clearly that's a question to which you'll need the answer by the time you reach England's fair shores."

He was right. He was also . . . engaging with her in a way she'd never imagined. A verbal foray of dizzying directness veiling a deeper purpose; she wasn't foolish enough to miss his underlying objective.

"The man I want as my husband . . ." She didn't need to follow where he'd led, yet she couldn't back away from the challenge, couldn't not reply. However, like him, she'd never thought to put her requirements into words. To formulate them clearly. "He . . . would have to be a gentleman, and I mean in temperament, not just station. He would need to value women, ladies—me—need to acknowledge and appreciate my strengths and my achievements."

His gaze was on her face. "You have achievements?"

"Several." As *A Young Lady About London* she was one of the most popular columnists of the day. "As well as paying due deference to my worth, he should be able to provide all the usual, accepted things. I have no ambition to live in a cottage."

The sound he made suggested he couldn't imagine her doing so.

"Other than that . . . he would need to be courageous, enough to let me be myself, and while he might be protective, he would need to be careful not to attempt to stifle me."

"Stifle you?"

"He would need to learn not to get in my way."

"Hmm. It's been my experience that to protect someone, one often needs to stand in front of them."

"True, but not in the sense of blocking the one protected unnecessarily. Protection should never become obsessive prohibition."

He frowned. "So—a gentleman of substance who worships at your feet, who will leap to protect you from any danger, but who will otherwise allow you free rein. Your hypothetical husband is not destined to have an easy life."

"No." She glanced at him, took in the quality of his frown, managed to keep a straight face. "The position will be a challenge."

They reached the far side of the deck. In concert they turned, and, even more slowly, ambled back toward the stairs. Showers were threatening to close in once more.

"You haven't yet described your preferred physical attributes. Ladies always have preferences."

She was no exception, but how to avoid the obvious? "Tallish, well set up, strong and in good health, but as we all know that handsome is as handsome does, I would place greater emphasis on character and personality than on physical beauty."

"What traits in particular would you look for?"

"Loyalty. Devotion. Courage. Intelligence. Slow to anger, quick to forgive. An active man. Someone who has lived, who has an appreciation of life." She glanced his way, met his gaze levelly. "That's sufficient definition to recognize him . . . should I find him."

The stairs lay ahead. They both slowed, halted. Eyes locked on his, she waited . . . but then he looked over her head, across the deck, and she remembered Hassan standing in the shadow of the bridge.

Rafe's gaze returned to her face and she smiled, adding, "Thank you for your escort and for sharing your views. It seems we both have matters to consider."

He held her gaze for a moment, his blue eyes unreadable, then his lips quirked, reluctant and wry. "Indeed. It seems we both have chances we might take, and decisions to make as to whether to seize them."

She squelched the urge to correct him. It was *a* chance. And whether to seize *it*. They were talking of one and the same thing.

Imagining the prospect . . . made her feel faintly giddy.

She inclined her head, stepped toward the stair. "I'll leave you to your cogitations." While she retired to face her own.

In the early afternoon, Loretta sat in the salon and pretended to work at her embroidery. Esme had retired for a postprandial nap. Rose and Gibson had taken over the stateroom's sitting room to sew and mend. Hassan and Rafe were up on deck, as far as she knew.

Which left her free to return to her unfinished cogitations.

Looking back on their amble about the deck and the singular conversation she and Rafe had shared, she was tempted on the one hand to think she couldn't possibly have interpreted his words correctly, yet on the other hand she knew she had.

They'd been talking of marriage. Between them. Her and him.

There was no other explanation, no other motive for him to have taken such a curious conversational tack other than to test the waters. And his cast had worked. Not least because the possibility had surfaced in her mind, too.

Interestingly, the one point she hadn't revealed, the one subject he hadn't inquired about—the attraction she felt for him, her hypothetical husband—was currently providing her strongest motivation. That attraction—the overwhelming need to learn much, much more of such physical interaction, to experience much more of the scintillating sensations, and even more of the strange connection she'd sensed flowing beneath—was pushing her to step forward and engage. Boldly, as a Michelmarsh would.

She was, she was discovering, a Michelmarsh to her soul—wild and abandoned when in pursuit of a desired goal.

The very fact she desired Rafe Carstairs was a wonder in itself. After all her years of feeling not the faintest compulsion to spend time with any male, she had started to believe she never would. But Rafe definitely made her want, and some elementally female part of her positively gloried in the discovery.

Luncheon, taken in the salon with the others, had proved notable for the way in which he hadn't met her eyes—or she his. If she weren't so prosaic, she might have said the atmosphere between them had crackled, yet no one else had seemed to notice.

Or at least had given any sign of noticing.

She wasn't entirely sure she believed them.

She heard someone in the bar, looked up, and saw the object of her thoughts walking toward her, the pack of cards in one hand.

His eyes met hers.

She simply sat, her needle poised, and watched him draw near. That was something else he and she hadn't touched on, the dangerous allure that hung about him, tangible as a cloak, a temptation to sin that had her Michelmarsh instincts prodding and pricking to make her reach out and touch. Stroke.

Provoke.

She smiled, coolly arched a brow. "Piquet again?"

As before, he shifted the table between them, swung one of the armchairs to face her and slouched into it. He dropped the cards on the table. "Possibly." His eyes trapped hers. "Or you could tell me about London. You spend most of your year there, don't you?"

"In recent years, yes." She hesitated, then looked down at her work, set her next stitch. "Not, however, entirely by choice."

"You don't like town?"

"I'm not averse to it in limited doses. However, over recent years, my sister-in-law Catherine has been determined to do her duty as she sees it and get me suitably wed, so we've spent all the Season, and all the Little Season, too, in town. That, to my mind, is rather too much."

Rafe was in wholehearted agreement. Yet . . . "I thought one of the principal occupations of ton females, married or not, was the observation of the marriage mart and all associated activities as pertaining to their relatives, connections, and general acquaintance."

Loretta grinned. "Both my sisters are already wed and my nieces are babes-in-arms." She glanced up, met his eyes. "And as we discussed earlier, my requirements of a husband suggest that he would be wise enough to be engaged elsewhere through much of the year, so me spending so much time in the capital seems unnecessary. To my mind, I'm unlikely to meet him—my hypothetical husband—there."

He humphed. "So what does interest you when in London, and how do you occupy your time when in the country?"

"In London, aside from all the balls, soirees, parties, and dinners Catherine ensures I attend, I spend my time viewing exhibitions, visiting and corresponding with friends, and I have, I've been told, a decidedly unladylike penchant for reading news sheets. I have also been known to engage in political discussions, which, apparently, is behavior acceptable in an earnest older matron, but not in one of my tender years."

He snorted.

She nodded. "Precisely my thoughts."

He watched her lips curve in a rather secretive smile. When she said nothing more, he prompted, "And in the country? How do you fill your time there?"

Somewhat to his surprise, she hesitated, but then went on, "I correspond. A lot. And of course I still have the news sheets to read. But otherwise I ride, and walk, and do all the customary things ladies do in the country—visit nearby villages and neighbors. That sort of thing."

He couldn't put his finger on what she was concealing. Before he could think of a way to probe, she looked up.

"You must have spent some time in London before joining the army. What do you remember of the ton from then?"

A deliberate distraction, or . . . He inwardly shrugged. "I only spent six months on the town. Other than friends, the only group I truly remember were the grandes dames. There was one, Lady Osbaldestone. She terrified me. At Waterloo, when the Cynsters rode with us, I learned she terrifed them, too."

Loretta grinned. "I know her. She's not so terrifying."

"Perhaps not to you. Who are the others currently holding sway over the ton?"

She told him, refreshing his memory of those he knew, painting vivid verbal vignettes of those he hadn't previously met. From there their talk ranged more widely, covering topics—the Corn Laws, the Peterloo riots—that he'd heard about, but hadn't paid attention to. Somewhat to his surprise, she had a remarkably deep and detailed knowledge of the social upheavals of recent times. If she hadn't admitted to devouring news sheets and talking to peers and members of Parliament, he would have wondered.

He decided she simply had an excellent memory for details. He already knew she was innately curious.

Then Esme wandered in and joined them, and while all personal revelations came to an end, he remained and allowed Esme, aided by dry comments from Loretta, to entertain him with her opinion of the Prime Minister and his closest advisors.

The minutes to dinnertime sped by.

That night was the last they would spend on the *Uray Princep*. Ulm, their immediate destination, lay not far ahead.

"We will reach there by noon tomorrow," the captain informed them as they sat around the table in the dining room, ready to partake of a celebratory dinner organized by Esme.

She had invited the captain, the first mate, and the purser to join them. All three had accepted, fascinated by her and her larger-than-life persona.

Esme raised her glass, filled with the finest wine on board. "To journey's end for you, and our thanks to you and your excellent crew, who have made our time on your vessel such a pleasant one."

They all raised their glasses and toasted the three sailors, all of whom blushed and disclaimed.

The captain proposed another toast, one to undemanding passengers.

They all laughed and drank, and then the cabin boys brought in the platters and the dinner began.

At the end of it, they took their leave of the captain and his crew.

With a sigh, Esme led the way into the salon. The rest of them, all pleasantly replete, trailed in her wake.

Rafe brought up the rear. Once the four women had settled on the window seats and in the armchairs, he and Hassan drew up straight-backed chairs and joined them. He let his gaze travel the circle of faces. "We need to make plans for tomorrow. By all accounts the distance from Ulm to Strasbourg, where we'll hire a boat to take us down the Rhine, can be covered in a carriage in one day. Given we'll reach Ulm at noon tomorrow, I suggest we put up at a hotel there, organize a carriage, and leave the following morning."

Esme was nodding. "That's the wisest course. No need to risk an inn in some out-of-the-way place, which we would have to if we leave Ulm straightaway."

"Precisely. Of course," he continued, "that assumes there are no cultists waiting for us in Ulm, but it isn't on any major highway, and if it's true the cult hasn't realized we're on the river, then there's no reason they'll have thought to send men to such a backwater."

"My memories of Ulm are somewhat hazy. I don't believe we ever stayed there. However," Esme said, "at this time of year we should have no difficulty finding a suitable hotel. It might be off all the highways, but it's rather more than a village."

"Indeed. I don't expect any trouble finding a carriage, either. In Ulm, we simply need to be on guard, and otherwise put one foot in front of the other." He drew breath, went on, "However, from Ulm onward our journey is likely to be more fraught. Increasingly dangerous. It's best we discuss our subsequent plans now, here, where we're safe and there's no one to overhear."

Esme nodded. Loretta, alert, had her attention fixed on him.

He glanced at Rose and Gibson, confirmed they, too, were listening intently. He didn't need to glance at Hassan.

"We've been lucky—far luckier than I imagined we might be—in avoiding the cult this far. As far as we can tell, Ulm will be safe, and the road from there to Strasbourg is a relatively minor one through the forests. Just outside Strasbourg, however, we'll join roads coming from more major towns, and Strasbourg itself, as a town on a number of highways, will be sure to contain cultists watching all traveling carriages and the major hotels. Once there, we definitely will not be safe, and from there onward, on our trip down the Rhine, we'll be increasingly exposed. Many of the major towns on the Rhine are also on major highways. The cult is sure to have men stationed there, and the closer we get to England, the more concentrated the cultists are likely to be, the more tightly woven the cult's net."

He paused, then went on, "If we leave Ulm at first light,

my best guess is that we'll reach Strasbourg by midafternoon. Once there, I propose we find a small but decent inn close to the river. I'll ask in Ulm for recommendations. When we reach the inn, the rest of you can remain there with Hassan while I organize passage on a riverboat down the Rhine."

"As to that," Esme said, "in this season we should have a choice of available berths."

"I'm hoping to find one of the faster boats with an experienced captain and crew." He hesitated, then added, "Given I feel certain we won't escape the cult's notice while on the Rhine, we'll also need our chosen crew to be amenable to supporting us in fighting off cult attacks if need be."

Loretta frowned. The thought of cult attacks, of men with swords attacking Rafe and Hassan . . . "I vote that we find a quiet, modest inn in Strasbourg, one where the cult is unlikely to accidentally stumble upon us, and then take however many days we need to secure the right boat, with the right crew."

"I second that motion." Esme caught Rafe's gaze. "Even going downriver, we'll be on the Rhine for days, perhaps a week. It makes sense to take the time to make the best preparations we can for the journey."

Rafe took in Esme's determined expression, then glanced at Loretta.

She arched her brows, her own determination clear.

He nodded. "Very well. That's what we'll do. We'll find a bolt-hole in Strasbourg, and take whatever precautions we can to make our trip down the Rhine as fast and as safe as possible." He rose, looked down at them, his gaze touching each face. "Of one thing we can be certain. Once we're on the Rhine, the cult will spot me, and the chase will be on in earnest."

Time, it seemed, was of the essence. Loretta waited in her cabin until the boat quieted around her, then tugged on her pelisse, slipped out of the stateroom, and headed for the stairs.

Rafe's review of their plans had sparked a sense of urgency; if he and she were to come to any decision regarding what seemed to be flaring between them, they needed to make a start on their decision-making process. There was no point—indeed, no sense—in leaving the matter pending, unresolved.

Once they reached England. . . .

Climbing the stairs to the observation deck, she looked up at the night sky. Muttered, "If I'm going to embrace my inner wildness, better the transformation be over and complete before I see Robert and Catherine again."

Before she joined their household again.

Stepping onto the deck, she wondered if, given how much she'd already changed, she could ever live under their roof again.

She doubted it.

"Forward." With her whispered direction ringing in her head, she determinedly set out across the deck, her goal the large, commanding figure leaning on the rail on the starboard side. One swift glance around the deck confirmed they were alone.

He turned to face her as she neared, straightened.

She'd never seduced a man, never even set herself to tempt one into kissing her. She really had no idea what to do, how to go about it.

Their last exchange on the deck replayed in her mind. Although nothing had been openly stated, the directness of his tack had surprised her—enough to have had her following instinctively. . . . Two could play at that game.

Her eyes locked on his, she slowed as the distance between them shrank, but she didn't halt—not until she'd walked into him. Her breasts met his chest. She reached up, clasped his face in both palms and tugged him down as she stretched up on her toes, and kissed him.

Pressed her lips to his in blatant demand.

Her strategy proved sound. After an instant of surprise, he kissed her back.

His arms closed around her, locked her to him as he bent his head. She parted her lips, lured him deeper, and he came.

She sighed in relief, pressed closer in expectation. She needed to know more, experience more, and more was here, within her reach.

Within the steel bands of his arms, inside the thoroughly masculine cage that enclosed her. That held her trapped, albeit willingly. His strength wasn't rocklike but tensile, like a well-tempered blade, flexible yet unbreakable, supple yet ungiving.

Her senses waltzed as she drank in the sensations. The hardness of his muscles, the solidity of his heavy bones, the alluring masculine heat of his body. The wide planes of his chest, the breadth of his shoulders, the long, hard columns of his thighs braced on either side of hers as in large part he supported them both.

His hands had spread over her back, holding her, then, at the flagrant invitation she poured into their kiss, infused into the heated duel of their tongues, urging her closer.

She went. Gladly.

She had only one aim. More.

More of whatever it was that sparked and arced between them, that sent thrills of anticipation licking over her skin, shivers of excitement slithering down her spine, and sharp awareness sizzling along her nerves. Heat bloomed and spread beneath her skin, then sank in, down, pooled low in her belly.

Sliding her hands back from his cheeks, she gripped his nape with one, sank the fingers of the other into his thick hair. Ruffled the silky locks, then clung. Clung as he kissed her back, and she tasted fiery need, desire, and passion.

One of the hands at her back eased, drifted lower. Smoothly slid over the full curve of her derriere, a slow, exploratory caress that had her senses reeling. Then he gripped, lifted her against him. His tongue brazenly filling her mouth, distracting and demanding, he tilted her hips to his so she could feel the rigid column of his erection riding against her taut belly.

She gasped through the kiss, clung and gloried.

More. She wanted more. More of this.

More of his passion.

Rafe was lost—for long moments utterly lost—in the fiery demands of the kiss. Of her. Lost in the sensation of her curvaceous, intensely feminine body pressed to his. Of her softness, her warmth, filling his arms. Given, surrendered, pressed on him like an offering.

Want was a solid thud in his blood, need a lash that scourged him.

Desire flashed, flared, then roared to a conflagration, potent, red-hot, urgent and demanding.

When had passion ever been this acute, this desperate, this overwhelming?

The dizzying realization shook him. Enough for sanity to briefly resurface in his desire-razed mind.

The reins of his control were almost gone, frayed and flapping. He seized the ragged remnants, gripped harder, hung on.

His lips melded with hers, his tongue captured by the honeyed delights of her mouth, he struggled to find wit enough to think.

Reason was well nigh beyond him, yet . . .

They'd talked of their plans. Yes, he remembered that. Talked of the impending danger. Talked of the cult waiting, close ahead.

Too close. Danger and threat, to her and the others, were far too close to indulge in this. To allow him to indulge and be distracted.

He wrenched his lips from hers, raised his head. High enough so she couldn't drag him down, couldn't lure him back to her succulent sweetness. He was breathing hard. So was she.

Eyes closing, tipping his head back, he struggled to slow his whirling wits. "We can't do this."

His voice was all gravel.

Opening his eyes, he looked down, into her face. Into her wide eyes, periwinkles drowning in passion.

Her lips, swollen and slick, parted. "Why not?" She appeared to be struggling to marshal a frown.

"Because it's not the right time, not a good place . . . and we're going too fast." That was another truth, one equally important. He dragged in a breath, set his jaw, and forced his arms to move, to set her back on her feet, then ease her back from him, putting space and cool air between them.

Her frown materialized. Before she could think of words to go with it, he continued, "This sort of exchange . . . leads rather quickly to the other." She was quick; she'd know what he meant. What he was alluding to. "And if I'm not yet sure about us, you can't be either." A brutal truth, but one that clearly needed to be stated.

Of course, especially after the last few minutes, he was as close to certain as he could possibly be without being one hundred percent sure, but she couldn't possibly have made up her mind—to anything. Not so soon.

For some reason he couldn't at that moment formulate, that she had to be certain—logically, rationally certain— was fundamentally important to him.

She opened her mouth.

"No—don't argue." Easing back along the rail, he ran a hand through his hair. "Please—just go to bed." He met her eyes, voice even lower said, "Don't just stand there. Tempting me."

Her lips had firmed. At his words, her lashes flickered, then she tilted her head slightly, regarding him. "I tempt you—just by standing here?"

"You tempt me just by breathing."

She blinked.

"Please." His accents had grown clipped, his tone more terse. "Just . . . go below."

He didn't want to think of her in her bed.

She looked at him as if debating whether to glare, then she let out an exasperated sigh. "You are an extremely *irritating* man."

With that, she spun on her heel and stalked back across the deck.

He watched her go. Felt the warmth of her flow away.

Tried, hard, not to even think of surrendering to his reckless instincts, following her downstairs, and deflecting her from her bed into his.

This time when the agonized sound shook her from a restless sleep, Loretta instantly knew what it was.

Flinging back the covers, she grabbed her robe, slid her feet into her slippers, and headed into the stateroom.

Shrugging on her robe, she belted it, then opened the door into the corridor. As before the narrow passageway lay in darkness. Two steps took her to Rafe's door. She opened it and went in, shutting the door behind her.

As before, he lay on his bunk, largely wrapped, trapped, in his tangled covers. One long leg lay free, bared to midthigh.

The night was cloudy; what light leached through the cabin's porthole was weak. Her mouth still dried, her breath still caught as she stared at his leg while her mind absorbed the implication. Bare shoulders. Naked leg. He lay naked beneath his sheets.

Shaking aside her tantalized fascination, she walked to the side of the bunk and looked down at him. Her eyes had adjusted to the dim light. He was clearly still fast asleep.

Clearly still in the grip of his nightmare. His head twisted violently. He muttered something, then his body turned partly away from her. She noticed the dampness of the hair clinging to his brow, then his features contorted and his body stiffened as if in pain.

Gripping his shoulder, she shook him. "Rafe."

She might as well have tried shaking a mountain.

His body contorted again, a raw sound escaping his clenched teeth.

"Rafe!" She couldn't yell, but infused his name with every ounce of command she possessed.

She called his name, poked his chest, pinched him. All to no effect.

"Damn it!" She could feel her own emotions twisting every time he twisted in the bed. Jaw firming, she gathered her robe and gown, hitched one hip onto the edge of the bunk, and leaned over him.

Leaned her forearms on his upper chest, pressing to hold him in place with her weight as she grasped his face between her palms, held it steady, bent and pressed her lips to his.

Hard. Hard enough to jolt him and break the nightmare's hold.

His lips parted. He stilled, then his arms were around her, trapping her against him. His lips broke from hers only to return with crushing force, covering hers, forcing them apart, ravenous and greedy.

Her wits went flying.

He turned, and she was beside him, sunk in the mattress, trapped between the hot, hard, living wall of his body and the cool wood of the cabin wall.

She locked her hands on his shoulders, not to push him away but to hold onto him. To anchor herself as her world spun.

On a mental gasp she kissed him back—met him, clashed with him in the maelstrom their kiss had become.

Hot, wild, delicious. The taste of him drew her in, the texture, the heat. The glorious sense of reined power that thrummed beneath his skin.

She wanted it. Her fingers flexed, digging into the resilient muscles defining his shoulders.

She wanted him. The knowledge lanced through her, sharp, exciting. Igniting desire, sending it careening through her.

Passion soared and rode its wake.

Like a wall of flames it rolled through her, spreading decadent heat that swelled and filled her. That melted, then coalesced, then built to a raging inferno, a molten furnace, empty and aching.

Yearning.

That was the only word to describe what she felt, a need so potent it drove her. Relentlessly propelled her on.

Releasing her grip on his shoulders, she spread her hands and reached as far as she could, running her palms over the long planes of his back, over the bunched muscles of his upper arms.

His hands shifted in concert. Up her back, to her shoulder, to her breast.

His fingers closed and she shuddered. They eased, searched, found, and tightened—and she moaned into their kiss, riding a wave of exquisite sensation, one he fed, one his talented fingers sent lancing through her again and again.

Those wicked, clever hands shifted, drifted, stroked, sculpted, caressed.

Not possessing but learning. Not compelling but persuading.

Heat built within her, as insistent as a heartbeat.

Clinging to their kiss, savoring the answering heat and hardness beneath her palms, she gave herself to it. Drank it in and let it swamp her.

Rafe sensed her surrender, that evocative, elementally primitive, moment of triumph. Everything male in him gloated, savored . . . then moved on.

Moved in. Blindly he searched and found the buttons closing her nightgown. Seconds later, the bodice gaped enough for him to slide his hand beneath and palm her breast. Soft flesh, already firm, firmed even more at his touch. He kneaded and possessed the swollen mound, then circled her nipple, stroked, caressed, then trapped the tight bud and squeezed.

She arched in his arms. He drank in the evocative sound she made, one every scintilla of maleness within him gloried in. Fed on.

Pressing her back, he shifted his attention to her other breast. Continuing to kiss her, to plunder her willing, wanton lips, he drove her on, until she gasped through the kiss and moaned her pleasure.

He took that as an invitation to push aside the fine material and bare her breasts, to slide his lips from hers, tracing a path down the long column of her throat to taste the tortured peaks—to lick, lave, then suckle first one, then the other, until she writhed against him, until the hand sunk in his hair gripped wildly and she arched beneath him on a strangled shriek.

Loretta couldn't breathe. Her lungs had locked tight under the onslaught of sensation. Sensation of a sort she'd never felt before, had never even dreamed existed.

Intense. Lancing sharp.

Mesmerizing and addictive.

She only wanted more. This, he, was a drug she couldn't get enough of, would never gain her fill of.

With her lips, with her tongue, with her body she pressed him, caressed him, and urged him on.

Wherever on led, she wanted to go there, to reach whatever peak her giddy senses insisted loomed ahead, beckoning, but as yet beyond her reach.

He could take her there, she knew it. Would take her there. That was the promise implicit in the hard body pinning hers, in the heavy rigid rod of his erection pressing against her hip.

With wild abandon she embraced that promise, embraced him, and drew him on.

She heard her own heartbeat thudding in her ears in the same instant he reached down and his hand cruised her calf, skin to skin. Her breath suspended as that questing hand rose, beneath the fall of her nightgown rose inexorably higher, gliding over her knee, up the quivering tautness of her thigh, to brush, then touch, the curls covering her mons.

Her body quivered on the cusp of revelation.

Anticipation streaked lightning fast down her nerves.

The heated emptiness within her swelled, a compelling imperative.

She grasped his face between her hands and kissed him. Drew his tongue into her mouth and caressed.

His fingers firmed, slid further, past her curls, dipped between her thighs.

He touched her there, gently yet insistently exploring the soft flesh. She sensed slickness that made his fingertips glide, slip, slide over her, around and over the increasingly sensitive lips.

Until on a gasp she eased her thighs wider.

He stroked deeper. Pushed in, pressed, and her world shook.

His questing finger probed, then retreated, and she thought she'd lose her mind.

She couldn't breathe but through him, through their kiss. Her heart thundered. She was clinging to reality by a gossamer thread.

With a deliberation that curled her toes, he slowly, heavily, intently pushed that single finger deep inside her.

The sound she made was half sob, half moan. It echoed in her head even as her body arched, begged.

He gave her what she wanted, what she hadn't known she did. His hand flexed between her thighs, his finger thrust, steady and sure, within her sheath, and her world changed. Her senses expanded. Reality was suddenly all sharp-edged sensation, gilded and glowing.

Overflowing.

Sensation rushed through her, caught her, buoyed her, then propelled her up and up . . .

On a smothered cry she shattered, senses fracturing into shards of cataclysmic brightness, the eruption of a sensual nova.

As it faded, undiluted pleasure poured through her. Washed through her.

Leaving her floating on a golden sea, his lips on hers her only anchor to reality.

Rafe inwardly gloated. Unrepentantly, arrogantly triumphant. She'd given herself to him, and now she was his. All his.

His to pleasure, his to savor.

He reached for the belt of her robe, tugged . . .

She was wearing a robe?

A tap on his calf finally registered as a slipper.

Slippers, too?

A moment of giddy disorientation ensued before his mind realigned and he grasped the unwelcome truth. Once again nightmare had converted to dream, and then, to his utter disbelief, into reality.

Her lips still clung to his, her mouth a lush cavern of enticing delights. Even as, shocked, stunned, he desperately grappled, fighting to releash impulses he hadn't known he would need to contain, her body arched to his, inviting, inciting.

He groaned, and she swallowed the sound. Her hands— small, feminine, greedy hands—stroked and slid, setting fires searing beneath his skin.

The scalding wetness of her arousal burned his hand.

Another second and he'd be lost.

A second more and she would be, too.

Where he found the strength he didn't know, but he managed to pull his hands from her. Managed to ignore the evocative perfume that sank to his marrow, wreathed his brain, and threatened to overwhelm his good intentions.

Sinking his palms into the bedding, he braced his arms and dragged his lips from hers.

Straightening his arms, he hung half over her, his breathing harsh, beyond ragged, and stared down at the luscious phantom who'd proved to be flesh and blood.

Hot flesh, hot blood.

Closing his eyes, he hung his head, fighting to wrench his thoughts from their obsession.

Two heartbeats passed. Opening his eyes, he glanced at her face.

Her lids had risen to reveal eyes darkened by passion, sultry with banked heat. Her expression was all languid pleasure.

She caught his gaze, stared at him for an instant, then fractionally tilted her head. Smiled like a siren. "Don't stop."

Her hands shifted on his skin again. Before he could react they drifted lower. She stroked, and he all but hissed.

"Don't stop?" The words were guttural, choked. He shifted to seize her hands, found he couldn't without crushing her again; he gave up and pushed back instead. "We shouldn't even have got this far."

Shifting, twisting around, he sat up as well as he could, infinitely grateful for the sheets twining about his waist.

Feeling as if he'd been clouted over the head, he ran a hand through his hair. Clutched tight as he realized. "Damn it! This wasn't supposed to happen. Not yet."

"But it has, so stop arguing."

Although her tone was the epitome of lazy reason, even in the dimness, even without looking, he could feel her frown.

After an instant's fraught pause, she went on, "I know there's more. I know what should be and I want it all. Now."

Lips compressed, he shook his head. "No. This can't happen yet. You're not sure—you can't be. We first spoke of this less than twenty-four hours ago. You can't have considered adequately and made a logical rational decision yet."

He paused, stunned at what he'd just said. She was offering and he was refusing . . . why?

"Don't be ridiculous." Now her tone snapped. "I know what I'm saying. I know what I want."

"No." He looked at her, all but glared at her. "You might know what you want, but have you thought of the consequences?"

The part of him that was Reckless groaned. What was he *doing*? She wanted him, and he was denying them both?

She struggled up on one elbow and definitely glared; he could feel the heat of her rising temper. "You might have spoken about it—alluded to it—first, but did it ever occur to your overwhelmingly arrogant mind that *I* might have *already* been thinking about it—about us, the possibility, about you and me—about this?"

If he let her argue, she would win.

Time to roll out the heavy guns.

He narrowed his eyes on hers. "Listen, and listen well." He'd summoned his commander's voice. He wielded it like a weapon. "If we go on with this, if we go further, the result will be marriage. No question. No option. If I bed you, we will wed. There is no other outcome that I will accept—that I could accept. And marriage is not an issue that should be decided in a moment of lustful madness."

Inwardly he blinked. That hadn't sounded like him.

Refocusing on her face, he saw she was eyeing him belligerently.

"I'm twenty-four. One year away from being declared an old maid." Her tone was cutting. "We are not under my guardian's roof, or your roof. You know perfectly well that if I wish it, there's no reason—"

"Which just goes to show how much you know."

Was it possible for a man to be honorable and cowardly at the same time?

He wrestled with the sheets, dislodging her. Finally managing to fully sit up, he swung his legs out of the bunk. Dragging the sheets with him, he stood, wrapping them about his waist. Anchoring them with one hand, he grabbed her hand with the other and all but yanked her off his bed. "Come on."

She tumbled and rolled and came to her feet, hair tousled and wild, her nightgown still gaping, giving him a totally unnecesary view of the flushed mounds of her breasts. "What—"

"Here." He tugged at the side of her robe. "Do this up."

Her glare reached volcanic proportions. Her expression was all smothered fury as she slapped away his hand, but to his intense relief she yanked her robe closed and rebelted it. "So you're refusing me?"

"No. I'm denying you—defying you. Delaying you. It's for your own good."

The sound she made reminded him of an irate tigress about to tear her prey limb from limb.

"Come on." Setting his free hand to her back, he propelled her to the door. "You need to get back to your cabin."

She had no option but to move her feet. She halted facing the door. "Why are you doing this?"

He didn't like to think. Didn't want to think, because if he did he would see, and what he would see meant . . . "Because it's the right thing to do."

The glance she threw him informed him she wasn't impressed by his snarl. "You are going to regret this."

She didn't know the half of it. Reaching around her, he opened the door, gestured her through. "Off to your own bed, Beauty."

The look she bent on him would have scorched steel. "You are the most vexing, irritating man I've ever met."

With that, thank heaven, she stepped into the corridor. He hung in the doorway, watched her stalk to the stateroom door, open it and, without a single glance back, pass through. The door softly clicked shut.

He sagged. Relief was not what he felt.

Confusion, yes. Plus a very wary, very vulnerable feeling in his gut.

He'd been reckless all his life, yet when it came to her, to her safety, to her future, to her feelings . . . to doing whatever it took to have her in his life as he wanted her . . .

"Damn!" Gritting his teeth, he stepped back and closed the door.

He'd finally met a woman who could tame Reckless.

Nine

December 10, 1822

The following morning, Rafe stood at the rail on the main deck and watched Ulm draw near. He scanned the banks as the captain maneuvered the *Uray Princep* to come alongside the wooden wharf.

Moving to where the gangplank would roll out, he fervently prayed that everyone aboard had put the tension that all but vibrated through him down to concern over what his party might encounter in the town.

Loretta knew better, but she was keeping her distance, quiet and tense herself—in her case from reined temper. The glint in her eyes whenever they met his made her mood abundantly clear.

It took effort and considerable concentration to focus on the matter at hand, on the possibility of danger lurking in Ulm's streets, and on getting his party to safety within one of the town's hotels.

He'd already made his farewells to the captain and crew, had tipped them generously, sincerely grateful for their services. The instant the gangplank touched the wharf, he went down it and swiftly scouted the area. Finding nothing to cause alarm, he returned to help Hassan assist the four women ashore.

Unable to avoid it, he offered Loretta his hand to help her off the raised gangplank. He wasn't sure she wouldn't reject his help. Instead, she gripped his fingers, let him steady her down the two steps, then released him.

Leaving him feeling the phantom touch of small, smooth hands sliding across his skin.

He hadn't thought he could get more tense. He'd been wrong.

Gritting his teeth, he turned his attention to their luggage. Once everything was piled onto a cart pushed along by a porter, with Esme on his arm, he led the way off the wharf, through the wide gate in the town walls and into the cobbled streets.

It was no great distance to the Wurttemburg Arms, the hotel Esme's guidebook declared to be the best the small town had to offer. A largish rectangular structure in good solid stone, the inn met with his approval.

As Esme had predicted, with winter closing in there were few other travelers about. Little by way of cover in the streets, but against that he had no difficulty securing the best rooms at the hotel—a suite at the front for the ladies, an adjoining room for their maids, and flanking rooms for him and Hassan.

"We are delighted to welcome you to our town." Standing by the door to the suite's parlor, their host, a genially rotund man, bowed low to Esme. "Anything you wish, my lady, please ask."

Esme smiled. "An early luncheon, I think. Once we've had a chance to sort out our luggage."

"Our dining room is at your disposal. Shall we say in half an hour?"

Esme glanced at Rafe, who nodded. "Thank you." The manager bowed himself out, shutting the door behind him. Esme looked at Rafe. "Luncheon, and then what?"

"Then while you all relax here in safety, I'll go and organize a carriage to take us on."

That had been his plan, but Esme, it transpired, had another idea. Sadly, a better idea—one he couldn't easily argue against.

He'd still tried.

And lost.

Half an hour after they'd finished a surprisingly tasty lunch, Rafe strolled the short distance to the hostelry the innkeeper had recommended—with Loretta on his arm.

Stiff with the effort of not reacting to her in any overt way, not responding to the pervasive awareness of her that permeated his senses, he guided her along the pavement of Ulm's main street.

Although she hadn't suggested it, she'd been quick to support Esme's contention that if he were to venture on the streets, then he needed his disguise as a courier-guide, and that meant taking Loretta with him. Alone, he was more likely to attract the notice of any cultists lurking in the town.

He hadn't wanted to spend any more time than absolutely necessary close to her, not until the events, the sensations, and the temptations of the previous night had faded from both their minds. He'd suggested taking Rose or Gibson instead, but Esme had decreed that to appear at all authentic he had to take Loretta, or her. And she really ought to rest.

So it was Loretta on his arm as he neared the open doors of the hostelry. Somewhat to his surprise, she appeared to have put aside her earlier displeasure. She was doing an excellent job of appearing oblivious to any undercurrents between them.

Jaw firming, he strove to follow her lead.

They turned into the hostelry and halted. A boy working on readying a carriage saw them, bobbed his head, then turned and shouted for his master.

A large, heavyset man came out from a tack room.

"Good afternoon." Rafe's German was passable, whatever Esme might think. "I wish to hire a carriage to convey a party of six to Strasbourg."

Negotiations ensued.

Although Loretta didn't speak German, she could follow well enough. The stableman suggested a large traveling coach. She and Rafe went deeper into the stable to inspect it.

When Rafe arched a brow at her, she nodded her approval; the carriage would hold them all, and was comfortable and clean.

The stableman assured Rafe that with the horses he would have put to, his driver would deliver their party to Strasbourg in an easy day's journey. As the three of them walked back to the stable door, Rafe arranged for the carriage to call at the inn at seven o'clock the next morning. He also arranged for four outriders as guards.

Halting by the open door, Loretta drew her hand from his sleeve to allow him to step into the tiny office beside the stable to negotiate the charges. She could still hear the exchange; the amounts involved made her mentally raise her brows. Although Rafe was good at bargaining, the overall outlay was considerable. Especially with the four guards.

When he and the stableman emerged from the office, she accepted Rafe's offered arm and they took their leave of the stableman and started back down the street.

She hadn't forgotten the previous night, but had decided she was in no mood to let his idiocy distract or deflect her. She would set him straight on that subject later. Now, however . . . frowning, she glanced at his face. "I must remind Esme to repay you for the monies you've outlaid on our behalf."

He'd been scanning the street; his watchfulness seemed an ingrained habit. He met her eyes. "No need." He looked away again. As she opened her lips to argue, he added, "Consider your company, and that of your outrageous relative, recompense enough."

Eyes forward, she tapped her fingers on his sleeve while deciding how to broach what might be a sensitive subject. "You were an army captain. I've always understood that a captain's stipend isn't all that much."

"I believe I mentioned I'm as rich as Golden Ball."

"I thought you were exaggerating."

"I wasn't."

That caused her a moment's pause. Allowed curiosity to come to the fore. "How?"

"The five of us who went to India were Hastings's—the Governor-General's—personal appointees. Aside from a significantly greater stipend, that also gave us considerable scope for trading on our own behalf. We invested in several highly successful ventures. By the time we quit India, we were all extremely wealthy."

His gaze touched her face, then he went on, his voice lower, "I'm more than warm enough to stand the reckoning, and you, Esme, Rose, and Gibson have provided Hassan and me with a disguise good enough to get us this far without any major clash with the cult. To me, that's invaluable. Added to that, you've tended my wound diligently and all of you have provided us with company of a sort we wouldn't otherwise have had."

Still she frowned. "All that may be so, yet this was Esme's trip."

"Which she's allowed me to appropriate for my mission." The Wurttemburg Arms lay just ahead. Slowing, he caught her gaze, for a moment searched her eyes, then to her surprise he ducked his head and kissed her—too briefly for her to properly react. "Let it go." He mumured the words as he straightened. "That's a battle you're not going to win."

Steadying her nerves, quelling the warm, fluttery anticipation his kiss had provoked, she shot him a more direful frown, humphed, but let him guide her to the inn door.

She pretended not to notice the smile that curved his lips.

Decided that ignoring it, and the subject of their discussion, would be in her best interests.

Because he was right. She needed to save her powder for the more important engagement—the private tussle brewing between him and her.

Late that evening, in a highly dissatisfied mood, Loretta paced her room. Arms folded, she halted before the fireplace, fixed her gaze on the flames, and felt like growling.

As far as she could see, she faced a simple choice: go to Rafe's room, to the left of the suite she was sharing with Esme, and resume their engagement—the one he'd summarily terminated—or alternatively accede to his high-handed decree that now was not the time. That she needed more time to think before she could declare her own mind. That regardless of what she thought and felt and wanted, they had to wait . . .

Until when? Until he decided she'd thought enough?

Until they reached England?

She knew what she thought about that.

"He wants me—at least he didn't deny that. Not that he could." Not with his erection acting as an excellent barometer of his lustful thoughts. "And what," she muttered, "was the point of raising the prospect of us marrying—as he undeniably did—if we're not to proceed to make up our minds?"

She was sure she was in the right about his—their—intended direction; his subsequent actions supported her conclusion. He was insisting on giving her time to consider, and reconsider, before they took what he considered an irrevocable step. She, however, didn't see that same step as irrevocable, not if it proved that they didn't suit, but she would allow that, honorable gentleman that he was, he would deem it an unbreakable commitment.

All very well, but how was she supposed to make up her mind about whether they would suit, whether what might exist between them was of sufficient power and intriguing wonder to make her finally contemplate matrimony, if they didn't take that step?

If they didn't explore the connection between them further?

"Aargh!" She swung about and started to pace again. The frustration she felt was novel, not something she'd had to cope with before.

If she'd been able to revert to her previous self—the self that had been perfectly willing to hide behind a prim and proper façade—she might have been able to go along with his conventional and no doubt proper decree. Unfortunately, she couldn't. The Loretta who'd been willing to live within the constraints of proper reserve had died.

Slain by exposure, however brief, to passion and desire.

Thanks to Esme, she'd lost Loretta-the-demure's clothes, and now, thanks to Rafe and her reaction to him, she'd lost Loretta-the-demure altogether.

Of course, Loretta-the-demure had always been a construct, a façade she'd fashioned for her own convenience, but she doubted she could resurrect even ghostly remains. Loretta-the-demure was gone. Forever. She had no patience with such restrictions, not when it came to this. To Rafe. To Rafe and her. Whatever Rafe-and-her proved to be.

"I have to find out, that's all there is to it." She swung around and headed for the door.

Crossing the suite's parlor, she tapped on Esme's bedchamber door. Hearing Esme's voice bid her enter, she did, shutting the door behind her.

Propped up on a mound of pillows, her novel open in her hands, Esme arched an inquiring brow. "Yes, dear?"

"I have a problem and I need advice." Loretta stalked to the armchair angled beside the bed and sat down.

"How wonderful." Esme shut her book and smiled encouragingly. "I'm all ears. Do tell."

Loretta cast her incorrigible relative a warning glance, but Esme's eager response made it easier to broach the issue at hand. Esme and Richard had shared a long and loving union; if anyone knew the best ways for a Michelmarsh female to approach the matter of marriage, Esme did.

After gathering her thoughts, Loretta began, "Matters have reached a point where in his mind the next step, once taken, makes a wedding unavoidable. However, to my mind, I cannot make a reasoned decision to marry until after that step, and possibly several after, have been taken."

"Ah, yes." To her credit, Esme kept her lips straight. "That step. And yes, I can see the dilemma." She paused, clearly considering. Her expression grew more serious as she did. "Sadly, I must advise that that dilemma is one you will need to deal with—you cannot avoid it. It arises because of the sort of man he is, and really, you wouldn't want the dear boy without that streak of chivalrous loyalty. It's a part of him you can't and won't want to excise, so you'll have to find a way around it."

"But how? I want to go forward and learn what I need to know, and he's clinging to propriety."

"Not so much to propriety as to what he believes to be the honorable path. But tell me this—what is it you need to learn from this next step?"

The question gave Loretta pause. She knew what she wanted, but did she know why? "I need to learn . . . whether what's between us is powerful enough, potent enough, intriguing and mesmerizing enough to hold me. To keep my attention not just because it's new and not something I've experienced before, but because it, and even more what feeds it, is something I crave and will keep craving . . . I suppose until death us do part."

Esme regarded her shrewdly. "From any young lady that would be a good answer, but from a Michelmarsh it's an excellent answer—indeed, exactly the right answer. And regardless of all social conventions and exhortations to the contrary, you are correct—you are following the right path. Michelmarsh females have never done well in marriages that failed to satisfy the criteria you described. You do not wish to know what happened to my aunt Gertrude— or to her husband. She was the last Michelmarsh female to defy our heritage and make a match that did not satisfy our family nature's particular demands."

Loretta nodded. "So I'm right. I thought as much."

"Indeed, but before you go forging on, as I would encourage you to do—for what else can you do, after all?—I should point out there is one large and unavoidable consequence you might want to consider before you take that inevitable next step."

"What consequence?"

"That wedding he spoke of? If you take the next step and all the criteria are satisfied, that wedding will come to pass. There will be no avoiding it. Once you take the next step and learn your truth, if the answer is positive you need to be prepared to follow that truth, to honor it to the end of your days. As I have, as your father did, as your sisters and brothers—even Robert—will. It's not something that can be explained adequately to someone who has yet to feel it, but once your Michelmarsh heart is engaged, there will be no turning back."

Esme grimaced. "That's the brighter side of the coin. The darker side is that if you take your next step and the answer is negative, as soon as you realize you must pull back, pull away, and let him go. More, cut him off, however harsh and cold you have to be." She paused, then went on, "The truth is, for a Michelmarsh, your next step is an all-or-nothing affair. If you win, you win it all. If you lose, you lose everything. You will not be able even to keep him as an acquaintance."

Loretta frowned.

As if reading her thoughts, Esme continued, "Which means, dear Loretta, that quite aside from your own wants and needs, you have to consider his. You have to take his mission into account—weigh the risk of learning that he isn't your destiny, and the effect that will have on any necessary interaction, in your scales."

After a moment, Loretta said, "That's not an inconsiderable risk, is it?"

"No. It's not. A positive answer will strengthen you both. A negative answer will make life very awkward, and will distract and weaken him."

Loretta growled, then pushed to her feet. "I'm not going to be able to just rush on and take that next step, am I?"

"Not if you want to do the best for him, no."

* * *

Her late-night discussion with Esme had left her with too much to think about to countenance confronting Rafe then and there. She'd retreated to her room, to her own bed, and had tossed and turned for the rest of the night.

Now she sat in the carriage she'd approved and, wedged between Esme and the window, rocked and swayed as the miles slid by.

Rafe sat opposite, his long legs bracketing hers. Rose sat next to him, with Hassan beside her, filling the opposite seat. Gibson sat on the other side of Esme.

Esme was such an experienced traveler that she could sleep sitting up. Loretta felt a stab of jealousy. She was tired, yet could barely nod off; her rest was fitful at best. Despite the dreariness of the journey, she didn't think Rafe or Hassan even dozed. As usual both remained alert and watchful.

Beyond the carriage, dark sentinels of the forest flashed by. Even when she roused herself enough to peer out, all she saw were trees. They paused only briefly to change horses, and for lunch at a village tavern, then rushed on, through the Black Forest.

Trees, and yet more trees.

With Rafe directly in her line of sight, her thoughts had little reason to wander. They remained fixed on him, circling the decision she had to make. To go forward now, or wait until later.

Much later, after they were back in England.

She appreciated all the points Esme had made, yet had to question whether waiting until she was once again under Robert and Catherine's roof wouldn't make matters significantly more difficult, especially with respect to taking that next step. Aside from all else, as she understood it her rejection of eight suitors had garnered her a certain notoriety, which would focus attention on her when she returned to London, and the last thing she would wish was to be dealing with Rafe, feeling her way forward with him, all under the glare of the ton's avid interest.

Yet when it came down to it, she wouldn't—couldn't—go

forward with him, couldn't agree to any more formal connection, until she'd learned the answer to her questions,
which she wouldn't until she took that next step.

Her thoughts went round and round until she felt like
screaming.

The alteration in tone of the wheels on the road came just
in time. The carriage slowed, then swung onto a larger road,
and at last the trees fell back, the forests ended, and the wide
swath of a river appeared to their left.

"The Rhine."

Rafe's murmured confirmation registered. She looked out
at gray water rippling under a brisk breeze. Saw the last leg
of his mission looming. Minutes later, the roofs of Strasbourg and the spires of its cathedral appeared ahead.

She was going to have to do something to break their
impasse. She was going to have to decide whether his immediate well-being as well as her own were worth risking
in pursuit of something more powerful and infinitely more
enduring.

She was going to have to decide just how wild, bold, and
reckless she could be.

The only certainty she felt as the carriage slowed to cross
a stone bridge and enter the town was that she was going to
act. She wasn't going to wait until England.

The Beau Rivage was a small inn catering to those who
lived in the country surrounding the town and had business
on the river. Half-timbered with a sound slate roof, it stood
facing one of the numerous minor quays.

The innkeeper at Ulm, apprised of their requirements—a
modest inn not in the town center but close to the shipping
offices—had suggested the Beau Rivage. The instant he set
foot inside, Rafe knew the man had steered them well.

Although the inn did not have suites, with the weather turning cold and sleety there were few other guests; it was easy
to hire one entire corridor of rooms. Rafe took a quick look,

confirmed the quarters were both adequate and defendable, then returned to the carriage to hand Esme and Loretta down.

Esme peered at the building through the thickening river mist. "It's rather small."

"In this case," Rafe said, taking her arm, "small means difficult to infiltrate because everyone knows everyone else on the staff." And despite the timber in the building, with the river so close and the chill damp fog increasing, there was little chance of anyone setting the inn alight.

Esme slanted him a glance. "You're sure we'll find cultists here?"

"I'm absolutely certain of it." They hadn't sighted any yet, but they'd avoided the town center.

He escorted both ladies and maids inside, introduced the innkeeper and his beaming wife, then followed his charges up the stairs and briskly assigned the rooms he'd chosen.

He felt grateful when no one argued. He stepped back from the door of Esme's room to allow two lads to carry in her trunk, then headed back to the room he'd selected as his own, the one nearest the inn's main stairs.

His bags and weapons had already been left there, courtesy of the lads and Hassan respectively. He made short work of stowing things, then sat on the bed and cleaned and prepared one of the pistols he'd bought in Vienna.

Setting eyes on the Rhine and then entering Strasbourg had been like crossing a boundary—one marking the start of the last leg of his long mission. Urgency had gripped him, a sudden sense of being in action, real action, as if he'd just obeyed the order to set foot on some battlefield.

Everything suddenly seemed much more immediate.

He wondered where his friends, the three other couriers, were. It was the eleventh of December. Had any or all of them reached England? Had the Black Cobra struck at them? Had they got safely through to Wolverstone?

Unanswerable questions that only added to his battle-ready tension.

The pistol primed and ready, he stood, slipped the weapon into his coat pocket, buckled on his saber, then went to the door.

He met Hassan coming up the stairs. "I'm going to the shipping offices. You're on guard."

Hassan merely nodded and went on to his room.

The stairs were narrow and turned at right angles to descend to the ground floor and the foyer before the door. Making the turn, Rafe continued quickly down. The foyer gradually came into view. He saw the hems of ladies' cloaks, and slowed.

The cloaks were familiar. The further he descended, the more of the ladies in question came into view.

Esme and Loretta. Waiting for him.

He stepped off the last stair.

Esme favored him with a bright, shiny smile that stated her determination louder than a roar. "Ready, dear boy?"

He glanced at Loretta, met her eyes. Determination was a poor description for the resolve he saw there.

Inwardly sighing, he offered Esme his arm. "The shipping offices are at the end of the quay and along the embankment."

It was too soon for the cultists to have organized an attack.

When they entered the office of the Golden Eagle Shipping Line two hours later, he was feeling a good deal more grim. They'd already visited the offices of three other shipping lines. As they'd foreseen, there were numerous boats for hire, but they'd been of the slow, launch-cum-barge variety, in this season carrying mostly cargo and wedded to a ponderous, town-by-town schedule.

Fronting the main desk, Rafe asked what passenger vessels the Golden Eagle was running down the Rhine.

The clerk, by his appearance a retired ex-riverman, glanced past Rafe to Esme, then looked down at his register and confirmed that the Golden Eagle, too, had only passages on slow vessels available.

Edging Rafe aside, Esme stepped up to the desk. She smiled at the clerk, every bit as old as she. "But, my dear man, there *have* to be faster boats. I've traveled on smaller vessels myself—quick, quite luxurious boats just for passengers. Where have they all gone?"

The man blinked. Under Esme's encouraging gaze, he somewhat cautiously admitted, "There are riverboats that cater for small parties, passengers only. During the season wealthy patrons hire them to cruise the Rhine on river excursions."

"Exactly!" Delighted, Esme beamed at him. "We wish to hire just such a craft."

"Ah . . . all such craft are in dock, out of the water now it is winter and there's so much less call for them."

"But I'm calling for one now." Esme opened her eyes wide. "Our need is quite urgent. There must be someone with such a boat available. To whom should we speak?"

The clerk appeared lost in Esme's eyes. After a moment, he cleared his throat. "My nephew—his boat, I think, is still in the water. It is a perfect vessel for a small party—I think you said you were six? His boat is as fast as anything on the river."

Rafe stepped forward again. Satisfied, Esme eased back and allowed him to further question the clerk about his nephew—in his twenties, young and eager—and his boat. The *Loreley Regina* really did sound like the perfect boat for them.

The price the clerk quoted was exorbitant, but Rafe had expected that. He was happy to pay as long as they secured what they needed.

There was, however, one catch. The *Loreley Regina* was moored downriver and it would take a full day before she could be ready to sail.

Deciding he wanted to see the boat by daylight before trusting it, the captain, and his crew with the ladies as well as his mission, Rafe arranged to have the captain bring his vessel in to the quay opposite the Beau Rivage at first light the day after the next. If on inspection boat, captain, and crew passed muster, Rafe would pay the captain half the agreed sum, with the second half paid at Rotterdam, their destination.

Throughout the discussion and negotiation, he was careful to remain in his role of courier-guide, using Esme's name and never mentioning his own.

With all as settled as it could be, Rafe ushered Loretta and Esme out onto the embankment.

"Quite fortunate, really," Esme said as she accepted his arm, "that the inn faces the river."

Rafe nodded, scanning their surroundings. The fog had thickened while they'd been inside. On the one hand, it hid them from any cultists' eyes; on the other, the dense, drifting mists were an effective screen for any skulking assassin.

Tension leapt, a tightening sensation between his shoulder blades. He needed to get Esme and Loretta back to the inn.

Beside him, Loretta shivered and drew her cloak closer about her. He fought down the urge to loop his other arm around her and draw her close.

"Let's get back." She glanced at Esme. "It's getting colder."

"Indeed." Esme waved with her cane. "I haven't seen this much fog since London. But we are further north than we were."

"And heading even further north," Loretta pointed out.

Esme nodded. "We must hope the river doesn't freeze."

Rafe could only pray. If the river froze, the roads would be impassable, too. He wouldn't be able to get through. He would have to leave Loretta and Esme. . . .

He cut off the thought, shook aside the vision. It was only mid-December. The weather wasn't that cold and, he thought, unlikely to get that cold this side of January. He made a mental note to check with the innkeeper.

At least the nippier temperatures had Esme and Loretta walking on briskly. Without further conversation, they retraced their steps along the cobbled embankment and down the quay to the Beau Rivage.

* * *

The fog remained, steadily thickening with wood smoke and the sulphurous taint of coal fires.

The next morning, seated at a table with breakfast spread before her, Esme peered out of the inn's dining room window at the dismal excuse for a day. "Is it always like this in winter?"

The innkeeper set a platter of pork sausages in front of Rafe. "Sadly. It is the forests, you see. They are all around, and so stop the wind from blowing the smoke away." He gestured at the scene beyond the window. "It hangs."

Which, Loretta felt, glancing out of the window, was appropriate. She was hanging, too—vacillating over, not if she would act, but when. Last night, every time she'd turned toward her door intending to open it and go to Rafe's room, she'd hesitated. Not because of him, or her, but because of his mission.

It was important; it would affect the well-being of many people. If she precipitated the next step only to discover that he and she didn't suit . . . her subsequent retreat might affect his ability to complete that mission. Did she have the right to potentially jeopardize it?

She didn't feel she did. More, when she'd consulted her feelings she'd discovered a strong commitment of her own to helping him succeed.

Of course, once they took the next step, if they were not suited, despite all he'd said she might yet persuade him that in the circumstances a marriage based solely on honor wasn't wise. He might agree to part with no fault on either side . . . then again, if the next step proved them incompatible in her eyes, she could simply not tell him, pretend all was well, and use his mission to avoid further incidents until they reached England and his mission was complete, and only then break the news to him that she wasn't going to marry him.

Scandalous and deceitful, yes. But any scandal wouldn't occur until they were back in England, and she couldn't find it in her to care. As for the deceit, if it ensured his mission's success, she would consider it justified.

Her Michelmarsh side was clearly growing stronger with every passing day.

"The cathedral, dear boy, is the one place I really must insist we visit." Sipping her tea, Esme fixed her eyes on Rafe. "Besides, you can't expect us to spend all day confined to our rooms when we haven't had any real excursion on land for nearly a week."

Rafe had hoped, but . . . lips setting, he nodded. "The cathedral, then. But just there and back."

He changed his mind an hour later, after their party had ambled down the fog-laden streets, through ancient squares lined with medieval buildings, and, skirting the town's center, found their way to the gothic splendor of the cathedral, then spent twenty minutes studying the fine carvings inside and out.

"No cultists." Halting beside Hassan halfway down the nave, Rafe watched Loretta examine a choir stall. "I'm not sure if we simply haven't seen them because of the fog, or . . ."

"If they had spotted us yesterday, they would have attacked the inn last night."

"True." Rafe scanned the side chapels, searching for any sign of potential attackers.

Hassan slanted him a glance. "The last cultists we saw were in Vienna, and they did not see us."

Rafe nodded, his gaze on the ladies as they started back up the nave. "It would be helpful to know if our disguise works . . . and here and now is a reasonable place to test it." He and Hassan had fought together for so long they usually thought along similar lines.

"The fog . . . we could use it to our advantage."

"And if the worst came to be, we could flee by carriage. The highways are good from here." Rafe straightened as the four women approached. He glanced around, confirmed no others were close, then faced them. "We've decided to see who else is in town. Remember, if you see any black scarves, don't react. Pretend you don't know what the sight of a cultist means."

"Excellent idea!" Esme claimed Rafe's arm. "Always a good policy to know the enemy's strength. And even more helpfully their weaknesses."

Rafe glanced at Loretta and saw her lips quirk, but they were all as intent and alert as he could wish when they filed out of the cathedral and descended the stone steps.

With Esme on his arm and Loretta strolling on his other side, he led the way down the street toward the main avenue of shops and businesses. From the smell, the fish market lay somewhere to their left. The fog was dense, distorting sounds as they walked deeper into the isle on which the town stood. The buildings closed around them, fog cloaking the eaves and hanging so low it was difficult to recognize landmarks and identify exactly where they were.

But as they penetrated deeper into the town, they encountered more and more people on the streets. Most were briskly striding, on their way to somewhere. Few were ambling, but with Esme's cane identifying her as elderly, their pace didn't seem out of place. Rafe kept them moving steadily as if they, too, were on their way somewhere, but just walking slowly.

The cultists, when they came upon them in the fog, were more obviously idling. The pair, both in the distinctive turbans, black scarves dangling, but otherwise swathed in European-style cloaks, were openly scanning the people passing by, occasionally searching faces.

They saw Rafe, saw them all, including Hassan walking with Rose to the rear of the group.

The cultists looked, then their gazes passed on to the next couple walking along.

Rafe held his breath as the pair passed by on the outer edge of the pavement.

He didn't look around, hoped none of the others would, either.

Only when they were around the next corner, did he glance

back and meet Hassan's eyes—and see the same question that had just occurred to him reflected there.

"Back to the inn." Rafe turned down the next street leading in the general direction of the quay on which the inn stood.

Halfway back, they passed another pair of cultists, with the same result.

Rafe was certain that if he and Hassan had been by themselves, the cultists wouldn't have been so patently disinterested.

They reached the inn without further incident. Esme, triumphantly thrilled, ordered a pot of tea. It was served in the inn's parlor, which at that time of day was deserted but for them.

"So!" Dropping into an armchair, Esme looked brightly up at Rafe. "They don't recognize you while you're with us. We"—she waved to include Loretta, Rose, and Gibson—"provide you with effective camouflage."

"So it seems." Rafe exchanged another glance with Hassan, then, as Loretta subsided into another armchair, he drew up a straight-backed chair and sat, too. "That, however, raises a question. Clearly the cult hasn't issued a sufficiently detailed description of me or Hassan to their own members. They're expecting us to be traveling as a pair—I saw them look more closely at two other men walking by. So"—he glanced again at Hassan—"the cult doesn't have an effective personal description of us. That being so, how did the locals we assumed they'd hired in Pressburg, in Vienna, and in Linz know to attack us when the cultists themselves can't identify us?"

Loretta stared at him, as did Esme, Rose, and Gibson. No one rushed to answer his question.

Eventually, Loretta stirred. "Perhaps those incidents were attacks by thieves. If they weren't cult-inspired, what else could they be?"

He met her eyes. "I don't know." After a moment, he grimaced. "As things stand, we're left to assume that three different groups of attackers, who attacked this party in three different cities, were nothing more than opportunistic thieves."

Ten

$\mathscr{E}$vening came and went. Later still, Rafe kept the first watch, seated on the inn's main stairs below the right-angle turn, from where he could see the front door.

He had plenty of time to think and brood.

In the chill small hours Hassan came to relieve him. Rafe stood, stretched, then, dropping a hand on Hassan's shoulder as the big Pathan settled on the stair, Rafe turned and went up. Reaching the first floor, he headed down the corridor toward their rooms.

The cult had yet to get wind of them. It seemed increasingly likely they wouldn't, at least not in Strasbourg.

He hadn't imagined they would be so lucky. If the gods remained willing and continued to steer him clear of any cultist who could recognize him, it seemed possible he might even gain England's green shores before encountering an assassin.

The old Reckless would have chafed at that, at the lack of action. Instead, with Loretta, Esme, Rose, and Gibson with him, Rafe would simply be grateful.

Reaching his room, he opened the door—and instantly came alert.

Light spilled from the lamp. It was turned low, but he hadn't left it burning.

Slowly, silently, he slipped past the door's edge, swiftly surveyed the room. No one. He exhaled, then quietly shut the door. Maybe the maid had come in to tidy.

He'd taken two steps deeper into the room before his gaze penetrated the shadows beyond the lamp's glow and he saw the figure lying on his bed.

Sable silk spilled across his pillow.

He hesitated, then walked closer, until he stood by the bed's side looking down at Loretta. She was in her night-gown—not a good thing—but the warm robe she wore over it was tightly belted; much better. Her slippers were on her feet. She lay on her side on the couterpane, her head on the pillow, one hand tucked beneath her cheek.

From the slow, steady rise and fall of her breasts she was deeply asleep.

His mouth had dried. He moistened his lips, then com-pressed them, trying to think of how best to handle this. How best to handle her.

His initial impulse was to leave her where she was, undis-turbed, and slink away to sleep somewhere else. Her bed, for instance.

But then Rose would go to waken her in the morning, and find either an empty bed, or him; either scenario would lead to difficult questions, ones with even more difficult answers.

So . . . he drew in a deep breath—and the subtle perfume that was simply her wreathed through his brain.

He gritted his teeth against the inevitable effect. Waited . . . shored up his control. "Loretta."

Nothing. Not even a twitch.

He tried again, louder. "Loretta?"

Not so much as a flicker of an eyelash. He didn't dare say her name more forcefully.

Steeling himself, he reached for her shoulder. Stopped. He stood between her and the lamplight. Waking to see him, a large, dark, masculine shadow leaning over her . . . she might react badly.

Girding his loins, he eased down to sit alongside her on the bed. He couldn't help but notice the delicate curves of her cheek, her jaw, the long, evocative line of her throat. Her skin showed porcelain white through the black veil of her hair, and tempted his fingers. Drew them.

Abruptly his senses were swamped by her—by tactile memories of her softness, of the curves he already knew, alluring recollections of her warmth, her scent, her lips. Her taste.

Shutting out the distraction, refocusing on what he had to do, meant to do, took effort. He shifted so the light from the lamp struck his face. Mentally gritting his teeth, ensuring his expression was as blank as he could make it, he reached for her shoulder. Closing his hand over the quintessentially feminine curve, he gripped lightly and shook. "Loretta? Loretta, sweetheart, wake up."

He didn't realize what he'd said until she eased over onto her back and opened her eyes.

For an instant, wide-eyed, she looked into his face. His heart stopped for that instant, then started to beat again as her lids lowered and her lips curved.

"Oh. Good. I've been waiting for you." A sleep-tousled siren, she stretched, all slow, sinuous suppleness, then delicately patted away a yawn. "I must have fallen asleep."

"Yes, you did. And now it's exceedingly late and you need to go back to your bed and fall asleep there." He started to rise—to put distance between them—but she caught his sleeve.

"No. Stay. I wanted to talk to you. I need to tell you something—"

"Loretta—"

"—and yes, I know it's the height of impropriety to come to your room like this, let alone fall asleep in your bed, but"—releasing him, she pushed herself up to sit against the headboard—"that I did should convey to you how set on talking to you I am."

She was entirely awake now. Lamplight fell on her face,

revealing the stubborn line of her chin. Her gaze met his, held it, belligerent determination etched in periwinkle blue.

He narrowed his eyes, his own jaw setting.

She narrowed hers back. She folded her arms. Her expression took on a mulish cast; from experience with Esme, he knew what that meant.

"Very well." His tone was ungracious. He didn't care. "Talk. I'm listening." Even as he said the words, he knew capitulation was a mistake.

How big a mistake . . . he was sure she would teach him.

Loretta considered him for a moment, then simply stated, "I came to tell you that whatever it is that's growing between us, I feel it, too, just as much as you, and I need to know what it is."

Unfolding her arms, she shifted forward the better to look into his face. "I need to learn more—about it, about what feeds it. Enough to know why I feel as I do." She searched his eyes. "What we discussed on the observation deck that day? You insist I must think, and weigh, and make a rational decision, yet I can't make any decision on that subject at all—not until I know." She gestured between them. "About this. About what it is, why I feel it. And that you feel the same. For the same reasons."

He held her gaze, but his eyes, his face, were unreadable. A long moment passed, then he said, "I don't have the answers."

"I didn't think you did."

"Then why are you here?"

He knew. She could see him steeling himself to deny her. She wasn't having that. Holding his gaze, she reached out and sank her fingers into his cravat. Clutched. Slowly drew him closer as she shifted forward.

She saw his summer blue eyes flare. She didn't give him a chance to think of how to stop her. She dropped her gaze to his lips. "I'm here to learn those answers."

Lids falling, she kissed him.

Brushed, stroked, pressed her lips to his, then parted them. Lured.

And he came. Reluctant, unwilling, but she'd expected that. Expected to have to take the lead in this, to make her demands plain. She did, boldly, her tongue touching his, tempting, caressing, until she felt his response. Tasted the hunger he tried so hard to hide.

Once she had, she knew there would be no turning back. Not for her, not in this, not tonight. She could see her goal mentally before her, burning bright. She wanted to explore his hunger. Wanted to learn of it, experience it, wallow in it.

Wanted to feel it devour her.

One hand remaining sunk in his cravat, she sent the other skating up to cup his nape, to hold him to the kiss that was steadily growing hotter, to the melding of their mouths that grew, heartbeat by heartbeat, more erotic.

More primitive, more provocative.

She wanted.

Him. This.

More.

Yet even as her body tensed and she tried to tip backward, taking him with her to the billows of his bed, she felt him holding back, hardened muscles all but quivering beneath iron restraint.

How to break it, rupture it?

How to conquer him?

She allowed their lips to part only enough to breathe, "If you want me in your future, don't deny me now." She kissed him again, harder, openly, brazenly challenging, then drew back just enough to meet his eyes. "I need to learn, and you're the only one who can teach me."

Their breaths mingled, laced with rising passion. Eyes locked on his, she spoke to the summer blue, to the heat that simmered behind it. "You're the only one I've ever wanted to learn from." She dropped her gaze to his lips. "And I need to learn about you, about me, about us. About this. Now."

She closed her lips on his, poured every ounce of need she felt into the kiss. Into him.

Gloried when he broke. When he shifted, when he effortlessly seized control of the kiss, and his hands rose and closed about her shoulders.

The tenor of the kiss changed. From hungry to greedy to ravenous.

To an exchange so primitively evocative, so searing, it curled her toes.

She leaned back and he followed. Lips locked, she fell back on the bed and he shifted and followed her down, pressing her down, caging and holding her.

Every sense she possessed sang with delight at the promise implicit in the rock-hard body suspended over hers. Thrilled, expectant anticipation poured through her, heated her, excited her. Wrapping her arms about his neck, she poured all she felt into the kiss, pressed the heady mix on him.

Rafe groaned. Drew her in, drank her in, and reached for more.

Deny her? Had he really thought he could? He couldn't find the strength to draw back from the kiss, to even mute it. Her demands, her wants, her encouragement combined into a potent elixir. He was addicted and couldn't get enough.

He was lost. He knew it. He was hers to command. Tonight she'd discovered that.

She'd already learned that much.

And he couldn't find it in him to deny her the rest. To let her see the rest. Explore the rest. Experience it.

Some primitive self he barely recognized wanted her with a passion beyond taming, a passion beyond reason, or civilized restraint.

A passion that burned in his gut, in his heart. That burned just for her, that only she could ignite.

She'd set fire to his tinder. Now they had to survive the blaze.

He surrendered, and took charge.

If her innocence inspired his chivalry, her unfettered brazenness provoked a more primal response. A blatantly sexual reaction.

He wanted her beneath him, wanted her cries of surrender filling his ears as he sank into her sheath and possessed her, as he took, demanded, and claimed every iota of passion she had in her, yet even now, even here, the commander that was an intrinsic part of him was willing to cede a battle in order to win the war.

She wanted to learn, was demanding he teach her, so he would. He would teach her of passion, of desire so sharp it scored the soul, of need that beat like a pulse beneath skin and demanded satiation.

He would teach her of fascination that transmuted to obsession, of sensation so bright it burned. Of wants so elemental that once evoked they would never die, but instead would bind her to him, would keep her his, from tonight until forever.

That was his battle plan, his campaign for the night, his goal. He set out to secure it.

Pressing her into the bed, using his weight to keep her pinned, he reached for the belt of her robe. One sharp tug and it unraveled. He pushed the halves of the robe wide, paused as his mind swiftly gauged the terrain, its possibilities.

His lips and tongue still engaged with hers, he shifted, turned so his hip rested alongside hers, stretched his long legs down the mattress, then brought one up to hold hers trapped. Angling his shoulders over hers, he settled on his elbows, his chest a breath away from the peaks of her breasts.

She wanted to learn, but he had no intention of losing any clothes himself. There was only so much temptation he could take.

His weight on one elbow, he raised his other hand to frame her jaw, held her steady as he deepened the kiss even further, as he settled to plunder her mouth in a fundamentally possessive fashion.

Loretta met him, matched him, invited and incited. This was what she wanted, to know all he could show her.

His hands found her breasts. Her senses leapt.

They closed, and she stopped thinking.

All but stopped breathing as, his touch screened by the fine material of her nightgown, he traced and weighed, then closed his hands and possessed.

His lips still holding hers, he kneaded, and her awareness skittered, scattered, her nerves awash with sensation. With sparking expectation.

His fingers tightened about one nipple and bright feeling arced and streaked through her.

Heat bloomed beneath her skin.

Turned to a fiery demanding ache when he released her and set his fingers to the buttons of her nightgown, and she waited.

Kissing him. Savoring the heady male taste of him, yet impatient and yearning for the heat of his touch.

It returned moments later, a gift of delight when he brushed the halves of her bodice wide and set one hard palm to her flushed and heated skin.

He cupped her firm swollen flesh and her senses exulted. Drawing back almost languidly from the conflagration their kiss had become, he trailed fire and flames over her jaw, down her throat, over the taut swell of the breast he held plumped in one hand. Then he closed his mouth over the tightly furled peak and suckled.

Her body arched. She barely managed to mute her shriek.

As he feasted—what other word was there to describe such heated, deliberate attentions?—strangled shrieks built in her throat. Unlocking the fingers still sunk in his cravat, she pressed her knuckles to her lips to hold the telltale cries back.

He took her precaution as an invitation. Lids heavy, lashes low, she felt more than saw the glance, one of heated summer blue burning with desire, he cast her, but then he focused his attention fully on her breasts—on teaching her of all he could make her feel, all he could wring from her just by caressing her artfully, too knowledgeably, there.

Wielding sensation like a whip, using heat like a brand, with his hands and his fingers, his lips, tongue, and teeth, with the scalding wetness of his mouth he stamped his touch on her, on her body and her mind.

Hands gripping his skull, she was writhing, gasping, one step away from moaning, a heartbeat away from begging when he raised his head, surveyed her gown, then set his fingers to undo the buttons that led steadily down.

Panting, she watched his face, let her eyes drink in the sculpted planes, the hard edge desire set to the angle of his cheekbones. Let her senses reach for and absorb the intentness in his expression, the strength of his drive, his passion, the control that, despite her victory in precipitating the exchange, still ruled him.

Could she break that control? Would she need to?

The questions had barely surfaced through the lust-filled clouds in her brain when with a flick of one hand, he bared her.

All of her.

She lay naked under his gaze. She told herself she should feel . . . at the very least uncertain. Instead, something inside her purred.

Her Michelmarsh self was well and truly free.

Drawing up one knee, the one further from him, she started to turn to him.

His hand firmed on her hip and he held her back. "No. Let me see."

What he meant was let him explore.

With his eyes, with a gaze that burned. Then with his hands, with a touch that seared and branded.

That made her writhe anew, that made her gasp, more intensely aware of her body, of her as a woman and him as a man, than she'd thought she could possibly be.

And her body . . . rose to him. Shamelessly responded to every heated, increasingly explicit caress, and blatantly begged for more.

This was what she'd wanted to know—the passionate heat, the compelling yearning. The furnace that burgeoned and grew within her, that ultimately reached some flashpoint and melted, and left her molten and needy, aching to be filled.

This, and more. She wanted it all.

Was determined to have it all.

She reached for him, surprised to discover he'd shifted lower in the bed. Irritated to realize he'd yet to shed his clothes, inwardly frowning, she plucked at his shoulders.

Rafe caught her hands, pressed them back to the bed. He had the reins firmly in his hands and had no intention of sharing them. He knew his direction, his purpose, knew his goal.

He wasn't about to let her distract him.

Even though beneath his clothes he burned.

Lust was a familiar flame, yet never had it been this hot, this scorching. This demanding. Ignoring it was impossible. Holding the greedy conflagration in check was just barely within his scope.

The silk of her skin was a potent temptation, drawing his lips across it a sensual delight. Exploring the taut slopes of her midriff, the evocative indentation of her waist, he supped, licked, drew in the subtle pleasure, a sweet fruit to feed his desire, to temporarily appease his passion.

He wanted, ached to take, much more. The primitive side of him, the innate self she called forth, wanted to devour her. To have her all. To possess her completely. He had to rein that self in, curb its more primitive passions, distract it with the promise of more, of a deeper, more complete surrender, later.

When the time finally came.

That time would not come tonight. Not if he could help it.

He set himself to woo her senses, to feed them, fire them, ultimately to overwhelm her with sensation.

That was his plan. He applied himself diligently.

He traced her legs, the sweet curves of her calves, the delicate arch of her small feet, the long firm lines of her thighs, muscles quivering with awareness, with reaction to his touch, to the languid trail of his fingers, the possessive sculpting of his palms.

The sweet globes of her derriere filled his hands, made his mouth water. Cradling them, holding her, he set his lips to her navel, kissed, with the tip of his tongue traced, then probed.

Heard her breathing fracture, and inwardly smiled.

Shifting lower, he bent his head and set his lips to cruise the taut swell of her belly, then with undisguised intent sent them skating lower.

Eyes closed, head tipped back into the pillows, Loretta felt sure her lungs would implode. She wasn't breathing. Her head was swimming. Her senses were reeling far beyond her control.

Too many muscles were tense and trembling, not locked yet aching for release. Too many nerves were focused on the sensation of his lips burning her skin, on the branding grip of his hands, the fiery tracing of his fingers.

She burned, and yet she felt each touch so keenly. She'd had no idea her body could be so sensitive, so attuned, so enraptured.

His lips brushed the curls at the apex of her thighs and she shivered. The tension holding her racked tighter.

Before she caught her next breath he drew back a fraction, then he shifted. Lifting one of her legs, he draped her knee over his shoulder, then shifted further, and did the same with her other leg.

The intimate pose made something inside her shake. Quake. What was he up to?

Lifting her head, she battled to raise her heavy lids. "What—"

She broke off as his fingertips touched her.

Lost what breath she'd managed to drag in as he stroked.

He caressed and probed. Still tense and tight, she eased back onto the bed. Her body knew this, recognized his touch.

She'd already been this way before. Closing her eyes, she followed the remembered sensations.

The silken brush of his hair against her inner thigh gave her an instant's warning, then his lips closed, hot and burning, over her slick, swollen flesh and she shrieked.

Soundlessly. She had no breath left.

Couldn't find any as he supped, licked, laved. Then he thrust his tongue into her.

She bucked, but he held her down. One heavy arm over her waist, he held her immobile as he tasted her. Thoroughly. As he possessed her there in a flagrantly intimate way, an intimate possession that reached far deeper than skin and bone, that burned through her flesh and traveled her nerves to her mind.

All of her writhed, caught in a net of indescribable pleasure. One that with every knowing lick, with every artfully gauged thrust of his wicked tongue, drew tighter. Until it pressed on nerves already stretched tight, until it built to a weight that threatened to fracture her senses.

Then it did.

With one last slow thrust of his tongue, he brought her soaring senses crashing down on her. Cataclysmic pleasure exploded within her, splintering all sensation into shards of bright glory that lanced down every nerve to bloom like a million pinpricks of heat beneath her sensitized skin.

Heat and pleasure rolled over her in a wave, submerging her in glory.

When her awareness rose to the surface again, she felt languid yet empty, as if a fever had raged through her, then broken, and left her hungry.

Her senses slowly returned, and she felt her lips curve. She could guess what she needed to make her feel complete. Full. Properly replete. It was an effort to lift her lids. While she struggled to open her eyes, she shifted her hands . . . her fingers touched his sleeve.

He was still wearing his coat.

Her returning senses reported that instead of rapidly divesting himself of his clothes, he was busily doing up the buttons of her nightgown.

She snapped her eyes open, glanced down to see her nightgown closed to her hips. She looked at him. "What are you doing?"

His expression was unrelievedly grim. "Getting you in presentable order so I can take you back to your room."

"My room?" She blinked. "You want to finish this in my bed?"

He briefly closed his eyes, then opened them and reached for the gaping sides of her robe. "No. We're not finishing this—not tonight. Some other night."

"When?"

"Later."

She really wanted to object to that answer, and even more to his dictatorial tone, but no matter how hard she tried to summon her determination, what he'd done, what she'd experienced, had sapped her will. Her spine felt as solid as seaweed.

When, her robe cinched, he swung her legs off the bed, then grasped her hands and hauled her to her feet, her knees wobbled.

Despite her earnest wishes, she wasn't up to arguing, not with him in one of his I'm-in-charge moods.

But she could manage a protest. She fixed him with a glare. "This is not what I was expecting."

His glare was harder, stonier. "You didn't experience something you hadn't before?"

"Well, yes, of course. But—"

"No buts." He grabbed her hand and towed her to the door. Reaching it, he glanced back at her. "This is how it has to be. Now be quiet and let me get you back where you should be."

She had certainly never before experienced the mix of latent pleasure and awakened temper that coursed her veins as he opened the door, looked out into the corridor, then drew her out into the dark passage.

Unfortunately the deadening pleasure was still dominant. He reached her door, opened it, and steered her inside.

He remained at the door.

She took two steps, then turned back.

He pointed, stern and immovable, to her bed. "Sleep."

She narrowed her eyes at him. He met them; she saw his lips firm, then he stepped back and closed the door.

She turned to eye her bed. It took effort to make her feet move, but she reached it, then sat, then flopped down. Reaching blindly, she found the covers she'd left pushed back, and dragged them up.

Despite a vague intention of lying awake and dreaming up ways to torment him, sleep came in like a tide and she drowned.

Rafe stood outside Loretta's bedroom door until he was sure she'd reached her bed, and was staying in it. The last thing he needed was her deciding to return to his room to argue his decree.

Letting out a long breath—equal parts frustration and relief—he ran a hand through his hair, then turned and slowly walked back to his room.

All in all, he was proud of himself. A trifle shocked as well.

Reaching his door, he glanced back along the silent corridor, then opened the door and went in. Closing the door, he shrugged off his coat, reached for his cravat. Glanced at the rumpled bed.

Even now he couldn't quite believe he'd managed to restrain himself, managed to refuse her. Exercising willpower of that magnitude in that particular arena had never been his forte. Yet with her. . . .

She was different. Significantly different from all others who had gone before. In a different league, on a different plane.

He knew what that meant, but didn't want to think about

it. Dwelling on it . . . would only make him more acutely aware of the vulnerability that caring for her and wanting her so desperately had already opened somewhere in his chest.

He could comfortably live the rest of his life without acknowledging that gaping hole in his personal armor, in his emotional shield.

One thing was clear. If he wanted to suppress the sense of emotional exposure that being with her sexually evoked, a feeling that would increase exponentially the instant he made her irrevocably his, he would do well to ensure they avoided any repetition of the past hours.

Not until they'd reached England and his mission was complete.

Grimly clinging to that as his goal going forward, he stripped, flung himself onto his bed, and willed himself to sleep.

The subtle scent of her clung to his pillow. Wreathed his brain. Lingered on his mouth and on his tongue.

The inevitable effect of his noble abstinence bit, sank its teeth deep.

He didn't get any sleep.

Rafe rose and dressed well before dawn, and, cocooned in fog, was waiting with Hassan outside the inn when the *Loreley Regina* materialized wraithlike out of the murk to glide alongside the quay.

Crew moved with silent efficiency, tying up the boat. A gangplank rolled smoothly out and a youthful sailor came striding down.

He proved to be the captain, a few years younger than Rafe. Most of his crew were of that age, but Julius, the captain, assured him all were experienced on the river, and were eager to pick up some extra money from the unexpected run.

Rafe spent half an hour on board. After inspecting the cabins and chatting with the cook, he took Julius aside and in general terms explained his mission and the potential for attack.

Julius looked even more enthused. "A little excitement on the journey never goes amiss. We will be happy to help you and your man repel these heathens."

Rafe suggested that further largesse would be forthcoming if the crew would take on the duty of keeping watch through the night. Julius assured him that he and his crew would be happy to oblige.

He was openly delighted when Rafe added a potential bonus for getting them to Rotterdam on time. "By the nineteenth of the month? I would suggest we go at our best clip on the earlier reaches, then we can adjust on the latter stages."

With all arranged to their mutual satisfaction, they settled on a departure within the hour.

Rafe returned to the inn. The pacing tiger within was somewhat placated to find all four women not only awake and dressed for the journey, but seated in the dining parlor breaking their fast. Their bags were stacked ready in the foyer.

He joined them, taking his customary seat on Esme's left, across the table from Loretta. He'd avoided catching her eye, but after thanking the innwife for the piled plate she set before him, as he turned back to the table, he couldn't resist glancing Loretta's way.

She caught his gaze, her own very blue and . . . serene?

He inwardly blinked, but before he could look again and confirm, her lips curving, she turned to speak to Esme.

Focusing on his plate, he tried to imagine what might be going through her mind to engender such a calm and assured air.

An in-control air. The observation filled him with a certain foreboding.

By the end of the meal, when they rose and as a company bade their hosts farewell, then turned to the door and the *Loreley Regina* waiting beyond, he'd started to wonder what she knew that he didn't.

He'd expected some degree of suppressed irritation, if not outright disgruntlement, over his rescripting of her previous night's plans.

Getting everyone settled on the boat, the passenger quarters of which were a scaled-down version of those they'd enjoyed on the *Uray Princep*, then watching for cultists as, the ropes cast off, the *Loreley Regina* slid down the channel around the isle that was Strasbourg to eventually join the much wider Rhine, claimed his attention. They'd been on the river itself for half an hour, and the spires of Strasbourg cathedral had vanished in the mists off the stern, when Loretta came to join him in the prow. There was no observation deck on the smaller boat.

He glanced at her. Grasping the rail, she was looking ahead, that disquieting smile still curving her lips. Wisps of hair had come loose from her topknot; she shook them back as she raised her face to the light morning breeze.

A memory of her hair sussurating like silk on his pillow as he'd pleasured her and she'd threshed in ecstasy burst across his inner eye. Silently clearing his throat, he clenched his hand more tightly about the rail and looked ahead.

Followed her gaze to where the river mists that had replaced Strasbourg's fog were thinning to the merest haze. Beneath his feet, he felt the river currents catch at the boat's hull, felt the powerful surge as they took hold.

"Do you feel impatient now you're starting the last leg of your journey?"

He considered the question, consulted his feelings. They were a lot more complex than mere impatience. "There's a lick of that, but just as much wariness. Anticipation, eagerness, and trepidation—an odd mix."

A familiar if unsettling one.

"Perhaps a wise one given the Black Cobra lies somewhere ahead."

She was right. He'd often felt like this in the moments before a charge.

Silence ensued, oddly comfortable even though he knew

she couldn't possibly be pleased with him. That somewhere beneath her calm, irritation had to lurk.

Eventually, she murmured, "If anything, this vessel, with just our party on board, is even more private than the *Uray Princep*."

He recalled all too well what had occurred, and had nearly occurred, on the *Uray Princep*. He straightened, grasped the reins. "Which brings me to a point I wanted to discuss with you."

She looked up at him, arched a brow.

"I know I was the one who raised the issue, which was all very well, but in light of the questions you have, we'll need to postpone any further discussions until we reach England and my mission is complete."

The narrowing of her eyes had him hurrying on, "I can't afford to be distracted, not with my mission entering a critical phase—the last leg of a long journey, as you observed. The closer I get to England, the more danger we'll all face. And my mission, bringing it to a successful conclusion, means a lot to me." He held her gaze. "You, of all people, know why."

The thought of James's death was still a raw wound across his soul.

She understood; the light in her eyes softened.

Suddenly perceiving a fate worse than any the Black Cobra might serve him, he hurriedly added, "However, while this is not the right time to be embarking on the sort of explorations you have in mind, that isn't to say I don't want to find the answers to your questions. I do." The truth was he already knew the answers, at least with respect to him, but wasn't ready to face them. Pushing the insight aside, he held her gaze, drew breath. Confessed, "I want to . . . court you, if that's the way your decision goes. I want to have time to devote to you, to your questions—to learning the answers you need to know."

A considering light had entered her eyes. She tilted her head, studying him.

"But from here on, my mission will take precedence over all personal matters. It'll make demands—ones I won't be able to put off or refuse. I'll be distracted, and . . ." He hesitated, then said, "The truth is I don't want us to make any precipitous decision and later have that rebound on you."

By "precipitous decision" he meant making love to her, properly and completely. Loretta knew her calm acceptance of his derailing of her night's intentions was confusing him, but this latest start of his only confirmed that her reading of him and his motives was correct. His behavior of the night and his latest declarations were all of a piece, all stemming from his apparently insatiable need to protect her, even from herself.

While she appreciated his tack, while she understood and to some extent agreed with his assessment of the relative importance of his mission, she was very far from agreeing with his conclusion. But now was not the right time to inform him of that, either; aside from all else, he was all but armored against her. Still holding his gaze, she inclined her head. "I understand."

He smiled.

She blinked. That smile was the first time he'd intentionally set out to charm her, and it worked.

He took one of her hands, in a courtly gesture raised it to his lips. "Thank you. Once we're safe in England, we'll revisit your questions. I promise. Until then—"

"Loretta?"

They turned to see Esme climbing the narrow companionway up to the deck. They went to help her.

Once on deck, Esme glanced around, then smiled at Rafe. "I came to find you two to make plans for our first halt. Mannheim. According to dear Julius, we'll be there by this afternoon."

The innkeeper of the Beau Rivage was standing behind the high counter at the rear of the foyer, polishing spoons and wondering why his wife always saddled him with the chore, when the front door opened. The innkeeper looked up, surprised to see a well-dressed Prussian step inside, glance left and right, then close the door.

The innkeeper set down the spoons and his polishing cloth. He knew the man was Prussian—his harshly arrogant mien and the style of his hair bore witness to his origins—while the set of his shoulders and the way he walked fairly screamed cavalry officer.

Like the Englishman.

Clothed as a gentleman, the Prussian halted before the counter and fixed the innkeeper with slate gray eyes. "You have a party staying here—six people. Two ladies, both English, their maids, also English, and their courier-guide and guard."

Somewhat glad said party had already departed, the innkeeper carefully nodded. "Such a party did indeed reside here last night."

The Prussian's eyes narrowed. "And where are they now?"

"They left this morning." The more he saw of the Prussian, the more the innkeeper was glad that was so.

The Prussian's hand rose. The innkeeper's gaze was drawn to the gold coin between the man's gloved fingers.

"Did they leave on the river?"

The innkeeper debated, his eyes on the coin.

The Prussian's hand dipped, rose again, and now there were two coins clasped between gray leather.

The innkeeper nodded. The party in question had left early; they were well downriver by now.

The Prussian laid the two coins on the counter, then produced another two. His eyes caught the innkeeper's. "Which boat?"

The innkeeper hesitated.

The Prussian sighed. "I can ask at the shipping offices and learn the answer—or you can tell me, which will be faster, and you will be richer."

The innkeeper grimaced. "The *Loreley Regina*."

No reaction showed in the Prussian's face. He laid the

second pair of coins down with the first, curtly dipped his head, then turned and left.

The innkeeper didn't move until the door snicked shut. Then he swiped up the coins, examined them, then slid them into his waistcoat pocket. Then he frowned. The man hadn't asked which way the boat had gone, upriver or down.

He puzzled over that for a moment more, then shrugged, retrieved his polishing cloth, and picked up a spoon.

Eleven

The *Loreley Regina* eased toward a mooring at Mannheim in the late afternoon. Storm clouds had been gathering all day, massing above the riverbanks, hanging threateningly low over the mountains further back. Daylight was already waning into a gloomy dusk.

On the deck, from the shadows beneath the overhang of the bridge's roof, Rafe looked back, watching the sections in the pontoon bridge that had been raised to allow them and a small flotilla of other craft to pass through slowly lower again. Julius had informed him they would remain tied up at the dock through the night, then, after taking on various provisions in the morning, they would set out on the river again.

From Esme's guidebook Rafe had learned that the town was part of the Duchy of Baden and had been burnt to the ground twice in its history. That explained the modern town visible through the encroaching drizzle. It looked airy and open, with broad streets set in a regular grid. He picked out remnants of old city walls now surrounded by public gardens.

Mannheim looked like a quiet country retreat. He seriously doubted the cult would have bothered sending any members or even hirelings there.

Hassan slipped into the shadows alongside him, hunching

in his thick coat. "The ladies are in the salon planning their next excursion."

Rafe grimaced. "I'd better go and play the voice of reason."

Hassan nodded. "I'll stand watch."

"Once it gets fully dark, the crew will take over." With his head, Rafe indicated the bridge. "Just ask Julius."

Hassan nodded and settled back against the bridge's wall.

Rafe headed for the forward companionway that led directly into the main salon, given over for passenger use. Reaching the stairs, he paused, scanned the river, the banks, and the town once more, then went down.

He stepped into the salon and was the immediate focus of four pairs of feminine eyes.

Esme wrinkled her nose. "Your shoulders are damp. It's closing in, isn't it?"

He nodded. "It'll be dark early, too."

"It's too late to do anything tonight," Loretta said. "We can go for a stroll tomorrow while Julius and the crew are loading their provisions."

Rafe hesitated, but then nodded. "That should be safe enough." He exchanged a glance with Loretta, then inclined his head to the group in general and headed for his cabin.

She might have agreed to his dictate regarding the two of them, but as far as possible he intended to play safe.

The dining toom of the *Loreley Regina* was a small paneled cabin situated between the salon and the galley. As the boat carried fewer passengers than the *Uray Princep,* the space was more intimate, with one good-sized table and built-in but luxurious padded bench seats. As both benches had walls at their backs, the seating was comfortable enough.

Their first dinner on board proved the cook was up to the task of meeting Esme's expectations. Loretta had less interest in the food itself, but had hoped to use the the time about the dining table to introduce Rafe to the realities of her, and therefore their, situation.

But with all six of them gathered about the table, she decided against raising the subject. While she had no secrets from Rose, and Gibson and Hassan would be no more than passingly interested in what she had to reveal, she needed Esme's help and she doubted her great-aunt would step up to the necessary mark in general company.

To her relief, her opportunity came when, the meal completed, they repaired to the salon. Rose and Gibson decided to take a turn about the deck, and Hassan elected to go with them.

Esme settled in one of the comfortable armchairs.

Loretta quickly sank into another and ignoring Rafe, who was hovering just inside the room, fixed Esme with a faintly concerned frown. "It occurred to me that this is the last leg of our journey—soon we'll be back in England. In my case, back in London."

Esme arched a brow.

"I wondered, in the circumstances, what I'll find when I return. What I'll face in regard to the matter that made my accompanying you so desirable. What my social situation might be." Seeing awakening understanding in Esme's eyes, she tilted her head. "Have you heard anything?"

Esme pulled a face. "I have—a letter from Therese Osbaldestone reached me in Trieste—but it's nothing more than you might expect, dear. Given all that's gone before, and that you will turn twenty-five next year, now matters have come to this pass you'll be expected to make your choice of the available offers that, as I understand it, are being discussed. It seems there's a list of sorts."

"A list?" She hadn't expected that. "Of potential suitors?" Rafe hadn't moved. He was listening avidly.

Esme nodded. "Indeed. And I make no bones about it— and Therese didn't either—you will have to, if necessary you will be pressed to, make your choice from that list." She grimaced. "To hear Therese tell it, the list is growing longer by the day and there are already wagers being placed in the gentlemen's clubs over who will secure your hand."

It was easy to look horrified. "But—"

"No buts." Esme wagged a finger at her. "The instant you set foot in London, you'll be back under Robert's roof and in his care, and you'll be sat down and that list will be placed before you, and you will have to choose."

Loretta stared. That was a lot worse than anything she'd expected.

By the door, Rafe shifted. When Loretta and Esme glanced his way, he said, "I'm going to take a turn about the deck before retiring. The crew will be standing the night watches instead of me and Hassan, so there will still be someone on deck, on guard, through the night." But not him.

Just in case Loretta thought to find him up there later.

Smiling, Esme waved graciously. "Thank you, dear boy. Sleep well."

Turning away, he caught Loretta's eyes, then inclined his head and quit the room. Heading for the companionway leading up to the deck, he wasn't sure what to think, how to interpret what he'd just heard.

Just how desperate was Loretta's matrimonial situation?

Had he been right in seeing a degree of horrified surprise in her eyes?

If so . . .

He'd been certain he knew the best way forward for her. For them. He wasn't so certain now.

With Rafe's footsteps fading, Loretta, once more staring at her great-aunt, felt forced to clarify, "Is there really a list?"

Esme opened her eyes wide. "Well, you did ask, dear. And I really don't think a list and wagers are things dear Therese would be likely to invent."

"No." Consternation, quite genuine, gripped her. "I had no idea it would be that bad."

"As I've lectured you ad nauseum, you are a Michelmarsh, dear. Females of our line are always considered highly marriageable. Added to that, while not a grand heiress, you are certainly very well dowered." Esme regarded her, then added, "And you should remember that the words most frequently associated with Michelmarsh young ladies are bold and passionate. To most gentlemen, those words have a connotation, an implication, beyond the social."

Loretta frowned direfully. "I am not going to consent to marry any gentleman who puts his name on a list."

"Of course not. However, apropos of your current situation, I believe it's my duty to remind you of one of life's great maxims." Esme caught her eyes. "If a chance that is right for you comes waltzing by, seize it. Do not let it slip past. You can never be certain that fate, as fickle as she's wont to be, will allow you a second chance at happiness—not if you refuse to grasp the first."

Held in Esme's gray gaze, Loretta understood what her incorrigible great-aunt was suggesting—indeed, advocating. As it happened, she was fully in agreement.

Jaw firming, she nodded. "Thank you."

"Not at all, my dear—that's why I'm here." Esme grinned roguishly, then pushed to her feet. "And now I'm going to retire." The sounds of footsteps on the companionway reached them. "And there's Gibson, just in time. Good night, Loretta dear—and sweet dreams."

Loretta didn't react to that last recommendation. She heard the others in the corridor, then Rose came in. She and Rose chatted, discussing wardrobe matters, then she let Rose go off to her cabin and more slowly headed for her own.

Closing the cabin door, Loretta looked at the porthole, at the darkness beyond, and wondered how long it would take for the others to settle in their cabins and fall soundly asleep.

An hour later, Rafe was still pacing his cabin, three strides one way, three back, when a faint tap sounded on the door.

He'd just reached the porthole. As he whirled, the door-knob turned; the door opened. Loretta peeked in, saw him, and whisked inside.

She was in her nightgown and robe, her hair down, soft slippers on her feet.

Her attire answered one of the questions circling in his

mind. He waited while she closed the door, then crossed to him.

Halting before him, she looked into his face. "You heard what Esme said." Her gaze turned inward as if consulting some prerehearsed speech, then she drew breath, said, "I understand your position—all you said about your mission, its importance, its demands, and how that impinges on any exploration of what's between us."

She refocused on his face. "But I can't wait." Jaw firming, she searched his eyes. "I'm not prepared to risk losing any chance we might have for a shared future by returning to London without knowing about us. Without having learned what I need to know. I'm not prepared to risk never knowing—and if that means I have to take a risk, take a chance—roll the dice—now, so be it."

When she tried to step closer, he seized her waist, held her back. "Was that true, what Esme said?"

"Apparently, yes!" She flung up her hands, then set them down on his shoulders. "I had no idea, but she assures me she had it from Lady Osbaldestone, and why would she lie to Esme?"

Why would Lady Osbaldestone lie? Because she was one of the arch-meddlers in the ton. Why would she lie to Esme, however? . . . that was a great deal harder to imagine.

Looking into Loretta's eyes, Rafe didn't need to ask what she wanted. What she expected. He glanced at the narrow bunk, around the small cabin. His jaw tensed. "This isn't how I would have had it."

One small hand flattened against his cheek. She turned his face back to hers. "I don't care." Her lips firmed. "You said it yourself—the further we go down the Rhine, the greater danger we'll be in. We're safe here. For tonight there's no danger. So it has to be now, it has to be here."

He drew a deep breath. "If we take the next step—"

"I don't want to discuss anything further. Not beyond the next step. I don't want to consider consequences—if this, if that." She framed his face with both hands, looked into his eyes. "I want you to make love to me, no strings, no expectations. I want it simply to be you and me together—I want to learn what could be, what we might have between us—honestly and openly, you, me, and our passions—and I can't have that, we can't be that, if you're going to hedge us in, surround us with contingencies."

She drew breath. "I need this—I need you. Now, tonight. And I don't care what the risks are—I'm willing to take them and pay whatever their price." She held his gaze. "Are you?"

She could have been him. She could have been Reckless. She spoke directly to that side of him—and to all the rest, too.

His hands were firming about her waist, his head lowering to hers even before he said, "Yes."

She met him halfway.

Their lips touched, brushed, locked. Fused.

And they were lost.

Why it should have been different just because he'd let his resistance fall he had no clue, but the desire that surged, the passion that leapt so hungrily in its wake, was nothing short of need incarnate. The slaking of abstinence, however long enforced, had never been this powerful. This overwhelming.

Her lips parted under his, welcoming, inviting, and he took. Supped, sipped, then settled to plunder. Her hands sank into his hair and she gripped and kissed him back, equally hungry, equally urgent.

His grip on her waist eased; he spread his hands, holding her to him. Urging her closer. She pressed closer yet, her body all evocative curves and alluring feminine heat, sliding, then fitting snugly against him, a deliberate provocation of his ravenous senses.

Between one heartbeat and the next desire ignited. Passion flashed, soared, hot and greedy. His arms locked about her, seizing, holding. He angled his head and deepened the kiss; in a tangle of tongues she met him, flagrantly challenged and dared him. Heat rose in a wall and bore down on them, crashed into them, filled them, overflowed, and swept them on.

"Clothes." Loretta tugged at his collar. "You have too many on." Her gasp was a command; desire sang in the sound. Her breasts were already aching, her senses flushed and needy, and she wanted him naked.

His lips closed over hers again; he found her tongue, stroked, sucked as if the taste of her was an ambrosia he had no intention of ever giving up.

But his arms released her. Even while he plundered her mouth, in a rush of grasping, greedy hands he and she together wrestled him out of his coat, out of his waistcoat, stripped off his cravat.

He had to let her go and step back to haul his shirt off over his head.

She seized the moment to dispense with her robe.

His eyes gleamed through the moon-drenched shadows as, flinging his shirt aside, he reached for her.

Lips throbbing, she let her robe fall where it would and reached for him.

They came together in a clash of sensual fire that left her mentally reeling. Inwardly gasping as her hands met his bare chest, as the weight and resilience of the heavy muscles banding it screamed *male* to her giddy senses, as his strength wrapped around her and he took control of the kiss, as his hand found her breast and kneaded.

In that instant she realized they'd stepped beyond some boundary, that he'd taken her at her word and come to her honestly, openly, just him, her, and their passions—with no reserve, nothing held back, nothing to mute his aggression and power.

Nothing to mute the delight that filled her, the certainty that welled, swelled and rushed through her. *His. Mine.* Two sides of the one coin, this was what she yearned for.

Grasping his head again, she wildly kissed him back,

dropped every last fading link to convention and gave herself over to him, to this, to her Michelmarsh self.

To bold and passionate pleasure.

It swirled around them, swept over them, slid through them, sending insidious heat licking over every square inch of skin they exposed. Every square inch of her he reverently caressed, every inch of him she gloried in.

Exploration she'd called it. To her reeling mind the description was apt. But the lead changed between them, leaving her wallowing in long moments of mind-stealing sensation as he feasted on her breasts, only to have him still, eyes closing as with lips and tongue and wicked little nips she returned the pleasure.

She'd never thought to feel so free. So free to feel, to exult in the physical, to reach for pleasure with such uninhibited abandon, to feel so moved to lavish pleasure and delight in return.

He sat and pulled off his boots, then stood and drew her to him. He divested her of her nightgown with a touch that spoke of reverence.

At her insistence, he allowed her to unbutton his breeches, then stepped back and stripped them away.

Her mouth dried as he straightened, as he stood bathed in moonlight, a golden god, the gilt wash glinting in the fine blond hairs that dusted his arms and legs, the deeper golden brown of the curling hair that swept across his chest, then arrowed down to his groin, casting mysterious shadows and drawing her eye.

Her breath caught. Her lungs seized.

He stood before her, his rampant erection declaring his desire. It was she who moved closer, drawn. She closed her hand about the rigid length, and felt him shudder.

He shifted nearer. His hands slid around her hips, skin to naked skin; he bent his head and took her mouth again, but he didn't deny her—didn't draw her hand away but allowed her to claim him, to with her hands trace and learn and know. . . .

Passion rose with their heartbeats, a crest of silent thunder rolling in and taking them under.

Hands gripped, slid away, stroked, then returned to claim again. A flush spread beneath her skin as touch transmuted to sensation, and sensation was all pleasure.

Their breathing harried, still they dallied, wanting each moment, stretching each scintillating second, drinking each other in.

No rush, no hurry. This night was theirs.

Rafe had never before felt such fascination, as if this were fresh, uncharted territory. As if this was the first time his fingertips had ever glided over a woman's naked thigh, the first time he'd gripped and felt sleekly rounded flesh fill his palm.

The unexpected novelty held him in thrall.

His heart beat in a cadence he didn't recognize, heavy with lust, yet deliberate and slow. Slow so his senses could take in the wonder, the absolute delight of the woman in his arms.

Yet beneath the slow dance of tactile possession, the heat still built.

And built.

Until on a gasp she broke from the seething conflagration the melding of their mouths had become, her fingertips sinking into his upper arms, her head tipping back as her body arched to his in need, in want, in unspoken entreaty.

He swept her up in his arms, laid her on the bed, and covered her. Spread her thighs with his and settled between. Caught her mouth with his, caught her hands and pinned them one on either side of her head, held her down as desire erupted, raged, and ripped through them.

Ravaged them.

She kissed him back as ferociously, as temptestuously as he kissed her. Her body arched beneath his, hips tilting in primitive evocative invitation.

One touch confirmed she was ready.

He set the aching head of his erection to the slick entrance of her sheath. Felt the nails of her freed hand score his back. Felt her desperation, felt her need.

Felt his own need swamp him.

One thrust, and she was his.

The sudden sharp pain shocked her. Loretta clung for one second, her shriek muted by their kiss. She hovered, for that instant caught between two worlds, but then passion closed around her, tugged, and she let go, let herself sink into the heated tide once more.

Her body softened around his, accepting the heavy intrusion, his presence at her core igniting a flame that burned hotter than any she'd felt before.

The sudden tension eased, and he drew back.

In flaring panic, she clutched. "No!"

She heard a raspy chuckle as he reversed direction.

"Not a chance."

Those were the last words they exchanged. The last words either was capable of uttering.

Whatever her imagination had prepared her for, it had never come close to this.

Possession. Possessing.

Giving and taking in a rush of heat and flames, of sharp desire and scintillating passion.

Of a communion of the physical that reached to the soul.

And touched it.

Intimacy. She'd never thought it could encompass all this—the closeness, the yearning, the vulnerability.

The feel of his body moving over hers, the weight of him crushing her into the mattress, the rough abrasion of his hair-dusted limbs and chest over her sensitized flesh, over her tightly peaked nipples, the sensitive inner faces of her thighs.

The shivery reality wrapped around her, held her, impressed itself on her through the thrust of his flesh so deep inside her, the instinctive clutch and cling of her sheath, the rocking of her body as she cradled him.

As she held him and gloried, and surrendered and claimed.

Pleasure and delight welled, and overflowed, spiced with a blossoming joy unlike any she'd felt before, a giddy feeling verging on euphoria.

And over and through it all sensation swelled, pressure and friction, slickness and heat.

Pressing her on, driving her higher, filling her until she thought she would burst.

Until her nerves and senses imploded, the climax both familiar yet not. Deeper, brighter, a cataclysm of sensation that shattered her, shredded her, hollowed her out, then flung her into some void.

Open and empty, naked and helpless, she clung, then was swept away on a tide of ecstasy.

Rafe gritted his teeth, eyes closed, held on, but he couldn't hold back, couldn't keep himself from her, from sealing their implicit pact and giving himself to her. His body was no longer his but hers. Her sheath rippled, clutched, clung, and he surrendered.

Thrust deep and, on a long muted groan, emptied himself into her.

He collapsed on top of her, unable to move. Stripped of every last iota of strength, of will, of resistance, by a glory so deep it transcended ecstasy.

Only when his heart had slowed, when his blood had cooled to a mere simmer, could he summon the strength and wit to move, to force his weak arms to push his body up from hers.

He looked into her face. An angel's face filled with un-shielded bliss. Her lashes fluttered. He saw the glint of her eyes, then her lids lowered. Her lips curved.

She raised one hand and weakly patted his chest, then reached up and stroked his cheek. "Lovely."

Her tone made the simple word golden.

She wriggled. He withdrew and lifted from her and she turned on her side, nestling her cheek on his pillow.

It was his bunk, and narrow. He managed to wedge himself against the wall, pulling up the covers, gathering her against him, spooning his long body around hers.

With a sigh she settled in his arms.

He brushed his lips to her temple. "Sweetheart, you'll have to go back to your cabin."

"Hmm." A whisper of sound. "Later."

He looked down at her. Later.

He tried to make himself insist—tried to find the experienced lover who would have charmingly urged her up and steered her to her own bed.

Couldn't find him.

He lay down, gathered her close, and accepted what he knew to be fact.

He wasn't going to let her go.

Not now, not willingly.

Not ever.

She woke in the small hours. He sensed her start of surprise, relished the all but instantaneous acceptance of her position in his arms.

Relaxing again, she lay still, silent.

Eventually, he raised his head and brushed a kiss to the edge of her jaw. "We need to get you back to your cabin—the crew get up early."

She sighed, hugged his arms around her for an instant, then slipped from the bed. He followed.

He pulled on his breeches, then, ignoring the chill air, helped her into her robe; she'd already donned her nightgown.

Loretta found her slippers and slid her cold toes into them.

Taking her hand, Rafe led her to the door. He paused with his hand on the knob, glanced back at her.

He studied her eyes, then softly said, "I don't want to argue with you, but as far as I'm concerned, the upshot of the last hours is that we will wed, as soon as we're safe in England."

She studied him in return, replied, "We'll see."

His eyes narrowed. "There's no seeing about it. You wanted to know, to learn, to experience, and I gave you what you wanted. Now—"

She held up her hand; frowning, he stopped. "No arguing, remember?" she said.

His expression hardened. "Loretta—"

"You're rushing me. I learned, I experienced, and now I have to think about what I learned and experienced." Not least because she'd experienced something more than she'd expected. More than she'd anticipated, and she wanted to know if that unexpected element was what she thought and hoped it might be.

She smiled placatingly and patted his chest, her fingers lingering on his bare skin. "I'm not disagreeing with you, but you're jumping ahead several steps and I prefer to go slowly."

When he simply looked at her, she stretched up and touched her lips to his. "This isn't an end, but a beginning. Now open the door."

He did.

She whisked past him, looked back at him. "My cabin is two steps away. I won't get lost." She let the warmth that lingered around her heart infuse her smile. "Go back to bed, and dream of me."

With that, she slipped into the shadows of the corridor.

Rafe remained at his door. He heard her door open, then quietly shut.

Slowly, he shut his cabin door. Stared at the panels.

Dream of her?

Clearly he wasn't going to get any more sleep.

❧ Twelve ❧

*R*afe stood in the nave of the Mannheim cathedral and watched Loretta's face as she gazed at the windows high above.

There was nothing all that striking about the windows, nothing to account for the dreamy expression that all through the morning had haunted her face. Whenever she caught him looking, her eyes smiled and her lips curved, as if she knew something, understood something, he didn't.

That look, that smile, were unsettling.

"I've seen all I wish to." Quitting the altar, Esme glided toward him.

Loretta joined her, Rose and Gibson falling in in her wake.

Rafe stood back and waved them on. Hassan was waiting by the main doors. Rafe scanned the side chapels as he followed the women up the nave. Although the crew of the *Loreley Regina* had reported a quiet night and neither he nor Hassan had detected any sign of cultists, they weren't about to let down their guard.

The ladies reached the door and Hassan led the way down the stone steps to the street. They hadn't bothered with a carriage; the river and wharf were only a short stroll away.

Esme, Loretta, and Gibson paused on the steps, turning back to look up at the intricately carved façade. They pointed and exclaimed, then consulted Esme's guidebook. Rose walked on to join Hassan on the pavement.

Emerging from the shadows of the cathedral's maw, Rafe halted at the top of the steps and scanned the street. It was midmorning. There were no other visitors in sight, but a smattering of locals walked briskly past, intent on their business. There was no one loitering . . . other than a man, a European, possibly a local, lounging in a doorway opposite the cathedral, shoulder propped against the wall, his stance radiating the impression he was waiting for someone.

Except that he was watching the three women on the steps.

Rafe didn't consider that suspicious. Loretta looked striking in a dark gray pelisse trimmed with periwinkle blue, a matching blue cap perched atop her dark hair. The coat was expertly cut to showcase her figure. Esme, too, with her exquisite style, still drew appreciative glances.

Rafe waited for the man's lingering gaze to move on.

It didn't. And the longer Rafe watched, the more definitely he sensed that the man was specifically and intently watching the three women.

Slowly, deliberately, Rafe descended one step.

The movement caught the man's attention; his gaze deflected to Rafe.

They stared at each other, then the man straightened, looked away, then stepped out of the doorway and walked briskly off, away from the cathedral and away from the river. Rafe watched until the man turned a corner and disappeared, then, inwardly frowning, continued down the steps to where the three women were concluding their study of the cathedral's stonework.

Esme shut her guidebook as he approached.

"If you've seen all you wish . . . ?" Rafe glanced at Hassan. For once his friend had failed to notice the watcher; he'd been too absorbed talking with Rose.

"Yes, indeed, dear boy." Esme handed the guidebook to Gibson, and tightened her grip on her cane. "We've had a most satisfactory morning."

"In that case, let's head back to the boat." Rafe's every protective instinct was on high alert. The man might have gone, but to where? To whom?

Most importantly, why had he been watching them?

The cult?

Yet the man had spared barely a glance for either Rafe or Hassan.

Shaking aside the confusing conundrum, Rafe shepherded his flock back to the wharf. The *Loreley Regina* was due to depart in half an hour. Regardless of the nature of the man's interest in them, they'd be gone before he could organize anything.

Later that afternoon, Esme patted Rafe's arm as they left the ornate Augustinekirche in Mainz. "Thank you, dear boy."

They'd made unexpectedly good time down the river, arriving in Mainz at noon. During luncheon, Esme had explained her desire to visit a short list of sights in the town, if Rafe could see his way to accommodating her.

He'd felt obliged to consider it. When consulted, Julius had advised that with the unexpectedly strong currents augering well for their speed, and the fact that Rafe did not wish to reach Rotterdam too soon, it might perhaps be wise to dally now, when it seemed safe to do so.

Although reluctant to spend time ashore where they'd be more exposed than when on board, Rafe had agreed to the excursion. Like Mannheim, Mainz wasn't on any of the major highways, and they'd yet to sight any cultists anywhere, yet to see any evidence the cult even knew where he was.

They'd already viewed the Marktbrunnen, a large renaissance fountain capping a well in the market square, and the Mainz Dom, the cathedral, then had ambled down to take in the roccoco brilliance of the Augustinekirche.

Esme sighed. "Richard and I stopped in Mainz frequently. I'm so glad to be able to see these sights one last time."

"This is your trip." Rafe steadied her down the church

steps. "And we haven't seen any sign of cultists, so . . ."

Pausing on the pavement while Esme consulted her list and Loretta and Gibson sought direction from the guidebook, he studied Esme's face, saw the genuine pleasure she drew from her memories reflected in her expression, and decided that, in this instance, capitulation had been the right choice.

"If we continue on," Loretta said, pointing to a passage in the guidebook, "then we should reach the ruins of the Roman theater, and the Drusus Stone."

Rafe waved. "Lead on."

The women turned in the direction Loretta indicated. She and Esme led the way, Gibson and Rose behind them. Rafe and Hassan brought up the rear.

Their stroll was punctuated by pauses to admire various buildings. They eventually reached a parklike area in which they found the remarkably well-preserved remains of a large Roman amphitheater.

Although the day was cool and the light breeze carried a definite chill, the rain clouds held off. They spent some time exploring the stage and the tiers of stone seats, then walked the short distance to the Drusus Stone. The monument erected to the Roman commander by his men had been enclosed within the relatively recently built citadel. Weathered and worn, the monument stood on the edge of an open courtyard, presently deserted.

Rafe and Hassan stood back and watched as the women walked about the stone, reverently touching the ages-old rock.

Studying the large edifice, Rafe murmured, "Either Drusus was a highly respected commander, or . . ."

Hassan grinned. "Or his men hadn't yet been paid."

They exchanged grins, then Rafe folded his arms and settled to wait.

A sound to their right had both of them looking.

Then moving.

With a muttered curse Rafe swung between the five—no,

seven—men determinedly approaching the Drusus Stone and the four women clustered at its base. The men had had their sights fixed on the women. When Rafe, with his naked saber in one hand, and Hassan, similarly armed to his right, appeared across their path, the men slowed. Halted.

All seven held knives, mostly short swords, but the man at the rear held a saber.

One glance over the others' heads at that last man and Rafe recognized him as the man he'd seen in Mannheim. By his stance and that sword, Rafe was willing to wager the man was a Prussian ex-cavalry officer turned mercenary. "Wonderful," he muttered beneath his breath to Hassan. "If you can, avoid killing."

The six other men looked like local bully boys, heavy and meaty, yet mean enough and belligerent enough to be dangerous in a fight.

The local who'd been walking at the rear with the Prussian pushed forward. He looked at Rafe and Hassan, then gestured with his knife. "We just want the woman." He spoke in heavily accented English. When Rafe didn't react or respond, the man made a dismissive gesture. "She is just one old woman. What do you owe her? You are just her guards. Let us have her, and you can have the young one, and the other two. We will let you go, and you can say we were too many for you." He paused, his eyes hardening. "Which we are."

No, they weren't—not in an open area like the courtyard. Without exchanging so much as a glance, Rafe and Hassan glided apart, affording each other greater space to move. Even while one part of Rafe's brain absorbed the fact that the gang was after Esme, not Loretta, not him, Reckless was stretching in anticipation.

The Prussian recognized the change in Rafe's and Hassan's stances. "Attack!"

As if his order was a prod applied simultaneously to the rears of the other six men, they yelled and charged.

Rafe grinned, swung his saber, and followed it up with his boot. Three-to-one odds required inventive methods. One well-placed kick to the side of an opponent's knee and the man was writhing on the ground screaming.

Hassan had dealt similarly with another, which left them fighting two men each. Better odds already.

But their attackers were determined. Swearing, they squared off, then in concert came for them again. Rafe met their ferocity with a snarl of his own. As he beat back the knives trying to slash at him, from the corner of his eye he checked on the women standing together at the base of the stone. They were white-faced, but not hysterical.

Snapping his attention back to the threat before him, he caught a glimpse of the Prussian—just his coat as he disappeared around the other side of the monument.

Rafe cursed and redoubled his efforts. Momentarily throwing back the pair facing him, he glanced at the women—saw Loretta, her face set in determined lines, seize Esme's cane.

The Prussian came around the monument.

Loretta swung the cane.

The heavy silver head caught the Prussian on his temple. He staggered against the monument, and Gibson and Rose were on him like furies.

Rafe saw Loretta raise the cane over her head again, but was forced to swing his attention back to the two men trying to incapacitate him.

They were all trying not to kill. He pressed harder, mind awash with fear over what was going on at his back, by the foot of the monument.

Hassan, too, had seen. The snarl that contorted his dark face was fearsome.

Clash by clash, blow by blow, Rafe and Hassan wore their opponents down, beat them back. When it came down to it, the pair of them were in far better fighting shape. Able at last to risk pushing in closer, Rafe pulled his knife and used the hilt to knock out first one opponent, then, finally, the other.

One glance showed Hassan with only one opponent still standing. Leaving him to it, Rafe whirled and raced toward the melee about the base of the monument.

The Prussian, arms raised to protect his head from the slapping, scratching, cane-wielding women, saw him coming. Abandoning all defense, he lowered his arms, seized both Rose and Gibson. Loretta swung and hit him full in the face. The man roared, then heaved, and flung the two maids—into Loretta.

Knocking her back into Rafe.

He went down beneath a welter of feminine limbs, heavy skirts, and petticoats. Three wriggling bodies held him trapped.

Frantic, he grabbed Loretta and bodily lifted her up and off him—saw the Prussian start for Esme, shocked and clinging to the monument's worn stone.

Then the Prussian's gaze lifted; a split second later he glanced at Rafe. Then he turned on his heel and fled.

Still flat on the ground, Rafe looked up and back as Hassan limped up. "Wounded?"

Breathing heavily, Hassan shook his head. "Just twisted." He stood looking after the Prussian. "He didn't see. If he'd realized I couldn't follow . . ."

Struggling to his feet, Rafe met Hassan's eyes, then he gave Loretta his hands and hauled her to her feet. Rose had already scrambled up. She helped Gibson up, then rushed to support Hassan.

Loretta bent and swiped up Esme's cane, then hurried to Esme, Gibson on her heels. Rafe followed.

Backed against the cold stone of the monument, her slender figure slightly hunched, Esme looked suddenly frail. Her expression was blank. Too blank. The hand she gave Loretta visibly trembled. Loretta took it, curled Esme's fingers about the cane's head. She glanced at Rafe. "Back to the boat."

He was about to nod when a sound drew his attention toward the men he and Hassan had left strewn at the edge of the courtyard. The four they'd knocked unconscious had revived, and were quickly assisting the two with wrenched knees away, heading as quickly as they could for the twisting streets of the old town.

Rafe cursed beneath his breath. Hassan sent him an inquiring look. Disgusted, Rafe shook his head. "No—let them go."

With his twisted knee, an old injury, Hassan couldn't move fast enough to give chase, and Rafe didn't trust the Prussian not to still be keeping watch, ready to pounce again if Rafe left the women with only a hobbled Hassan to guard them. Besides . . .

He glanced again at Esme, then gently took her arm. "Let's head back to the wharf."

By the time they reached the *Loreley Regina* Rafe had worked out the basic elements of an effective response.

Although deeply shaken, Esme, he was perfectly certain, possessed a spine of steel. She just needed a few minutes to recover her composure. Leaving her ensconced in an armchair in the salon, with Gibson brewing tea and Loretta chafing Esme's hands, Rafe went to find Julius. Rose had gone to help Hassan to his bunk. Rafe knew how to fix his friend's injury, but he suspected Hassan would rather have Rose tend him.

Locating Julius, Rafe spent a few minutes learning about the local authorities, and discovered he held an unexpected ace. Julius's uncle was the local chief of gendarmes.

Julius and the crew were shocked to hear of the attack. "I and those of us who can be spared will come with you."

Rafe accepted the offer gladly. In the towns along the river, the captains and crews of the riverboats were largely viewed as locals. "I need to speak with her ladyship first. I'll come and fetch you once I've learned what I can."

He returned to the salon to find Esme greatly recovered.

Hands wrapped about a deep tea dish, she met his eyes, her own puzzled. "They were after me. Why?"

Pulling up a straight-backed chair, he set it in front of

her and sat. "That's what we need to work out." He glanced at Loretta, sitting beside her, then met Esme's gaze. "Who might want to harm you?"

Esme pulled a face. "I have no idea."

Loretta leaned forward. "Did Richard have any enemies? People who might not know he's dead?"

Esme sipped, then shook her head. "Not that I ever heard, and Richard used to share everything with me." After a moment, she added, "I'm sure that when he died he was not at odds with anyone."

Lifting her head, she looked at Rafe. "But whoever was behind the attack today . . . do you think they could have been behind all the other attacks, too? Even in Buda, remember? Until today we assumed all the attacks since we met were directed at you, dear boy, but what if, all along, the target was me?"

Horrified, Loretta met Rafe's gaze, saw that he was wondering the same thing. "All along?"

He grimaced. "There've never been any cultists involved in the attacks—we just assumed they were behind them because we had no reason to think anyone else would want to attack our party. But now . . ." He inclined his head to Esme. "It may well be that all the attacks have been instigated by someone else."

"But who?" Loretta looked from him to Esme. "Who would want to harm you?"

Esme lifted her shoulders in a helpless gesture.

Loretta looked at Rafe. "Ransom? Could that be what they're after?"

He stared at her for a moment. "If they were locals targeting travelers with a view to ransom . . ." He shook his head. "If that were so they would be fixed in one town, not following Esme, a single traveler, up the Danube and down the Rhine. They've followed us over half of Europe. The Prussian who you struck?" He nodded at her. "He was in Mannheim, watching us outside the cathedral."

"Has he been following us from Buda?" Esme frowned.

"But how could anyone have known I would turn up there?"

Loretta's blood chilled. "I think they followed us from Trieste."

Rafe and Esme stared at her. "What makes you think that?" Rafe asked.

Loretta looked at Esme. "The day before we left Trieste, I happened to meet Phillipe in the marketplace." To Rafe, she said, "He was our courier-guide from Paris to Trieste. He became entangled with a contessa there, and we parted company." She looked back at Esme. "But that day he told me to beware because he'd heard there were men—not nice men—asking after two English ladies, one old, one young, traveling alone." She grimaced. "There were quite a few travelers who met that description in Trieste, and as we were leaving the next morning I didn't give his warning further thought. Looking back . . . those not-nice men might have been looking for us."

"If they picked up your trail there . . ." Rafe frowned. "Why there?"

"Because," Esme said, "that was the one place at which people knew we'd halt. The rest of our trip, both before Trieste and since, has been more or less impromptu, decided as we've gone along. But I was determined to visit Trieste again—other than Paris, it was our only certain stop."

"And we remained there for nearly two weeks," Loretta said. "There were letters waiting for us, and others we sent home from there."

Rafe nodded. "So Trieste was the one place someone in England might have learned you would halt at."

"Yes, but . . ." Esme shook her head. "I can't imagine why anyone would hire thugs to follow and attack me. To what purpose?"

Silence descended, then Rafe drew in a breath. "Let's look at this from a different perspective. If not an enemy as such, is there anyone who would benefit from your disappearance, or your death?"

Esme blinked, then opened her eyes wide. "Other than my

legal heirs . . ." Her voice faded. Her expression stilled, her gaze growing distant.

Loretta and Rafe waited, their gazes fixed on Esme's face.

But then she shook herself free of her abstraction. Frowning, she looked at Rafe. "I suppose . . . but I really can't believe it." She looked away. "I need to think."

Following her gaze, Rafe looked out of the window at the town beyond. It was still afternoon, but the light would soon fade. He rose, looked at Esme. "While you think of who might profit from you vanishing or dying, I'm going into the town with some of the crew to see if we can hunt down the man Loretta hit." He glanced at Loretta. "Your last blow cut his brow. He'll probably have a black eye."

"Good." She sounded quite fierce.

Suppressing a grin, he continued, "Hassan will remain aboard with the rest of the crew. You'll be safe on the boat."

Loretta looked up. "Take care of yourself, too."

He met her gaze, inclined his head. With a last glance at Esme, he turned and left.

An hour later, backed by Julius, two of his crew, and several local gendarmes, as well as their chief, Rafe cornered the Prussian in the back of a smoky tavern in the seediest quarter of the town.

Earlier, they'd tracked down four of the locals Rafe and Hassan had injured. Given sufficient incentive, the four had delivered up the other two locals, including the leader of their pack. The chief of gendarmes was delighted to finally have a reason to throw the man in jail. Angry, surly, but gutterwise, when Rafe had asked, the man had given them the name of the tavern where he was supposed to meet the Prussian.

With gendarmes at every exit, Rafe walked into the tavern, spotted his quarry in the far back corner, and strolled over.

The Prussian had been gazing into a stein of beer. Sensing a change in the atmosphere, he glanced up. Tensed to rise, but then, seeing the figures behind Rafe, he eased back, remaining in his seat.

Rafe drew out the chair facing him and sat. He studied the Prussian, taking in the contusion and swelling around his left eye. Noticed the man's fingers tightening on the stein's handle. "If you fling that at me, I'll make sure your eyes match."

They'd both been cavalry officers; they were much the same size and build. A fair enough match, except the Prussian was bloodied and bruised, and Rafe was not.

A tense moment ticked by, then the Prussian deflated. He slumped against the grimy wall at his back. "I was hired."

"So I supposed. Who hired you?"

"You think I know his name?"

Rafe considered that. Considered the man before him. He had good features, clean cut, a trifle harsh. And getting into the Prussian cavalry hadn't ever been simply a matter of putting down one's name. "Yes. You're too intelligent to work for someone you can't identify. What if they decided not to pay?"

The Prussian's lips twisted. He inclined his head. "True."

"So who was it?"

The Prussian sighed. "An Englishman. His name is Sir Charles Manning. I met him years ago in Vienna, at the Congress. He knew . . . that once the wars were over, I would need . . . employment. Recently he contacted me."

"He told you Lady Congreve was in Trieste."

The Prussian nodded.

"And he asked you to . . . what?"

"Dispose of her. He did not care what was done as long as she did not return to England—as long as nothing more was ever heard of her."

Rafe held the man's gaze. He was tempted to ask if he'd made other people vanish, too . . . but what he saw in the man's gray eyes made him suspect the answer was one he wouldn't want to hear. As it was . . .

He pushed back from the table and rose. With one hand

indicated the man who stood just behind him, close enough to have heard every word. "Allow me to introduce the chief of gendarmes."

Another benefit of Julius's uncle being the chief of gendarmes was that he understood the imperatives of river travel. They'd lost time enough in Mainz; Julius wanted to put back onto the river as soon as possible.

He left Rafe with his uncle and returned to the boat.

The uncle, grateful for his prisoners, summoned a magistrate to take Rafe's testimony. By the time Rafe had finished, and, with a copy of the Prussian's information verified by the magistrate in his pocket, returned to the wharf, the *Loreley Regina* was ready to sail. Julius gave the order to cast off as soon as Rafe stepped on board.

Pausing by the rail, Rafe watched as the boat nosed away from the wharf, watched as the town's spires slowly slid away astern. He felt the currents catch and grab, then the sails rose and the *Loreley Regina* gained speed.

Closing his eyes for a moment, he breathed in the cleaner air, savored the tang of the freshening breeze. Opening his eyes, he turned and went down to the salon.

Esme was still sitting where he'd left her, staring out of the window at the banks slipping past. Instead of the tea she'd earlier held, she now sipped from a glass of brandy.

Loretta was there, too, standing before another window; she turned and looked at him, a question in her eyes.

He gave a slight nod, then turned his attention to Esme. Crossing to her, he again sat in the straight-backed chair facing her. When she shifted to look at him, then arched a brow in question, he said, "I take it you know a gentleman by the name of Sir Charles Manning."

She grimaced. "So it was he. He was the only one I could think of who might be . . . black-hearted enough for such a deed."

"The Prussian said Manning hired him to dispose of you—he specifically instructed the Prussian to ensure you never returned to England and that no more was ever heard of you."

"How *dreadful*." Loretta sank into the armchair alongside Esme's, her gaze trained on Esme's face. "Why would he do such a thing?"

Esme's gaze turned agate hard. "Money. Why else?" She sipped, then explained, "I stand in the way of him making a great deal of it."

"How?" Rafe asked.

"There was a company set up, decades ago now, when the new mills were springing up everywhere." Esme sipped again, then went on, "The companies running the mills, all sorts of mills, needed housing for their workers. Their idea of housing was generally along the line of hovels. However, in a number of towns this company—Argyle Investments—bought up land not far from the factories and built decent, livable cottages. Because the company was run by gentlemen who, shall we say, had a certain clout, the milling companies were persuaded to do the right thing and pay for their workers to live in these better cottages. The milling companies paid Argyle Investments, and the workers had decent roofs over their heads."

"Argyle owns the cottages?" Rafe asked.

Her expression distant, as if she were looking into the past, Esme nodded. "All went well for many years. Indeed, as far as the milling companies and their workers are concerned, all is still well. However, within Argyle Investments the years brought inevitable changes. To make matters simple, from the first there were only ever one hundred shares in the company. They were divided equally between the ten farsighted gentlemen who founded it, of whom Richard was one. Over the years, as those gentlemen passed on, their shares were divided between their heirs, some of whom sold them. Richard bought some. Those of the original shareholders still alive bought others. Just over a year ago the four remaining original shareholders discovered that Sir Charles Manning had taken an interest in the company. He had amassed a holding of forty-six shares, becoming the major shareholder. As such he called a meeting, and informed the remaining original shareholders of an astonishing deal he had brokered with a company wishing to build a new foundry. In return for one of the largest tracts of workers' cottages Argyle owns, the company was prepared to hand over a staggering sum."

Esme's lips twisted. "Sadly, Sir Charles hadn't done his research, or rather, had chosen to ignore what he'd learned. The founders of Argyle had never intended the company to make profits of that magnitude. What profits have been made over the years have either been plowed back into making improvements to the cottages, or buying land and building more. But Sir Charles wasn't interested in workers' cottages. If the money had been intended to rehouse the workers displaced, perhaps something might have come of it, but no—Sir Charles insisted that the money from the sale should be returned to the shareholders. A capital return on their investment, in more ways than one."

"I take it the other shareholders were opposed?" Rafe asked.

"Implacably. As Richard told it, there was a row of biblical proportions that ended with Manning storming from the room vowing he'd take control of the company one way or another." Esme sighed, then looked down into her glass. "Richard died a month later. Oh, it wasn't in any way connected—he'd been fading for some time. However Manning, of course, saw it as his chance. He came up to see me in Scotland."

A cold smile playing about her lips, Esme drained her glass. "I had barely put Richard in the ground, and Manning was there with an offer to buy the shares. I do believe he thought to bamboozle the grieving widow and leave with Argyle in his pocket."

Rafe felt his own lips curve. "And?"

"I sent him to the rightabout in no uncertain fashion. Among other things, I told him it would be a cold day in hell before I let him get his hands on Richard's shares." Esme grinned. "It was most satisfying."

For a moment, all was silent, then Rafe asked, "Why you? Why target you and your shares, rather than any of the others?"

Esme held up a finger. "Ah—there we see the craftiness of the man. The other three shareholders have sole male heirs who think as their fathers do, and who will continue to keep Argyle as it is, as far as they are able. The heirs know of their fathers' wishes and will honor them. So twenty-nine shares are beyond Manning's reach."

"He needs five?" Loretta asked.

Esme nodded. "And that's where the twenty-five shares I now control come in." She looked at Loretta. "Those shares are now mine. Richard willed them to me, trusting me to see to it that they would be voted correctly. When I die, my heirs are you and your siblings. That's common knowledge—I have no other blood relatives. There's five of you. Manning is banking that each of you will get five shares. In that, he's correct."

"So if you'd died on this journey," Rafe said, "then Manning would have had five separate chances to pick up the shares he needs."

Esme nodded, her gaze returning to Rafe. "And given the present situation regarding Loretta's future, all the speculation within the ton, I rather suspect that Manning has a very real interest in who will win Loretta's hand. He will assume that the successful candidate will control her shares."

Rafe studied her eyes. "Am I right in assuming that in that, he isn't correct?"

Esme smiled. "I do like you, dear boy. And yes, you're right—Loretta will control the shares she'll inherit from me, as will her sisters. So along with Robert and Chester, they'll have to sharpen their wits and sit at the board table and make sure the right decisions are made. The other original shareholders agreed with my view that the female perspective won't go amiss."

Rafe imagined they hadn't dared argue.

Silence fell. He and Loretta exchanged glances, then both sat back. He imagined she, like he, was trying to digest all they'd learned enough to define their best way forward.

Esme, he suspected, was slightly tipsy.

And, he also suspected, sunk in the past.

Eventually, Rose and Gibson arrived to rouse their respective mistresses to change for dinner.

Rafe got to his feet. He looked down at Esme. "One thing—how likely is Manning to persevere?"

To his surprise, Esme's gaze was sharp and clear. "Everything I know of him says he will, increasingly intently. However, there's one point that stands in our favor—one I wish to think rather more about before we discuss this matter further."

Rafe frowned; giving her his hand, he helped her to her feet. "What point?"

Esme opened her eyes at him. "Why, dear boy, with that Prussian in jail and unlikely to correspond with him, until he learns otherwise, Manning will assume I'm dead."

Thirteen

*L*ater that evening, a glass of brandy in his hand, Rafe
stood at the window in the salon and looked out at
the lights of Bingen. The *Loreley Regina* had tied up
at the town's wharf just before they'd sat down to dine.

The weather was too inclement to walk the deck, sleet and
icy winds sweeping past. He was glad he'd arranged for the
crew to stand the night watches, allowing him and Hassan
to rest decently at night. After the day just passed, he was
doubly glad of that.

Loretta walked into the salon. He glanced around, one
brow arching as she came to join him.

Esme had eaten little, then risen from the table and declared she was retiring immediately. Such a happening was
unusual enough to concern them all. Loretta had accompanied Esme down to the stateroom.

Halting beside him, Loretta sighed. "She's resting on her
bed—not sleeping, but thinking. When I asked whether she
wanted to see any sights in Bingen, she said she'll think
about that later, that she has more important decisions that
need to be made first. When I asked what those were, she
said she'll tell me, and you, in the morning. Then she shooed
me out." Loretta's lips quirked. "She told me I could help by
distracting you."

Taking a sip of brandy, Rafe raised his brows. He stared out into the night. After several quiet minutes, he asked, "Do you have any idea what she has in mind?"

"No. But I should warn you that of all the willful and independent ladies of my acquaintance, Esme has it in her to be the most outrageous of all."

Loretta had no idea what Esme was thinking, what she might decide on, but the possibility that her great-aunt's decision might curtail her time with Rafe—the time she could seize to explore the nature of their connection before they reached England—spurred her to action.

One day at a time; one night at a time.

When the boat fell silent, in nightgown, robe, and slippers once more, she slipped out of the stateroom and down the dark corridor to Rafe's door.

She raised her hand to tap.

The door opened. Rafe stood framed in the doorway. He grasped her hand, tugged her inside, and closed the door.

"Sssh." Rafe turned to face her. Expecting—anticipating—her, he'd been listening intently. "I heard someone else in the passageway." Someone who had gone into Hassan's room further down and across the corridor.

"I didn't see anyone." Loretta stepped closer.

Without conscious direction, his hands slid about her waist as she pressed nearer, reaching up to twine her arms about his neck. Oh, yes, he'd been expecting her. Her nearness, her warmth, the promise in her slender frame as she leaned into him fired his hunger. The inner Reckless purred.

"I've been thinking." Through the shadows, she searched his eyes. "I need to explore more."

He'd expected that, too. "Just as long as you acknowledge one thing." Eyes locked with hers, he backed her toward the bed. "As far as I'm concerned, we're as good as affianced. Betrothed. Heading for the altar."

Her brows rose haughtily. "Are we, indeed?"

Halting before the bed, he held her gaze. "To my way of

thinking, you made your choice—accepted my proposal—last night."

Her gaze remained level. Her lips took on a subtle curve. "I see."

He didn't. He had no idea what was going through her mind. Her intensely female, ergo unpredictable, mind. "Just as long as you agree to that, you can explore all you like."

She tilted her head. After another unnerving moment of assessing him, replied, "I'm not agreeing, but neither am I disagreeing. As I told you last night—or was it this morning?—you're rushing ahead too fast. I'll need time to catch up."

What did she expect? He wasn't called Reckless for no reason. But the compulsion to decree their relationship determined, settled, recognized, and acknowledged sprang from a deeper imperative. And he knew it.

"Catch up?" He reached between them and tugged the belt of her robe free.

"I need time to explore, to learn and see, and reach my own decision in my own way, in my own time."

He didn't need further exploration. Didn't need to look deeper into his own motives, his own emotions, to know that regardless of what he might find there, he really didn't want to know. Didn't want to have to face that reality.

Not if he could help it. Not if he could avoid it.

He set his jaw. "What exactly are you searching for—and how long do you intend to withhold your agreement?" Sliding his hands beneath her parted robe, he closed them about her waist, then, irresistibly tempted, reached further, the fine material of her nightgown tantalizingly screening her hips, her curves; closing his hands, he urged her nearer.

Lips curving, she came, arms tightening about his neck, face tilting up to his. "Last night was a beginning, a first act, as it were. I'm looking for more than a mere repeat—I'm looking for a wider, more far-reaching experience. Greater depth, greater intensity, a deeper engagement. More on all counts."

He was sorry he'd asked; Reckless didn't need further encouragement. But her answer gave him an inkling of a strategy—a way he could turn her exploration to his advantage. He could use it to support his own cause.

"As for time," she went on, "while we're on this journey, we're outside our accustomed worlds. I see no reason we need to decide anything until we return to those worlds at our journey's end."

"I don't agree. We're still ourselves, not different people."

She looked at him for a moment, then softly said, "Speak for yourself." Then she stretched up and kissed him.

This time he let her lead—let her think she was. He took advantage of the clear invitation of her parted lips, sank into the honeyed sweetness of her mouth. Took his time glorying in the taste of her, revelling in having her in his arms again.

Letting desire build, but slowly.

Her body was taut and supple beneath his hands, spine slightly arched as she pressed into him. Her breasts cushioned his chest, her sleek thighs warmed his, her belly cradled his rampant erection.

He told himself to go slowly, to savor and stretch the moments out . . .

The better to snare her.

To let desire thicken and grow, let passion seep into the exchange so slowly she slid into its grip without truly knowing. Without realizing that want and need could bind as surely as emotions.

That hunger could become an addiction.

He waited until she made the next move, until, sunk in the kiss, as unwilling to break it as he, she lowered her arms and shrugged off her robe. He drew it away for her, let it fall.

Welcomed her back into his arms. Angled his head and drew her yet deeper into the heat of their kiss.

Into the slowly rising maelstrom of passion and desire. Into the waltzing whirlpool of their senses' giddy delight.

Once she was whirling, his hands on her back he stroked, tracing the planes, sculpting the curves of her hips and derriere. He cupped one ripe globe and urged her closer yet, tilted her hips so he could—slowly—shift suggestively against her, the movement redolent with blatant passion, yet utterly, unquestionably reined.

At her command.

Hers for the asking, the taking, the wanting.

His to deliver.

Loretta ached, longed, yearned for more. For his touch, skin to skin. For the thrust of his body into hers that the evocative pressure of his erection against the tautness of her belly presaged.

Hands sliding from his nape to frame his face, she kissed him, her tongue tangling with his, stroking, teasing, wordlessly encouraging, but if he wasn't hurrying, she wasn't about to rush him. This was what she wanted—exactly what she needed. The chance to study, to examine and assess what drove him. A chance to learn which emotions she could sense investing his touch, infusing each caress with hidden meaning.

When one hard hand slid between them, then rose to boldly cup her breast, her senses leapt. Equally bold, she pressed the already swollen flesh into his palm, held back a shudder of pure delight when he closed his hand and kneaded.

There was nothing tentative in his touch. He fondled and caressed with expert intent, then through the fine linen of her gown circled her nipples until both were hard and tight, then he closed thumb and finger about one and squeezed . . . until she broke from the kiss on a gasp.

Head tipping back, she felt her senses sway, felt her lips curve as the buttons of her bodice slid undone, helped by long, strong, experienced fingers. Raising her head, from beneath heavy lids she watched his face as he opened her gown all the way to where the placket ended at her navel.

Passion was already etched in his features, desire stamped in his expression. Yet there was more to see, to sense in the weight of his summer blue gaze as, her gown gaping, he pressed the halves wide, baring her breasts. The weak moonlight washed over her. He stared for a moment measured by the heavy thud of her heart, then he raised his hands, cupped her breasts, and possessed.

Possession. As her lids closed on an aching wave of pleasure, she listed that among his motives. His desires.

Then he bent his head, set his lips to her heated, aching flesh, and ripped her wits away.

Sent them whirling.

She clutched his head, all thoughts dissolving as feeling—raw and primitive—rose in a wave and crashed over her. Washed through her, then returned with the hot tug of his mouth about her nipple.

Searing sensation lanced, speared through her. Then receded as he lapped, laved.

Only to return again, stronger, hotter, on the next wave of his worship. Cresting on a gasp, knees buckling, she clung to him, grateful for the steely arm that tightened, banding her waist, holding her upright as the resulting wave spread and sank in, diffusing heat and pulsing need beneath her skin, and deep to her core.

Awakening her.

She'd intended to watch him, to learn what he felt and why, but she suddenly saw herself through different eyes—eyes opened by passion, by a hunger too visceral to be denied.

Yes, she wanted him, inside her, buried to the hilt within her, but she wanted, as she'd told him, that deeper experience, that greater intensity.

Instinct insisted. Why she wasn't sure, but she wanted him like that, unfettered, unrestrained, unleashed.

She was wondering how to lead him to that, wondering what the path might be, when he raised his head and kissed her again, blatantly sank into her willing mouth again. Conquered again, languid and assured, then he drew back and murmured, his breath an intoxicating caress over her throbbing lips, "Will you stand naked in the moonlight for me?"

"Yes." The word had passed her lips before she'd thought. Then she did. "Why?"

His lips returned to hers, and she didn't think he would answer, but then he drew back and trailed kisses along her jaw. "Because I ache to see you." He whispered the words by her ear. "To know you . . . like that."

On the words, he straightened, raised his head. His hands cupped her shoulders and eased the gaping nightgown off.

She raised her lids, looked into his eyes. Held by the naked passion in his gaze, she lowered her arms, let the sleeves of the gown slide, felt the material glide in an evocative caress down her back. He followed the fall with his hands, brushed her hips and sent the garment sliding down to puddle about her feet.

He took a half step back.

The storm had rushed past, whipping the clouds before it. Leaving the moon to sail free in the winter sky, its radiance steadily strengthening. Slanting through the porthole to his right, moonbeams played over her naked body.

She should have felt chilled, but she didn't.

His gaze heated her as, with slow deliberation, he surveyed what he'd revealed. Like a gossamer caress, his gaze traveled over her bare shoulders, over her breasts, peaked and swollen, heavy with that increasingly familiar ache. Unshielded, his gaze swept over her midriff, over the indentation of her waist, over her belly, then swiftly down her legs to her feet before, slowly, wending back up to come to rest on the dark curls shadowing the apex of her thighs.

Her breath tight in her chest, her eyes, her entire attention, fixed on him, she felt like a piece of precious porcelain, or some creature spun out of the finest crystal, something so delicate and rare and exquisitely beautiful that she—her body—of itself possessed the power to ensorcel him.

He, his gaze, all she saw in his face made her feel . . . that powerful.

The tension that held him, the desire darkening his eyes,

were a revelation. Possessiveness and more lived in his face, plain for her to see. Along with something else—something more akin to worship and reverence—that elusive something she sensed in his touch, that called to her heart and her soul.

For one instant, in the wavering moonlight, she could almost touch it.

Then he moved.

To her, yet he made no move to seize her. Instead, raising one hand he set one fingertip to her shoulder, then traced lazily around the curve and down, laying a tracery of fire beneath her skin, over the swell of her breast, down its side, slowly down her body. . . .

She broke. Closed the distance, threw her arms about his neck, threw herself against him and kissed him.

Passionately.

With a demand Rafe felt to his soles.

His senses reeled at the contact. His hands closed about her waist, but before he could even catch his breath she pulled back and commanded, "Now you."

He would have chuckled, but desire had sunk her talons deep. All he could manage was, "As you wish," in a voice so gravelly he wondered if she would make out the words.

Not that she'd waited for them. She was already wrestling with the ties at his throat. He dealt with those at his wrists, then leaned back and stripped the shirt off over his head.

Before he'd even freed his hands, she fell on the buttons at his waist.

He caught her hands. "Boots first."

It took him less than a minute to ease both off; she all but jigged with impatience. The instant he straightened, her small fingers caught the last button at his waist and slid it free.

The flap of his breeches fell open. His erection sprang free, proud, fully engorged.

The look on her face distracted him; the sheer fascination investing her features made him inwardly blink.

Her eyes fixed on the object of her interest, she waved vaguely at his breeches. "Take them off."

He complied, thanking his stars he'd had the sense to ease the closures on the ends of the legs earlier, so all that was required was for him to strip them off one leg, then the other.

The instant he straightened, she reached out and closed one small hand about his erection.

One glance at her face, at the expression in her eyes, had him shutting his, then biting back a groan.

Her fingers eased, then drifted. Her other hand joined in.

Exploration. Learning.

Every muscle tensed to unbending iron, shackled under an inflexible will, he waited out her curiosity. Gritted his teeth, spine rigid, raised his head, and bore with the delicate touches, the gentle caresses.

Eventually he realized she was watching him, his face, as she stroked, then lightly squeezed.

He cracked open his lids, just enough to see . . .

Joy. Fascination. Delight.

She saw him looking, smiled—a madonna's smile full of secrets and yearning—then she eased one hand from his turgid member, raised it, and, still holding his throbbing erection in one hand, with the other stroked his shoulder, his chest, traced lovingly down to the tight disc of one nipple . . .

He broke. Reached for her. Seized her arms and hauled her against him.

Felt her shock as if it were his—that indescribably erotic jolt of sensation when naked female body met naked male.

Loretta trembled—with soaring, searing anticipation. She'd wanted to, had needed to, learn, and she was learning. Feeling, experiencing, seeing.

Starting to know, to understand, but as she melted into his arms, into him, felt the sensuous glide of her body against his as, one hand still closed about his erection, she stretched up against him, wound her other arm about his neck and gave him her lips, she wanted yet more.

She offered her mouth and he took. Plundered.

Gone was all restraint, yet he was still in control. He knew what he was doing, was too experienced in this to harm her in any way, yet the sheer strength in his hands, the way he molded her body so flagrantly to his and rocked into her hand, was both a thrill and a warning.

She'd come to him, offered herself to him, blatantly encouraged him to take—and now he would. Now he would take what he wished of her, physically possess her, fill her and make her his.

She couldn't wait. Could feel the compulsive beat in her blood, could swear she felt it echo in him. Through the kiss, through the evocative, provocative thrusting of his tongue, through his bold, explicit caresses, through his touch that was no longer gentle but driven, it gave notice of what was to come.

Then one hard hand eased its grip on her bottom. Skating that palm over flushed and dewed skin, he reached between them, pressed against her belly, then his fingers tangled in her curls, stroked through them and reached further.

Probed the hot, slick wetness between her thighs.

Left her sensually reeling, gasping as with just the right pressure, just the right touch, he sent fiery need arcing through her. The furnace deep inside her yawned, empty and molten and aching.

Needing. Wanting. . . .

He drew his hand from her, caught her wrist, drew her hand from him. Broke from the kiss and in the same breath closed his hands about her hips and hoisted her up.

"Wrap your legs around me."

Even before the gravelly order ended she had. Instinct had her firmly in its grip, an age-old anticipation searing her nerves, heightening and tightening at the flex and slide of naked skin, at the exquisite abrasion of harder, hair-dusted limbs against her silken flesh.

He held her against him, their faces almost level. His eyes locked on hers, he eased her down, so the throbbing flesh between her thighs parted and slowly eased over the engorged head of his rampant erection.

She shivered at the first touch, eyes wide, held her breath as he eased into her, forging steadily deeper as he drew her down. She caught her breath on a hitching sob, senses slowly splintering at the feel of him filling her, hard and heavy and oh so real; quivering on the cusp of delight, she clung as he sheathed himself in her surrendered body.

He thrust in the last inch, seating himself fully within her. And it was more—a clearer, harder, more unrelenting sensation, an even more undeniable possession.

A moan shuddered in her throat. Swallowing it, from beneath heavy lids she forced herself to meet his gaze, to look deep into his desire-darkened eyes and see . . . his jaw tightened and he lifted her hips.

Raised her until she almost lost the fullness of him, then brought her down, thrust up and in, and filled her anew, stretching her as a sound of surrender and entreaty combined escaped her.

He heard. He understood. Hands gripping her hips, he lifted her and brought her down again, setting a steady pace, one she discovered she had no ability to influence. All she could do was wrap her arms about his neck, cling and clutch and allow him to fill her, pleasure her, as he willed.

As he wanted, as he wished.

And he did.

Pleasure rose in a hot wave and washed through her, flooded her and filled her and still he continued to relentlessly press the potent combination of desire and delight, of passion and possession, upon her, into her, through her.

Until she thought she would die, drunk on unadulterated glory.

That her body would implode under the sheer weight of sensation—under the swirling mass of tactile stimulation and the underlying emotions that, with every heated breath, every powerful thrust, only swelled and heightened.

They were both panting, gasping, lungs burning. Caught

in the conflagration of their needs, in the powerful, merciless vise of their joint passions. Blind and deaf, she clung, aware only of the pounding pace, of the accelerating, relentless drive to completion.

In talons of steel, it gripped her, gripped him, and forced them on.

Desperate, she forced open her heavy lids, saw the glimmer of blue beneath his lashes. Saw the same yearning desperation she felt, the same raw hunger reflected in his face, in his harsh features.

Locking one hand about his nape, she levered up in his hold, and kissed him. Crushed her lips to his, plastered her body to his and deliberately sank down hard as he thrust up.

The change in angle was the trigger.

He hit a spot inside her that made her cry out. Knife-edged pleasure lanced through her, sundering her fragile hold on reality, flinging her up and out into a featureless void, sending her senses careening, her nerves unraveling as she soared on a crest of near violent pleasure.

Fingers sinking deep, head flung back, her body a taut arc, she soundlessly screamed.

Ecstasy erupted, welling from where they joined. It poured up and overflowed, sweeping her from the pinnacle of fractured need into an uncharted sea of blissful, golden satiation.

Rafe clung to her, held on, but couldn't deny her call—couldn't hold back from the rippling contractions of her sheath, the siren's call that ruthlessly beckoned him on . . .

She was delight; she was life. She was the promise of all he'd ever dreamed he might have, the embodiment of his future.

Head bowed, muscles straining, he held her hips immobile and thrust deep, groaned, and felt his reins slip.

Let them go, held her tight. Sunk to the hilt in her body, her limbs wrapped about him, he surrendered and let her have him, let her take him and possess him as he had her.

Let the circle close. Felt it click.

He shuddered, acknowledging the change, the capitulation, the reality, felt the knowledge sink to his bones.

She was his and he was hers, and nothing but death could now part them.

Long minutes passed. All he could hear was the rasp of his breathing, the thready sibilant race of hers.

All he could feel was the golden aftermath of pleasure, the heady glow of receding ecstasy.

She lay slumped in his arms, limp and heated. He'd slumped back on the bed, still holding her close.

Eventually she stirred, tried weakly, ineffectually, to wriggle.

Summoning the dregs of his strength he lifted her from him, tumbled her onto the bed, then followed her down, spooning around her, wrestling the covers up and over them.

He lay beside her and sleep dragged them down.

An hour or so later, Rafe surfaced from the warm wings of slumber as he usually did—in good time to leave the lady's bed and find his own for the rest of the night.

Except . . .

Opening one eye, he saw a delicate shoulder, ivory satin peeking through a broken veil of dark silk, and relaxed. With his senses reached for the body wrapped in his arms, registering its warmth and softness, then he allowed his limbs to fall leaden once more.

He closed his eyes on an inward, quietly gloating smile.

They were in his bed, and he had no wish to let this lady—his lady—go, not until dawn tinged the sky and he was forced to.

Surrendering to the pleasure still fogging his mind, he let his thoughts free, let them roam.

Wondered, fleetingly, what progress he'd made—whether the night's interlude had strengthened the sensual bonds with which he sought to bind her to him. Enough so she would accept his suit without further argument . . . that led to the question of what had happened, and where they were now . . . what had changed . . .

It didn't require much consideration to reveal the uncomfortable truth.

He might have succeeded in further enthralling her, but not without cost.

Ignoring the truth, the reality of what he felt, had just grown immeasurably harder.

Fourteen

've made up my mind and I will not be swayed." Seated in one of the salon's armchairs, Esme looked up at Rafe.

He stood before her, his mind scrambling in the wake of her latest decree.

Her lips lifted faintly. "I'll be perfectly safe, dear boy." With a wave, she indicated the plump, matronly nun seated in the other armchair. "You can trust dear Henny to make sure of it."

Dear Henny—Henrietta Wimplethorpe, apparently an old and dear childhood friend of Esme's, now the abbess of a nearby convent—beamed cherubicly. With her soft blond hair and apple cheeks, she looked more like a Helga—or her convent's patron saint, Hildegard of Bingen.

Dragging a hand through his hair, Rafe decided the second allusion was more apt. There was a shrewdness behind the twinkling blue eyes regarding him. Measuringly.

"Esme's right, you know." Hildegard—Henny—aimed her sunny smile at him. "The convent's impregnable—it's withstood sieges, marauders, and all manner of attackers through the ages. And we still keep the place locked up tight. It's a closed community, which"—she glanced at Esme—"sounds like just what's needed."

"And you'll do much better without me, dear boy. Especially on this last stretch, when you will have to travel faster, and possibly have to duck, weave, and scuttle to avoid cult pursuit. At my age, ducking, weaving, and scuttling is beyond me."

"But . . ." He didn't know why he was arguing. Esme was right in that her relative lack of mobility might become a liability the closer they got to England. Yet . . .

As if she could read his mind, she continued imperturbably, "And you said it yourself—it's possible Manning will persevere, that he will learn that the Prussian failed him and have another villain in his pocket to throw against me. On this penultimate leg of your mission, you can't afford the distraction of having to defend me against Manning's hired thugs."

He exhaled through his teeth. "It's just . . ."

"That you accepted the mantle of Esme's protector in Buda, and your honor and loyalty make you reluctant to yield it up." Henny spoke with the authority of one used to guiding others. "Entirely understandable, indeed, to be lauded. However, in this case, you need to bow to the greater call on your devotion—completing your mission successfully must take precedence over all else."

Looking into Henny's eyes, old and wise and very sure, he had to acknowledge that an abbess would unquestionably know all about devotion.

He dragged in a breath. Forced himself to incline his head. Tried not to think of what accepting Esme's plan would mean for him and Loretta. Parting now, after last night and the night before, after what he'd realized in the still depths of the night when he'd woken and found her in his arms . . . just the thought caused a painful wrench somewhere inside him.

Lips compressed, he shifted his gaze to Esme, fighting the urge to glance at Loretta seated on the window seat to his right, and nodded. "Very well. Hassan and I will see you to the convent, then go on alone."

Esme opened her eyes wide. "No, no, dear boy—you misunderstand. Only myself and Gibson will remain here—Loretta and Rose must go on with you."

Battling the urge to clutch his head with both hands, Rafe stared at her. "That's . . ." *Perfect*, Reckless purred. "Not possible." He glanced at Henny. "Such a situation would be highly improper."

Henny pursed her lips. "Irregular, perhaps, but not out of the question, and in this instance, with Rose by her side, Loretta's reputation wouldn't be at risk." Henny blinked up at him. "The circumstances are rather difficult, after all."

"But . . ." Rafe ran his hand through his hair again. "What possible reason could there be for Loretta to travel on, rather than wait here with you?"

"Because," Esme replied, her tone suggesting she was explaining the obvious, "without Loretta to bear witness to my wishes, how do you imagine prevailing on my man-of-business to act against Charles Manning? Dear Henny has agreed to provide me with safe refuge for the nonce, but I cannot remain—indeed, much as I adore Henny, do not wish to remain—in the convent forever. My safe release will depend on removing the threat Manning poses, and to accomplish that, you will need to persuade my representatives to act in my absence."

Hands on his hips, Rafe looked down at her. "You could give me a letter stating your wishes—that you wish your people to respond to the situation as I describe it."

"Oh, I've already written such a letter, dear boy, but I speak from experience when I tell you that without Loretta, my flesh and blood, and indeed one of my heirs, standing before him and stating unequivocally that I did indeed write that missive and that it does indeed represent my wishes, Heathcote Montague will not budge. Why, when I was trying to manage things from Scotland, the stubborn man posted all the way up into the Highlands just to confirm that the missives he was receiving were indeed from me and correctly represented my wishes. He's the definition of cautious when it comes to his clients' business. I daresay that's why he's so highly thought of."

Rafe could detect nothing but calm certainty in Esme's eyes. She was speaking the truth, at least as she knew it. He didn't dare glance at Loretta to see how she was taking her relative's maneuvering.

"Besides," Henny said, glancing at Loretta, "the convent is no place for an active young lady." She looked at Rafe. "As I said, we're a closed community. No one visits us, and we rarely venture out. All very well for Esme, especially as she and I have so much catching up to do. But for Loretta . . . she'd be climbing the walls in a week, and her Rose with her."

Finally, Rafe glanced at Loretta.

Shifting her gaze from Henny, she met his eyes. After a moment's silence, she lightly shrugged. "Unless you have some strong counterargument, it appears Rose and I will be traveling on with you."

Loretta understood Rafe's difficulty; she, too, felt torn. Riding back in a hired carriage after parting from Esme and Gibson at Henny's convent deep in the forests a short way from Bingen, she still felt the tug of conflicting emotions.

On the one hand, she was hugely relieved that she would be traveling on with Rafe—aside from all else, after all that had passed between them, and even more all she hoped would come to be, what she was almost certain she would learn if she pressed hard enough, the instant the possibility of being left in the convent had loomed, one question had risen, screaming, in her mind: what if he was injured again?

She was highly conscious of the warmth of his large body as he sat in the carriage alongside her. Who would continue to tend his arm, to salve and rebind it, as he was loath to do and had to be constantly reminded? If she didn't, who would? Could she trust Hassan to insist in the face of Rafe's tetchiness?

As for the prospect of any worse befalling him . . . that she wasn't prepared to contemplate. Not at all.

The relief she'd felt when Esme had declared and insisted that she travel on with him had been acute.

But she didn't like leaving Esme either.

Henny had arrived immediately after breakfast in reply to a letter Esme had apparently dispatched by courier the previous night, requesting asylum. Gibson had already had their bags packed.

After their discussion in the salon, there'd been no sense in dallying. As Esme had pointed out, they'd already spent more time in Bingen than Julius had allowed for; the boat needed to get on.

She, Rafe, Hassan, and Rose had accompanied Esme, Gibson, and Henny back to the convent. They'd stood at the gates and hugged and kissed—Esme had insisted on tugging Rafe down and kissing his cheek, too. Then she'd gone inside with Henny. Loretta had stood beside Rafe and waved until the door of the convent had swung shut and sealed Esme away.

But Esme was now safe, as safe as she could be, which was also a relief. Over their travels, Loretta had grown deeply fond of her outrageous and incorrigible great-aunt.

Although the sky was overcast, the clouds had remained high and the rain had held off. The day wasn't as cold as the one before—it was a good day for traveling.

"Here we are." Rafe leaned forward as the carriage slowed, then opened the door and stepped down to the wharf.

Out of habit, he surveyed their surroundings before turning and handing Loretta down. Leaving Hassan to climb down and assist Rose, he led Loretta to where the *Loreley Regina* bobbed at dock, the crew waiting, eager to be off.

"I hope she'll be all right," Loretta murmured as he assisted her up the gangplank.

"Esme's a suvivor. She'll probably drive Henny to distraction, but . . ." He stepped down to the deck. "As soon as my mission's complete, I'll go to London, meet with her Mr.

Montague, and then I believe I'll pay Sir Charles Manning a visit."

Leading the way into the prow, Loretta glanced back at him. "That would be . . . very kind."

Strolling after her, his eyes on hers, he shrugged. "It's the least I can do in recompense for the many good things your estimable relative's interference has brought me."

Looking into his eyes, she read the message therein, then smiled her secretive smile and halted by the rail to watch the roofs of Bingen slide away.

In the early afternoon, they started the descent down the stretch of river known as the Rhine Gorge. The river swung north. Where until then the river banks had been low lying, strips of meadowland running back to meet whatever hills and mountains marched nearby, now cliffs rose directly from the water on either side; the river rushed between with increased force, whipping into small whirlpools close by the rocky shores, sweeping the boat on in unexpected surges.

Julius and his crew handled the challenges with a mixture of gusto and aplomb, checking and resetting their sails, constantly shifting position to ride the currents safely. To them, guiding the small riverboat through the tricky waters was a game, one they relished and were confident of winning.

Standing by the prow rail beside Loretta, Rafe watched the river rush giddily past. The shadows cast by the cliffs swallowed them. Although the heights afforded excellent vantage points to watch boats barreling down the river, they were moving too fast for any direct attack. He suspected this day and the next while they rushed down the gorge would be their last relatively safe stretch.

That they'd managed to get this close to England without any clash with the cult was due entirely to his wisdom in choosing to travel via the rivers, combined with a healthy dose of luck. He suspected their luck would run out when they reached Bonn, if not before.

Until then, however . . . if his time in the army had taught him anything it was that life was too short to waste good times.

Shifting his gaze to Loretta's face, he studied her clear profile. "Does your family retire to the country for Christmas, or remain in town?" He wanted to know; the answer would be relevant later.

She glanced briefly at him. "We usually congregate at one or other of my sisters' houses. One's in Berkshire, the other in Oxfordshire." Looking back at the cliffs, she added, "I wonder if it's snowed yet."

"It's the fifteenth of December, so it might have."

Loretta regarded him as he leaned on the rail alongside her. "You've been in India for years—are you looking forward to a white Christmas?"

His brows rose; he considered, then replied, "Yes, I am. It's been a long time since I spent Christmas with family. The thought of a snowy Christmas takes me back to those days."

"You have brothers and sisters, like me. At Christmas, what games did you play?"

They swapped anecdotes, some clearly fond family tales, others too unexpected and particular to be drawn from anything but personal experience. Many were revealing, but if both of them noticed, neither drew back. They exchanged tit for tat, memories of being children in England and Christmases long past while the Rhine swept them deeper into its gorge, on between soaring forested cliffs.

Then Rafe spotted the first castle. Delighted, Loretta retrieved the guidebook Esme had left with her, flicked it open.

As the boat surged, dipped, canted, then whisked on, she read from the book while Rafe played lookout, scanning the heights for stone towers and crenallated battlements.

"Look!" Rafe pointed. "That's the Loreley Rock."

Loretta gazed at the massive outcrop jutting out from the right bank. Frowned. "I thought it would be more . . . impressive. Are you sure that's it?"

Rafe nodded. "Julius described it to me."

They studied the rock, took in its heavy, watchful presence as the boat followed the river in a wide arc around its base.

"It must be the legend that lends it significance," Loretta concluded. "Without that cachet, it doesn't seem all that remarkable."

At that moment, Julius looked out of the enclosed bridge and hailed them. "Come inside." He beckoned. "Up here. The next section is dangerous."

Keeping hold of the rail, they made their way quickly to the bridge. They climbed two steps to find Julius at the helm in the center, with two crewmen watching the river closely from the forward corners of the bridge.

"Hold on!" Julius yelled, never taking his eyes from the river ahead.

Grasping a window ledge, looking ahead, Rafe saw the river's surface ripple and churn. Although the water to either side appeared smoother, Julius steered the boat into the dangerous currents.

The boat pitched. Loretta's hold on the door handle slipped. Before she staggered Rafe clamped her to him, his arm about her waist, her back to his chest. He held her steady as the boat wallowed, then rolled, then shot ahead.

"The channel for boats is very narrow through here," Julius called back. "It is the most dangerous part of the river." Abruptly, he hauled on the wheel, righting the boat as it listed wildly, then one of the crew pointed and yelled. Julius swung the wheel the other way.

Under his expert steering, the *Loreley Regina* rocked and rolled, but overall continued surging on.

"Luckily," Julius continued, "the passage is short and fast. It doesn't last long."

Just as well. Loretta was grateful for small mercies. Grateful, too, for Rafe's arm snug about her. She relaxed back against him, knowing he was strong enough to hold her, and would, even if her feet went out from under her.

The warmth that stole through his coat and through her pelisse was soothing, too.

Comforting and reassuring.

The *Loreley Regina* slowed; a minute later the boat rode steadily, stably, onward once more.

They thanked Julius. He grinned and snapped off a salute, then they returned to the forward deck.

Once again at the prow rail, they were joined by Hassan and Rose.

"We were in the salon," Rose replied in answer to Loretta's query, "but the crew warned us. Bumpy old ride, it was."

Just ahead, the cliffs drew back from the river leaving a narrow strip of land just wide enough for small townships on both banks.

"That's St. Goar." Nose in the guidebook, Loretta waved to the cluster of houses on the left bank. Above the town, a castle crowned the thickly treed cliff. "This book doesn't mention that castle. But to the right we have St. Goarshausen."

They all studied the small town as the boat slid by. Rafe and Hassan noted and commented on the square defensive tower that stood guard toward one end of the town.

Loretta looked further along and up. "And that"—she pointed to a castle just beyond the town, perched on the point where the cliff swept back to the river's edge—"is Burg Katz."

The castle gradually came into full view as they rounded the next gentle curve. A sizeable edifice, it dominated that portion of the river, with a clear view south to the Loreley Rock and a similar view north along the next stretch.

Rafe and Hassan speculated on the military implications of its position.

The boat sailed on. The light was fading, the shadows lengthening as a winter's dusk took hold. Peering ahead, Loretta pointed at another, even larger castle perched on a height a little way back from the river. "I think that's Burg Maus."

Rafe glanced at her. "Burg Katz, Burg Maus?" When, brows rising, she glanced at him, he explained, "Castle Cat, Castle Mouse." He grinned. "I wonder what significance that has. Were the families actually the Katz and the Maus, or do the names allude to something else?"

The question resulted in some very inventive answers.

"Oh, here it is." Looking up from the guidebook she'd been scouring for any suggestion of the true origins of the Cat and Mouse designations, Loretta swung around and looked back at the castle rising above St. Goar on the opposite bank. "That's Burg Rheinfels."

"At least that name makes sense," Rafe said.

Having straightened from the prow rail to look back, he noticed the boat's sails had been lowered. That, indeed, the boat had slowed.

As if in answer to the question forming in his brain, the rattle of the anchor chain reached them.

Julius swung down from the bridge and came toward them. "We will halt here for the night. This is a peaceful spot and as we need nothing in the town there is no need to tie up there." He met Rafe's eyes. "The river is too strewn with sandbanks and submerged islands to allow us to safely navigate the channels by night."

Rafe nodded. "How are we faring with respect to our schedule?"

Julius grinned. "From here on, the river is swift and our way is fast. We should still reach Rotterdam on the nineteenth, as you wished."

"Good." Rafe glanced at the mists rising off the river now that the daylight had fled, then turned to Loretta, Rose, and Hassan. "Let's go down and stay warm."

By his calculation, they had that night, and if they were lucky the next, before they encountered the cult and the tension induced by his mission increased exponentially. They had been amazingly lucky; he held no illusions that such luck would hold.

Back in the salon, Rose settled with some sewing in an armchair at the rear of the room. Hassan sank into the chair alongside her.

Leaving them quietly chatting, Rafe followed Loretta to

the pair of armchairs in the prow. Reflecting on the insights their earlier conversation about their childhood exploits had revealed, he waited while she sat, then lounged in the other chair and returned to that subject. "Tell me about your sisters and brothers—what are their lives like now?"

The more he learned of her, her background, her family, the better placed he would be to ensure his claim to her hand met with no unnecessary resistance.

Nothing loath, Loretta replied. "Robert is the eldest. He and his wife, Catherine, make their home in London. They have three children—"

Describing her married siblings' households brought them and their spouses vividly to mind. The more she spoke, the more she remembered and sought to convey, the more she saw, the more she understood—the more clearly she saw what it was she was searching for.

What it was she wanted of life. Of a husband, of her future.

What it was she wanted of Rafe.

No one who knew her three married siblings and their spouses could doubt that an emotion deeper than mere affection linked each couple. Even Robert and Catherine shared that deeper bond.

Loretta hadn't, until then, defined, even in her own mind, why she'd refused to agree with Rafe's decree that he and she would wed. Why she was still holding aloof, holding back from that decision.

A decision Rafe wanted to insist she'd already made.

She hadn't, and no matter what he thought, she did have alternatives.

If at the end of this journey, she returned to London, to Robert and Catherine's household, only to discover that the social pressure to choose a husband had become too great, she would simply seek refuge with one or other of her sisters in the country. They would shelter her, and if this journey had taught her one thing it was that she didn't lack for spine when she had need of it. It wasn't in her nature to cause difficulties if she didn't care about the issue, but if she did . . . she was confident, now, that she would act. She would retire from society until she reached the age of twenty-five, and was officially declared an old maid, on the shelf. Thereafter, the pressure to marry would largely evaporate, and she could continue on as she had before—writing her vignettes and amusing herself with being an aunt to her siblings' offspring.

She'd been happy enough before, and would be again. A lesser happiness than her sisters and sister-in-law had claimed, but she would cut her coat to suit her cloth and be content.

So her alternative life was real. It was there, ready for her to claim if she wished.

Prior to meeting Rafe, that alternative had been her first and, to her mind, only available choice. Now . . . while she spoke, she studied Rafe. He was leaning forward, drinking in all she let fall, asking questions that by their very nature revealed an inherent understanding of sibling interaction.

Studying his eyes, the clean lines of his face, she acknowledged that her previous first choice had slipped very definitely to second place.

What now stood in first place, what encompassed her most ardent desire for her future life, was . . . a relationship with Rafe that held that same element of deep connection that her siblings enjoyed with their mates.

That was what she'd been searching for—instinctively, intuitively—in their physical interactions. Some hint, some clue, that he and she might within them possess the necessary ingredient for that deeper bond. She knew what she sought went by the name of love, yet that word described such a broad gamut of feelings and reactions that it seemed wiser not to evoke it.

Wiser instead to search for the evidence of its existence. For its shadow, as it were.

So she'd started to search, and was determined to keep

searching. What she'd found . . . was thus far inconclusive. What she sought might be there, in his heart and in hers, but she wasn't experienced enough to be certain. Not yet.

But if what she sought was there . . . pursuing her agenda, devoting herself to the task of revealing it, confirming it, then strengthening and protecting it, was self-evidently the only reasonable choice she could make.

Tilting her head, she looked into Rafe's eyes. "What of your brothers and sisters? Are they married with families, too?"

His lips twisted. He leaned back in his chair. "They are, but I've been away so long . . . rejoining the fold will be like walking into an unknown world."

"What about in India? Were you close to other English families out there?"

He shook his head. "I lived mostly in barracks, or in bachelor lodgings in Calcutta and Bombay. In between fighting, Hassan acted as . . . my majordomo, I suppose you might say. In the early years we spent a lot of time in the field, putting down uprisings and the like, then securing trade routes for the merchant caravans. And in the last months when we moved to Bombay, we spent all our days pursuing the Black Cobra and the cult."

She approached the subject from every angle she could think of, but the answer remained the same. Rafe had no experience of married life to draw on—of the sort of married life his contemporaries might have. The concept of what she sought might well be a complete mystery to him.

Consequently she jettisoned any thought of asking him directly what he felt for her, yet him not knowing what love, the sort that applied in marriage, was did not in any way preclude him from feeling it.

Clearly discovering whether love could be the foundation stone of a marriage between them rested solely on her shoulders.

When the darkness outside had closed in and they rose to

change for dinner, she headed for her cabin determined to prevail. To unearth the truth, for both their sakes.

After dinner, a rather relaxed affair now there were only the four of them at table, they repaired to the salon and, at Rafe's suggestion, indulged in several games of whist. To Loretta's amazement, Rose proved surprisingly adept; when questioned, she revealed that in Robert's often quiet household, the staff had taken to playing the game to fill their evenings.

An hour sped by, then by general consensus, they retired to the lower deck, to their cabins.

But not to their beds.

In her cabin off the stateroom's sitting room, Loretta, still fully dressed, vacillated over whether she was brazen enough to invite Rafe to her cabin and her bed—and, if so, whether to change into her nightgown first, or later, which presumably would mean not at all—when the sound of a door opening and quietly closing reached her.

Going to the cabin door, she eased it open—and heard the stateroom's main door, the one into the corridor, quietly shut.

Emerging into the sitting room, she stared at the corridor door, then crossed to the other smaller door that gave onto the tiny cabin tucked behind the principal cabin Esme had occupied. Loretta scratched on the panel. When no answer was forthcoming, she opened the door and peeked in— confirming that Rose was no longer in the cabin. No longer in the stateroom.

Loretta smiled fondly. That made things simpler.

Turning to the corridor door, she opened it—

Rafe filled the doorway.

Swallowing a gasp, she reeled back, waved him in. He stepped past her. She shut the door, turned to face him.

His hands, already sliding about her waist, firmed. He smiled, blue eyes improbably innocent under raised brows. "Were you expecting me?"

Hands rising to his shoulders, she frowned him down. "I was coming to invite you here . . . to my cabin."

"I decided to save you the journey." He glanced at her open cabin door, at the bed visible beyond it. When he turned back to her, his expression had left innocent far behind. "Your bed's bigger than mine."

He drew her closer until their bodies met, until heat streaked through her, familiar and sweet. "And," he murmured, seductively deep as he lowered his head, "there's a great deal to be said for a good-sized bed."

His intention to demonstrate didn't need to be stated. Loretta twined her arms about his neck and met his lips with hers. Kissed him with all the beguiling passion she could muster, then parted her lips, invited him to take, boldly challenged him to conquer.

She was getting better at this, the giving and the taking, more confident and assured, and if her wits still suspended beneath the onslaught of his passionate response, they no longer vanished or vaporized.

Both wits and will were still hers, able to be deployed in the pursuit of her need. In pursuit of the answer, in pursuit of her goal.

She still gasped when his hand found her breast and closed, then eased and fondled. Even through the heavy silk of her winter dinner gown, she felt the heat of his touch, the passion that flowed as he caressed, the possessiveness when he kneaded her soft flesh, then found her nipple and tweaked, squeezed . . .

"The cabin." The words came out as a sultry instruction, a directive more than a request.

His lips curved against hers. "As my lady commands."

Somewhat to her surprise he stepped back, but then he caught her hand, and with his other hand still at her waist she was twirling. Whirling. He waltzed her, literally, around, then through her cabin's door, swirled and nudged it shut behind them, then slower yet no less powerfully, he continued to dance with her in the moonlight.

To circle and glide, press closer and retreat, moving her effortlessly around the small room.

She'd forgotten what an excellent dancer he was, how gracefully and powerfully he moved. One hard thigh parted hers as he swung her, holding her tightly, close, as the smallness of the cabin limited their turns.

Their bodies shifted, silk against suiting, a sibilant herald of impending delight. A promise. The wide window spilled moonlight into the cabin, limning them in silver, casting his eyes in mesmerizing shadow as, moving to a beat that resonated in her blood, he . . . seduced her.

She laughed softly and gave herself up to it, this new dimension in which he wanted to play. Curious, she followed his lead, let her body speak for her as they whirled tighter and closer, faster, more intent.

Then he stopped.

And kissed her.

Framed her face and filled her mouth.

And fed her passion.

Whipped up, stirred up, heightened by the dance. Raised and stoked and brought to a heady simmer. Distilled and condensed to an intense liquor that slid, all fiery heat and glory, down her veins.

His hands left her face, slid away, then glided down her back. Drawing her in, settling her against him, molding her to him. No gentle touch but a claiming. A seizing accomplished with grace, with skill.

He held her with the kiss, his tongue a hot brand against hers, stirring and stoking the passions that rose, inexorably, to his call.

Buttons at her back slid free. Her gown eased. Cool air washed over her heating skin as with an expert's touch he opened the gown all the way down to the curve of her hips.

Easing back from the kiss, he raised both hands, curved them about her shoulders, then slid the gown down, eased the sleeves down her arms, helped her draw her hands free. Their breaths mingled. Their breathing was rushed, pulses already racing. She glanced at his face, saw his heavy lids shielding the blue of his eyes as his gaze lowered, following the folds of material down as his hands eased the silk over her hips.

The gown fell with a soft *whoosh* to the floor.

Forgotten.

By him as his eyes feasted on her curves, on her breasts, already peaked under the near translucent shimmer of her chemise.

By her as she watched, fascinated anew at the naked desire that limned his features.

Chest expanding, he drew a tight breath, then raised his head, raised his gaze, to her eyes. Looked into them for an instant, then stepped nearer, closer. His hands rose and once more framed her face, tipped it up so he could kiss her again. Could with lips and tongue draw her into the magic again, into the slowly whirling spiral of desire.

He only touched her face, her lips, her tongue, her mouth, yet she felt the kiss, its warmth, its heat, its ineffable promise slide through her body.

Felt its touch, and quivered.

Her body sensed him, his nearness. Like a beacon his warmth called to her, drew her like a lodestone. She edged nearer, raised one hand and skimmed it across his chest.

Realized he was still fully dressed.

Raising both hands, she gripped his lapels.

Releasing her face, he caught her wrists. Breaking from the kiss, murmured across her lips, "Not yet."

"When?" was on the tip of her tongue, but he kissed her again, hotter, harder, with just enough conquerorlike domination to keep the word unsaid.

He drew her hands up, draped them over his shoulders, drew her nearer, into him. Set his hands to her body, screened only by gossamer silk, locked her hips against his thighs. Angled his head, sank into her mouth, set a beat that thudded through her veins, and commenced a dance of a different sort.

One that screamed of passion, of lust, of desire so potent it swept her into a furnace of hungry, greedy need. Straight into a maelstrom of heated yearning that left her gasping and clinging, needing and wanting.

Waiting for fulfillment.

Aching for completion.

His hands touched, traced, and fire bloomed beneath her skin. Passion rose like a hound to its master's call and fell on her, devoured her.

Consumed her.

Physical sensation was his to command as his hands roamed and the fires raged . . .

When she was all but incandescent with need, when she grasped his face and kissed him like a fury, pressing her demands, telling him of her need in language as blatantly flagrant as his touch, Rafe set his fingers to the ribbon ties of her chemise, with two quick tugs stripped it from her.

Set his hands to her naked skin and felt her burn.

For him.

It was a giddy moment, but he clung to his purpose. Lost in her mouth, with her body a flame between his hands, his senses lost in the wonder of her, it was tempting to let his reins fall, let her passions and his sweep them on, but still he clung. To that small voice of sanity that yet lived in his reeling brain, beneath the clouds of lust, the ever-thickening fogs of desire.

He'd come to her cabin with a plan. One he needed to follow.

She was trying to see too much, trying to see beyond his emotional shield, but that way lay disaster.

He knew what she was looking for, what she sought to find amid the caresses and the gasps. It would be better, infinitely better, if she never found it, never saw it—if she did, he wouldn't be able to pretend it wasn't there.

Yet she was determined and dogged. He needed to distract her—and romance and seduction were his only options.

But it was winter. No flowers.

They were on a boat. No music.

And he couldn't sing worth a damn.

Which left seduction.

And the passion that flowed in its wake.

He was determined to give her both. In quantity. In soul-clutching, heart-stuttering quality.

Deliberately he closed his arms around her, locking her nakedness against his fully clothed form. He knew the effect feeling his woollen suiting against her sensitized skin would have on her. Was banking on her response.

It was everything he'd wished for. She shuddered, her breath hitching as she surrendered and greedily pressed nearer, the raspy abrasion of fine wool igniting fires beneath her skin.

In seconds she was so hot and desperately eager she made no demur when he drew his mouth from hers, closed one hand about her swollen breast. His other arm banding her waist, he bent her back over it, lowered his head and set his mouth to her breast.

She shrieked at the contact. Clutched his head and moaned as he drew the turgid peak deep into his mouth and suckled.

He feasted, ruthless, relentless, and impossibly greedy, feasting not only on the taste and texture, on her wild heat and passion, but on the sounds he drew from her, the inarticulate sounds of delight that fell from her lips and spiced the night.

Rose and Hassan were tonight in the cabin furthest away. For the first time he could freely rejoice in the sweet sounds of her surrender.

The fingers of one hand rolling and tweaking one tortured nipple, his mouth latched about its mate, he suckled fiercely. At her shattered cry he shifted his other hand from her waist, sent it gliding lower. Hand splayed, fingers spread, he cupped her bottom, kneaded possessively, then tipped her, locked her hips against his thighs and suggestively rolled his hips, thrusting the heavy rod of his erection against her belly.

And felt her nerves unravel.

Felt her will, her ability to do anything but follow, but appease any and all demands he might make, crumble.

The bed was at her back, close. Unlike his bunk, hers was a proper bed, with headboard and footboard and a mattress piled with feather quilts and comforters, with pillows mounded at the head.

But the mattress was too high.

He tore his mouth from her breast, found her lips again, kissed her deeply, possessively, felt her melt.

Nearly as desperate as she, from beneath the screen of his lashes, he scanned the room, searching. . . .

There—thank God. The chair from the dressing table. The seat, he judged, was the perfect height, and wide enough, deep enough for their purpose, the low, wide, arched wooden back perfect for her to cling to.

They'd nudged the chair aside when they'd waltzed. It now stood positioned before the window seat, spotlit by moonbeams.

The heat in his blood was a pounding roar, one that found a ready echo in her.

He steered her, backed her to the chair.

Wrenched his lips from hers, spun her around, gripped her hips, and lifted her. Set her down, kneeling on the chair, facing the window.

She gasped, shivered. Straightened as if to turn.

He stepped behind her, close, reached around and closed his hands about her breasts, and reminded her of all she'd already learned.

Of the heat, the yearning, the sensations evoked by his hands, his fingers, his lips and his tongue, and the flaring need that burned in their wake.

Loretta felt it all, wits and will all but drowned beneath a turbulent sensuous sea, beneath waves of need that welled, swelled, and crashed through her.

This wasn't merely possession but passion unleashed, unbound and unrestrained, given free rein to plunder.

Head back, eyes closed as his hands moved freely, flagrantly over her sensitive skin, blatantly stoking the fires anew, she knew no more than a pounding erotic need to feel him within her.

She felt no chill even though the air was cold, felt no modesty, poised naked before him while he was fully clothed.

Felt nothing more than the need that scoured her and left her hollow and hot and waiting, panting, gasping, head swimming as with the long fingers of one hand dipping between her thighs, stroking and teasing the swollen flesh, then circling her entrance, he sent his other hand stroking over her bare bottom, caressing, fondling, assessing.

Heated dew flashed over her skin. Her flesh burned in the wake of his touch. The abrasion of his trousers shifting against her was an erotic stimulation all its own.

So sunk in the sensations he sent rolling through her, she was only dimly aware when his hand left her bottom and his hips shifted behind her.

A second later she realized he'd opened the placket of his trousers, that he'd released his erection.

Her hands gripped the back of the chair tight as he eased her up on her knees, his fingers gripping and anchoring her hips, tipping her torso forward.

Anticipation flashed. Her nerves ratcheted tighter than an overwound spring.

She lost her breath when the rigid rod of his erection pushed between her thighs, when the broad head nudged into her softness.

Then he thrust in, with one long powerful stroke filled her, and she rose on her knees on a keening cry of pure passion.

He drew back and thrust in again, powerful and sure.

She sobbed, and clung, arms braced, fingers clenched, overwhelmed by the pleasure.

By the sensual delight of feeling him there, of feeling full and filled and taken as he rocked her. Completed her in this most primitive way, thoroughly and deeply. Overwhelmingly.

The shifting friction of his trousers against her naked skin punctuated every thrust, heightened every sensation, deepened the claiming.

She understood it now—why he'd chosen this position, this way, this path. If she could have smiled she would have, but command of her features was far beyond her.

All that mattered as she rocked and rode the pounding beat of his thrusts was feeling this, knowing this, letting the passion and the moment take her, fill her, sweep her away. . . .

The sense of clamping about him, about the solid length of him, was so much more evident in this position, impinging much more strongly on her mind, rising through the haze, making her infinitely more aware of her own sensual self, of her own real involvement, her own taking, her own giving.

Her sheath's clutch and release, acceptance and claiming, was both instinctive and deliberate. She shuddered under the onslaught of his passions and hers, writhed and rode the escalating beat, the heavy pounding tattoo of their joining. Tipping back her head, she shook back her hair, gasped as he pushed her on.

And then they were there—at the pinnacle of sensation. High and bright, where the air seemed rarefied and cataclysmic pleasure beckoned. If she would reach for it, if she would dare . . .

He thrust deep and hard and pushed her over—tipped her into a searing web of scintillating sensation that cinched tight, then ruptured, exploded and fractured, shattering her into sharp glittering shards, those myriad fragments of exquisite delight all that was left of her body and her mind.

Esctasy rushed in to fill the void.

To fill her, soothe her, buoy her, leaving her floating in sensual bliss.

Her body no longer hers but his, she waited, only dimly aware, for him to find his pleasure and join her.

Instead, his thrusts slowed, then he withdrew from her.

She was too wrung out, too physically drained to protest when he lifted her in his arms and carried her to the bed.

Rafe had no idea why he was doing it, why, instead of

seeking release in her wholly surrendered body, there in the moonlight before the window, some part of him was insisting he needed this instead—to feel her beneath him, surrendered and open, willingly and knowingly his to take.

That having enjoyed the sight of her bent before him, her body offered up, his to fill, that he take this, too, savor this, too—the inexpressible delight of having her wrap him in her arms, welcome him into her body, and take him to her heart.

He wanted to be there.

Reckless assured him this was the way.

He stripped in seconds, then joined her beneath the covers. Settled her amid the mound of pillows, spread her thighs wide and sank between. A small remnant of sanity was howling from some distant corner of his mind that this was dangerous; he blocked it out, ignored it.

This was important, watching her as she crested again, as she opened to him again and, knowing it was him, accepted and embraced him, and let him possess her.

Reaching down, he drew one of her knees up, curled her leg over his hip. As he settled himself on his elbows, his chest abrading her breasts, she drowsily, languidly, raised her other leg and draped it over his thigh, raised her arms to his shoulders, slid one hand to his nape.

Her lashes fluttered, barely opening as she lifted her face and drew him down, offered him her lips.

He dipped his head and took, devoured, kissed her until they were both heated and reeling again.

With one thrust joined their bodies, and felt their tension leap, felt the inexorable rise of desire, the rake of its claws as he thrust deep into her mouth, deep into her body, and rode her.

Deep, powerfully, hard, but not fast. There was no rush; he wanted to savor every scintilla of her surrender.

Wanted to experience every nuance of the joy of her warmth, her welcome, her unalloyed, unrestrained acceptance.

She held him, undulated beneath him, rode with him into paradise.

The way was clear, untrammeled and easy. All he had to do was follow the path, and let the flames have him.

Surrender to them as they licked over his flesh, burned away all inhibitions and reached for his soul.

He broke from the kiss, breathing ragged, eyes nearly blind.

Their breaths gusted and mingled, heat to heat, sweetness and passion. They rocked unrestrained, both reaching, racing. The musky scent of their loving rose and embraced them, clouding his senses, racking his arousal one notch higher.

From under weighted lids, he glanced at her face, saw the faintest of smiles curving her lips.

Saw unalloyed delight in her expression.

Saw it tighten as passion laid hold and she tensed, then arched beneath him, nails digging in, scoring as, head back, she shattered.

As beneath the covers her thighs gripped his flanks and her sheath clamped tight and drew him on.

Into the maelstrom of sensation, of sharp, biting, slicing pleasure. Into the explosion of consciousness that soared through his body, streaked along every nerve, pounded down every vein to take him. Shatter him.

Empty him and remake him.

That, at the last, left him wracked, wrecked, and struggling for breath, hanging over her.

Her arms tightened, tugged, and pulled him down.

With a grunt, he gave in, surrendered.

Felt her arms close around him, felt the gentle stroke of her hand.

Felt peace sink into him and take him.

He woke in the night. Found himself lying beside her, with her head on his shoulder, her body cleaving to his.

Bliss still lapped him. Certainty dwelled within him.

He didn't want to be anywhere but where he was.

Then she stirred, sleepily wriggled, glanced up, then

stretched up and kissed him. One sleek thigh rose to slide across him.

She held him to the kiss, and the kiss went on.

He knew it was dangerous.

He no longer cared.

A storm had blown up. Clouds had swallowed the moon. Wind raked the river, then strafed hail across the deck.

The savagery, the howls, and drumming rain were a distant counterpoint, a contrast of sounds as in the cocoon of her covers they gasped and clung, loved again, came together and rose and shattered again.

Slumped again, sated beyond imagining, secure and satisfied in each other's arms.

She slid back into sleep, snug in his arms and transparently content.

He held her, and wondered where his plans had gone.

Less than a mile away, the Lorelei was reputed to have lured sailors to her—to their deaths, to their loss, to the ultimate surrender.

Tonight, in the shadow of the siren's rock, Loretta had done the same. She hadn't had to sing; she'd simply had to be. He hadn't been able to resist her lure.

So now he lay in her arms, his defense in tatters. Facing the reality he'd fought to deny, had thought to deny forever.

But she knew, now—he'd sensed it in her kiss, in her touch, in the way her eyes had held his, in the soft caress of her hand on his cheek as she'd given herself to him again. As he'd given himself to her. Again.

And now that she knew, he knew, too.

The truth, it seemed, couldn't—wouldn't—consent to be hidden. Locked away.

He'd have to get used to it. He'd have to find a way.

Because he couldn't retreat. Couldn't let her go.

He couldn't imagine his life without her.

❦ Fifteen ❦

As soon as the fog thinned sufficiently the next morning, the *Loreley Regina* got underway.

Still determined to see what sights there were, Loretta took Esme's guidebook into the enclosed bridge.

"Boppard." Standing at the helm, Julius pointed to the left. "See the twin towers? That is the St. Severus Church."

Standing by the window, Loretta peered through the murk, and picked out the twin spires. Noticing the boat was heading for the bank, she glanced at Julius. "I thought we weren't stopping."

"We aren't, but I must swing this way to come around the next curve—it is almost . . . how do you English say it?—a dog-leg?"

Loretta tried to look ahead, to follow the banks, but they disappeared into the low-lying mist.

By the time they'd negotiated what Julius informed her was the largest bend along the entire Rhine, Rafe had joined them and the mists were lifting, blown away by a crisp breeze.

Although Rafe paused to exchange comments with Julius, the only member of the crew on the bridge at that moment, Loretta was acutely aware of him—of the glance he cast her, of the weight carried in every heartbeat during which their gazes locked.

Then Julius spoke, and Rafe turned to him.

She drew breath, calmed her giddy heart. Great heavens! This was worse than before. She was at a loss to understand why their most recent engagement had affected her—and him, too, it seemed—to such a degree. As if, between them, some shield had fallen, been stripped away, leaving them . . . more sensitive to each other, their nerves more alive to the other's nearness, the other's thoughts, their awareness excruciatingly heightened.

It was unsettling . . . and exhilarating.

Eventually Rafe left Julius and approached her. His blue eyes held hers for a moment, and again she was conscious of the thud of her own heart, then he glanced at the guidebook.

"So . . ." He lounged against the window beside her. "What can we expect to see today?"

She told him. Lahneck Castle was soon visible above the right bank, but what they could see through the lingering wisps of mist was not impressive. Soon, however, on the left as they approached Coblenz, they saw a much more eye-catching edifice towering above the river.

"Stolzenfels Castle," Loretta pronounced. By the time she'd read out the description of the multiple walls and battlements, and the towering keep, Coblenz itself was sliding toward them.

Rafe shifted nearer so he could read the guidebook over her shoulder. Again their gazes met, just for an instant, and a shiver of awareness streaked over her skin, yet it wasn't the same as before. The novel sensation suggested closeness, something more private, more personal, something neither he nor she had ever shared with any other.

Why she was so sure of that she didn't know, but as she drew in a tight breath, raised her head and stared unseeing out at Coblenz—and Rafe did the same—she was sure, to her heart sure, that he hadn't been down this road before.

Such closeness stunned and amazed her. That indefinable sense of drawing near a large and potentially dangerous beast, one who had grown addicted to her touch. Who was skittish rather than nervous, wary of her intentions yet who was willing to chance them just to feel her touch again. Just to gain what soothed his beast's soul . . . her lips curved at the imagery; she straightened them, but the notion, she sensed, wasn't that far off the mark.

He darted a glance at the guidebook, then pointed. "That must be the fortified wall."

She read, nodded. A minute later, she pointed, "Those towers must belong to the Basilica of St. Kastor, and that building over there must be the Church of St. Florian."

They continued picking out sights as they sailed past Coblenz.

"And that"—Julius pointed ahead to the left—"is the Moselle River. It marks the northern boundary of the town."

Rose and Hassan emerged onto the forward deck, looked around, then spotted them and came hurrying into the bridge.

"Right brisk it is out there." Rose blew on her hands. She peered out through the windows. "Is there much to see?"

They continued playing "spot-the-castle," as Rose put it, then repaired to the dining room for an early luncheon. They dallied over the platters, exchanging stories of strange meals in strange places. The tales Rafe and Hassan told trumped anything Loretta or Rose had experienced. Both women hung on every word, then exchanged glances and demanded to hear more.

A mizzling rain had closed over the river, although as Julius had predicted the currents remained swift and the winds in the right quarter to carry the *Loreley Regina* rapidly on.

Eschewing the grayness outside, they went into the salon. Swapping the guidebook for the pack of cards, they played several games of enthusiastic whist, then a crewman looked in to convey a message from Julius that the sights looming ahead were worth seeing.

Rescuing the guidebook, they trooped up to the bridge, and spent what remained of the afternoon watching picturesque villages slide past. The gorge now lay behind them and the mountains had drawn back from the riverbanks, leaving the river cutting a northwesterly swath through a fertile plain.

They'd passed Linz am Rhein, and the town of Remagen with its shrine to St. Apollinaris overshadowed by a last, towering castle, when, leaving the wheel to another crewman, Julius came to speak with Rafe.

"You said you feared your enemies—this cult—would have watchers at Bonn?"

Rafe nodded.

Julius grimaced. "We must put in there—we are low on supplies. But we are making good enough time for us to anchor here for the night. We are far enough away from the town to be safe, yet close enough that tomorrow we will reach the dock just after daybreak, and be away soon after. Our business will not take long."

Rafe hesitated, then nodded. "If we must, we must, and better there than further along. The closer to Rotterdam we get, the more likely we are to encounter cultists in greater numbers."

"After this halt we will not need to tie up at any town before Rotterdam. If the winds stay fair, and in this season there is no reason to think they won't, we will be there as you wished, on the nineteenth of the month."

Rafe smiled. "You've done well. We'll stay below tomorrow morning until Bonn is behind us."

That evening, they dined quietly, discussing Bonn and the reality of the danger looming ahead. To alleviate the tension—or at least hold it back—they played whist for an hour, then forsaking even that, retired.

Rose followed Loretta into the stateroom, then halted.

Loretta glanced back, saw Rose clasping and unclasping her hands, and arched a brow.

"I thought to mention," Rose blurted out, "that Hassan and I . . . we've decided to tie the knot. After this is all over, of course, and after you and Mr. Rafe wed, but . . ." Blushing, Rose waved vaguely at the stateroom door. "In case you'd noticed . . . I thought I should say."

Loretta beamed. "That's wonderful, Rose—and thank you for telling me. Not that I wondered—in the circumstances, what you wish to do is for you to decide—but . . . oh, I'm so sincerely happy for you." Whisking back, she enveloped Rose in a hug. "Good luck to you both. He's lucky to find such a treasure as you." She paused, then added, "If you're sure he's the one?"

"Oh, I am—I am." Rose hugged her back. "And good luck to you and Mr. Rafe, too."

"Thank you." Loretta stepped back, tugged her gown into place. Lips quirking, she nodded at the door. "You can go. I won't need you again tonight."

Rose's face lit. "If you're sure?"

"I am. Go." Loretta shooed.

Her face wreathed in smiles, Rose turned and went, slipping out of the door and closing it quietly after her.

Loretta stared at the door, her own smile fading.

If you're sure? Luckily, Rose hadn't asked her that question in relation to Rafe. However . . .

"I am." She murmured the words, felt them resonate inside her. She was sure, yet . . .

She knew—in her heart, to her soul, knew that he felt that something special for her. She'd sensed it, tasted it, felt and experienced it last night, had seen it—or the effect of it—in his eyes that morning.

Had felt the evolving, deepening, and strengthening shift in the current that had linked them throughout the day.

What she still didn't know was whether he knew.

Whether he recognized the feeling, the emotion, for what it was.

It was important that he did.

After you and Mr. Rafe wed.

She no longer doubted that they would. Yet until he acknowledged what it was that linked them, what power it was that would underpin their marriage, some inner instinct warned that she'd be wise to withhold her final agreement.

Men like Rafe Carstairs were the epitome of stubborn, at least when it came to subjects they wanted to avoid.

Her vision of him as a wary and wily beast returned to her mind. If he could gain the succor he craved yet remain unleashed, he would.

If she let him.

She nearly snorted, then remembered something she'd packed away . . . its time had clearly come.

Swinging around, smiling in suddenly eager anticipation, she walked into her cabin and shut the door.

Ten minutes later, Rafe tapped on the stateroom's door. He'd gone up on deck to check that the spot Julius had chosen in which to anchor was reasonably safe. Reassured on that point, he'd come straight back down.

Straight to Loretta.

He was willing to wager that Rose had already tripped her way down the corridor to Hassan's cabin. Hassan had told him of their plans, and while he wished them nothing but happiness, he wished his own future was equally definite.

The thought had sent him striding to the stateroom's door to knock almost imperiously. When no answer was forthcoming, he frowned, opened the door, and looked in. The sitting room was empty, the lamps unlit, but a sliver of lamplight glowed along the base of the closed door of Loretta's cabin.

Entering, he shut the main door, then crossed to the last door between him and his intended. Halting before it, he raised his hand, hesitated enough to restrain his impatience, then rapped lightly.

"Come in."

The faintly sultry, decidedly languid tones rushed over him like a caress, and set every instinct on high alert.

He hesitated, then, jaw tightening, grasped the doorknob, turned it, and walked in.

She was lying on her side across the bed, propped on one elbow facing the door, a smile of welcome on her face, her long, luscious body encased in a confection composed of feathers, wisps of satin, and scraps of lace.

Beyond his control, his gaze swept from her shoulders, the ivory curves peeking through a froth of lace and feathers, past the ripe curves of her breasts outlined in sheening satin, past the indentation of her waist, the evocative curves of hip and stomach, the long svelte lines of her thighs, to her calf, half revealed beneath a ruffle of lace and feathers, to the tiny feathered slippers on her feet.

Lamps on side tables flanking the bed cast a warm, loving glow over her dark hair, her porcelain skin. Gilded her curves.

His mouth had dried. Breathing was difficult. He managed to shut the door behind him. Cleared his throat, gestured. "Where . . . ?"

"Esme. Paris. What more need I say?" Her smile was an open invitation.

He took one step foward. Halted. Seized the moment to get his baser self under more rigid control.

Her eyes on his, she moved, slowly, sinuously, rising to her knees.

Revealing to his fascinated senses that the nightgown was even more alluring than he'd thought—almost insubstantial across her upper breasts, leaving the ripe mounds to beckon and tease behind a shifting drift of feathers anchored on open lace. At her sides, panels of the same lace framed two slits that ran up her thighs, up the sides of her hips to just below her waist.

Whoever had designed the nightgown knew a great deal about men. Whatever Esme had been thinking when she'd bought the garment for Loretta, he didn't want to know.

On her knees, Loretta, all siren, beckoned him to the side of the bed. His feet moved of their own accord, and took him to her.

"This time," she murmured, fingers closing around his lapels as she drew him the last inch closer, "I get to lead."

He couldn't think of a worse idea but, as her lips pressed, all voluptuous temptation, to his, he gathered she wasn't interested in his opinion.

His reservations.

He clung to the latter, but he couldn't deny her as with those delicate lips and the tip of her wicked tongue she lured him into the exchange, until he accepted her brazen invitation, and sank into her mouth and claimed.

All she offered. That reality, as ever, sent his senses reeling, set his desires aflame, his passions slavering. His hands closed about her, satin shifting seductively under his palms, teasing his fingers with the tactile promise of what lay beneath. Skin so fine it made satin seem coarse.

The nightgown had been designed by some sorceress to pander to a man's lusts, to heighten male anticipation; he wasn't proof against the magic. Hands spreading, fingers splaying, he seized—

Loretta pushed his coat over his shoulders, restricting his reach.

Holding to the kiss, an incendiary duel of heat and rising passion, he shrugged off the coat—discovered his waistcoat hanging open and shrugged it off, too. Her fingers were busy with his cravat. Leaving her to it, he closed his hands about her hips, sank his fingers into the firm flesh beneath the sliding satin, then eased his hold and sent his hands skating around and upward to close about her breasts.

The feathers and lace distracted him, confused him.

Her lips still locked with his, she drew his cravat off, tossed it aside. Leaning into him, into the kiss, flagrantly pressing her breasts into his hands, she seized his shirt above his waistband and tugged.

Then she rocked back on her heels, broke the kiss. Eyes dark with passion, lips swollen and sheening, demanded, "Off." She tugged at the shirt.

Determination was stamped in her expression, echoed in her tone. Muttering a curse, he grabbed the shirt and hauled it up over his head.

Felt her hands grip his waistband as he did.

Felt the buttons give as he whipped the shirt off his head, then wrestled to free his arms.

Even as he dropped the shirt, she closed her hands about him. Locked her fingers about his erection and stroked.

His eyes closed. He clenched his fists, fought for the strength to endure her touch, her eager, exploring caresses, curious, innocent, yet lascivious all at once. He had, he reminded himself, experienced far worse, more expert and demanding torture, yet for some reason with her . . . her simplest touch felt infinitely more intimate. More meaningful. More passionate, laden with her own brand of sultry heat.

At least she was only touching. . . .

The thought had him forcing his eyes open. His gaze fell on her face; he took in the wonderment in her expression, an open delight as she stroked and fondled. . . .

His arousal racheted up another excruciating notch; he was already as hard as he could get. Fully engorged, under her hand he felt like hot marble, impossibly straining.

If he didn't get her hands off him . . .

He caught them, one in each of his, drew them from his throbbing erection as he placed one knee between hers on the bed, drew her hands up level with his head—as she looked up, lips parted, he swooped and locked his lips over hers.

Kissed her voraciously.

The instant she was caught, he released her hands, set his own to her sinfully clad body, intending to sweep them beneath her bottom and lift her to him . . .

She wrapped her arms about his neck, kissed him with such fiery demand she stole his breath—momentarily seized his wits. Before he could reclaim them, she tipped back, tumbled back across the bed, taking him with her.

With neither purchase nor balance to resist, he landed atop her in a welter of limbs and feathered satin. Gritting his teeth, he pushed up. Ignoring the lust spearing through him at the sensation of having her satin-encased form undulating beneath him, he rolled to the side so he wasn't squashing her.

But she followed.

Used her weight to push him further, tipping him onto his back. Rising on her knees, tugging the skirts of her gown free, she slid one sleek thigh across his hips, and straddled him.

Bracing her hands on his chest, she looked down at him.

Her slow, sultry smile was that of a cat eyeing an entire bowlful of cream.

He stared up at her, a touch dumbfounded, increasingly wary.

Beyond aroused.

Concealed beneath the fall of her gown, cradled against one delicate inner thigh, the most aroused part of him twitched.

She felt it. Smile deepening, she looked down, then gathered and lifted the folds of satin to reveal his errant, still engorged, still throbbing, member.

"Ah, yes." Lustful anticipation laced the words. She glanced up at him, met his eyes. "My turn, I believe."

She might as well have licked her lips.

He wasn't entirely sure she hadn't as she wriggled back down his legs, then gripped his trousers and tugged them down.

There was, clearly, no point in resisting. Thanking heaven he'd worn trousers and shoes, he toed the later off, heard them fall to the floor, then lifted his hips, helped her free his legs.

Managing to anchor his legs the whole time, she stripped the trousers from his feet, and triumphant, flung the garment aside.

Then she turned back to him. To a slow, thorough perusal of all she'd uncovered.

He lay back and looked at her, encased in the gossamer-fine, provocative, evocative confection of satin and feathered lace, perched across his hips like a lustful angel. Swallowed. His mouth was dry; his chest felt tight. Her words echoed in his head. Her turn?

Bad idea. Very bad idea.

Just how bad he looked set to learn as, leaning forward, she set her hands on his chest just below his shoulders, used her weight to hold him steady as she bent her head and pressed her lips to his.

Kissed him, all sweetness and slow, intoxicating pleasure.

Why she imagined he'd move he didn't know.

He lay there and drank in the promise of her kiss. Let her show him her flavors, gift him with her textures.

Mesmerize him with her passion, blind him with her desire.

When she moved on, sliding her lips to his jaw, then down the line of his throat, he sighed, and let her. Hands at her sides, he didn't try to guide, but simply held her, and thrilled to the sensations she sent sliding over his skin as she shifted over him. As with her lips, her hands, her tongue, her teeth, she kissed, caressed, licked, laved, and nipped her way down his body.

Inevitably she found scars; with loving care, she tended them with lips and tongue, with the soft waft of her breath, the brush of her fingertips.

Eyes falling closed, he drew in a shuddering breath as she edged lower, her lips skating across the tensed muscles of his abdomen.

Tension heightened, inexorably tightened as she slid lower still. Delicate fingers again wrapped around his erection. He felt the press of her breasts through the feathered lace as she held the rigid rod against her, then she tilted the head aside so she could place a hot open-mouthed kiss on his navel.

Lust closed viselike around his spine, fierce talons sinking deep.

Even as she shuffled lower yet, his mind was awash with thoughts, images, hopes, and contradictory fears.

Would she? Surely not. But what if . . .

He felt the warm wash of her breath across the sensitive head and stopped breathing. Fists clenching tight, he told himself he wasn't going to look, wouldn't . . .

His lids cracked open, he glanced down his body, and saw. . . .

A sight that rocked him to his soul.

She was lightly tracing the veins, the bulbous head, but the look on her face . . . she was studying his erection, examining it, delighting in it as if it were some precious prize.

He must have groaned; her eyes flicked up to meet his.

She looked into his eyes, then smiled.

Put out her tongue and licked.

He jerked, closed his eyes, groaned again—deeper this time.

Felt the soft exhalation of her delighted laugh—an unbelievably erotic sensation—then she licked again, slower, more deliberately, and he stopped thinking.

Could only feel as she tasted him. As she explored and learned.

His hands had risen to cup her head. By an inhuman feat of will he managed not to sink his fingers into the dark silk of her hair, grip, and guide her . . . but his reins were fraying, his control thinning to a wisp, more hope than reality.

When she slowly licked across the broad head, then circled the rim with the tip of her hot tongue, he'd had enough. Could stand no more. Not without . . .

Incipient panic gave him the strength to open his eyes, lift his shoulders and, as gently as he could, tighten his grip on her head and draw her away.

She caught one of his hands in hers. Twined her fingers in his, drew his hand from her head and pushed it down to the bed.

"No." The word fell from her lips, clear, firm, decisive. She met his eyes, her own radiating certainty. "You have to let me." Her lips curved. She leaned forward on her knees and stretched up to brush her lips over his. Whispered across them, "You have to let me have my way with you tonight."

From close quarters, she held his gaze. "This, tonight, is my turn to explore and learn what pleases you." A bewitching, beguiling smile on her lips, she eased back, softly said, "My turn to show you how much I love you."

His chest swelled. He lay there, searched her eyes—saw that the words had been deliberate, no accident, no light, airy, half-conscious statement.

She'd meant every word.

He lay on his back on her bed, and his world, his universe, rocked. Quaked.

As if she understood, she drew back to her previous position astride his thighs, closed one hand about his straining erection, then bent her head and took him into her mouth.

His eyes closed; his body bowed. A groan was ripped from his chest as she took him deeper.

As she confirmed all she'd said in sensation and pleasure.

Lorettta devoted herself to the task, and discovered just how much pleasuring him rebounded on her. Having him at her sensual mercy was one delight. The sense of control—of leading in this dance at least as far as he would let her—was a different sort of joy.

Holding him in her mouth, suckling, curling her tongue around his solid length, she let her hands roam, stretched them up over his ridged abdomen, over the wide muscles of his chest.

Possessed by touch as she did by suction.

Gloried in her power, in his all but helpless response.

He was magnificient, and he was hers. All hers. She'd spent the day thinking about the previous night, about what it had revealed, and how. About what he'd shown her of the ways to communicate in this arena. About how to return the favor—the pleasure and the wordless commitment, the promise, the unspoken vow.

Tonight, as she'd stated, was her turn. Her turn to communicate that wordless commitment, that unspoken vow. To worship, to pleasure, to give.

Eventually the pressure of their passions grew too great. She felt the urgency pounding through him, through her, felt the throb of aching need between her thighs reach fever-pitch.

Releasing him, she rose up on her knees, gripped the skirts of Esme's scandalous gift and with a silent thank you to her great-aunt, drew the slithering folds up and off over her head.

He reached for her, gripping her waist. She sensed his intention to roll her beneath him and stopped him, gripped his wrists in both hands. "No—like this." Shuffling forward on her knees, she positioned herself over his straining member. "I know it can be done—show me how."

His grip tightened. One glance showed his jaw locked, his features like hewn granite, his eyes a burning blue. But then his fingers eased enough to slide to her hips.

And he showed her.

How to take him in, how to envelop his hardness in her slick softness, how to use her body to flagrantly caress him.

How to ride him.

He held her, showed her, taught her, guided her—showed her how to love him this way.

Showed her how to ride him until their hearts beat as one, until their breaths were ragged gasps and their senses spun.

He surged up, locked his lips over one turgid nipple and suckled powerfully. Head tipping back, she cried out, and rode him even harder.

Until he burned at her core, hot and hard, and she tightened and tightened, then he thrust up, deep, one last time, and on a rush of pure pleasure she melted.

Releasing her breast, he locked his lips on hers, claimed her mouth in a searing kiss. Locked her hips to him and rolled her to the side, rolled her beneath him.

With one powerful thrust resheathed himself fully within her.

Then he rode her.

Into shattering bliss, into exquisite oblivion.

Into the heaven that waited for them, in each other's arms.

In the depths of the chilly night, Rafe's mind swam back to consciousness. His body remained sunk in a sated, bliss-filled warmth he never wanted to leave.

Thank God he wouldn't have to. He tightened his arms around Loretta, breathed in her scent, felt it wreathe through his mind and sink to his bones, then relaxed, eased his grip. There was no need to physically lock her to him. She wasn't leaving either.

She'd claimed her turn, her right, and claimed him.

My turn to show you how much I love you.

She'd said the words and meant them. In uttering them she was braver than he. That one little, four-letter word still held the power to make him quake.

But . . . *my turn* she'd said. Which implied she knew, had correctly interpreted and understood, all he'd unintention-ally, helplessly, revealed the night before.

He lay still, her body, warm and sated, curled against his, and wondered how he felt about that.

If even though he hadn't said the words, hadn't uttered them out loud . . . if she knew, and he knew she knew . . . where did that leave them?

She seemed to know.

Sadly, he didn't.

He wasn't sure how to deal with that emotion—that mas-sive, powerful, all-encompassing emotion that some ancient scholar had in some fit of idiocy described in a word of only four letters.

That emotion was so overwhelmingly powerful it quali-fied for seventeen letters, at least.

Yet no matter what label was put on it, the result remained

the same. When it came to acknowledging it, working with it, managing it, he had no clue. He wasn't sure what it meant, how it would affect him.

He didn't know what he ought to do about it, for it, with it.

Most pertinently, he wasn't sure he, being him, could do very much with it at all.

The morning brought distraction, but not in a way any of them would have wished.

As Rafe had told Julius, he, Loretta, Hassan, and Rose remained below deck as, soon after an early breakfast, the *Loreley Regina* tied up at the dock in Bonn.

A thin fog hung over the docks. The winter sun was struggling to thrust even a ghostly grayish light through the heavy clouds.

Soon after Julius and some of the crew had departed for the warehouses, another crewman came down to tell them that the crew left on watch had spotted Indian-looking men wearing turbans with black scarves wound around them.

Rafe thanked him, and he left.

The minutes crawled by; the tension grew.

To break it, Rafe suggested a game of whist.

They gathered in the salon, in their usual spot in the prow where the windows on either side of the vessel let in enough light to see.

The dock lay alongside. After peering out, Loretta drew the lace curtain across the dockside window, relieving Rafe of that concern. Even if cultists strolled past on the dock, they wouldn't be able to spot them through the lace.

They settled to their game.

Nearly an hour later, they heard the men returning.

Julius looked in, saluted. "We have all we need." He nodded at Loretta. "I gave your letter into the post, m'amzelle." To Rafe he said, "We will be putting out shortly—there is another vessel ahead of us that must go first."

"Excellent." Rafe relaxed, leaning back in the armchair.

Julius left, and Rafe looked at Hassan. "If we escape detection here—"

A heavy thud sounded on the narrow walkway on the starboard side, the side facing the dock. Simultaneously the boat tipped, then righted; there seemed little doubt what had happened.

Both Rafe and Hassan leapt to their feet, heading for the door to the walkway.

"No!" Loretta swung to face them. "Go down. Go and stand in the corridor where they can't see you."

Rafe and Hassan hesitated, caught by the instinct to defend and protect.

"Aar—" Rose clapped a hand over her mouth. Eyes round, with her other hand she pointed at the mahogany brown face pressed to the port prow window, the uncurtained one facing the river.

Black eyes stared at them. The apparition wore a turban wound about with black silk.

Rafe swore and raced for the walkway door, Hassan at his heels.

The cultist's gaze tracked them, then he whirled and disappeared toward the dock.

Loretta yanked aside the curtain over the dockside window, knelt on the window seat and tried to track the man.

All she saw was a boot as he leapt up onto the dock and vanished.

Five minutes passed before Rafe and Hassan returned to the salon. As they did, the prow of the *Loreley Regina* swung out into the river.

Both men came to join Loretta and Rose as they stood at the front of the salon and watched the docks fall behind, and the river open up before them once more.

Once they were underway, Loretta glanced at Rafe.

He met her gaze, his own heavy with concern. "The dock was crowded. They—there were two of them—disappeared before any of us got more than a glimpse."

She nodded, then, sensing there was more behind the men's hugely increased tension, raised her brows.

Rafe exhaled, ran a hand through his hair. "They not only know we're on the river. They know we're on this particular boat."

The cult also now knew that he and Hassan had two women with them. Rafe hadn't stated that, yet of all the aspects now in play, that weighed on him the most.

They kept watch, a tense watch, throughout the rest of the day. They saw no likely cultists as they slipped past Cologne, but at Dusseldorf they spotted a lone cult member sitting on a pile of rope on the dock.

He was watching the river, but idly.

Given the speed the *Loreley Regina* was making downriver, with the wind holding steady from the stern, they concluded that the news of their sighting at Bonn hadn't yet reached that far north.

Later, after dinner, Rafe paced the stateroom's sitting room. Rose had gathered her things and decamped to Hassan's cabin at the end of the corridor, leaving the stateroom to him and Loretta. Given how he felt, he was grateful.

"With any luck, they'll expect me to leave the boat now that I know they've spotted us on it." Eyes narrowed, he stared at Loretta, seated in one of the armchairs. A lady's traveling writing desk balanced on her knees, she'd been scribbling on and off since they'd settled in the sitting room.

She looked up, met his gaze. "That would be fortunate, given we have to halt at anchor every evening."

They were presently at anchor in what Julius had described as a secure merchants' basin off Duisberg. The town's docks were some way away, back along the river, and the riverbanks were too distant, and the currents between too strong, to imagine any attackers swimming out to the *Loreley Regina*. In addition, the crew were on watch. Now they'd sighted the enemy—indeed, had had one board and then escape—they were very much on their mettle. Rafe knew their party was as safe as he could make them, yet still . . .

This, he suspected, lips twisting as he resumed his pacing, was one of the outcomes of that four-letter-word emotion.

Stifling a sigh, Loretta closed her writing desk and set it aside. She'd been trying to jot down ideas for her last *Window on Europe* vignette, but Rafe's imitation of a restless, prowling beast was an irresistible distraction.

Standing, she turned down the lamp, then blew it out, plunging the room into moonlight and shadow. Rafe halted as she turned to him. Smiling wryly as much to herself as to him, she walked to him, took his hand, wound her fingers with his, and drew him to her room.

Shutting the door behind them, she turned and went into his arms.

They closed around her, his head bent to hers as she stretched up. Their lips met, brushed, touched, then they sank into each other's mouths, into each other's embrace, and let the moment have them.

Let the night enfold them, let passion rise up and sweep them away, knowing this night might be the last of their journey in which they were free to indulge. During which they were safe enough to indulge.

During which they could strip each other bare, join, and let the glory take them.

Unrestrained, unshielded.

During which they could with complete and utter focus concentrate on the other, on their wants and needs, on satisfying both, on reaching and seizing, then clinging to that ultimate glory.

It left them wracked, sated and limp, in a tangle in her bed.

Gently, with those reassuring touches only lovers could share, they disengaged and settled to sleep.

Boneless, at peace, Loretta slid into sated slumber.

Rafe held her close.

And listened to the night. To the occasional creak, the whistling of the wind. The almost silent slap of the river wavelets against the hull.

Physically sated he might be, but he was mentally too tense, too on guard, for sleep.

As the dark hours rolled on, his mind circled. To the start of his mission, to the start of this long journey. To his thoughts and feelings then. And how they'd changed.

Yet another outcome of that unnameable emotion.

He now had so much more to lose, something so precious he would give his all, even his soul, to protect it. She, her life, her love—they were inviolate, something he could not conceive of ever allowing to be harmed. But along with that bone-deep determination came a yearning, a hope beyond all other hopes, that he would live through the coming clashes and survive to join his life with hers. That he would live to have a chance to explore all he felt for her, long enough to learn how to cope, how to manage, how to acknowledge and admit to that too-powerful emotion, out loud, to her.

To say the words and admit to the truth that already lived in his heart.

That already invested his soul.

And that was one thing he'd been wrong about. Yes, with that emotion came vulnerability of a sort he, the warrior in him, hated to embrace, yet simultaneously, out of the hope, the yearning, and the determination it engendered, that emotion gave him strength.

A strength he'd never felt before, one he'd yet to test. But if its power was anything like that of the emotion that gave it birth . . .

The chances were he'd find out. Soon.

And alongside the new—his recently acquired hopes and dreams—ran the older imperatives: his loyalty to his friends, his duty to his country, and his devotion to seeing James MacFarlane avenged.

As the faint gray light of dawn seeped into the cabin, he held Loretta close, and with his cheek on her dark hair, thought of those things, his most prized possessions, his deepest vows.

Those were the things he would fight for, that he would face the Black Cobra and battle for. And of them all, the one he would give his soul to keep safe was his future with her. Reckless would never be reckless with that.

≋ *Sixteen* ≋

*B*y the following afternoon, they'd left the main channel of the Rhine and were on the Lek, the arm of the river that eventually flowed past Rotterdam.

Rafe stood on the bridge looking out at the passing riverscape. He'd come up to consult with Julius and his crew over what they might expect once they reached their destination. Although some miles from the open sea, Rotterdam was the biggest seaport in Europe; its many shipping basins played host to merchantmen and fishing fleets from all around the globe.

If anything, the river currents had strengthened and the *Loreley Regina* was running fast before a stiff breeze. Although they'd all helped mount a close watch on the numerous small town docks they'd whisked past, as well as on the surrounding river traffic, they'd sighted no more cultists.

With a nod to Julius, Rafe headed for the companionway. Descending, he walked into the salon to join Loretta, Hassan, and Rose, who were waiting in the armchairs about the small table they'd used to play whist.

"Julius says," Rafe reported, dropping into the chair alongside Loretta's, "that we'll reach the port of Rotterdam tomorrow, in the late afternoon or early evening. Quite aside from the vagaries of wind and currents, we'll soon have to slow to tack between vessels anchored in the river."

"Will we halt tonight?" Hassan asked.

Rafe shook his head. "Apparently that's unnecessary. Although to hear him describe it, the river will be an obstacle course, in these reaches all vessels mount running lights, and accepted practise is for vessels to keep moving until they reach their intended destination. Speaking of which, Julius agrees that putting into the usual passenger docks would be foolish. Because we'll have to slow for the last stretches, it's certain the cultists in Rotterdam will be warned of our arrival before we reach there. Julius predicts that the cult will have a welcome waiting for us at the *Loreley Regina*'s customary dock."

"What's the alternative?" Loretta asked.

"The consensus is that we'll all be better off if the *Loreley Regina* avoids all the basins set aside for passenger vessels and instead slips into one reserved for merchantmen. Apparently smaller craft occasionally put in there to unload cargo they've brought downriver. The crew consider it highly unlikely the cult will be patroling the trade docks—there are simply too many to cover, even with a small army."

He paused, then grimaced. "I know why Wolverstone organized each courier's route independently and so secretly, but I could wish that, at this juncture, I had some idea where the others are—and even more pertinently if they've recently passed through other embarkation ports on the Continent, like Calais, or Le Havre, or better yet further afield, and so have forced the Black Cobra to spread his available forces along the Channel coast. I'd love to know if any or all of them have already reached Wolverstone, or if they're still in the field providing active distraction—which will mean the difference between us facing a thinly spread cordon of cultists, or instead running headfirst into a concerted force."

"The other three were decoy missions." Hassan shrugged. "Their reason for being was to draw the cult away from our path."

"True, but . . ." After a moment, Rafe grimaced again. "I am carrying the original letter and it must get through.

I think from now on we have to operate on the assumption that the Black Cobra will oppose us with all force at his disposal—and that that will result in a significant gauntlet for us to run."

Silence fell as they digested that, considering, imagining, then he continued, "Our goal is to be in Felixstowe by the evening of the twenty-first—three days from now. On that evening, our guards will meet us at the Pelican Inn. Assuming we disembark in Rotterdam tomorrow—on the evening of the nineteenth—that gives us two full days to reach our rendezvous. According to Julius and crew, we may be lucky and find passage across the Channel immediately—in which case we'll reach Felixstowe a day early and have to go to ground there—or, and they consider this more likely, we'll need that extra day to find suitable passage. The trip across the Channel will take between ten and fifteen hours, depending on the type of vessel we take, the tides, and the prevailing winds."

He glanced at the other three faces, all now familiar to him, even Rose. "Let's assume Julius puts us safely off at one of the Rotterdam trade docks early tomorrow evening. What do we do next? How should we go on?"

"Finding passage onward is our primary concern," Hassan said. "Perhaps Julius and his men can suggest what areas of the docks would be most useful for finding transport across the Channel."

"Before we get that far," Loretta said, "there's another point we ought to consider." She met Rafe's eyes. "As you stated, we'd be wise to assume the Black Cobra's men will be everywhere, searching for us. So before we even step onto Rotterdam's docks, we should consider whether there's any way we can shore up our disguise."

He pulled a face. "After Dusseldorf, us traveling together will no longer afford us much cover. If they spot two tall men with two women, they'll come sniffing closer."

"Well, even if you leave us behind, they'll still recognize the two of you"—Rose nodded at Rafe and Hassan—

"perhaps even quicker, so there's no point suggesting we separate from you." The statement was a declaration of belligerent intransigence.

Loretta mentally applauded; she'd been about to make the same point, albeit more subtly. After studying Rose's face, Hassan floated the idea of disguising himself and Rafe as sailors. Rafe allowed it might be possible, but questioned whether securing passage might then prove more problematic.

When, frowning, the other three fell silent, Loretta evenly stated, "There's one thing we can do that will make us much less noticeable, especially if this fog also hangs thickly about the docks in Rotterdam."

A certain stillness seized Rafe. He hesitated as if debating whether he wanted to hear her idea, but then he arched a brow. "What?"

"We can split into two couples and make our way separately." She leaned forward. "Think about it—in the area about any docks, in the taverns and shipping quarters where we'll have to go to find passage onward, other than groups of men, what's the most common sight?" She answered the question herself. "A sailor with his woman for the night."

Rafe's lips quirked downward, but he didn't argue. She was perfectly certain he wanted to, but in this instance, his mission had to come first.

To smooth his way to agreeing, she went on, "I concede that splitting into two couples will make defending against attack more difficult, simply on the basis of numbers. Against that, however, we'll stand a much better chance of slipping past the cultists unnoticed—without having to defend against any attack at all."

Sitting back, she raised her hands. "As I see it, that's our only better option. Continuing all four together would be tempting fate—the cultists in Rotterdam will have been warned to look specifically for our party. And leaving me and Rose behind could well be the worst thing you could do."

Neither Rafe nor Hassan argued. They exchanged a long glance, then after a tense pause, Rafe turned back to her. "Let's say we split up on the dock—what then? Do we stay apart until Felixstowe?"

She nodded. "As two separate couples we have a much better chance of all four of us reaching the Pelican Inn."

His eyes on hers, he said nothing for a full minute, then grimaced and nodded. "All right." He glanced at Hassan. "We part on the dock and go our separate ways, each finding our own way across the Channel."

Equally reluctantly, Hassan nodded—forced himself to nod. "If they realize we've separated, it will at least force the cultists to follow two separate trails."

Rafe studied his henchman. "No heroics—under no circumstances are you to draw cult attention your way."

Rose humphed. "You can rely on me to make sure he doesn't."

Her belligerence was still very much on show. This time Rafe seemed more comforted than confronted by it; he inclined his head Rose's way.

"So assuming we part on the dock, what next?" Loretta reclaimed their attention.

"If we're separating, then we should look for passage in different quarters—Julius and the crew can advise us on that. But we can also put another degree of separation into play." Rafe looked at Rose. "Do you know England's east coast at all?"

"A little. Not well."

"Harwich lies across an estuary from Felixstowe—there's a regular ferry that connects them. You and Hassan can make for Harwich, then get the ferry across. Loretta and I will make directly for Felixstowe."

Leaning forward, hands clasped between his knees, Hassan nodded. "And then we go to the Pelican Inn. And then?"

"The men we're supposed to meet are Christian Allardyce

and Jack Hendon. On the evening of December twenty-first, they'll be waiting in the inn's taproom. You can trust either man implicitly, but don't trust anyone else."

"How will we recognize them?" Rose asked.

"I suspect they're ex-Guardsmen." Rafe glanced at Hassan. "You know the type."

The big Pathan nodded. "Cavalrymen like you. Will anyone else, the cult, for instance, be able to guess those men—men with those names—will be the ones we will look for?"

"I doubt it." Rafe considered, then shook his head. "I can't see anyone of Wolverstone's caliber being that indiscreet. If an Englishman of the right build walks up and introduces himself as either Allardyce or Hendon, you should be safe in trusting that they're who they claim to be. But, and I can't stress this strongly enough, don't trust anyone else. We can't tell what friends Ferrar might have rallied to his cause."

After a moment, Hassan rose. "I will go and ask Julius and the crew about the different areas around the docks, and ask them to recommend different ways in which we might go to find passage to Harwich or Felixstowe. I will not tell them we plan to go separately."

Rafe nodded and rose, too. "I'll go and fetch the maps. I want to go over the dangers we may face." He glanced at Loretta and Rose. "Let's meet back here in half an hour."

With Rose, Loretta nodded, stood, and followed Rafe down to the cabin deck. He went into his cabin. She led Rose to the stateroom. "We may as well start packing. I'll speak to Julius about sending on my trunks."

"I was thinking"—Rose followed her into the sitting room and shut the door—"that it might be best if we took . . . well, no bags at all. Nothing we can't easily carry, and better if it looks like we're not travelers."

Struck by the suggestion, Loretta nodded. "You're right. The less we look like travelers, the less likely the cultists will consider us too closely."

She led the way into her cabin. "Let's see." Opening the armoire, she looked at her clothes, then regarded the twin trunks set against the wall. "If we squash everything down, we should be able to pack all my things and yours into the trunks, then I'll carry my embroidery bag and you can take your knitting bag, not with embroidery or knitting but with just the things we'll need for a few days."

Loretta glanced at Rose, saw her nodding. "I'm sure that the ladies wherever we're going will be willing to lend us some clothes."

They returned to the salon half an hour later to find Rafe poring over several maps spread on the small table. Hassan joined them with a scribbled list of directions.

After some discussion, they agreed that Hassan and Rose would hire a cart and travel out of Rotterdam. Rose felt more confident about dealing with English sailors from the fleets of smaller craft that frequented the docks on the river's lower reaches. Julius and the crew had told them of a dockside inn at which they would likely find a helpful captain from Harwich.

Rafe and Loretta would remain in Rotterdam and search for an English captain at one of several taverns Julius had suggested as more likely to be playing host to the crews of larger fishing vessels from the Felixstowe fleet.

With that decided, Rafe and Hassan speculated on the form of cult hurdles they might find themselves facing.

"We have to expect that Ferrar will have hired mercenary captains to patrol the Channel. All we can hope is that they'll be stretched too thin to worry about fishing boats." Rafe met Rose's and Hassan's eyes. "That said, we'll need to take the captain we each hire into our confidence, at least to the extent of explaining about the cult and the possible dangers. We'll need the support of captain and crew to avoid the cultists' boats and, if necessary, to hide us from cult searches. They can't help if they don't know, so we'll

tell them. You know the tack to take—appeal to their patri-
otism, and"—he drew money pouches from his pockets—
"pay them well. Half when you hire them, half on getting
off the boat in England, with the promise of a sizeable tip
if they get you there quickly, without fuss, and above all,
in safety."

He dropped a large pouch before Hassan, then a somewhat
smaller one in front of Rose. When she looked up, surprised,
Rafe said, "In case you and Hassan get separated. If that
happens, you go on to Felixstowe and the Pelican Inn." He
glanced at Hassan, then at Loretta as he dropped yet another
purse on the table before her. "If something happens and
we're forced to part, that's where we'll meet again."

"Where we'll *all* meet again." Loretta picked up the purse.
She met Rafe's eyes, then Hassan's, then Rose's. "At the Pelican Inn in Felixstowe."

By the time night fell, and they made their way to their respective cabins, Rose and Hassan to Hassan's, with Rafe following Loretta through the stateroom to hers, the tension
had escalated dramatically.

They'd spent the last hours dicussing various aspects of
what might come. Hearing of Loretta's and Rose's decision regarding what they would carry with them, Rafe and
Hassan had elected to follow suit. They would leave their
bags with Julius to send on, and would each carry a shoulder
satchel, a visual suggestion that they were town-based mes-
sengers rather than travelers.

Hearing Rafe shut her cabin door, Loretta reached up to
pull the pins from her hair; her gaze landed on her trunks,
packed and left ready against one wall. A sign of their impending departure, and of the dangerous times looming.

Their journey along the rivers—their relatively slow passage up the Danube, the increasing pace as they'd come
down the Rhine—had all been leading to this, to the rapids
as they rushed into the last turbulent days of Rafe's mission,

as they raced into and through the gauntlet of opposition the Black Cobra would amass and hurl against them.

Hardly surprising they were all on edge.

That in each of them tension had racked to such a level that it transcended all artifice—stripped away all social veils and left reality revealed in a stark, harsh, uncompromising light.

Left them unequivocally sure of what they wanted. What they needed.

Of what was, in the end, important.

Laying her pins on the bedside table, her hair a rippling veil over her shoulders and back, Loretta turned and saw Rafe shrugging off his coat.

They hadn't bothered lighting a lamp. Although diffused by the river fog, the moonlight was strong enough, yet the soft light left Rafe's eyes and expression shadowed, poorly lit.

She walked to him. Instantly felt his attention swing to her. Fix on her. Halting before him, she looked into his eyes, met the summer blue darkened with need.

Holding her gaze, he shrugged off his waistcoat.

She placed her palms on his chest, felt the latent heat. His gaze lowered to her lips. She pushed her hands up over his chest as she stepped nearer and he lowered his head.

Stretched up and met his lips as they found hers.

They kissed, and it was different. Direct, open, unflinchingly honest. No shields, no veils—no time to waste with either.

Passion was a steady beat in their veins, desire a heat that never truly left them.

Love a hunger neither wished any longer to deny.

It swept up and filled them, a tangible force that caught them, commanded them. That made them burn.

That had her wrapping her arms about his neck and clinging to the ravenous exchange while he pulled her tight against him, then sent his hands racing over her body, quickly, expertly divesting her of gown, petticoat, chemise—then she drew back and, with heat and that hunger a steady flame beneath her skin, returned the favor.

Until their bodies touched, skin to naked skin. Until their hands claimed, possessed, until their senses reeled, filled with pleasure, with delight, with each other.

Until their pulses pounded and hunger became a ravening compulsion that sank talons into them both.

They fell on the bed in a tangle of driven limbs and slick, passion-dewed skin. He flicked the covers over them as urgency whipped, spread her thighs wide as passion ignited. Settled heavily between.

His eyes locked with hers. From a distance of mere inches he held her gaze as their breaths mingled and their senses clamored.

His body lay hot and heavy on hers. Hard, hair-dusted muscle and heavy bone held her pinned, captured, beneath him. Then his spine flexed.

She caught her breath on a gasp, arched beneath him as with one long, smooth thrust, he joined them. Held his gaze, breathlessly clung to the steady blue flame of it as he withdrew and plunged in again. Deeper. Harder. She closed her arms about him as, cradled in his, she opened herself to him, as she raised her knees to grasp his flanks, and abandoned and wild, willful and certain, she gave herself to him and surrendered.

To the glorious potent power that linked them.

She drank it in. He settled to a relentless pounding rhythm of thrust and retreat and she rode with him. Lids falling, rocking to his beat, she stretched up and set her lips to his, offered her mouth and lured him to take, to lay claim and plunder.

To sink his tongue into her softness to the same primitive, driving rhythm with which their bodies joined.

Rafe locked his lips on hers, sank into the heady sweetness of her, the provocative lushness of her mouth, the scalding slickness of her sheath. And savored.

Clung to the promise embodied in the act, the shattering joy of possessing such bounty freely offered, touched, clutched at both the wonder and the hope.

The hope that having discovered this, recognized and claimed this, seized and acknowledged this, that having linked himself so irrevocably body and soul to her no earthly entity would ever be powerful enough to wrench them apart.

Their climax roared down on them. Their senses expanded and it swept in and filled them, effortlessly caught them, harried and pushed them, rushed and whipped them up the highest of highest peaks, then wracked them and wrecked them.

Shattered them, then succored them.

Filled them with a glory so unutterably wondrous it sank to their souls.

And left them floating in bliss, at peace.

Left him slumped over her, holding her close, pressing his lips to her temple in wordless promise.

Eventually, he lifted from her, and they settled to sleep, her head on his shoulder, one hand spread protectively over his heart, his arms around her, his cheek against her hair.

He dropped one last kiss on the dark silk, then closed his eyes, one hope for the looming dangerous days a whisper in his mind.

He hoped. He prayed. That fate protected lovers.

That those who loved freely fate would shield under her wing.

That hope was a distant memory when, with his hand locked around Loretta's, Rafe stood on a deserted dock alongside Hassan and Rose and watched the *Loreley Regina* slip away.

Fog closed around them, so dense that within just a few yards the boat was a mere ghost. A few yards more and it disappeared altogether.

It was early evening, but the dock in one of Rotterdam's trading basins was already silent, devoid of other life. The warehouses fronting it were all shut; the navvies had long ago trudged back to their homes in the narrow streets of the dockside quarter. The only sounds to reach the four of them were the distant echoing blare of a passing barge's horn and the constant *slap-slap* of the river against the pylons. The area was weakly lit by the shrouded glow of lights on boats bobbing at the dock or anchored nearby; larger flares shone dim and hazy in the streets beyond.

Rafe glanced at Loretta. Tendrils of fog curled around them both, icy fingers reaching beneath their cloaks. She shivered.

He looked at Hassan, then held out his hand; his old friend gripped it. "Take care. And Godspeed."

Hassan nodded solemnly. "And you." Their hands parted. "We will see you in Felixstowe."

Loretta and Rose embraced, hugged hard, then releasing Rose, Loretta tugged Hassan near and hugged him, too. "Be careful, both of you."

Releasing Hassan, she stepped back.

Rafe gave Rose a quick hug. "Take care of him," he whispered. "Don't let him do anything daft."

"I won't," Rose whispered back. More loudly she said, "You just make sure you both make it to Felixstowe in one piece."

Rafe looked from her to Hassan, then gave a last nod, took Loretta's hand, turned and walked away.

At the end of the dock, he and Loretta paused and glanced back, but could see nothing but fog.

He gripped her hand a touch more tightly. Met her eyes as she glanced his way. "The trick is not to worry about things you can do nothing about. From now until Felixstowe, it's just you and me, and we need to concentrate on staying alive."

She regarded him for an instant, then, lips firming, nodded.

Gripping his hand back, she turned to the street before them, and by his side, walked into Rotterdam.

They found one of the taverns Julius had recommended. It was still early; the main room wasn't crowded. Trying to appear as inconspicuous as possible, Loretta allowed Rafe to settle her at a small table not far from the door, tucked back against the front wall. The table was beyond the circle of light thrown by the lamps suspended above the bar; they both clung to the shadows. A serving girl came and they ordered pies and ale. Loretta was quite keen to try the brew, but it proved so bitter she wrinkled her nose and, once Rafe had emptied his mug, swapped hers for his.

He accepted the exchange with a look, but no comment. This wasn't the sort of tavern in which one could order wine.

By the time they'd finished their meal, the tavern had started filling. Rafe closed his hand over hers on the table, gently squeezed. "Stay here, and keep your eyes down. Stare into the empty mug, and don't meet any man's gaze. I need to speak with the barkeep."

She nodded. Grateful for the shadows, she raised her eyes just enough to track him as he made his way through the increasing press of bodies to the bar. He hailed the barkeep, asked for another mug of ale, then leaned on the bar and engaged the man in what appeared to be an open and animated conversation.

Eventually, the barkeep nodded, then turned to attend to some other customer.

Rafe made his way back to the table. Setting down his freshly filled mug, he reclaimed his seat.

She leaned close, her shoulder brushing his. "What did you learn?"

"That Julius and crew steered us well—according to the barkeep, at least three different English fishing captains are likely to drop by tonight. They're regulars." He sipped his ale, then met her eyes. "I don't want to tell more people than necessary about our need to cross the Channel, let alone to where, so I told the barkeep that I was thinking of contracting for a specific supply of fish, and asked what he knew of the three captains, how experienced they were, what their vessels were like—whether they were solely fishermen or sometimes engaged in other trade."

He paused, then went on, "I chose the oldest—not that old, only middle-aged, but he runs his own small fleet and has never been known to engage in goods shipping, let alone passenger ferrying."

"So no one would expect one of his boats to be carrying passengers?"

Eyes on his mug, he nodded. "The barkeep's agreed to send the man my way when he arrives."

"So all we have to do is wait?"

"Wait, and be patient."

Not so easy when their nerves leapt every time the door opened. Every time a chilly gust blew in, Loretta expected to see a mahogany face beneath a black-silk-encircled turban peering her way. The face pressed to the window of the *Loreley Regina,* dark eyes fanatically gleaming, remained in her mind.

An hour ticked past. Only the steady pressure of Rafe's hand on hers allowed her to bear it without shifting, standing, doing something that would draw attention their way. But if he could sit slouched in the shadows, so still he seemed barely sentient, she could do her part.

Eventually, he shifted, straightening in his seat. "Here he comes."

A grizzled, rather stern-looking man wearing a captain's cap shouldered through the now dense crowd. He halted before their table, a brimming ale mug in one hand. He nodded to Rafe, then his gaze shifted to her.

Forgetting Rafe's instructions, she met the man's gaze—saw a frown slowly form in his deep-set eyes, remembered and looked down.

Rafe stirred, drawing the man's attention. "You're Johnson?"

The man met his gaze, then slowly nodded. "Aye. Walthar at the bar said you wanted to speak to me about some fish."

Rafe swiftly assessed all he could see in the man's face, all he could read in his expression and his stance. The risk seemed worth taking. "That's what I told Walthar. However"—with his boot, he pushed out a chair he'd kept by their table—"if you're a loyal Englishman, I'd ask you to sit down, listen to my tale, and see if you can help me with what I really need."

Johnson considered him for a long moment, then, moving with slow deliberation, he set down his ale mug, drew out the chair, set it down opposite Rafe, and sat.

Folding his arms on the table, leaning on them, he met Rafe's eyes. "I was in the navy for ten years—got out in '13. Went back with my own boat in '15 to assist with getting the troops to Waterloo. I was in the thick of it at Corunna, way back then." He eyed Rafe, then raised his mug. "You?"

"I was there—both at Corunna, and at Waterloo."

Johnson sipped, nodded. "You've the look of a cavalry man. Guards, was it?"

When Rafe nodded, Johnson pursed his lips, then set down his mug. "So. What's landed you here—and what can I do for you?"

Rafe told him, in sufficient detail for Johnson to grasp the importance of his mission, the danger posed by the Black Cobra cult and its members, and the urgency of his and Loretta's situation.

His reading of Johnson proved sound. When he heard of Loretta's involvement, he sent her a look part awe, part disapproval, part pending paternal protectiveness. But he made no comment. He listened until Rafe fell silent. Then he stared at the table for some minutes, before fixing Rafe with a direct look. "How do I know any of this is true?"

Rafe pushed aside his cloak, enough to expose the hilt of his saber. Johnson saw, clearly recognized the style of weapon. "Aside from that," Rafe said, "what possible benefit to me could there be in fabricating such a tale?"

Johnson grimaced. "There is that." He drained his glass, set it down with a clack. "Right, then—so how can I help?'

"We need to get to Felixstowe as quietly as we can, by the evening of the twenty-first at the latest. Can you get us there?"

Johnson's gaze flicked Loretta's way. "Just the two of you?"

"Yes. Just us. Our party had to split up to avoid detection by the cult."

Johnson nodded. "My son—he's captaining my ship through the winter months—mentioned he'd heard something about foreigners offering large sums for boats, captains, and crews willing to sail under their orders up and down the coast." Johnson snorted. "Told him I wasn't interested in taking orders from anyone, much less foreigners. He agreed, but said others had taken the money." Johnson shrugged. "Understandable—it's lean pickings for some this time of year."

"Those will very likely be the boats we'll need to avoid."

"Aye, well, most on both coasts know my boats—know I deal in nothing but fish. With luck, my boy will get you into Felixstowe in good order."

"How soon can we leave?"

"Ah." Johnson tugged at his earlobe. "Won't be tonight, nor yet tomorrow—my boats, along with the rest of the Felixstowe fleet, are in the Channel at present. They'll be back tomorrow afternoon, but with the tides as they are there's no way you'll get a boat out—mine or anyone else's—until the early tide day after tomorrow."

"The twenty-first," Rafe said.

"Aye. But if you take that tide, in the small hours it'll be, you'll be in Felixstowe before nightfall."

Rafe grimaced, but nodded. "That's all we need. Where and when should we meet you tomorrow?"

Johnson raised his brows. "Here? The dock I use isn't far. How about at this time, or so? My boy and I'll be here, having a drink. We can meet with you, then all leave together."

"An excellent plan." Rafe drained his glass, set it down, and reached for his purse. "Now, what do you usually make from the fish you take in a day?"

Johnson shook his head. "No need for coin. I'll do it— well, have Ned take you—on the strength of your story."

But Rafe insisted, and when Johnson reluctantly named a price, counted out and pushed across double the amount. "You may feel you owe the country, but you don't owe our cause your son, or your boat, and it will be dangerous."

Johnson stared at the coins, then shook his head resignedly and took them. "I can't say it'll go amiss, but the boy— he'll be thrilled to see action. Too young for Waterloo, he was, but he's always had a hankering for getting involved in some derring-do."

Rafe met Johnson's eyes. "No need to tell Ned, but I'm sure you'll understand when I hope that our journey will prove entirely uneventful." He reached for Johnson's mug. "Let me get you another ale, and we can drink to that, then"—he glanced at Loretta as he rose—"it'll be time to retire to our lodgings."

Loretta smiled up at him, then gave her attention to charming Johnson while Rafe went to the bar.

"I thought you said we were going to find lodgings? Well, you said 'retire to our lodgings,' but I assumed that's what you meant." After trudging down innumerable cobbled streets while clinging to Rafe's arm and doing her best to imitate how she imagined a woman of the docks might behave, Loretta couldn't keep a certain waspishness from her tone.

"I thought the same, until we passed the first pair of cultists and I realized that they're no doubt keeping a close watch on all hotels or inns, and seeking a room above a tavern might well be even riskier." Not least because drawing attention to her was the last thing he wanted to do.

Sighting danger ahead, Rafe smoothly drew Loretta to him, ducked his head as he backed her into the alcove before a darkened doorway. Kissed her lustily, pressed her to respond.

He heard footsteps at his back draw near, pause . . . he tickled Loretta and made her squirm, the strangled sounds that escaped their fused lips thoroughly misleading. For good measure, through her cloak and skirts he gripped her bottom and squeezed, openly kneaded.

The footsteps resumed, passing on and down the street. When he judged the cultists were far enough away he raised his head.

With Loretta, he looked, but the cultists were disappearing into the fog. Seconds later they were screened from sight.

He exhaled, stepped back, grabbed her hand, wound her arm in his and started strolling once more. "We need to get off the streets. The longer we're out here, the fewer other couples there are around and the more we stand out and attract their attention."

After a moment, she leaned in; her warm breath brushed his throat as she murmured, "The area near the dock we came in on—didn't Julius say that was the wool merchants' quarter?"

He nodded. "Lots of wool gets shipped in and out of Rotterdam."

"So there must be wool warehouses." When he glanced at her, she smiled meaningfully. "If we seek shelter in one, at least we should stay warm."

Finding a wool warehouse took another fifteen minutes, but the search took them away from the area the cultists were patrolling—a very good thing. It didn't take much effort to open the warehouse door; alongside more conventional lessons, Rafe had learned to pick locks at Eton.

Loretta, however, was impressed.

While he prowled the warehouse checking for other doors, she plundered open bales, constructing a fluffy pallet on which to rest, then pilfered yet more fleeces to fashion a heavy blanket beneath which they could stretch.

Eventually sliding between the sheets she'd made of their cloaks, he gave very real thanks that she was a resourceful and understanding woman.

She snuggled close. He raised his arm and drew her closer so she could rest her head on his shoulder. She did, then with a sigh relaxed against him.

After a moment, she raised her head, kissed his jaw, then settled down again. "Just promise me one thing."

He glanced down at her. "What?"

"That you'll wake me in an hour or so, so I can keep watch and you can get some sleep."

He stared at her.

When he didn't reply, she gave a little snort. "Yes, I worked it out. We can't both sleep just in case the cultists somehow find us. One of us needs to be awake at all times." Shifting her head, she looked up at him through the shadows. "I trust you to keep watch over me while I sleep. It's only fair that you do the reverse—and you need to sleep. God knows what we might face tomorrow, and you even more than me will need your wits about you."

She held his gaze. "So promise me that—that you'll wake me in an hour or so and let me keep watch while you sleep."

Resourceful, understanding—and far too intelligent. Trapped in her gaze . . . he could do nothing but nod. "All right. I promise I'll wake you."

Her smile was worth the small capitulation; radiant, it warmed him. "Good." She patted his chest, settled her head down once more, spreading her hand comfortingly over his heart. He felt her smile, heard her soft, "Good night."

He smiled too, reluctant, yet . . . he pressed a kiss to her hair, then, one arm bent behind his head, he looked up at the ceiling and settled to wait out his watch.

Loretta shook him in the darkness before dawn.

He came instantly awake, felt her lips at his ear as she whispered, "I heard someone go past whistling. They didn't stop here, but I suspect we'd better be on our way."

He nodded, reluctantly threw back the wonderfully warm covers. They rose, quickly bundled themselves back into their cloaks, then put back the fleeces as they'd found them, and crept out of the warehouse.

They headed for the docks—the same trade docks they'd come in at. Fishermen and navvies were up with the dawn, and the taverns near the docks were open and ready to provide hearty breakfasts.

Rafe chose a tavern a trifle more refined than the rest, and after a quick reconnoiter, risked hiring a room and requesting hot water so they could wash and use the facilities. When they came downstairs, a substantial breakfast was ready and waiting in the tiny parlor.

They ate, and felt much better.

But the instant they were back on the streets, they saw cultists.

"Is it just my imagination," Loretta asked, as they emerged from yet another runnel down which they'd ducked to avoid closer inspection, "or are there more of them? Even more than yesterday?"

"There are more." Grimly, Rafe took her arm. He didn't add that some they'd seen that morning had been cult assassins; their appearance signified a significant deterioration in his and Loretta's situation. "We need to find shelter—somewhere we can see out the day in reasonable safety." Complete safety was something he couldn't even imagine.

But finding such a place . . .

"You said the cultists aren't Christian." Loretta glanced at him. "Would they be likely to search in a church?"

When he looked at her, she pointed . . . to a small stone church wedged between two other buildings.

He raised his brows. "It's worth a try." He glanced carefully around. "No cultists in sight. Let's see if the door's open."

It was. They spent the day in the rear pews of the old church, surrounded by the warmth of old wood, the chill of stone, and the musty smell of old prayer books and kneelers. The church remained quiet, its ancient silence undisturbed; they took turns napping, stretching out along the pew, head in the other's lap.

They left the church as the last of the daylight faded, and the smothering fog grew thick once more. By a circuitous route they returned to the tavern where they'd arranged to meet Johnson, backtracking frequently to ensure no one was following, then circling the tavern until Rafe was convinced that Johnson hadn't in any way—intentionally or unwittingly—betrayed them.

"No cultists watching," he finally declared. "Let's go in."

They claimed the same table they'd occupied the previous night. The same serving girl brought them the same food.

Unappetizing though the heavy mutton pie was, Loretta forced it down. She would need energy for whatever was to come; the last thing she needed was to faint from hunger at some critical moment.

Rafe seemed much less sensitive to the fare's shortcomings. He broke the coarse pastry, scooped up the filling and steadily ate.

Loretta poked at a piece of something unidentifiable coated in thick gravy. "I expect you've had much worse rations than this in your years of fighting."

Rafe swallowed, considered the pie in front of him, then raised his eyes to hers. "Much worse."

"So what was the worst?" If she could keep him talking, she might be able to get the pie down without thinking too much about it.

His smile suggested he understood; he obliged, regaling her with descriptions of dishes that rendered the unpalatable pie, in comparison, delicious.

She managed to adequately clean her plate. He'd ordered watered ale for her; she sipped, grateful to be able to replace the taste of stewed mutton with the less objectionable taste of hops.

The dinner hour was long past and the tavern had grown crowded again when Johnson arrived. He saw them, nodded their way, ordered ale for himself and the younger man by his elbow, then, mugs in hand, they made their way to Rafe and Loretta's table. With respectful nods, they drew up stools and sat.

"This is my son, Ned." Johnson tipped his head toward the younger man. "He'll get you to Felixstowe and those heathens be damned."

Ned looked thoroughly delighted; Rafe inwardly sighed.

He was getting too old to watch over wet-behind-the-ears youngsters. The last one he'd schooled had been . . . James.

The thought sobered him. He leaned on the table, caught Ned's eyes. "Make no mistake. They may appear to be light-weights, but they wield knives like devils. They're danger-ous—it would be a mistake to think otherwise."

Ned's grin faded a trifle, but he nodded, still eager. "We saw a few of them on the way here. There are so many In-dians and such like on the docks, I thought nothing of them until Da pointed out the black scarves."

Rafe nodded. Glanced at Johnson. "As long as you know the enemy, and respect what they're capable of."

Johnson grinned. "He's steady enough behind the wheel, never fear." He clapped his son proudly on the shoulder. "So—I've checked the tides and we'll be able to get you off in the wee hours." He glanced at the room, at the many sailors surrounding them. "I'm thinking it would be best to remain here until closing time at midnight, then we can head straight to the dock."

Still grinning, Ned bobbed his head. "I've left orders to have the boat ready to set out the instant we have the tide."

Rafe glanced at Loretta. He and she were one step away from Felixstowe and the safety of his waiting guards. He had little doubt that once they made contact with Wolver-stone's men, whatever happened, they would prevail.

Turning back to Johnson and Ned, he nodded. "You've planned well." He raised his mug to them both. "We're in your hands."

They all drank, then a commotion at the bar had the other two men turning. Rafe saw it was only two sailors arm wres-tling, and turned his attention to Loretta.

Meeting her eyes, seeing hope building, still banked but there, beneath the table he found her hand, squeezed, leaned closer to murmur, "I hope Hassan and Rose have been equally fortunate in finding passage to Harwich."

She squeezed back. "Who knows? Depending on who they found to take them, they might already be there."

Lifting her hand, he raised it to his lips, briefly kissed. "We can hope." He wasn't just talking about Rose and Hassan.

She knew. She smiled. "Yes, we can."

∾ Seventeen ∾

Johnson's boat, a good-sized fishing trawler, went by the moniker the *Molly Ann*.

They boarded her in the coldest, blackest hour of the night, just after the town's bells had tolled one o'clock. The fog had thinned somewhat, enough to see the black water of the river rippling beneath the gangplank.

After leading them aboard, Ned introduced his crew, all of whom were more his age than his father's. Johnson clapped Ned on the back, recommended the crew to be on guard, then, with gruff wishes for Rafe's and Loretta's safety and the successful completion of Rafe's mission, he left.

Ned conducted Rafe and Loretta to the prow, where a triangular section of planking designed to mount a forward anchor stretched from rail to rail, creating a small open compartment underneath. "This is probably the best place for you both. You can see me at the wheel"—Ned turned to point—"but you'll be out of sight of any other boat, and out of the wind and spray, too."

A young sailor rushed up with an armful of cushions. He bent and stuffed them into the space, quickly patting them down. Straightening, he blushed. "It's a fair ways to the other side—you'll be cramped enough as it is."

Loretta smiled and thanked him, which made him blush

even more, then she inclined her head graciously to Ned, and sank down, then wriggled back under the overhang.

Rafe thanked Ned, then joined her.

Seeing them both stowed, Ned grinned, saluted, and walked off to oversee his craft.

Rafe smiled to himself, caught Loretta's questioning look. "The enthusiasm of youth."

She gripped his arm, lightly stroked over the spot where the bandage still covered his wound. She'd yet to miss a day of her ministrations. Rafe closed his hand over hers, then settled to watch the crew at work.

They upped anchor and slipped away from the dock as the bells tolled two o'clock. Ned guided the boat between the others anchored in the basin; they passed many other medium-sized fishing vessels readying for sailing, but none had yet got underway.

The *Molly Ann* was the first vessel into the main channel; under sail, with the night inky black about them, her running lamps reflecting off the dark water, she rode the river out toward the sea.

Beside Loretta, Rafe stirred restlessly. She glanced at him. He was sitting with his arms about his knees, but glancing out and about; she sensed his frustration that he couldn't see what was around them and therefore couldn't adequately guard against danger.

She faced forward. "Once we meet with our guards, what then? Do you have any idea where they'll take us, or when?"

He frowned. "I assume . . . I'm certain that eventually they'll escort us to wherever Wolverstone is waiting, but I don't know where that is, or when we'll go there." He settled, considering. "As I'm carrying the vital document, I would think they'll want to get us to Wolverstone immediately, but with the other three possibly close by, too, there may be a need for delay. In which case they'll have to have somewhere to hide us, somewhere highly defendable against cult attack." He paused, then grimaced. "The truth is, once we meet with our guards, our immediate future will be in their hands."

"What about once you hand the document to Wolverstone?"

"That's . . . even harder to predict. It may take some time for him to focus the necessary attention on Ferrar."

"So what will you do while you're waiting? It's nearly Christmas, so assuming you get your letter to Wolverstone in the next few days, what then?" She looked at him, met his eyes.

He held her gaze for a moment, then, lips twisting, looked ahead. "As I mentioned, I haven't told my family that I'm returning. Given the risks of the journey, it seemed wiser to wait until I reached England safely, and my mission was complete. Time enough then to let them know I'd returned. So they're not expecting me for Christmas." He glanced at her. "What about you?"

She smiled. "My family's been expecting me and Esme to return this past month, but they know what she's like, so won't be surprised if we don't appear. A letter to my brother and sisters to let them know Esme and I are safe, and where we are, and that due to a vital patriotic mission involving the Duke of Wolverstone I've been delayed but will be home shortly, will serve to allay all concern. Indeed"—she widened her eyes—"a letter like that will cause boundless curiosity."

He reached over and took one of her hands, drew it across to cradle between his. "So what will you do for Christmas?"

She met his gaze, softly smiled. "I'd thought to spend it with you. If you'd like me to."

"I'd like you to." He raised her hand to his lips, pressed a kiss to her knuckles. "This Christmas, and the next, and all the Christmasses to follow, I'd like you to spend them with me, by my side."

"Well, then." She leaned her shoulder against his. "We have that to look forward to."

They didn't say more, but sat in companionable silence thinking—she hoped—of their shared future, planning, imagining . . . rather than dwelling on what dangers and threats currently lay between them and all they desired.

They saw the beam of a lighthouse, felt the ocean swell lift the hull, and knew they'd left the Continent and had started across the Channel itself.

From their position in the prow, they saw various of the crew draw Ned's attention to something some way off the starboard side.

Leaving the wheel to his first mate, Ned picked up a spyglass, looked, but then shrugged, spoke with his men, and returned to retake the wheel.

Sometime later, when the boat was steadily forging through the waves and dawn was a pale glimmer on the eastern horizon, Ned came walking to the prow. Spyglass in hand, he halted by their hiding place.

"Just as well you stayed out of sight." He kept his gaze up as if scanning the waves, but tipped his head toward starboard. "There were Indians with black head scarves on a flotilla of boats keeping watch on all the vessels coming out of the river mouth, and those leaving from up the coast, too. Howsoever, they didn't give us, or any of the other fishing boats, more than a cursory look. Scanned our decks, but didn't bother coming closer. They concentrated on the passenger boats, the ferries, and the private launches. Saw them come right up alongside one, hanging over their rails and looking at all the passengers."

Rafe exchanged a glance with Loretta, then looked back at Ned. "Are they keeping pace, or have they stayed by the coast?"

"They stayed—they're still searching. They're far behind us now, but some of those boats are fast, so it might be best if you stayed out of sight."

"We will." Rafe grimaced at the thought, but there was no alternative.

Ned all but imperceptibly nodded. "At least the winds are

better than I'd hoped for—we're going at a good clip, faster than I expected. At this rate we should be in Felixstowe by late afternoon."

"Excellent." Rafe watched as Ned turned and made his way back to the wheel, then looked at Loretta, met her blue eyes. Arched his brows. "Looks like our luck's still holding."

Daylight was waning toward a slatey-gray dusk and the breeze had whipped up to a stiff cold wind carrying the promise of ice and sleet when Ned left the wheel and, spyglass in hand, came striding toward the prow. As he neared, Rafe saw the concern in his face, the worry in his eyes.

Sensed that their luck had run out.

Ned halted by the prow, head up, brought the spyglass to bear as if he were searching ahead.

"What is it?" Loretta asked.

Ned spoke without looking down. "There's a line of ships—trawlers, yachts, even frigates—between us and the coast. Looks like some sort of blockade." He paused, then went on, "There are men on board all the boats—not just crew. Some are English ruffians of one stripe or another, but others are foreigners, Indian-looking with turbans and black scarves like before. The sailors are manning the ships, but the other men are giving the orders. They're stopping and searching all boats from the Continent looking to put in along this stretch."

"They're physically searching the boats?" Rafe asked.

"Yes. And we're not fast enough to outrun them."

Rafe swore. Stretching out his legs, he started massaging the cramped muscles. "How close are we to England?"

"Close," Ned said. "Even without a glass you can see the line of the land, the spume of the breakers."

"How far are we from the nearest enemy ship?"

"About a nautical mile."

Rafe frowned. "Where exactly are we in relation to the coast?"

"Wait there." Ned turned away. "I'll fetch a map."

By the time he returned and, crouching, spread a map on the deck in front of their hiding place, Rafe was itching to stand.

"We're here." Ned glanced over the gunwale, then pointed again. "The nearest ship, the one waiting to intercept us, is here."

To Loretta's surprise, Rafe glanced only briefly at the map, then he looked up, studied the sky, then looked at Ned. "In these conditions, can you swing to the southeast?"

Ned nodded, frowned. "But they'll follow, and there's nowhere we can put you ashore until Walton-on-the-Naze, and they'll come up with us long before then."

"We're not going that far." Rafe stretched up, peeked over the gunwale at the ship ahead of them, then sat back and focused on the map. "You need to take this course." He traced a path on the map. "Let them think you're running south to Walton, but as you pass the mouth of Hamford Water, if you slip us over the side in the clinker, I'll row in. Once we're closer to shore, the breakers will catch us—with the tide running our way, we'll get in easily enough. Meanwhile, you and your crew sail on and away. The boat following will follow us, not you—either go on to Walton or back out to sea, whichever you think is safest." Rafe handed over a purse, the rest of the agreed fee and a sizeable tip, then glanced again at the vessel lying in wait ahead. "If they try to follow the clinker in, they'll run aground, so the best they'll be able to do will be to send a rowboat after us."

"But . . ." Ned's concern was back in full measure. He glanced at Loretta, then back at Rafe. "Hamford Water's all marshes. Once you get through the mouth and behind the Naze, it's hard to find your way."

"Unless you had a bird-watching uncle who used to haul you all around Hamford Water every summer for years." Rafe glanced at Loretta; the look on his face, in his eyes, reminded her that his nickname was Reckless. He grinned.

"I never thought I'd be so grateful to Uncle Waldo, but"—he looked back at Ned—"night or day, I can find my way through there."

Ned hesitated, but then agreed to the plan.

Loretta didn't argue. One glance over the gunwale at the vessel drawing ever nearer—at the black-scarf-bedecked figures on its deck—and she was ready to quit Ned's boat whenever Rafe gave the word.

The next minutes went in brisk preparations as the clinker, suspended over the water at the ship's stern, was brought aboard and readied for launch over the ship's starboard side.

Loretta was touched by the sincerity of the crew, who paused by their hidey hole to bob their farewells and wish them luck.

Then Ned, who had retreated to the wheel and was watching the nearing vessel closely, called out a warning, and swung the wheel to the left.

The *Molly Ann*'s prow swung across the waves. The sail swung, was adjusted by ready hands, then swelled, puffed taut, and they started to run.

"Come on." Rafe took Loretta's hand and eased out of their cramped quarters. "We need to get ready to go over the side."

Dusk was deepening toward night when Rafe dropped from the boat's rail into the clinker, bouncing, suspended over the rushing waves.

Gripping the side of the smaller boat, he steadied, then, planting his feet wide, rose and reached up as the crew passed his satchel and Loretta's embroidery bag down. He stowed both beneath the crossbench, then, bracing his booted calves against the edge of the bench, reached for Loretta.

It was dangerous to attempt such a maneuver while the boat was running under full sail, bouncing every time it hit a wave crest, but they had no choice. Far better face this danger than the cultists in the boat swiftly following in their wake.

Rafe held his arms up, out, watched Loretta being lifted over the boat rail by one of the crew. The man held her until she got her feet on the deck's outer lip, held her until she gripped the rail . . . then he let her go. She held there for a moment, then lifted her eyes to Rafe's.

"Come on, sweetheart. I'll catch you."

She leaned forward, and let herself drop. Rafe caught her, wobbled, but managed to slowly ease her down. He heard her exhalation of relief when, her feet finally on the boards, she slid from his grasp and dropped onto the rear bench.

He quickly sat facing her, checking the oars, then looking around. Ahead. Through the deepening gloom, he could see the spray where the waves were breaking against the shore, but then came a relatively sprayless section—the opening of Hamford Water—then the spray gushed up once more from the waves breaking on the southern promontory's shore.

He looked up. The first mate was standing by the rail, squinting in the same direction. Then the man called to Ned. Immediately, the boat's speed slackened, then rapidly fell away as the main sail was loosened off.

Rafe glanced back at the pursuing boat. Earlier he'd used the spyglass to check, and almost wished he hadn't. The boat didn't carry just cultists, but assassins as well. They would definitely give chase.

At the moment, however, Ned and his crew had run hard enough to give him and Loretta a reasonable chance to make it into the marshes. After that, Rafe would have to rely on his wits to elude their deadly pursuers.

The boat slowed, and slowed.

Finally, the first mate gave the order and the crew waiting on the winches bent to their task. "Hold on!" Rafe warned Loretta. She grabbed the clinker's sides with a white-knuckled grip as it jerkily fell, bit by bit, until with a splash they were in the water.

With quick flicks, the sailors released the ropes.

With one oar, Rafe pushed away from the boat's side, then raised a hand in salute. "Thank you! Now go!"

Grabbing the oars, he bent and put his back into forcing the rowboat through the rolling swell. Once the clinker gained a little momentum and slid out of the boat's wave-shadow, the waves caught it and pushed it on.

They heard a "Good luck!" come over the water. Loretta twisted around and raised her hand in farewell.

Then the main sail on the boat filled again, and it drew away, steadily gaining speed.

Loretta turned the other way and peered back through the deepening twilight. "The other boat is coming on, but I think it's slowing."

Rafe glanced up from his task, confirmed it. "I need you to watch the shore and guide me, so I can row without looking around."

Loretta instantly faced forward, peering past him at the shore.

"Can you see the tower to your left?"

"Yes. A tall round tower?"

"That's the Naze Tower. We need to keep it on our left, and aim for the space further to its right where the water runs differently—flatter because it's rolling in and there's no shore for it to break against. Can you make that out?"

"Yes." Her voice grew stronger. "I can see it. At the moment, it's almost directly behind you."

"Good. The waves are going to push me off course a little—tell me which way to correct to keep heading for that spot."

He put his back into rowing while she kept her gaze trained on the shore, every now and then directing him a little to the right to keep on course.

Because she was facing the shore and was so absorbed, she didn't see the boat that had been pursuing them—a small frigate—draw nearer and nearer, but then veer to the south, slow, and come to a halt, bobbing on the waves. Clearly a local captain who knew of the shoals and tricky shallows at the mouth of the marsh.

As he rowed, Rafe prayed that the captain, knowing of

the marsh, would convince the cultists that there was no point pursuing them . . . but that was one prayer that went unanswered. Through the increasing spume as they neared the shore, he saw two rowboats lowered over the frigate's side—with two cultists as oarsmen in each, and an assassin in each prow.

Mentally cursing, he redoubled his efforts.

Loretta signaled for another correction, and he leaned back, hauling the oars through the waves—felt the give, the sudden easing of resistance as they slipped past the line where the surf met the calmer waters of the marsh.

The crest of a last wave caught the hull, lifted it and sent it sliding between the low headlands.

Rafe looked around, desperately locating landmarks, even more desperately making his next plans.

The deeper they went into the marsh, the darker the night became. The dense blackness as yet unbroken by any moonlight or even a glimmer of phosphorescence worked to their advantage. To Rafe's relief, memories washed through him with the ease of old friends, and guided him. All he needed was the lay of the surrounding land to have a reasonable notion of where he was; silhouetted against the stars, shapes triggered recollections, even in the otherwise pervasive dark.

His senses remembered the different sounds of the water as it slid, softly sibilant, beneath the hull, told him whether he was in a deeper channel, or had strayed too close to a marshy hillock. He used the oars to check depth, then push them on.

Although in this area the advantage of terrain was his, the instant he'd seen the assassins in the rowboats, he'd jettisoned any thought of trying to eliminate their pursuers. Four cultists, and he would probably have made the attempt, but six in all, with two being assassins . . . it would have been too risky even if he hadn't had Loretta with him.

So stealth and guile had to be his weapons. He had to

use both to gain as much of a lead over their pursuers as he could, enough to allow them to escape.

God only knew what waited for them ahead, but he'd deal with one problem at a time. Luckily, after deserting them for several hours, luck had again swung their way. The wind had picked up, whistling through the reedy grasses, the eerie sound masking the dip and drip of his oars.

Since slipping into the marsh, neither Loretta nor he had spoken. When she'd glanced his way, he'd caught her eye and signaled her to silence. Sounds carried all too well over water, wind or not. She'd swung around on the stern bench and kept watch, peering back over the marsh behind them.

He rowed as fast as he dared, which in these conditions wasn't that fast. He paused constantly to check the landmarks he recalled, to make sure he was where he thought he was, in the channel he thought he was. The last thing he needed was to run the clinker aground on some spit, and have to splash about refloating the boat.

From the cries and curses that reached them on the wind, at least one of the pursuing boats had either accidentally or on purpose made landfall, only to discover that there was precious little firm footing. It was easy in the dark to mistake the squelchy marsh islands peppering the channels for true land.

Rafe doggedly followed the course in his head, one drawn from his long-ago memories. Grim, tense, he prayed the channels and islands hadn't changed too much in the decade and a half since he'd last seen them.

His relief when he came upon the outlet of the stream more or less where he'd thought it would be was acute. He swung the prow of the clinker into it, then, bending forward, rowed harder, pushing the small boat upstream.

Gradually, the banks of the stream closed around them.

Loretta allowed herself to breathe a touch easier. The banks were now high enough to conceal them, and the stream wound along, quickly hiding them from any pursuers. It was like traveling along an open tunnel cut through the land. Gradually she realized the stream was growing shallower, and shallower. She wondered where Rafe was taking them, but even now didn't want to risk a question. Although they'd evaded their pursuers, they couldn't be far away.

Then they rounded another bend and a jetty loomed ahead, a denser black against the night sky.

She looked at Rafe, pointed. He glanced over his shoulder, then nodded. He changed course, and made for the jetty.

Expertly he turned the boat, and it slid slowly, silently, into the jetty's shadow. Just beyond, the ground rose, and further back yet, a thatched roof was discernible against the sky. After shipping the oars, he stood, gripped the slatted ladder fixed to the jetty's side, signaled her to silence again, then waved her up. She rose; he helped her to her feet, then held the boat steady as she climbed.

Stepping onto the jetty, she turned, and took her bag and his satchel as he passed them up. Instantly felt the weight in the satchel. He was wearing his scabbarded saber, and was carrying pistols and shot; nothing else could be that heavy.

He swiftly climbed the ladder, then reclaimed the satchel. After scanning the area, he passed the satchel's strap over his head and one shoulder, then crouched to tie up the clinker.

Loretta looked up at the sky. The moon had finally risen, but was screened by scudding clouds. Only faint light seeped through.

Rafe rose, caught her in a quick, reassuring hug, then he released her, grasped her hand, and started walking quickly up the grassy bank, away from the stream.

Before them lay a small hamlet—a few houses behind hedges, a small village inn with a shop beside it. She read the script above the inn door. The Beaumont Arms.

Rafe strode on, past the inn and on down a lane. More cottages lined it, scattered here and there. Lights glowed behind the curtains in some of the windows.

Loretta tugged at Rafe's hand. When he looked inquiringly her way, she pointed at the nearest cottage.

He looked, but shook his head. Leaned near to whisper, "It's too close to the stream and the rowboat." He looked ahead, along the lane, then turned back to add, still speaking low, "I know a place we can hide."

As if she needed convincing, from a distance a curse reached them, borne on the shifting wind.

She nodded, tightened her grip on his hand, and beside him walked quickly on into the night.

Rafe led Loretta to Stones Green, an even smaller hamlet a mile further north from the jetty at Beaumont. Although they'd started off in a lane, he'd soon climbed a stile and set off across the fields, before joining another lane.

They crested a rise, and, descending, saw the first cottages ahead, but before they reached the first, he turned sharp left down a track so narrow it would be near impassable in even the smallest gig. Thorny hedges almost met over his head.

He hoped the shortcut he'd taken would buy them enough time.

He was hoping even harder, indeed, praying, that his Uncle Waldo hadn't died while he'd been overseas. He walked swiftly to where a massive fir loomed dark and dense by the side of the track. Ducking under the thick branches that drooped nearly to the ground, he drew Loretta into the tiny porch of the cottage tucked into the lee of the tree.

Crouching, he slid his fingers behind the ivy that draped the cottage's walls and into the crevice at the corner of the porch. Relief washed over him as he touched metal. Drawing out the key, he fitted it into the heavy lock, turned the key, and opened the door.

Loretta stared at him. He waved her in, then followed her over the threshold. She halted immediately. The room inside, the parlor, lay in absolute darkness. Setting a hand to her back, he urged her a foot further inside, then quietly closed the door and locked it.

Turning back to the room, to Loretta, a denser shadow ahead of him, he murmured, "Wait here. I'll open the curtains over the opposite windows—that should let in some light."

Not much, but enough for them, with their eyes already adjusted to the night, to see well enough to avoid the furniture.

He crossed the room without knocking over anything, pulled aside the curtains, then turned. In the increased illumination, he saw Loretta looking around her.

"A lamp?" She glanced at him.

He waved at the sideboard, but said, "Not yet."

She froze. "Are they still following us?"

"I don't know, but I don't want to take any chances." He pointed to the stairs leading up. "There's a bedroom above—we can watch the lane from there."

She nodded. Clutching her bag, she waited until he came to lead the way, then followed him up the stairs.

The bedroom was as he remembered it. "This is my uncle Waldo's hideaway—he's an avid birdwatcher, and this is where he stays when he comes to study the birdlife on the marshes."

The stairwell had been lit by a small landing window, but the bedroom lay in darkness. Loretta waited in the doorway until Rafe drew aside the curtains covering the windows facing toward the lane. Enough light seeped in for her to see the big bed against one wall. She set down her bag on the bed's end and went to join Rafe as he stood looking out of the window.

Might they see us? The words were on her tongue, but as she neared the window, she realized there was little danger of that. The heavy branches of the fir draped across the window; although they could peer past the needlelike leaves, she doubted anyone glancing that way would see them.

As if he'd read her mind, Rafe murmured, "You can't see the cottage from the main lane—the tree covers it."

His breath warmed her ear. She reached for his hand, gripped it, and stared back at the rise where the lane into the hamlet was clearly visible.

Five minutes passed uneventfully, then Rafe leaned close to murmur, "Why don't you lie down on the bed and rest?" When she glanced at him, he continued, "I'll keep watch for a while, then join you."

She hesitated, but now they'd stopped moving, tiredness dragged at her. She nodded. "All right, but tell me if you see anything."

Rafe squeezed her hand, then released it. He kept his gaze trained on the exposed stretch of lane. He heard the bed creak, then heard her sigh.

Swiftly, he glanced at her, saw her lying on her side, her hand beneath her cheek, her eyes closed, her cloak gathered around her, then looked back at the lane.

It was too dark to read the face of his fob watch. By his best guess, close to half an hour had passed when two men came over the rise, almost running down the lane. Seeing the hamlet before them, they slowed, taking stock, then they moved quickly on, jogging past the opening of the track and on toward the visible houses.

At no point did either man glance toward Waldo's hideaway.

The house was hard enough to find in daylight. Rafe told himself that, yet he still waited for what he estimated was another half hour before he accepted that they were temporarily safe. Leaving the window, he shrugged off his satchel and laid it aside, then eased himself down onto the bed beside Loretta.

Mentally blessing Waldo, he stretched out, closed his eyes. Heard Loretta's soft breathing, inwardly smiled.

He fell asleep a heartbeat later.

A manor house outside Needham Market

Alex woke to the sound of a small brass bell.

It was still dark—late night at a guess, not even early morning. Someone had lit a small lamp; the glow diffused through the room.

Sitting up, Alex looked toward the source of the light. M'wallah stood at the foot of the bed, his dark face impassive.

Even before Alex's brows rose, Saleem stepped out from behind M'wallah. "Carstairs has landed."

Alex waited, then, voice hardening, prompted, "And . . . ?"

"As you directed, the boat he was in was pursued and pushed off course, but before our vessel could come up with it and board, Carstairs was put over the side in a rowboat. He had a woman with him, as our men in Bonn reported, but there was no sign of his man, the Pathan, or the other woman." Saleem fixed his dark gaze on the bedpost beside Alex's head. "Our men gave chase—six men in two rowboats, two assassins among them. They followed Carstairs into what proved to be a marsh. Our men could not at first find the way. By the time they did, Carstairs had got well ahead. The two assassins went on in one boat, hoping to come up with him, and sent the others back to report. The rider they sent just rode in with this news."

Alex sat perfectly still for an instant, then snarled, tossed back the covers, and reached for a robe. "Where, exactly, did he land? Show me!"

Within minutes a map was spread on the manor's dining table. Alex leaned over it.

Saleem consulted with the drooping rider in his own

tongue, then pointed. "Here. This is where he came ashore. Where he went after, we do not yet know."

Alex studied the detailed map, looked from the marshes north. "You say the ship he was in ran south, so it was making for Harwich or Felixstowe."

Again Saleem spoke to the rider, then reported, "The captain of the vessel we had hired, the one that gave chase, said the ship Carstairs was on was one of the Felixstowe fishing fleet."

Alex's brows rose. "Felixstowe . . . so most likely we are correct in thinking he's coming this way . . ."

A long moment passed. Neither M'wallah nor Saleem was foolish enough to interrupt the Black Cobra's cogitations.

Then Alex straightened. "I want all our men in the field— every last one except for my guard and you two. We will wait here, at the center of our web. I want our men, all of them—call back all those who are anywhere else—and put every last man in a cordon, a net tight enough not to allow anyone through unobserved. From here." One long finger jabbed at a village just north of Stowmarket. "To here." The finger traced a path southwest to Sudbury. "We know the puppetmaster lies somewhere north and west of that line, so to reach him Carstairs will have to cross it."

Alex looked at Saleem. "I want our men in a line close enough to maintain visual contact, one with the other. When Carstairs crosses our line, I want him taken, and I want to be informed. Immediately."

Saleem's dark eyes gleamed. He bowed his head. "It will be as you say, illustrious one."

"Go." As Saleem left, Alex glanced at M'wallah. "We are in a good position here—close enough to our line to be quickly and easily reached. There is no need for us to move."

M'wallah bowed low. "And your guard? What should I tell them?"

Alex smiled. "To sharpen their swords." Looking back at the map, expectation and anticipation welled. "This is the final game we will play with the puppetmaster—it has commenced, and I have no intention of losing. The instant Carstairs reaches our line—the instant he touches our web—he will be trapped, and like a spider alerted, we will ride out, the elite with you, Saleem, and me, at their head. We will triumph."

Studying the map, Alex murmured, "The puppetmaster will not imagine we can put so many men into the field. He doesn't know that we've guessed the position of his lair, and so can predict the direction this last vital courier must take. So in acting as I've ordered, we'll be doing the unexpected." Alex smiled. "And as I have so often proved, the unexpected usually wins."

~ Eighteen ~

Rafe woke to see the sky beyond the window, beyond the drooping branches of the fir, lightening to a pearlescent midgray. As he watched, clouds scudded past, darker, thicker, distinctly threatening, but at least it wasn't raining.

Turning his head, he looked at Loretta, still asleep beside him. He didn't think she'd moved all night. He didn't think he had either.

Pushing aside his coat, he reached into his waistcoat pocket, pulled out his fob watch. Nearly half past six. He rewound the watch, tucked it back.

His shifting had jiggled Loretta. She stirred; her lids rose. She looked into his eyes, then her expression eased. Yawning, she rolled onto her back. "I take it we lost them?"

"For now. Two assassins followed us, but they went straight on down the lane. They had no idea we'd stopped here." Staring at the ceiling, he weighed his thoughts, then said, "I've a nasty suspicion I'm the last one in—the last courier to reach England. Were I Wolverstone, that's what I would have done—used the others to clear the way, leaving me with the vital document to come in last, and hopefully therefore encounter least resistance."

"*Least* resistance?" Loretta turned her head to stare at him. "But we've seen so many cultists already."

"Exactly, and it's not just men the Black Cobra's throwing our way, but money, too. Setting up two naval blockades, one on either side of the Channel, would have cost a significant sum. That suggests the Black Cobra is desperate. That for the fiend and his cult, stopping me from reaching Wolverstone, or passing on the document in any way, is imperative." He met her eyes. "They're going to do anything and everything to stop me."

Her chin firmed, then she looked past him to the window. "In that case, we'd better get moving. The sooner we reach your guards, the better."

He led the way downstairs, alert, wary, but there were no surprises waiting for them. They took advantage of the pump in the kitchen to wash, shivering at the water's icy bite.

Waldo clearly hadn't been in residence recently; there was no food of any kind in the cupboards. Cheeks rosy from the cold, fully awake, but sadly hungry, they slipped out of the cottage, locked the door, and put the key back in its hiding place.

"Once this is all over, I'd like to meet your uncle Waldo," Loretta said.

"When this is over, I'm going to present him with a magnum of his favorite whisky."

"Do they make magnums of whisky?"

"I'm sure they can be persuaded to." Taking her hand, his satchel over his shoulder, Rafe set off along the track.

Not back to the lane, but away from it.

Carrying her bag in her other hand, Loretta glanced back, then focused on Rafe's face. "What's your plan?"

"We missed the rendezvous at the Pelican last night. I doubt Allardyce and Hendon will leave Felixstowe, at least not immediately. As I don't know where to find Wolverstone, we'll need to get to Felixstowe and find them."

Loretta looked around, then back at him. "Aren't we going in the wrong direction?"

His smile was grim. "We can't head directly to Felixstowe, because that's what the cult will expect us to do. We're going to have to circle around."

Elveden Grange, northern Suffolk

By seven o'clock that morning, the dining room of Elveden Grange was a hive of activity. Grim-faced men pored over maps spread over the large table. Deep voices posed questions; others suggested answers. The breakfast dishes arrayed on the sideboard lay largely ignored as the all-male company made plans.

On learning at one o'clock that Rafe Carstairs had failed to make the arranged rendezvous at Felixstowe, but that others of his party had arrived there, Royce Varisey, Duke of Wolverstone, had sent a rider to summon the Cynsters. Longtime friends of the four couriers coming in from India, the Cynsters had a real and personal interest in the game underway. And, as Royce had prophesized, he would need them today.

Devil Cynster, his five cousins, and Gyles Chillingworth had answered the call, riding over from Somersham Place. They'd arrived at five o'clock, along with Colonel Derek Delborough and Major Gareth Hamilton, the first two of the couriers to reach their goal. The third, Major Logan Monteith, had remained overnight at Elveden; he and his lady had arrived only the day before.

Also helpfully staying under Elveden's roof were six ex-colleagues with whom Royce had worked for years; he was immeasurably grateful to have their many talents at his disposal that morning.

Standing at the head of the table, he picked up the salt cellar and rapped smartly, calling the group to order. As the talk died, he glanced around the table. "Thank you for coming. Before we discuss any plan of action, let me bring you up to date with what we know."

Riders had been back and forth to Felixstowe several times already, racing through the dark watches of the night.

"Allardyce and Hendon, at Felixstowe, have confirmed that, as of five o'clock this morning, Carstairs and the young lady traveling with him had yet to arrive. However, Carstairs's man, Hassan, arrived at the rendezvous as expected last evening, along with the young lady's maid. Hassan reports that in order to evade capture at Rotterdam, the four, who until then had been traveling together, split into two couples. I'm not clear at this point when, why, or where Carstairs and Hassan joined forces with the lady and her maid, but at this juncture that's of little moment. What is pertinent is that Carstairs and the lady have not reached Felixstowe."

"Have they reached England?" From down the table, Delborough arched a brow. "Do we have any idea?"

"As to that, the last rider brought unexpected news. Hendon has been haunting the docks, hoping to either find Carstairs or learn something of his fate from the fishing fleet as it came in. The first thing he learned was that, through yesterday afternoon and evening, the Black Cobra mounted an effective blockade off the coast, searching all vessels heading for Harwich and Felixstowe. Hassan and the maid didn't encounter the problem because they came in the day before. But Carstairs . . . Hendon heard from a few fishermen that they'd seen another boat run from the blockade. It was chased off-course, but got close enough to shore to put a rowboat over the side. The fishermen saw the rowboat, with a man and woman in it, and chased by two other rowboats manned by what sounded like cultists, make it into the marshes inland of the Naze." Leaning over the map, Royce pointed. "Here."

"So Rafe slipped through the blockade and . . . what?" Gareth glanced at Royce. "He's got a lady with him and was running from at least four cultists?"

"According to those watching, there were six pursuers. However, the boat that ferried Carstairs across the Channel escaped while he was rowing in. The fishermen identified the vessel as the *Molly Ann*, one of the Felixstowe fleet. Hendon quartered the harbor, and found the *Molly Ann* tucked away on a minor dock. The young captain was suspicious at first, but Hendon convinced him of his bona fides—aside from verifying all that the others had said, the captain added that Carstairs knows the marshes. It was his idea to put in there—he was confident he could use the difficult terrain to his advantage, and so lose the cultists."

"Rafe has a talent for pulling off apparently harebrained forays." Logan Monteith straightened from the table, his gaze scanning the map. "Assuming he's succeeded and evaded capture, where's he likely to be?"

"Holed up?" Vane Cynster queried. "Or will he keep moving?"

"He won't head for Felixstowe," Delborough said. "At least not directly."

Gareth nodded. "Because he'll assume that's where the cult will expect him to go. So he won't go there."

"Perhaps not," Royce conceded. "But like the three of you, beyond the rendezvous with his guards, he doesn't know where he's supposed to head." He sighed. "I didn't give him even a specific destination, because all those months ago I couldn't be sure how this mission's details would run."

"Unavoidable," Devil Cynster said. "But while he doesn't know where you might be, he does know where I am." He glanced at Royce. "He might make for Somersham Place."

Royce met Devil's eyes, then nodded. "You're right." Leaning over the table, resurveying the map, Royce pointed again at the marshes. "He was here last evening. He might be holed up in some safe place and be waiting for the cult to lose interest, he might have found somewhere to rest for the night and already be moving again, or he might have kept moving all night."

Delborough shook his head. "He's got a lady with him, so he's not moving that fast."

"The cult know where he was," Gareth pointed out. "They'll have known for longer than we have."

"Indeed." Royce nodded. "I think we can safely assume that the Black Cobra and the bulk of the cult—his remaining forces—are going to be concentrated. . . . most likely between us and Ipswich." He waved a hand across that section of the map. "They have men in Felixstowe already, but they can't know Carstairs doesn't know his destination. Although the Black Cobra might keep some men there, given the blockade, he'll assume Carstairs will now bypass Felixstowe and make for here, meaning in this general direction, as the other three of you did."

"So the Black Cobra—the real Black Cobra—is somewhere between us and Ipswich and the marshes south of it." Del glanced at Royce.

Royce met his eyes. "If cultists capture Carstairs, are they likely to kill him and take the scroll-holder to their master, or will they take Carstairs himself, alive?"

Del glanced at Gareth, then Logan, then looked across the table at Devil, before returning his gaze to Royce. "I'd wager my life on the latter. Even more so if Rafe still has the young lady with him."

Royce nodded tersely. "That's my reading of this, too. So Carstairs won't be in mortal danger until he's in the presence of the Black Cobra."

"So what's our plan?" Devil asked.

Royce's expression was all lethal intent. "We let Carstairs run wherever he may—we go after the Black Cobra."

"It's after ten o'clock. Where the devil has the damned man gone?" Alex paced the drawing room of the manor house outside Needham Market, cold fury investing every stride.

"He has not gone to Felixstowe." M'wallah sat on a stool, a map spread on his knees.

His hand on his scimitar's hilt, Saleem stood at the older man's shoulder. "His man is there, with the guards sent to meet Carstairs, but neither Carstairs nor the young lady have reached there."

Alex halted, eyes narrowing. "Could it be a ruse? Could the man have the letter, and Carstairs be a stalking horse?"

Saleem exchanged a glance with M'wallah, then carefully said, "We do not believe that is likely, illustrious one. The men waiting for Carstairs searched all night—why, if they had the letter already? Were that so, surely they would have taken it immediately to the puppetmaster and left Carstairs to lead us further astray."

Alex considered, then conceded with a nod. "True. But none of our men have sighted him yet."

Watching Alex, pacing again, bite a nail, Saleem fixed his gaze across the room and reiterated, "Our cordon is in place from northeast of Stowmarket to southwest of Sudbury. The instant Carstairs attempts to cross our line, we will have him. Our men will bring him here, to you. We have only to wait and he will fall into your trap."

M'wallah looked up from the map. "We assumed, oh, illustrious one, that Carstairs would travel on through the night, fleeing our men. If that were so, he would indeed be nearing our cordon. But what if he had to rest? The lady might not have been able to carry on."

Alex halted, then, after a moment, slowly nodded in agreement. "Yes, you're right. I forgot about her. And I shouldn't." A slow smile curved Alex's lips. "Especially as I strongly suspect she will be the key to breaking Carstairs."

A tap sounded on the door. M'wallah called, "Come."

A young cultist pushed through the door carrying a tray loaded with teapot and cups. He set the tray down on a table near M'wallah. The older man rose, poured tea into a delicate cup, then lifted the milk pitcher and tipped—only a small amount of milk dribbled out.

The old man raised his head, with his dark gaze pinned the young cultist.

The young man cowered. "It is all we have, excellency."

Alex, who had retreated to the window, looked around, saw. Stared for a moment, then waved toward the door. "Go and fetch more. We are not moving yet."

Bobbing and bowing all but to his toes, the young man backed toward the door.

Saleem turned to him. "Do not go into the town itself—we do not need to let these locals know we are here. Find somewhere nearby, beyond the town, where you can buy or steal some milk."

Close to terrified, the young cultist nodded, and slid out of the room.

Holding the reins of the gig he'd hired in one hand, Rafe drew out his fob watch, glanced at the face, then tucked it back into his pocket.

"What time is it?" Loretta asked from beside him.

"Ten-thirty." Rafe glanced at her, then looked ahead. "We'll stop in Hadleigh. We both need to eat."

Loretta nodded. She was feeling light-headed. Their last meal—and it hadn't even been that decent—had been at the tavern in Rotterdam, and they hadn't eaten much during the preceding day, either. If they were to match wits with the Black Cobra, they needed sustenance.

Rafe had led her west along the track to another lane, and eventually to another hamlet, Goose Green, near the road between Harwich and Colchester. There he'd hired a gig, and driven them not toward Harwich and so closer to Felixstowe but southwest toward Colchester. As he'd explained, that wasn't the direction in which the cult would expect him to go. But he'd soon turned off the road back onto the small country lanes. Exhibiting a reassuring sense of direction, he'd tacked through the quiet byways, eventually passing through the small village of Dedham. Exercising all caution, they'd crossed the main road between Colchester and Ipswich, then plunged back into a haphazard network of country lanes.

Once Rafe had been sure they weren't being pursued, he'd paused to consult his map, then turned the horse north toward the village of Hadleigh.

Five minutes later, they crested a shallow rise and saw the village ahead of them.

"It's near a minor crossroads, but we're far enough from any main road—the village itself should be safe enough." Rafe added, almost to himself, "Assuming there are no cultists actually stationed there."

Tense, eyes scanning the pavements, the tiny connecting lanes, they trotted along the main street, then, steeling himself, Rafe took the risk of turning beneath the archway into the inn yard.

A quick survey showed no cultists lounging anywhere. A lad came running to take the horses. Rafe stepped down, rounded the gig, and lifted Loretta down. Taking her arm, he caught the ostler's eye. "We're stopping for a late breakfast. Have you seen any foreigners around? Indians or the like?"

The boy shook his head. "No, sir. None."

Rafe tossed him a coin, which the boy deftly caught. "Let me know if you or any of your friends spot one." With his head Rafe indicated the inn. "I'll be inside."

The boy grinned, tugged his forelock. "Yessir."

Still feeling as if his senses wanted to be searching everywhere around, Rafe guided Loretta up the steps and through the inn's side door.

A rotund innkeeper came sweeping up to them. With a manufactured smile and the application of a little charm, Rafe organized a private parlor and requested a late breakfast.

Loretta glanced at him, then informed the innkeeper, "A large breakfast, with a large pot of tea."

The innkeeper smiled and bowed them into the parlor. "Indeed, ma'am. Right away."

Following Loretta into the parlor, Rafe scanned the small room, waited until the door shut, then walked to the window.

It looked out over the inn's rear garden, but was screened by a large tree. Safe enough.

"I didn't see hide nor hair of any cultist." Loretta placed her bag on a chair by the window. "And if that lad didn't know of them—"

"We might be safe—at least for the moment." Rafe removed his satchel and left it with her bag, then trailed her to the table and held her chair.

"At least long enough to eat a decent meal." She sat.

He took the seat diagonally to her left, facing the door and the window.

Their meal arrived, borne by the innwife and a small tribe of serving girls. When all the platters were deposited and displayed, Loretta smiled and declared they were satisfied and would ring for anything more they required.

The gaggle of females withdrew, and they settled in unexpectedly pleasant peace to eat.

Not that they relaxed.

When Rafe finally heaved a huge sigh and pushed away his empty plate, Loretta, sipping a last cup of tea, arched a brow at him. "What next?"

He studied her for a long moment, then said, "We have to make a decision. Do we run and hide? We could, for instance, go to London, take refuge at some place like Grillons, then send word to the Cynsters. They'll know how to contact Wolverstone. That's one option, but it will give the cult more time to track us and try to take the letter."

She studied his face. "Such a course would prolong your mission."

"And extend the time we'd both be at significant risk from the cult."

"So what's our other option?"

He frowned. "I believe we have two. At this time of year the Cynsters will be at Somersham Place—that's in Cambridgeshire, this side of Cambridge, so not too far away. They're involved in this and will know where Wolverstone is, so we could try to go there. However, I'd wager they'll have been involved in the later stages of the other couriers' journeys. If so, the cult will know of them—there might even be cultists watching the roads, waiting for me to head that way. So"—he grimaced—"I don't think that's a wise option either. Which leaves us with our original direction—go to Felixstowe, meet with my guards, and learn where we're supposed to go next."

She lowered her cup. "The Black Cobra doesn't know that you don't know where Wolverstone is, does he?"

He shook his head. "So I'm hoping he'll expect me to head on toward wherever the other couriers went, and won't imagine that I'll circle back to Felixstowe." Sitting up, he pulled the map from his pocket.

She moved the platters to the far side of the table and he spread out the map.

"We're here." He pointed at the spot marked Hadleigh. He paused, then with his finger traced a route northward via a series of tiny lanes to another village. "I think we should go here, to this village."

Leaning forward to peer at the map, she frowned. "Why there?"

"Because Somersham is here, Felixstowe is here, and that village lies on the road between, and I'm betting that wherever we need to go, wherever it is that Wolverstone's waiting, it's somewhere in that general area—between Somersham and Felixstowe. Given I'm the last courier carrying the vital evidence, I can't see it being any other way.

"As for why that particular village, although it's on the road, it's so small there's no reason the cult would be watching it." He glanced up, met her eyes. "I propose to leave you at an inn at or near there—something quiet and small, off the main road if we can find such a place. Somewhere no one will imagine you might be. I'll leave the gig there and hire a horse, and ride back to Felixstowe—I'll be approaching from the last direction anyone would expect me to come from, and I'll be a lone rider on a horse, not part of a couple."

She'd opened her mouth to protest, to argue, but as his

words sank in, she closed her lips. After a moment of thinking, of studying his eyes, his face, lips compressing, she nodded. "All right. I don't like letting you out of my sight, but you'll make better time on horseback, and be safer without having to protect me as well."

He smiled, a charming smile that warmed her. "Good. With any luck, the cult will be scouring the area around the marshes and will have given up on Felixstowe by now." He rose, drew back her chair as she stood.

Crossing to the window, she handed him his satchel, lifted her bag. "So, how long to Needham Market?"

An hour of driving as briskly as possible down the narrow lanes saw them nearing the outskirts of Needham Market. From a rise outside the hamlet of Barking, they'd seen the roofs of the village ahead, but then woods closed in about the narrow lane, a mixture of trees including sufficient pines and firs to provide protection from the cold wind.

The sky was an unrelieved steel gray as Rafe guided the gig over a wooden bridge spanning a tiny stream.

Almost immediately a large clearing opened to the left of the lane. A many gabled, white-painted lathe-and-plaster Tudor building sat comfortably sprawled on a wide lawn, the white of its walls stark against the black of the timber beams. Just ahead by the side of the road, a post supported a swinging sign proclaiming the place to be the Laughing Trout Inn.

Rafe slowed the gig. After one comprehensive survey, he glanced at Loretta.

At her encouraging nod, he turned the horse past the post and into the gravel drive that led to a small forecourt before the inn's front door.

Halting the horse, Rafe sat and took stock. "This looks promising."

"Indeed. It doesn't look like they get much traffic here."

"The main road must be at least a quarter of a mile further on." Rafe glanced toward where they'd seen the village roofs. "And the village itself is further west along the road."

Tying off the reins, he climbed down, then went to lift Loretta down. Feeling her slender, supple form between his hands, sensing her passionate vibrancy even just for that instant, reminded him of how lucky he was, not just to have her with him, his in all but name, but that they were so close to the end of his mission and she had remained safe. Unharmed, unthreatened.

As her feet settled on the gravel and he reluctantly released her, a middle-aged man appeared from around the back of the inn.

The man nodded. "Good day to you, sir. Will you be stopping long, or just for a meal?"

"At least for the rest of the day." Rafe waved at their horse. "If you could unharness him and rub him down, I'll settle matters inside, then I'll be out to take a look at your hacks. I need to ride to a meeting, but will be back by nightfall."

"I've just the horse for ye." The man saluted. "Just ring the bell and the missus will help you. The stables be 'round the back."

The man led the horse and gig away. Rafe followed Loretta across the gravel to the front door.

She tugged the dangling chain of the bellpull. He pushed open the heavy door, held it for her, then, ducking slightly to avoid the wide lintel, followed her into a black-and-white tiled hall.

The inn was ancient, but in sound condition, spick and span, and, just like the motherly woman who bustled out to greet them, warm and welcoming.

"Good day, sir, ma'am—I'm Mrs. Shearer. And what can we do for you today?"

It was the matter of a few minutes to hire a private parlor and a large bedchamber in which Loretta could wash and perhaps later rest. While she followed Mrs. Shearer upstairs to view the accommodation, Rafe went out and around to the stable. It didn't take long to approve the mount Mr. Shearer had saddled and ready.

Returning to the inn, Rafe went into the parlor. A large room, its door lay directly across the wide hall from the front door. Loretta was still upstairs. He prowled the room, checking the view from the wide window, reassured to see it merely looked over the private lawn to the thick wood bordering the stream.

The inn seemed utterly isolated.

Setting his satchel on the sofa, he opened it. Reaching to the bottom, he withdrew the scroll-holder. Considered it. Hefting it in his hand, he weighed his options, then turned and scanned the room. His gaze landed on the tall dresser set against the wall behind the door. He smiled, crossed to the far end of the dresser, the end close to the room's corner; reaching up, he set the scroll-holder on the dresser's overhanging top, behind the raised, ornate front edge.

Stepping back, he viewed the result. Not even a man as tall as he could see the scroll-holder; only someone as tall as he could reach it.

He'd intended leaving it with Loretta, but having it would mark her, and might land her in unnecessary danger. This was much better. He doubted Mrs. Shearer, house-proud though she clearly was, would be dusting up there this afternoon.

With one problem off his mental slate, he turned to address another. Returning to his satchel, he rummaged.

The satchel was resting innocently against the sofa cushions and he was standing looking out of the window when Loretta returned, Mrs. Shearer in her wake.

He arched a curious brow at their hostess. "It seems blissfully quiet here—is it just your husband and you running the inn?"

Mrs. Shrearer smiled. "My husband and me—we own it—and our son helps about the place. It's quiet now, but we get a lot of customers come for the fishing." She tipped her head at the window. "There's a stream in the woods there that leads to a lake full of trout, so we're busy for most of the year. Just these winter months that it's quiet."

Rafe nodded. "I imagine any fisherman once he's stayed here would remember and come back."

Mrs. Shearer beamed. "Aye, that seems the way of it." She looked at Loretta. "Now, miss, would you like a tray of something?"

"At the moment, a pot of tea would be welcome. We ate a late breakfast, so I really don't want any luncheon. Perhaps some scones and jam a little later."

"Oh, you'll like my scones—fresh from the oven they'll be. But I'll get that pot for you now." Mrs. Shearer bobbed, then whisked out of the room, closing the door behind her.

Rafe eyed the door, then glanced at Loretta. "Did she interrogate you as to my intentions?"

Loretta grinned. "Not yet, but doubtless that will come." Her smile faded as she looked at him.

Feeling grim himself, he walked to her, took her hands in his. "I don't like to leave you here alone, but . . ."

She squeezed his fingers. "It's best that you do."

He glanced at the door, then releasing her hands, stepped to the sofa. "While I'm gone, I want you to keep this with you at all times." Lifting the satchel, he slipped the strap over his head and shoulder, then picked up the small pistol that had lain hidden under the bag. Turning to Loretta, he held it out, balanced on one palm. "It's small, but effective."

She reached out, with one finger traced the fine silverwork on the handle.

He tipped his head, looked into her face. "Do you know how to fire a pistol?"

Jaw firming, she gripped the handle, lifted it from his hand. "I point it." She used both hands to do so, aiming at the side wall. "And pull this piece—the trigger."

"Yes, but you need to cock it first—like this." He showed her, had her prepare to fire, then ease the hammer back several times. "Best you don't cock it until just before you fire it. You won't want it going off accidentally."

"No." Loretta stared at the deadly little pistol she held rather gingerly, the barrel now pointing at the floor. She glanced at Rafe. "Best I don't need to use it at all."

Turning, she opened her embroidery bag and settled the pistol in among her few clothes. Leaving the bag on the sofa, she faced Rafe. "Thank you."

He closed his hands about her shoulders. His gaze roved her face as if drinking in each feature. "I'll be much happier if you don't have to use it. Take care." He drew her to him, bent his head and kissed her—not with overt passion, but with a deep sense of earnest desire, with profound hope, and one simple want.

One wish.

She kissed him back.

His hands rose, framed her face, tipped it more fully to his so he could deepen the caress.

Lifting one hand to cup the back of one of his, she clung to the promise embodied in the unshielded, heartfelt exchange.

He pulled back, broke the kiss. They both felt the wrench.

He looked into her eyes for one last instant, then released her and stepped back. "I won't be long."

"I'll be waiting." She followed him with her eyes as he walked to the door.

Rafe didn't look back, just opened the door, strode across the hall and out of the front door. Shutting it behind him, he instinctively scanned the small forecourt and surrounds, but other than Billy, the Shearers' son, holding the big bay gelding Rafe had hired, there was no one and nothing to disturb the pervasive tranquility.

Reassured, Rafe strode to Billy, took the reins, vaulted to the saddle, and rode for Felixstowe.

Inside the parlor, Loretta examined the pistol she'd tucked into her embroidery bag. While it fitted well enough, it would be awkward to retrieve it, let alone cock it before pointing it and firing.

She puzzled over it for a full minute—trying not to dwell on the fading hoofbeats outside—then an epiphany struck. Taking her embroidery bag with her, she whisked out of the parlor and hurried up the stairs.

Mrs. Shearer would be returning with her pot of tea soon.

When she rushed back down the stairs a minute later, she carried her cloak and muff as well as the embroidery bag. She'd left the pelisse she'd worn earlier upstairs, and had draped a woollen shawl about her shoulders.

Flitting back into the parlor and shutting the door, she quickly set her stage. Cloak draped over the arm of the sofa with the muff sitting in that corner, as if in preparation for a turn about the grounds. She sat, and settled her embroidery bag on her other side. The pistol was no longer in it, but in her muff.

No one thought anything of a lady's muff; it was one of those items that was next to invisible, but the pistol had fitted perfectly into the inner pocket, as if the pocket had been made for the purpose.

She'd just relaxed on the sofa cushions when a tap on the door heralded Mrs. Shearer and her tray.

"Here you are, miss." Mrs. Shearer eased the tray onto the small table before the sofa. "I've just put a few pieces of shortbread on a plate there, in case you'd like a nibble of something."

"Thank you, Mrs. Shearer. That looks wonderful."

Mrs. Shearer glanced about the room. "Is he off, then?"

"Yes—he'll be back in a few hours." Loretta poured, aware of Mrs. Shearer hovering, struggling with her curiosity and her conscience.

In the end, Mrs. Shearer shifted closer and lowered her voice. "I hope you don't mind me asking, miss, but I couldn't help but see that you wear no ring. You're not eloping, or anything like that, are you?"

Loretta smiled. "Sadly, no. Mr. Carstairs is a friend of my

family and is escorting me into Cambridgeshire to visit with friends, but he has business to attend to near here. However, he's unsure how long his meeting will take, and so we can't be sure if we'll be heading on this evening, or staying the night."

"Oh. I see." While not overtly disappointed at not having an elopement to assist with, a hint of that emotion colored Mrs. Shearer's tone. She straightened. "I'd best get back to my scones—ring when you're ready for them, miss, and I'll bring some right in."

"Thank you. I will." Loretta watched the door close behind her hostess, then smiled, sat back, and sipped her tea.

And wished she'd left her embroidery in her embroidery bag.

The way her mind was already circling, imagining, supposing, simply worrying, she would give a great deal for anything powerful enough to distract her until Rafe returned.

❧ Nineteen ❧

At just after one o'clock, M'wallah slid silently into the drawing room of the manor house outside Needham Market. The tension in the room was thick enough to cut; it had been escalating steadily with every minute that had passed and still they'd heard nothing of Carstairs.

M'wallah's patron, and route to greatness, paced incessantly back and forth before the windows, arms crossed, features set in an expression of cold, contained fury.

Saleem stood in the shadows by one wall, more patient, more deadly. Saleem met M'wallah's eyes.

M'wallah allowed his glee to show.

Saleem straightened.

Alex sensed the change, whirled to face M'wallah. "What?"

M'wallah bowed low—extra low. "Oh, illustrious one, fate, as ever, has consented to shine her bountiful light on your endeavor. The young one you dispatched to fetch milk—mindful of the injunction placed on him by Saleem, he circled the town and found an insignificant inn at which they were happy to fill a jug with milk in return for our coin. The woman there was preparing a tray for a guest lately arrived—a lady traveling with a gentleman. The woman was telling her husband that the couple had no real luggage, only what they were carrying with them. She described the gentleman as tall and handsome—a military man.

"Our young one was no fool—he asked nothing, for it was clear the woman knew nothing to the point. He paid for the milk and departed the inn, but went only so far as the surrounding wood and kept watch. Shortly after, he saw Carstairs—and he is quite certain it was Carstairs— come out, mount a horse, and ride away from the inn. He did not see where Carstairs went, but he is sure the captain did not ride through the town. It seems likely the captain is headed toward Felixstowe." M'wallah paused, then some- what gleefully added, "The lady, however, remains at the inn."

"Excellent," Alex purred, expression transformed by ex- pectant intent. "Bring me this enterprising young cultist so that I may question him and thank him personally." Alex looked at Saleem, met his eyes, smiled in overt anticipation. "Inform my guard and saddle our horses. At last, we ride."

Royce paused at Stowmarket to confer with his troops. They gathered in Gipping Way, the main street through the town.

Seventeen large men on horseback, with assorted grooms and others, also mounted, made for quite a show. The pris- oners they'd collected, cultists with their distinctive black- scarved turbans, added an element of the bizarre.

Devil sat his huge black stallion and, grinning appre- ciatively, watched while Royce, exercising his authority as Lord Lieutenant of the County, persuaded the innkeeper to open the cells beneath the inn that were used to hold miscre- ants. Subsequently, Lucifer, Demon, and some of his grooms escorted the seven captured cultists down into the bowels.

"We must remember not to forget them," Devil murmured as Royce swung up to his saddle.

Settling his gray gelding, Royce replied, "I seriously doubt Kent, the innkeep, will allow us that option."

They'd all agreed that the best way to scour the area was to form a cordon of mounted men, each riding within sight and sound of those flanking him. They'd started outside Bury St. Edmunds, and swept southeast, their immediate goal Ipswich, and if they hadn't found Rafe and the Black Cobra by then, further to Felixstowe and to the marshes where Rafe had come ashore.

They weren't traveling as fast as they might wish, but their search was thorough. Every cottage, every farm, every barn and haystack, was checked and cleared. They'd come upon the cultists just outside Stowmarket.

Lucifer and Demon reemerged and went to their horses.

"Right," Royce said. "So the cult has strung a line of men from outside Stowmarket to, according to our prisoners, Sudbury. They're waiting for Carstairs to run into the line, reasoning—correctly as it happens—that his ultimate goal lies beyond."

"If they're still waiting for him," Logan said, "then they haven't yet captured him."

"Indeed." Royce nodded. "At this point, that's excellent news. As we're now inside their line, there's a chance we'll find Carstairs before any cultists do. But the best news is that we now know where to find the Black Cobra." He, Charles, and Gervase had interrogated the prisoners before they'd brought them into the town. "According to our captives, the fiend is quartered at their current base—a manor house just north of Needham Market. They were dispatched from there in the small hours, and told to bring Carstairs, should they seize him, to that place."

"So the Black Cobra's waiting at this manor house?" Del's eager tone matched the anticipation, the heightened expectation, that had invested every man's expression.

"Yes." Royce's tone conveyed coldly focused intent. "I suggest, gentlemen, that we adjourn to this manor house, and pay our compliments to the Black Cobra."

No one bothered even to voice agreement. Royce and Devil spurred forward; the others turned their horses and formed up in their wake.

The townsfolk of Stowmarket watched the cavalcade thunder out, and wondered who had fallen foul of that warriors' brigade.

Patience, sadly, had never been her strong suit. Loretta strolled the lawns beyond the inn's parlor windows, her cloak wrapped about her, her hands inside her muff, her right hand closed about the butt of the pistol.

At least she was armed. And she was alert. She scanned the woods bordering the lawn, but neither saw nor sensed any danger.

If she hadn't come out into the cold, clear air, she would have gone quietly insane. Never had she been subject to such worry before—not for herself, but for another. For Rafe.

She knew he was capable, coolheaded, and quick-witted, that he was accustomed to keeping himself safe, yet . . . she still worried. Incessantly.

It was driving her demented.

At least the fresh air, spiced with woodsmoke from the inn's chimneys, the silence broken by the occasional birdcall from deep in the wood, presented her senses with some degree of distraction. Walking briskly helped, too.

She reached the rear of the lawn and, with the chill starting to penetrate her cloak and clothes and touch icy fingers to her flesh, reluctantly turned and started back toward the front of the inn, intending to return to the warmth of the parlor. She was halfway across the lawn when a tall, willowy lady came around the front corner of the inn.

The lady saw her, smiled, and came walking toward her.

Loretta noted the pale, milkmaid complexion, the very pale blond hair, the easy, confident quality of the lady's smile, and relaxed a trifle.

The lady halted. With a yard between them, Loretta halted, too.

The lady met her gaze, inclined her head politely. "Good afternoon. I'm Mrs. Campbell. I'm staying nearby." She waved vaguely toward the town, then smiled engagingly. "Frankly, I've been starved for company, but then I heard one of the servants say that a young lady had just arrived here, and I wondered if you would care to share a pot of tea?"

Loretta smiled. "Thank you. I would welcome the company." And the distraction. She held out her hand. "Miss Loretta Michelmarsh."

Mrs. Campbell touched fingers. "Michelmarsh? I believe I've met your sister, Margaret." She smiled deprecatingly. "That would have been some time ago, however—in our first season."

"Margaret is my eldest sister." Which meant Mrs. Campbell was older than she looked, somewhere around thirty. Loretta waved to the front of the inn. "We should go inside— it's getting rather nippy."

"Indeed." Mrs. Campbell turned and, side by side, they continued toward the forecourt. "Mrs. Shearer makes lovely scones—I took the liberty of asking her to bring some to the parlor for us, along with the tea."

"Lovely." Loretta shivered as they rounded the inn. "I could use some warming up."

They entered through the inn's front door and proceeded into the parlor to find the tea tray waiting on the small table before the sofa.

Carefully laying her muff with the pistol still inside in the corner of the sofa, Loretta undid her cloak, swung it off, then draped the folds over the sofa's arm.

Mrs. Campbell had made herself comfortable on the sofa's other end and was already pouring the tea.

Loretta accepted the cup and saucer Mrs. Campbell offered her. "Thank you." She sat. "I have to confess I'm in need of distraction. My escort—we're traveling on to join friends—has deserted me for business. Until he returns, I'm very much at loose ends."

"Men!" Mrs. Campbell smiled, then sipped. "Are you come from London, then? Have you heard of His Majesty's latest start?"

Loretta considered lying, but Esme always maintained that the most successful route to prevarication lay in skirting the truth. "No, I haven't. I've been abroad and only recently landed. I'm expecting to spend Christmas in the country, although eventually I'll return to London. I live with my brother and his wife there."

"Ah, I see. So where did your travels take you?"

That topic made for easy conversation. Loretta started with Paris, followed their peripatetic route through France, Spain, then across southern France to Italy and Trieste. "Then we headed north to Buda. It's on the Danube, so we came home largely by river—up the Danube, then down the Rhine."

"That must have been quite an adventure."

"It was." Before Mrs. Campbell could ask how they'd crossed the Channel and where they'd landed, Loretta brightly asked, "So tell me—what is His Majesty's latest start?"

Mrs. Campbell set down her cup, settled back in her corner of the sofa, and smiled engagingly. "It concerns Carlton House and the Pavilion, as so many of His Majesty's starts do."

Loretta smiled encouragingly, pretended to listen, and wondered how much longer Rafe would be.

Rafe rode into Ipswich, apparently nonchalantly, in reality itching to look every way at once. Since leaving the Laughing Trout Inn he'd spotted two groups of cultists, both heading back the way he'd come. Seeking to avoid their notice, he'd ridden closer to other travelers, but such camouflage hadn't been necessary; as he'd foreseen, the cultists' attention had been fixed on those traveling away from the coast, not, as he was, toward it.

Those sightings had kept him tense and wary, but he'd yet to spot any cultists in Ipswich.

"Ho, there! Carstairs?"

He jerked his mount to a halt. Swinging the horse

around, he saw a tall, blond gentleman come striding out of a hostelry.

Rafe hesitated.

As if understanding his quandry, the man grinned. "You're a sight for sore eyes, man—we thought we'd lost you. I'm Jack Hendon." Striding up, Hendon offered his hand. "Allardyce and your Hassan and his Rose are in the inn over there, having lunch."

Gripping the proffered hand and shaking it, Rafe closed his eyes, then opened them. "Thank God." Immediately, his horse pranced. Releasing Hendon's hand, he tightened the reins. "I hope they're nearly finished, because I have to get back."

"Hassan and Rose said you had a Miss Michelmarsh with you?"

Rafe nodded. "I left her at an inn on the outskirts of Needham Market."

"Perfect." Hendon grinned again. "That's on the road we have to take. Let me fetch the others and we can be on our way."

Rafe dismounted, and with Hendon walked across and down the street to the front door of the Bell and Anchor Inn. He waited ouside while Hendon went in to collect the others.

Still on edge, he was scanning the street when the inn's door burst open and Rose rocketed out, closely followed by Hassan.

"You're safe!" Rose flung her arms around him and hugged him.

Beaming, she released him, then Hassan was there, gripping Rafe's hand, clapping his shoulder. "We were worried when you didn't arrive."

Rafe nodded. He'd been worried, too.

Hassan stepped back, making way for a tall, dark-haired gentleman with steady gray eyes.

"Christian Allardyce." He offered Rafe his hand. "Your other guard, and like Jack, very glad to see you."

Rafe gripped, shook. "And I'm inexpressibly glad I didn't have to go all the way to Felixstowe to find you."

"What happened?" Allardyce asked.

Rafe shook his head. "I'll tell you while we ride. I left Miss Michelmarsh at the Laughing Trout Inn, just this side of Needham Market. The inn seemed safe enough, but I've passed two groups of cultists headed that way—I'll feel more like talking once I know she's safe."

"In that case"—Jack Hendon waved them all on up the street—"let's fetch our horses and be on our way."

Royce and his troops located the manor house outside Needham Market easily enough. In a smooth, slick, and swiftly executed operation, they overran the cult's nest, subduing some twenty cultists and taking control of the building.

They isolated the man in charge, and sat him at the kitchen table. While the others moved through the house, searching and examining, and grooms kept watch over the rest of the captured cultists, trussed and deposited in the cellar, Del, Gareth, and Logan stood against the kitchen wall and watched while Royce, Charles, and Deverell interrogated the commander.

Who seemed very low on the cult's tree.

"The Black Cobra is gone—that is all I can tell you." The man's eyes bulged. There was little doubt as to his fear.

"Yes, but . . ." Charles—one very real source of the man's fear—tested the edge of his hunting knife. "You must know where your leader's gone. It really would be in your best interests to tell us."

The man shook his head. "You do not understand. We here are only foot soliders of the cause. The illustrious one would never tell us, share with us, such things. The Black Cobra is all-knowing and all-seeing. We follow wherever the illustrious one leads."

Royce grimaced. "More fool you." He rose, looked at Charles and Deverell. "He's telling the truth. They don't know . . ." He looked back at the man. "How long ago did your leader leave?"

"An hour ago—not more." The man's relief at being able to tell them something was palpable.

"How many men all told?" Deverell asked.

The man hesitated, as if realizing he was revealing useful information, but then he shrugged. "The guard—now twenty men. Plus M'wallah, the illustrious one's advisor, and Saleem, the guard captain."

"So including the Black Cobra, twenty-three, correct?" Royce held the man's gaze.

Resigned, the man nodded. "Twenty-three rode away."

Royce looked at his head groom, gestured to the cultist. "Take him down and put him with his fellows. Then lock and bolt the cellar door, and barricade it with that dresser as well. We'll leave them here for the moment."

The burly groom nodded. "Aye, Y'r Grace. I'll see to it."

Lucifer appeared in the doorway leading into the house. "There was a woman here—you only need to look at the bedroom. Silks and scents and candles all over."

Royce held up a hand, halting the groom and the prisoner he was leading away. "This woman—what happened to her?"

The cultist looked at him strangely. "Gone. Left."

Royce frowned. "With the Black Cobra?" Deverell had only asked about men.

The man hesitated, but then nodded.

"Do you know this woman's name?" Charles asked.

The man shook his head.

"I'm assuming," Royce's voice took on a lethal edge, "that you don't know the Black Cobra's name."

Rapidly, decisively—fearfully—the cultist shook his head. "We are only foot soldiers. The name of the Cobra is not for us to know." He hesitated, then, as if seeking to placate and convince them of his honesty, he said, "We knew one name—Ferrar. The other two . . . that was not for any to know, not even the guards who guarded them."

Royce's brows rose, then he nodded to his groom. "Take him down."

He turned to Del, Gareth, and Logan.

"None of those we've captured here are assassins," Del said.

"Given how many the three of us each faced, there have to be more," Gareth said. "Presumably they're among the twenty guarding the Black Cobra."

Logan grimaced. "We should probably anticipate that the Cobra's guards are all assassins, or at least of the group known as the elite—the better-trained fighters."

Royce nodded. "We can discuss strategy as we ride, but given the Black Cobra is only an hour ahead of us, and presumably headed to some particular place, then I want to get on the group's trail immediately."

No one argued. Royce led the way to the front door. Stepping out into the forecourt, with his gaze he sought Demon among the remounting riders. "With the condition the roads are in, a group of twenty plus riders shouldn't be hard to track."

Demon raised his brows. "That many?" He grinned, saluted. "I'll take point."

He urged his bay gelding onto the drive, moving to a jog-trot as the others formed up and followed.

They'd barely got one hundred yards from the house when an older man, by his attire and manner a neighboring squire out for a bit of game with his shotgun crooked over his arm and a pair of spaniels at his feet, stepped out of the woods lining the drive and hailed them.

Royce drew his mount to a halt.

Before he could say anything, the man bluffly declared, "I say—glad to see you've got those heathens in hand. Dab bit of work, capturing them like that—I was watching from the woods." The man squinted up at Royce. "You from the Lord Lieutenant, then?"

Royce looked down at the man, then inclined his head. "Wolverstone. I am the Lord Lieutenant."

"Oh! Well, then . . . glad you're keeping up with trouble on your patch."

"Indeed. But perhaps you can help us—have you seen their master?"

"Never set eyes on the beggar." The man raised his hand to shade his eyes as he looked up at Royce. "Did see her, though—the lady who's with them. Spoke to her earlier while I was on my way past—she saw me and came out to speak with me."

"Indeed? What did you speak about?"

"She wanted to know about the Laughing Trout Inn. It's a little place—a fisherman's inn tucked away in the woods a couple of miles southeast of here, on the other side of Gipping Way. Off the beaten track, but the Shearers keep it nice, and Mrs. Shearer's cooking is magic. Seems like the lady was after a good meal—said it sounded like just the place to satisfy her appetite."

Behind Royce, Charles leaned forward. "Did she tell you her name?"

The squire frowned. "Strange, now you mention it—she didn't. Very easy to talk to, she was, so it didn't strike me at the time."

"Did she say or ask anything else?" Royce asked.

The squire shook his head. "Just thanked me and went inside. I went on my way, but only minutes later I heard them ride out. A whole gaggle of 'em—don't know exactly how many, but through the trees I saw her, with a hard-looking heathen on her right and an old one with a long black beard riding on her other side." The squire frowned. "Vicious-looking lot. Don't know what a nice, civilized lady like her would want with such people."

Royce's brows rose. "That is indeed a mystery." He saluted the old man. "Thank you for your help."

The old man raised a hand in acknowledgment.

Leaving him calling to his dogs, Royce rode on. He glanced at Devil, equally sober beside him. "Down to Gipping Way with all speed, but after that, we'll have to go carefully."

He and Devil urged their mounts on, pushing to catch up with Demon, who was now well ahead.

They left their horses in a clearing just south of Gipping Way and, shadows slipping through shadows as the winter afternoon waned, went into the woods on foot.

Locating the inn wasn't difficult, but the instant he saw the large number of horses tied up out of sight at the rear of the stable, Royce signaled a withdrawal.

They gathered in a small clearing between the one in which their horses were tethered and the inn.

Royce spoke quietly. "It's possible they have pickets posted. We need them removed."

Charles, Deverell, Gervase, and Tristan held up their hands. Royce nodded. "Take a quarter each. Return here when you're sure all's clear. Go."

The four large men faded into the woods.

"Once we're sure all's clear, we need to secure the area." Royce nominated who would go where and watch what. "Next, we need to get what information we can on who is inside and where exactly they are—how many and who in each room."

Vane, Gabriel, Lucifer, and Richard Cynster volunteered to visually search the house.

"Team up with the others when they get back, search, then report back here." Royce looked at those still undeployed. "Meanwhile, the rest of us will remove those horses, so no matter what happens no assassins will ride away."

By the time they'd quietly moved in and removed all twenty-three horses from the rear of the stable, the teams sent to remove pickets and scout the house were drifting back to the small clearing.

Walking back from the further clearing where they'd left all the horses, Del frowned. "I would have expected twenty-four horses, but there were only twenty-three, and one had a lady's sidesaddle." He glanced at Royce, striding alongside. "The cultist at the manor seemed very definite—twenty-three men."

"I wondered the same thing," Royce admitted, "but perhaps one of the riders who left the manor rode on to Felixstowe or somewhere similar to carry some message on."

Del nodded. "Yes, that's likely."

They returned to the small clearing where all the others now waited.

Charles reported first. "No pickets. No one watching from the house, either. It's as if they're sure they're safe."

"If you think of it from their perspective," Vane said, "they have no reason to think they aren't—to imagine we're even following them, let alone so close."

Royce nodded. "So what's going on inside the inn?"

"The Closed sign is up in the window of the tap," Vane said. "There's no sign of life in the front room—the one that faces east to the lane."

"Nothing much clearly visible along the north face," Lucifer said. "The front door is shut, but through the two windows beside it I can see what I suspect are cultists in the front hall. Perhaps five or six. They seem to be standing guard, not moving about. Other than that, the windows of the bedchambers on the first floor are all curtained."

"There's more cultists in the rear rooms of the inn." Gabriel sounded grim. "I had to get around the stable, and slip across the yard to the laundry, but from there I got a glimpse into the kitchen. There are definitely cultists there." He nodded at Del and Gareth. "They may be your assassins— they looked significantly more capable than any cultist I've yet seen. They have what I assume are the Shearers—a couple and a boy who looks to be their son—tied to chairs around the table."

"Alive?" Logan asked.

"The woman appears unharmed, but both men have been beaten. That said, beyond bruises, cuts, and black eyes, they may well be all right—they don't look to be in serious pain."

"That's something, at least." Royce glanced at Richard, who'd scouted the last, southern, face of the building.

Richard met his eyes, then glanced at the others. "I think

you're going to need to see this. I found a good spot well screened by firs that gives a good view into the side parlor. Inside are two women—I'm assuming one is the lady from the manor. But there's a section of the room I can't see, not from anywhere. There could be someone else in there, but if there is, the women are ignoring him."

"What are the women doing?" Devil asked.

Richard met his gaze. "Taking tea."

They all looked.

"Anyone you recognize?" Royce asked Del.

Peering past a branch of spruce, Del shook his head. He looked at Gareth and Logan, but they shook their heads, too. Del turned to Royce. "We've never seen either of them anywhere—which means they could be either hostages or accomplices."

"There's another possibility," Logan whispered, his gaze on the parlor window and the unlikely sight beyond it. "We know Rafe was traveling with some young lady. Is one of those two Rafe's lady? And if so, where's Rafe?"

"Or are both of them simply hostages, or accomplices, or whichever, and Rafe and his lady are somewhere else entirely?" Devil shook his head. "There's no way we can tell."

"But what are they doing?" Gyles asked. "And where's the Black Cobra? Have we sighted any man who might be him?"

The collective answer being a resounding no, they concluded the Black Cobra was very likely in the parlor with the ladies—hostages or accomplices, whichever they happened to be—but because of the angle and the position of the window, he was hidden from their view.

"All right," Royce said. "What we have is the principal force of the Black Cobra—the central nest of vipers, as it were—here at the inn. Presumably they're here for a reason—it could be that they're waiting for something or someone, perhaps for Rafe, who's been captured and is being brought to them. Why here, we don't know. Why the ladies, we also don't know. But with the ladies in the parlor and the Shearers in the kitchen destined to be the first casualties if we attack, we can't make a move. As things stand, all we can do is watch and wait, too."

He glanced around, saw nods, heard no arguments. "But the one thing we can do is ensure that no matter what happens, not one of the bastards in there gets away."

Ten minutes later, a tight cordon of fighting men encircled the inn, ringing it with steel and well-trained muscle.

Satisfied, Royce settled alongside Devil to keep watch on the parlor, on the ladies within—who gave every appearance of amiably chatting while they daintily consumed scones and sipped tea.

❦ Twenty ❧

*R*afe couldn't explain the sense of urgency that gripped even tighter, sank its talons deeper, as he turned down the lane to the Laughing Trout Inn.

Jack Hendon and Christian Allardyce flanked him. Immediately behind them rode Hassan, with Rose up before him.

Hidden within the woods, the inn was still a hundred and more yards further on when two men stepped out from the trees bordering the lane and waved them down.

Rafe recognized one and hauled on his reins. "Cynster!"

Grinning fit to burst, Demon signaled him to silence and waved him to dismount, reaching for the bridle of his prancing mount.

Rafe swung down to the ground, slapped his hand into Demon's palm, and had it wrung. They briefly embraced; of all the Cynsters, Rafe had been closest to Demon. His gaze ranging ahead toward the inn, Rafe demanded, "What's going on?"

They all gathered around. The other gentleman who'd been waiting tipped a salute Rafe's way. "Tristan Wemyss, another of Wolverstone's colleagues." Rafe shook hands as Tristan continued, "We have the inn surrounded."

"Why?" Christian Allardyce asked. He and Jack Hendon were as puzzled as Rafe.

Tristan exchanged a look with Demon, then said, "Because we believe the Black Cobra's inside."

"What?" Rafe paled. His gaze locked ahead. "Loretta's in there."

"Oh, great heavens!" Rose clutched Hassan's arm. "The fiend himself has her."

Demon waved placatingly. "She's safe at the moment." He glanced at Rafe. "Which one is she—the blond, or the dark-haired one?"

Rafe frowned. "Loretta's dark-haired. But she was the only lady in the inn when I left, and Mrs. Shearer has brown hair."

"Mrs. Shearer's in the kitchen with her menfolk. Two ladies are in the parlor taking tea—presumably the dark-haired one is your Loretta. Also in the inn are the Black Cobra's guard, according to your colleagues mostly assassins, and we believe the Black Cobra himself, and his closest advisor and the captain of his guard, are also inside." Demon met Rafe's eyes. "They appear to be waiting for something, and at a guess that something is you."

Rafe nodded. "I need to get closer."

"I'll remain on guard," Tristan said. "Leave your horses here."

"I'll stay, too," Jack Hendon said. "We need to make sure no innocent accidentally stumbles into the action. The rest of you go on."

They did. Demon led them through the woods, then at a point where a stand of fir gave them better cover, they crept closer to the inn, to where, from behind a large tree, four men kept watch on the forecourt of the inn, its front door, and the front hall's lead-paned windows.

Rafe was welcomed with immense relief, not least by his close friend and fellow-courier Logan Monteith. Gabriel Cynster, another old friend, smiled and slapped Rafe's back. While Gabriel continued the watch, Rafe was introduced to Gervase Tregarth and Tony Blake, another two of Wolverstone's men.

Every impulse Rafe possessed was screaming at him to

rush in and seize Loretta, to keep her safe; contrarily, every experienced instinct was warning that rushing in without knowing the situation might prove fatal, for them both. He nodded at the inn. "So what's afoot?"

Logan drew him into a crouch alongside Gabriel, from where they, too, could scan the front of the building. "Ferrar's dead."

"What?" Rafe stared at his friend.

Eyes on the inn's façade, Logan grimly nodded. "Larkins—Ferrar's man—you remember him?" When Rafe nodded Logan went on, "Ferrar sacrificed him in order to get away with Del's copy. Then Ferrar himself took Gareth's copy—we'll explain how later. He was taking it somewhere, presumably back to his lair, when he was killed, too, and the letter taken."

"The copy was taken?"

Logan nodded. "Those here realized, then, that there was something else in the letter, not just the seal, that the real Black Cobra, whoever he is, didn't want to reach Wolverstone. But even though Wolverstone had had Gareth make another copy, so we've had the words to study, no one can see what the crucial point is. No names leap out at anyone, yet we're all now sure the Black Cobra is named in the letter. Yesterday, the Black Cobra sacrificed another man—Daniel Thurgood. He was Ferrar's half brother, who'd come after me and had seized my copy.

"Which brings us to here and today." Logan nodded at the inn. "It seems the Black Cobra wants every copy of that letter, and he's in there waiting for you to come back and hand the last—the original—over to him." Logan looked at Rafe. "Where is it?"

Eyes on the inn, Rafe replied, "I left it in the inn's parlor, on top of the dresser."

Gabriel glanced at him. "The parlor where we think the Black Cobra's waiting with the two ladies?"

"The parlor directly across from the front door. The window looks over the lawn on the opposite side of the inn."

Gabriel nodded. "That's the one."

Rafe's mind raced, considering, assessing. "I need to know exactly what's going on in the inn—who's doing what and where."

Gabriel glanced back. "Tony did the last circuit."

Tony Blake crouched on Rafe's other side. "We have men watching all four faces of the inn. There appears to be no one in the rooms facing the lane. As you can see"—he nodded at the façade before them—"there's men—cultists, most likely assassins—stationed in the front hall, but we can't tell how many. There have been sightings of people moving in the rooms upstairs—not looking out, but possibly searching. At the rear of the inn, in the kitchen, the innkeeper, his wife, and son have been tied to chairs, and are being guarded by at least five assassins. On the far side of the inn, the only room occupied appears to be the parlor. Royce, Devil, Del, and a few others are keeping a close watch on that room, but they can't see the area to the right of the window. They can see the sofa on which two ladies are sitting—your dark-haired Loretta and another with pale blond hair. Both appear English, both are taking tea, nibbling scones, and chatting—to all appearances oblivious of anything being wrong."

"So they may not know there are cultists in the inn?"

"We think the blond-haired lady arrived with the cultists," Tony said. "We're working on the assumption that she's a hostage taken from a nearby manor." He hesitated, then asked, "Is it possible your Loretta could feign supreme indifference to the cult, to the Black Cobra himself?"

Rafe nodded. "If it seemed the best thing to do." He frowned. "Mind you, I would have thought it more likely that she'd be arguing, giving him, or whoever else is in there, hell."

"We're not sure there is anyone else in the room with them. They don't seem to be interacting with or acknowledging anyone else." Gabriel looked at Rafe. "You know the room—could there be someone in the area we can't see through the window?"

Rafe visualized the parlor. "There's another armchair on that side of the sofa, and further back along the side wall, a sideboard, and then the hearth and the area before it, so yes, there's a significant section of the room that must be out of sight."

Tony cursed beneath his breath. "That's what we feared. We have to assume that the Black Cobra's in the room with them, possibly even with some of his assassin-guards."

After a moment, Rafe asked, "So what are we doing?"

Gabriel shifted. "We're sitting here watching, waiting for them to move."

"But they're waiting for me to arrive—they're not going to move until I do." His gaze on the inn, Rafe rose. "I'm going in."

"No—wait!" Logan stood, grabbed his arm. "You can't just go walking in there."

Rafe nodded. "You're right. I'll have to go back and get my horse. No need to tip them off that you're all out here."

He turned to march back through the trees.

"Wait!" Tony hissed. "You can't simply"—he gestured at the inn—"recklessly barge in there."

Rafe arched a brow, then looked at Logan. "Loretta's in there, very possibly trading insults with the Black Cobra. I'm not *not* going in." He glanced at Tony. "With all of you out here, no matter what happens, the Black Cobra is finished, and while the cultists don't realize you're here, the advantage remains with you. But we've reached a stalemate—one there's no benefit to us in prolonging. The longer we wait, the more risk one of them will see something and realize they're surrounded, and then the situation will rapidly deteriorate, especially for Loretta and the other lady."

Rafe looked at Gabriel, then at Christian. "At some point I have to return and walk into that inn as if nothing untoward

is going on. It's better I go in now than wait. None of us—
Loretta, the rest of you, or I—gain anything by waiting.
Once I appear, the Black Cobra will be distracted dealing
with me—he and his men in that parlor especially will
be concentrating on me. For those minutes, I'll be at least
equally in the driver's seat as he."

A second of silence ensued, then Christian nodded. "As
much as I'd like to say there's a better way, there isn't. You're
right. We need to bring this to a head, the sooner the better,
and to do that, you need to go in."

"*But,*" Tony said, exchanging an exasperated glance with
Christian, "Royce will have our heads, or worse, if we act
without warning him and the others."

Rafe glanced back at the inn, pulled out his watch. "Five
minutes." He glanced at the watch, then at Tony. "You have
five minutes to reach Wolverstone, then I'm riding in."

Tony went.

Rafe exchanged a glance with Hassan and Rose, then
turned and strode back through the wood.

On the opposite side of the inn, Royce was crouched alongside Devil behind a ridge formed by an old fallen branch,
watching the action, or lack of it, in the inn's parlor, when
Deverell appeared at his elbow.

Royce arched a questioning brow.

"Viscount Kilworth is here, asking to see you urgently."
Deverell looked toward the inn. "Apparently Minerva heard
his story and sent him on with one of your grooms. They
ran into our pickets, who brought Kilworth on. I left him in
the small clearing, but he's adamant about speaking with
you."

"Minerva sent him." Royce had to wonder why.

"There's nothing happening here," Devil pointed out.
"You may as well go and hear what Kilworth has to say."

After a second's consideration, Royce nodded and rose.
Leaving Deverell to watch beside Devil, he made his way
back through the wood.

Kilworth heard him as he stepped into the clearing. The viscount whirled. His face lit with relief. "Thank God!"

"Indeed. What is it?"

Kilworth grimaced. "Well, that's just it, you see. I'm not sure it's anything important at all, but Her Grace, Lady Letitia, and Lady Clarice all insisted I had to come and tell you." He spread his long arms. "So here I am."

Royce hung on to his temper. If Minerva *and* Letitia and Clarice thought he needed Kilworth's information. . . . "Just tell me what you told them."

"Well, that's another problem. It's . . ." Kilworth met Royce's eyes, then drew a quick breath and let it out in a rush of words. "It happened long ago and I have no idea whether it's true or not . . ."

His expression like stone, his temper reined with steel, Royce waited.

"I was at a ball," Kilworth said. "Years ago, when I was much younger. Looking about, you know, and I saw this young lady across the room, and she saw me and . . . well, I asked m'mother to introduce us, but Mama took one look, then scoffed and said that there was no more point introducing me to that one than in introducing me to Lavinia. Lavinia's m'youngest sister. I thought that was a strange thing to say . . . well, I understood the implication, but I knew m'mother exaggerated things, especially things to do with m'father. So at another ball I approached the young lady and asked her for a dance. She just looked at me— she really didn't need to do anything else, you see—then she smiled slyly and said she really didn't think that was a good idea."

Royce frowned. "Why didn't she need to do anything else but look at you—and from all of that, what did you deduce?"

"It was the eyes, you see." Earnest animation filled Kilworth's face. "Same as Roderick's—same as m'father's. No mistaking those chill blue eyes. But that's all I know— not exactly proof, is it? And there's no point asking the old man, because he won't say, but all in all, I'm fairly certain she's another of m'father's bastards."

He was missing something. Royce knew it. "Kilworth, why are you telling me this now?"

Kilworth looked at him. "Didn't I say? Her name is in that letter of yours."

"Your father denied he had any other bastards named in that letter."

"Bastard *sons*. He only mentioned sons. She's not a son. Well, he only focuses on his sons at the best of times, but a bastard daughter—"

"What's her name?" Royce managed not to roar.

Kilworth snapped to attention. "Mrs. George Campbell— Alexandra Middleton as was."

"Aside from her eyes, what does she look like?"

"Tallish, slender. Hair like Papa and Roderick—very pale blond."

Royce swore, swung on his heel, and raced back through the wood.

Rafe tucked his watch back in his pocket and reached to take the reins of his horse from Logan. He met Logan's eyes. "Wish me luck."

Handing over the reins, Logan slapped his arm. "You've that and more." He waited while Rafe swung up, then settled in the saddle. Looking up, Logan grinned. "Reckless rides again. Just take care."

Rafe dragged in a breath. They both knew walking into the Black Cobra's arms was literally dicing with death— especially for him, the last and vital courier. Jaw setting, Rafe inclined his head. Turning the horse, he nudged the gelding into a trot and started schooling himself—his expressions, his reactions—to those he would have had were he simply returning from conducting some business; that was the story he and Loretta had settled on to explain his absence.

He'd ridden into danger many times in his life, beneath

cannonades where one errant shell could blow a man to kingdom come. He'd faced death in foreign lands times beyond counting. That he might face death in an inn parlor in the quiet English countryside had never featured in his expectations.

As he trotted up the inn's drive, the sound of the horse's hooves on the gravel a sharp tattoo ringing clearly in the otherwise unbroken quiet, every instinct he possessed was awake, alive, alert—and screaming of danger. In the field he'd always had a type of sixth sense as to where, in which direction, immediate threat lay—and it was insisting imminent danger lurked beyond the inn's front door.

He wasn't looking forward to meeting it. He was a cavalryman; all his battles had been fought on the field with space enough around him to move. Fighting in constrained spaces, in a room with furniture and, worse, helpless innocents, was not all that far removed from his worst nightmare.

Regardless, he neither showed nor felt any hesitation in riding into the forecourt, slowing the horse, and swinging down to the ground.

He was being watched from multiple vantage points in the inn. He glanced around as if expecting a groom to appear and take the horse, then shook his head and tied the reins to the post not far from the front door.

He had little fear of dying. He never had had. One couldn't be reckless if one feared. He'd been a soldier all his life, and that's what soldiers did—gave up their lives if that's what was needed.

But this time he didn't want to die. This time, he actively wanted to live, desperately yearned to survive because now he had a reason for living, a future worth living.

With Loretta.

They both had to live.

For either of them to have the future they now craved, they both had to survive the upcoming engagement.

Yet if it came to it . . . he knew he'd give his life for hers, to secure hers. That was the only way he'd die today—if there was no other choice. But if there was no other choice to be made, he'd take that path, in an instant, without hesitation, and certainly with no regrets. She, above all, had to live, had to survive, even if he didn't survive to be with her.

She wouldn't agree, but he wouldn't be asking her permission.

The thought settled him. Gave him the certainty, the clear focus he needed, going into this battle. This fight within four walls.

With his usual nonchalant stride, he walked to the inn's front door, opened it, and stepped inside.

Instantly two sword points were leveled at his throat. One from either side, each held by an assassin. He let his expression blank—and hoped they read it as shock. Swiftly scanning, he saw four other assassins hovering in the shadows of the hall.

Another man—a much harder, more experienced, chillingly brutal-looking assassin—stood directly ahead of him, two paces into the hall.

He met the man's eyes. What had Tony said—a captain of the Black Cobra's guard?

With one finger, the man tapped his lips, then indicated that Rafe should shut the door.

Moving slowly, he complied, trying not to think about how solid the door was as it softly thumped shut and cut him off from the others outside.

The captain—Rafe decided to label him that—smiled, a totally unhumorous, unwarming sight. "Our leader, the Black Cobra, will be especially glad to see you, Captain Carstairs." To his men, he said, "Take his sword."

Rafe didn't react as the assassin to his right reached for his saber's hilt, then slowly drew the blade from its sheath.

The captain jerked his head, and both assassins stepped back, withdrawing their knives, but they didn't put the blades away. "You will do nothing that might lead us to hurt the young woman presently sitting with the Black Cobra—our illustrious leader calls her Loretta."

Lips setting in a grim line, Rafe inclined his head. So the Black Cobra was in the parlor.

The captain smiled again. "Just so." He seemed to relish having Rafe at his mercy. Then he glanced at the assassin on Rafe's left. "Search him."

Slowly, Rafe obligingly lifted his arms out to his sides. The assassin searched his pockets, his coat lining, patted his clothes, clearly looking for the letter. Rafe waited, but the assassin didn't search his boots—and so missed the knife he carried there.

Not that one knife would do him much good in this company.

The assassin stepped back, shaking his head.

Softly padding footsteps on the stairs had them all looking that way. An older Indian with a long black beard appeared. Stepping onto the hall tiles, he stared at Rafe and, frowning, came forward.

The man's black gaze traveled over Rafe, then returned to his face.

The Black Cobra's advisor? It seemed likely. The man wore robes of civilian style. The malevolence in his dark gaze was intense, almost tangible.

Eventually the advisor glanced at the captain. "I have had them search everywhere upstairs—the letter is nowhere to be found."

The captain considered, then looked at Rafe. Met his eyes. "We have not yet searched the young woman."

"She doesn't have it." Rafe uttered the words in his usual drawl.

Unsurprised, the captain raised his brows. "So where is the so-important letter, Captain?"

Rafe held his gaze. "I'm the only one who knows where it is. That shouldn't surprise you. Perhaps it's time you took me to meet your illustrious leader, so that he and I can discuss what he's willing to cede in exchange for the proof—such absolute and incontrovertible proof—of his villainy."

The captain considered him for a long moment, then

glanced at the advisor, who had been studying Rafe through narrowed eyes.

Some wordless communication passed between the pair, then the advisor glanced again at Rafe, and nodded. "I will go and inquire."

Turning, he headed for the parlor door.

Royce reached the fallen tree behind which he'd left Devil and Deverell to find that Tony Blake had joined them.

Before Royce could say a word, Tony informed him, "Carstairs has arrived. He's going in."

"*What?*"

Tony blinked. "It seemed the sensible thing to do—as he pointed out, we're at a stalemate. We can't move until they do, and they won't until he walks in. So he's going in. Any minute now."

Devil was staring at Royce. "What did Kilworth want?"

"He wanted to tell us who the Black Cobra is." Royce heard the cutting edge to his voice.

"Who?" three voices asked.

His gaze on the parlor window, on the scene inside, Royce felt a steely, warrior-calm take hold. "We've been watching the Black Cobra for the last half hour." He nodded to the scene in the parlor. "The blond. She's it."

The other three stared.

As had happened in other times, in other places, Royce suddenly knew exactly what to do. "We haven't much time. Tony—do another circuit at speed. Go to those watching in the lane first—send Charles to me here, with the rest to join Christian at the front of the inn. Tell Christian his men are to wait until they hear a commotion, then come in quickly and hard—I need his force to take down all the cultists in the front hall and in any corridors, or upstairs." Royce paused, then went on, "You join our men at the rear, and take the kitchen—again tell all there not to hold back. You need to account for all the assassins in the kitchen and free the Shearers as well. Then hold the room. Whistle like a warbler as soon as you're in position with those at the rear. Now go."

Tony went.

Royce glanced at Devil and Deverell. Gyles and Del were nearby. Charles would soon be joining them. "That leaves six of us to storm the parlor. We'll have to go through the window—luckily it's big enough."

Devil was already sizing up the window. "Big enough for two or even three of us at a time—we'll need to get inside quickly."

Royce nodded and hunkered down, intently watching the scene inside the parlor.

The parlor door opened and an older Indian appeared.

"Carstairs must have gone in," Royce murmured. "Tony will be in position within a few minutes. Once we hear his signal . . ."

Devil glanced at him. "We go in?"

Royce shook his head. "No. Then we wait. If there's one thing I've learned in all my years, it's that timing is everything."

Loretta was discussing the latest Parisian fashions with Mrs. Campbell when a tap on the door interrupted them.

"Come." Somewhat surprised that Mrs. Campbell had spoken the word at the same time she had—this was her private parlor after all—Loretta glanced curiously at the other woman, then looked back at the door.

Just as it opened, and a frightening apparition slid into the room.

An Indian man in robes. He was old, but how old was anyone's guess. His face was the color of walnuts, deeply lined, his hair, those strands that had escaped his black-silk-encircled turban, a straggling gray. In contrast, his equally scraggly beard was mostly black. A dead black. As for his eyes . . . when they met Loretta's across the room, her skin crawled.

His eyes were black windows through which a coldly malicious evil looked out upon the world and plotted pain and mayhem.

After the merest glance—enough to freeze Loretta—the apparition's gaze moved on to Mrs. Campbell.

The apparition bowed—deeply, in obeisance.

Loretta's jaw dropped. With an effort, she shut it, and turned her head to stare at her companion.

The old man straightened; at some point he had closed the door behind him. "The captain has arrived, illustrious one. We have searched him, and also searched everywhere else in this place."

Loretta glanced at the man in time to catch a lascivious glance thrown her way—realized with a sickening jolt that no one had searched her.

"But," the apparition continued, gaze again shifting to Mrs. Campbell, "we have found neither the letter nor its holder. The captain has suggested he should meet with you so that you may discuss the situation."

Loretta stared at Mrs. Campbell—at the woman who, until mere seconds ago, she'd believed was much like her or her sisters. Even as her mind scrambled to consciously accept that the conclusion her instincts were screaming was real—was the deadly truth—something in the woman's face changed.

As if a veil had fallen, revealing the true nature of what lay beneath.

"My God." Loretta was barely aware of the words that escaped her.

Mrs. Campbell turned her head and smiled—and there was nothing, not a shred, of feminine humanity remaining. "Yes, indeed, Miss Michelmarsh. I am your . . ." Pausing, she raised her brows. "And the captain's, most deadly enemy."

Transferring her gaze to the old man, she said, "How accommodating of the captain. I'm positively looking forward to discussing matters with him. Have Saleem bring him in. Two guards. And leave the door open."

"As you will it, oh illustrious one." The old man bowed even lower, then withdrew.

Loretta tried to will her all but palpitating heart to slow, to calm. If Rafe had returned . . . had he met with his guards? Was his appearance part of some plan?

Or were he and she on their own, facing . . . the Black Cobra.

It was so hard to take that in.

The door opened again and the old man reentered. He walked to stand by Mrs. Campbell's right, blocking what little heat came from the fire in the hearth behind him.

Loretta was suddenly very conscious of a chill.

Another man, a hardened soldier by the look of him, came in next—presumably Saleem. Behind him . . .

Rafe walked in.

Her eyes instantly met his, then she sent her gaze streaking over him, searching . . . but he walked with his usual sure-footed stride, moved with his customary horseman's grace. She could see no evidence of injury anywhere on him. Unharmed, her brain reported, almost giddy with relief.

And they hadn't even bound his hands, or restrained him in any way.

Two cultists—just a glance and she knew they must be those Rafe and Hassan labeled assassins—followed him into the room.

Saleem halted three paces in front of and a little to the right of the door. He put out a hand, halting Rafe beside and a fraction behind him. Saleem glanced over his shoulder, said something Loretta couldn't catch. In response the assassins took up positions on either side of Rafe, but behind him. From the way they held their arms, she guessed they were holding knives, poised to stab him if he made a wrong move.

Through the open door, she could see more assassins all but blocking the front hall. The attention of every assassin remained locked on Rafe.

Hardly surprising they hadn't bothered restraining him. They could kill him before he took a step.

The Black Cobra cult had taken over the inn while she'd

been sitting and chatting with Mrs. Campbell. Despite the very real fear slithering icily down her spine, Loretta threw the other woman a distinctly black look.

Rafe saw, and wondered, but he was too busy searching the room for the Black Cobra.

But . . .

Eventually, he brought his gaze to the only person in the room he couldn't place. He looked at the woman—the blond Tony had said had come from a nearby manor, who they'd assumed was a hostage . . . the woman Loretta did not like.

No hostage.

He knew the instant he met her eyes. No one seeing those ice-blue eyes, seeing the pure, undiluted, malicious malevolence that openly shone within them, could fail to mark their owner as evil.

Across his inner eye, his memory flashed a vision of James MacFarlane, beaten, tortured, and oh, so very dead, lying in the back of a cart in faraway Bombay. His jaw clenched. The cold fire of true hatred streaked through his veins.

That she was a woman became incidental. If he'd had his saber in his hand, he would have cut her down.

Sensing his comprehension, the Black Cobra smiled. Relaxing against the sofa, she considered him—as a cat might a particularly juicy mouse. "Welcome, Captain. We've been awaiting your arrival. And I'm glad to see that explanations are redundant, that you have realized that I am, indeed, the one you and your colleagues have been so assiduously seeking."

"We thought it was Ferrar." The longer he kept her talking, the longer he'd have to plan. His brain was already racing, weighing chances, risks, possibilities. Evaluating his strengths, her weaknesses. "Was it you who killed him?"

"Sadly, yes. Your friends in this country made that necessary—they'd taken too great an interest in him, and dear Roderick was never one to properly guard against danger. He never thought it could catch up with him."

"And Thurgood? I assume you sacrificed him, too?"

A flicker of some emotion, too fleeting for him to guess at, rippled through those ice-crystal eyes, but then they hardened. "That was regrettable."

Her tone suggested her namesake coiling, suggested that someone—very possibly Rafe himself—would pay for Thurgood's death . . . for forcing her to kill him?

Rafe registered the threat, but ignored it, too busy evaluating his options for saving Loretta. That came first. Saving himself came second, but if the chance was there, he'd seize that, too. As for the bitch of a Black Cobra, while he desperately wanted to behead her himself, if Loretta's or his life hung in the balance, he'd be happy to leave that to someone else.

There were at least three others outside who would do it in a blink.

Then again, simply killing her would be far too merciful.

"I believe," he said, "that you've been seeking something, too. Something I have." He'd evaluated all he could; it was time to get the battle underway.

"Indeed. The letter dear Roderick was so stupid as to pen." She glanced at Loretta, then returned her cold gaze to him. "I take it we don't need to threaten Miss Michelmarsh—or, heaven help her, harm her—for you to see the wisdom of handing the letter over, immediately, to me?"

"No. No need for threats. So undignified, don't you think?"

"I do." She inclined her head, watching him as intently as any snake. "I truly do."

Rafe had managed not to glance out of the window. He knew Wolverstone, Devil, and others were on that side of the inn, watching through the window. Knew they thought the Black Cobra was some man sitting to the blond's right, in the armchair that sat vacant to one side of the hearth.

He had to make them rethink. Had to make it clear just who the Black Cobra was. Shifting to stand formally at ease—as if addressing a superior—he kept his gaze locked on the woman seated at her languid ease on the sofa. "The letter isn't on me, or on Miss Michelmarsh. It's well hidden, and unlikely to be found—as your men have discovered. It is, however, near. I can retrieve it quickly. The question is: why should I give it to you?"

In one fluid, graceful movement, the Black Cobra sat up and leaned forward the better to fix her cold gaze on him. Not a trace of emotion showed in her face. Her voice was equally expressionless—not even cold, but truly devoid of all feeling—as she said, "You will give me the letter so you won't have to watch Saleem torture Miss Michelmarsh. He's really very talented and does so love his work." A flick of a glance went Saleem's way, a hint of approval, then her gaze returned to Rafe. "There's no one around to hear her screams, or yours. If you haven't yet realized it, the inn is entirely in our hands."

Loretta was staring at the woman, not so much in shock as disbelief. "You really are the Black Cobra."

The woman briefly met her gaze. "I always was."

It was a battle, but, as the Black Cobra returned her gaze to him, Rafe managed to subdue the rage her words had provoked. Jaw set, he paused as if considering, then took a risk—a reckless gamble instinct told him was worth the roll of the dice. "That answer might have worked in India, but you're a very long way from the safety you might have commanded there. And you've lost Ferrar. If you try such tactics here, now, you'll be hunted, and those already hunting you here in England are far more powerful than any opponents you've faced before—they're more than powerful enough to run you to ground."

Because he was watching for it, he caught the reaction—the flicker of uncertainty that so fleetingly marred her godlike assurance. After an instant of regarding him, she relaxed against the cushions again, but it was a studied pose. His words had hit a nerve.

"What, then, do you suggest, Captain?"

"I suggest. . . ." He looked at Loretta, then back at the Black Cobra; two could play at setting a stage. "I suggest that I surrender the letter to you on condition that you swear to leave us, and all others in the inn who are not your people, unharmed. You may tie us up if you choose. However, if you follow my advice, you will have no reason to fear pursuit. Once you destroy the letter, you will make it all but impossible for anyone to raise a hue and cry against you. Without the letter, the proof, without evidence of any serious crime committed here in England, gaining support for any action against you would be beyond the scope of anyone—even those presently arrayed against you.

"By taking the letter and leaving us unharmed, you will be able to walk untouched through the net those powerful men seeking your downfall will otherwise fling over you."

He'd been right; he could tell by the consideration that slid into her eyes. She feared getting caught, but was loath to lose what she saw as a game—especially one in which she was pitted against powerful men. She was a Ferrar to her soul. She craved power, craved acknowledged dominance.

If he could convince her . . . he chanced another throw. "Even your father would appreciate that—you sliding out of the net so smoothly."

Her eyes glittered; that arrow had found its mark.

A long, fraught moment passed, then she nodded. "Very well, Captain. I agree to your terms. Give me the letter, and I will agree to leave you, Miss Michelmarsh, and the inn-keeper's family, here, alive."

"To leave us all here *unharmed*." He wanted to give her the letter, but he couldn't make his capitulation seem too easy. Making sure those outside saw him hand the letter to her directly was the clearest indication he could give that she was the fiend they'd been chasing for so long. But she was too intelligent to risk a too-easy surrender; he had to wring from her a promise worth accepting. "And if you don't mind, I would much prefer you swore an oath to that effect."

Amusement, sharp-edged, flashed through her eyes. "Very well." She nodded. "I solemnly swear on my father's head that if you hand over the letter in question, then I will allow you, Miss Michelmarsh, and all those in the inn not in my train to remain here unharmed." She arched her brows, her gaze once again as cold as ice. "Is that sufficient?"

"Good enough." Good enough to excuse his next actions. He knew she'd never do as she'd said, oath or not.

"In that case, the letter, if you please."

"It's in this room." Rafe glanced at the assassin standing behind his right shoulder. "But I'll have to move to fetch it. No one else in here can."

She arched her brows. Looked at the assassin. "Let him."

The assassin lowered the short sword whose point until then had hovered a bare inch from Rafe's back.

Turning, he moved smoothly, unhurriedly, to the dresser against the hall wall. Going to its far end, he reached up, and retrieved the scroll-holder from where he'd hidden it mere hours ago.

He turned with it balanced between his hands.

The Black Cobra's eyes lit.

Still moving unhurriedly he walked back across the room, fingers flicking open the brass levers locking the scroll-holder's end in place.

Everyone was watching his fingers, the bright levers. No one said anything when he halted in not quite the same place he had been, but instead facing the hearth, his left shoulder to the assassin who'd previously been at his back.

He was now closer to Loretta, with no one between them.

He kept his gaze, his attention, on the Black Cobra as he opened the scroll-holder, reached inside, and drew out the single sheet it contained.

Eyes aglitter, she held out her hand.

Leaning forward, in full view of the window, he placed the rolled document in her palm.

Straightening, he waited, the scroll-holder with the lid hanging loose, its brass levers protruding, in his left hand. Not a great weapon, but it was better than nothing.

He watched as the Black Cobra unrolled the sheet, checked

the script, then turned the letter over and saw the seal.

The smile that curved her lips, one of the coldest calculation, sent a shiver down his spine.

Loretta surreptitiously shifted forward on the sofa. She wanted to stand and go to Rafe's side, but the tension in the room was so palpable she didn't want to add to it . . . but it was more than that. Rafe was watching the other woman like a hawk; his earlier tension hadn't left him—if anything, after Mrs. Campbell's agreement it had grown.

Encased in an aura of ice-cold confidence, Mrs. Campbell folded the letter, tucked it into her bodice, then raised her head. She looked at Rafe, her expression one of malignant triumph. "Thank you, Captain."

Without taking her gaze from Rafe, Mrs. Campbell tipped her head Loretta's way. "Thank you for your company, Miss Michelmarsh." A nasty smile lifted the Black Cobra's lips. "It truly was my pleasure to have made your acquaintance."

Smoothly, her gaze still on Rafe, the Black Cobra rose. Then she looked at her men. "You may kill them after I leave the room—sadly, I cannot afford to risk getting blood on this gown."

"What?" Loretta started to rise, felt the weight of her muff against her thigh and swiped it up as she sprang to her feet. Anger—fury, rage, and so much more—erupted from deep inside. "You promised!" Her voice rang. "You can't have us killed—you *swore*!"

Mrs. Campbell—the Black Cobra—favored Loretta with a smug smile and a pitying look. "I lied." Her smile turned infinitely superior; icy arrogance clung about her like a cloak. She shook her head. "It never fails to amaze me that people always forget that the female is infinitely deadlier than the male."

With that, the Black Cobra took one step toward the door.

"Wait!" Loretta uttered the word with such adamantine force that for one instant everyone was shocked into obeying.

In that instant, she thrust her hand into her muff, gripped the butt of Rafe's pistol, pulled it free of the fur sleeve, cocked the hammer, pointed the barrel, closed her eyes, and pulled the trigger.

The detonation rocked the small room.

Echoed and reverberated, shaking the glass in the window.

Loretta opened her eyes.

Silence gripped the room as the sharp retort of the pistol faded.

Everything stopped. All life, all movement, suspended.

Everyone stared at the Black Cobra, at the black hole in her left shoulder. At the red stain that grew and spread from it.

The Black Cobra watched, too. Then all color drained from her already pale face, her lids fell, and she slowly crumpled toward the floor.

Equally slowly, Loretta turned her head to look at Rafe.

Just as Rafe broke free of the shock. He had one instant to save them both. Cultists hated guns. They'd instinctively recoiled.

He smashed the open scroll-holder into the face of the nearest assassin, grabbed the man's long knife as he staggered. Whirling, Rafe swept Loretta up in one arm. Holding her to him, lifting her off her feet, he charged over the sofa, tipping it back so the seat flipped up, forming a barrier from behind which he could defend them.

At least for a minute.

Knowing the number of assassins in the front hall, he prayed a minute was all the others would take.

His first movement had broken the spell holding the cultists. Even as he'd grabbed Loretta, a wailing howl had erupted from Saleem's throat.

Rafe landed behind the sofa, pushed Loretta toward the wall, released her, and spun around to meet the enraged attack of the Black Cobra's captain.

He got the assassin's blade up just in time. Steel sheered off steel; sparks flew.

More assassins poured into the room, but before they could join their captain and overrun Rafe, the wide window to his left shattered.

The cultists cowered from the flying glass.

Before the debris settled, horse blankets were thrown over the jagged glass remaining in the window and men vaulted in.

Rafe left them to it and gave his attention to Saleem.

They hacked and slashed at each other. Rafe understood that the man was mad for vengeance against the one who'd slain his leader—but that was Loretta, who was squashed between Rafe's back and the wall. There was no way Rafe would allow Saleem to reach her.

There was also the matter of vengeance for a fallen comrade. Saleem might not have participated personally, but he'd been as responsible as his leader for every atrocity committed in the Black Cobra's name.

So Rafe looked to kill. Coldly, clinically, he searched for an opening. No matter how well-trained Saleem might be, he was better—and he was taller by a few inches, and had a greater reach.

He had no doubt who would win.

An opening came and he took it, cleanly, definitely. It was a better end than the man deserved, but it was an end.

Jerking the unfamiliar sword free, Rafe finally had a chance to glance across the room. Not a single cultist remained standing.

Chest heaving, he registered the sounds of fighting in the hall, and even more distantly deeper in the inn, but even that appeared to be subsiding.

A tall, dark-haired gentleman came striding back into the room, joining a taller, black-haired man who was checking the assassins' bodies.

The black-haired man rose. "These are all done for." He looked across at Rafe, grinned and nodded a wordless greeting. "I didn't check that one"—he pointed to Saleem—"but he looks very dead."

Rafe nodded. "He is."

The dark-haired gentleman walked over to the sofa. He held out his hand. "Wolverstone—Royce. Welcome home, and well done!"

Rafe took the offered hand, shook it. "Rafe Carstairs—and I'm very glad to meet you."

"We saw everything. You and your companion did a marvelous job. I couldn't have orchestrated it better."

Rafe finally registered the increasingly violent jabbing on his back. He shifted, allowing Loretta away from the wall. She hauled in a huge breath, shot him a glare. Unrepentant, he grinned. "Miss Loretta Michelmarsh."

"Wolverstone." Wolverstone reached for her hand, took it in his and bowed over it. "I'm delighted to make the acquaintance of such a coolheaded and resourceful young lady."

"Thank you." Loretta glanced, very briefly, around the room, then glanced—also briefly—at Mrs. Campbell, lying slumped on the floor before the hearth. She cleared her throat. "Is she dead? Did I kill her?"

Wolverstone smiled. "No—your shot was a trifle high. She's not that badly injured."

A crash sounded from down the hall. "The Shearers?" Loretta asked.

"They're alive and in reasonable shape. The father and son took some knocks, but suffered no major damage. But come." Wolverstone stepped back and waved them to the door. "Let's get you both out of here. Aside from all else, this is no place for a lady."

Between them, Rafe and Wolverstone helped her over the sofa and around the various obstacles that lay between her and the door, then cleared a path for her across the hall, shielding her as best they could from the results of the cultists' resistance. Rafe reclaimed his saber along the way.

Finally, Loretta stepped through the door, out onto the gravel of the forecourt. She drew in a deep breath and looked around, almost shocked to find nothing the least different in the woods, the sky, the sleepy lane.

A shaft of weak sunshine struck low through the clouds and bathed her unexpectedly in warmth.

She dragged in another breath, felt something inside her ease, dissolve. And started to shake.

Rafe's arm came around her, and he drew her close, against his chest, holding her, supporting her.

Then Rose came pelting out of the trees, waving wildly as she crossed the lawn. Hassan came around the building; a grin split his dark face when he saw them, and he came striding quickly to join them.

They met, all four of them, hugged and laughed and cried tears of relief. They were safe, all safe, and hale and whole.

Loretta met Rafe's eyes, and smiled, truly smiled.

Royce left the four travelers to their reunion and turned back into the inn. He and the others helped the Shearers set the inn to rights, moving bodies to the rear yard, tidying as best they could.

The one body no one touched was that of the Black Cobra. They left her where she'd fallen, slumped on one side, blood sluggishly seeping from what was, to their experienced eyes, a relatively straightforward, non-life-threatening wound.

At least one of them remained in the room at all times, just to make sure she didn't attempt an escape.

When Royce eventually walked back into the parlor, Del, Gareth, Logan, Christian, and Devil were gathered in the center of the room. Logan, Gareth, and Christian had just finished boarding up the window. Royce had just come from attempting to ensure that the Shearers were not out of pocket, but Devil had been before him.

Royce glanced at their prisoner. Alexandra Campbell's face had regained color enough, her breathing was quick and tight enough, to assure them she was conscious and listening. No doubt assessing if there was any way she could talk her way out of this, appeal to their chivalry, perhaps.

Looking at the other men's faces, Royce wouldn't give a sou for her chances. Every man there, and all the others gathering in the front hall, worshipped their ladies, even ladies in general, but when it came to villains . . . a fiend was a fiend no matter the gender.

Devil tipped his head her way and asked, voice low, "What now?"

Royce had been putting off the moment, waiting to make sure he had his reactions under control and could act impartially, as the law he represented demanded. Deciding to let instinct guide him, he turned, considered the fallen figure, then, soft-footed, crossed the room and crouched by her shoulders, tipping his head so he could see her face clearly, and she could see his.

After a moment, he said, "I know you're awake."

A shard of ice blue showed beneath her lashes.

He smiled. "I could, oh so easily, kill you now, and save us all the bother of organizing to deliver you to the authorities, and then making our case against you. Of course, that would spare you the ordeal of being tossed in a cold, dank cell, labeled a merciless fiend without conscience or remorse, and therefore being subjected to all the indignities that, as sure as the seasons, will follow."

He looked down at his hands, stretched his long fingers. Knew when her gaze shifted to them. He curled his fingers and hands. "Just one quick twist." He mimicked the movement. "You wouldn't feel a thing—not the slightest pain."

He kept his gaze on his hands, as if debating, deliberating.

"So do it." Her voice was deep for a woman, low, sultry, dark. When he glanced at her, she met his gaze. "Kill me now. You want to." Her lips curved. "All those others—your puppets—want you to. I don't know who you are, but I do know you're powerful enough that no one will ever question or challenge you."

When he didn't react, she went on, "What are you waiting for? Me to ask for absolution?" She chuckled, a dry, humorless sound. "I have no regrets. As you said, no remorse. Such emotions are for weaklings and fools."

He let his lips curve then. She'd answered the one question in his mind. "I'm Wolverstone. And I am very likely the one man in England who could kill you with impunity." He allowed a second to elapse, then let his gaze, his expression harden. "There's just one catch."

He looked again at his hands. "These hands"—he held them up, long-fingered, strong, and lethal—"caress my wife, stroke my children's heads." He shifted his gaze to her eyes. "I couldn't possibly sully them with the likes of you."

Her eyes narrowed to shards, shards that glittered with unrelieved hate.

His smile deepened. "No. I rather think I'll leave you to the dubious mercies of your jailers and the hangman."

Smoothly he rose, looked down at her dispassionately, certain, now, that his decision was right. "If it's any consolation, I daresay the crowd at your hanging will set a new record."

With that, he turned and walked away—and left the Black Cobra, pale and weak, lying, helpless, on the cold floor.

❧ *Twenty-one* ❧

No one had anticipated the triumph of the day, so the gathering that evening was impromptu and informal, but the emotions underlying it—the relief, the triumph, the need to share—were no less heartfelt for that.

Royce looked down the fully extended table in his dining room, smiling as his gaze touched the faces, so many familiar. So many old friends.

All animated, all engaged. All as one.

The Cynster ladies and Chillingworth's Francesca had arrived during the afternoon, drawn to share their waiting with Minerva, the Bastion Club members' wives, and the three ladies who had themselves directly contributed to the Black Cobra's downfall.

Each lady had been waiting in the forecourt, on the steps, or on the front porch to welcome her man when the combined party under his command had finally made its way back to Elveden.

Few homecomings had ever been so sweet. There'd been cuts and bruises, scrapes, and a slash or three to be tended; Charles got into trouble for trying to make light of his. That as a group they'd escaped with no substantial injuries was more a tribute to their comradeship, that they'd fought so determinedly shoulder to shoulder, each watching each other's back, than to their undoubted skill with arms.

To a man, the assassins had not surrendered. They'd had to be killed, and not one man of their party had stepped back from that necessity. Royce was proud of them all.

Of course, once the bustle of their arrival had faded, Minerva had decreed that everyone should stay to dine.

As everyone had been eager to hear of Rafe's journey and its triumphant conclusion, everyone had.

They'd foregathered in the drawing room. With every chair and perch occupied, Rafe had stood before the hearth and, with Loretta Michelmarsh seated in the armchair beside him, told their tale.

Loretta's great-aunt Esme was known to Minerva, Honoria, Clarice, and Letitia as a friend of Lady Osbaldestone's. Esme's relief—her release from the threat that held her trapped in the convent at Bingen—had therefore been promptly organized. Rafe, together with Gabriel, assisted by Christian, and Tristan, had been delegated to deal with Sir Charles Manning.

The end of the tale—not just of Rafe's journey but of Del's, Gareth's, and Logan's, too—had held all the ladies enthralled.

When the final piece of the puzzle fell into place and the identity of the Black Cobra was revealed, Royce hadn't been the only man smiling wrily, albeit very much to himself. To a woman, the ladies were so incensed that he was sincerely grateful none of them had been anywhere near the Laughing Trout Inn.

The female is infinitely deadlier than the male. Every man there knew that was true. All their wives were the kindest and gentlest of beings—unless someone threatened those they considered theirs, their husbands or their children. Woe betide any who didn't appreciate the tigresses within.

"It occurs to me," Royce said, catching Christian's eye, "that the major mistake the Black Cobra made today was in not applying the principle she herself exploited. She didn't treat Loretta as a potential threat. Didn't think she might have a weapon to hand, so didn't bother having her searched."

Wineglass in hand, Christian nodded. "She didn't imagine Loretta would react when she gave the order for their deaths, either, which was elementally foolish."

"Do you think so?" Honoria, seated at Royce's right, tipped her head in thought. "Actually, from everything we've recalled of her, Alexandra Campbell née Middleton has never been in love, has never had children, has never been touched by that particular emotion, so how would she know how a lady who loved would react?"

Put like that . . . Royce inclined his head. "Good point."

"Indeed. And you might be interested in something else we ladies recalled." Honoria leaned forward and looked down the table. Ignoring all formality—as they'd all been doing—she called to Letitia, further down the board. "Letitia, you put it best—about Shrewton and Alexandra."

"About what might have driven her?" Letitia's words had all the men about the table falling silent. She smiled and, with typical dramatic flair, with all conversation ceasing, claimed the floor. "Alexandra is the only child of Viscount and Viscountess Middleton, but she's definitely Shrewton's get. Indeed, she seems more like him in character and temperament than even Roderick was, and that's almost certainly what sparked her campaign to use Roderick and Daniel Thurgood, Shrewton's natural son, to advance her ends."

Letitia spread her hands. "Consider, as the daughter of the Middletons, Alexandra was minor ton at best, relegated largely to the counties, with no ready supply of slavering sycophants to pander to her ego. Imagine, if you can, Shrewton himself in such a position—his temperament would never stand for it. Alexandra's didn't either. She had to get out. Marriage to George Campbell was presumably her first step. But she couldn't control George, yet neither could he control her. He left her in his house in the north and spent all his time in London, gambling and otherwise enjoying himself. But Alexandra didn't stay left. She came to London, too, and, we assume, sought out Roderick. We can assume Thurgood—who seems to have shared her manipulative skills to some degree, and probably also saw himself as being owed by the Ferrars—had already attached himself to Roderick.

"So there we have the three, all Ferrars together, but Alexandra would have quickly realized that she was the strongest." Letitia paused and looked at Royce. "If you were to ask, and if Shrewton deigned to answer, I—indeed, all of us who know the Ferrars—would wager that were you to ask if he'd received a visit from Alexandra at some point while she was living in London, *before* there was any talk of Roderick going to India, then Shrewton would answer in the affirmative. She would, almost certainly, have sought her father's acknowledgment as the strongest, the most able and clever of his get. She would have craved that recognition—just as Shrewton himself is always so arrogantly insistent over having his own position recognized. And that position is about power. Just as he always demands that people acknowledge the power he's accumulated, so Alexandra would have wanted his acknowledgment of the power she wielded, including over his two sons, Roderick and Daniel."

Letitia shook her head. "But Shrewton wouldn't have given her that—nothing like that. He most likely wouldn't have given her the time of day."

"Kilworth said something," Royce said, "about Shrewton only focusing on his sons."

"Precisely. He is . . . I would say a complete misogynist only he's not even that. He doesn't hate women. He's simply utterly indifferent to us except as pawns or chattels."

"Ah—I see," Devil said. "Hence her comment about the female being deadlier than the male."

"Indeed." Letitia looked around the table. "What drove Alexandra Campbell to become the Black Cobra was all about striking back at her father—the father who would not, even privately, accord her the recognition that, by his lights as well as hers, was her due. So she took Roderick. She took Daniel. And she created an empire built on vicious, vindicitive, malicious arrogance above and beyond anything even Shrewton himself could achieve." With her customary histrionic facility, Letitia paused, glanced around the table, then declared, "And that's what the Black Cobra and her cult was all about."

For an instant, silence reigned, then Gabriel Cynster shuddered, and reached for a decanter. "I don't know about anyone else, but I'm glad it's all over, that the cult is no more and the Black Cobra's in jail, that the worst happened far from all our homes, and that our four returning colleagues"—he raised his refilled glass to the four: Del, Gareth, Logan, and Rafe—"succeeded in bringing it all to an end."

"Hear, hear!" echoed around the table. Glasses were raised in a heartfelt toast.

Then someone suggested toasting all those not present who had assisted in the adventure.

That list was long. It commenced with a somber remembrance of James MacFarlane.

"No longer with us, yet never to be forgotten." It was Rafe who said it. Standing, all the men raised their glasses and drank.

Royce noticed Minerva glance to right and left, then she grasped her wineglass and as one the ladies rose.

At Minerva's nod, Emily Ensworth proposed, "To James MacFarlane—a true hero."

Interspersed between their men, the ladies all drank, then, as one company again, everyone sat.

Royce felt his lips twist as, down the length of the table, his eyes met his wife's. He, for one, hadn't missed the message; when it came to matters such as this, not one of the men about the table would ever be alone.

They no longer fought alone, not in the wider sense.

The toasts continued in less formal vein, and soon real joy and laughter returned, sweeping away the lingering chill of the Black Cobra's tale.

Four of Royce's men had escorted Alexandra Campbell, sitting trussed in the back of a borrowed farm cart, to the jail in Bury St. Edmunds. She was now behind bars, guarded by a competent group drawn from Royce's, Devil's, and Demon's households, assisted by the somewhat dazed, but frighteningly eager local constabulary. There were cultists still free—a pair here, a trio there—but Del had agreed that they were unlikely to regroup and, lacking all officerlike direction, were more likely to disperse than seek to free their secretive leader, whom the majority of the cult had never seen.

The lower ranks of cultists had never known their leader was a woman, and her gender made an attack by them to free her even less likely.

Rafe looked around the table at all the faces he hadn't allowed himself to think about seeing. Not just Del's, Gareth's, and Logan's, and all the Cynsters', but also their until now unknown wives'. Wolverstone's, and all the rest. Even if he hadn't known them personally, he still hadn't let himself imagine meeting them. He hadn't let himself think beyond the final moment of the Black Cobra's reign.

But now he was there, beyond that moment, still living, more hale and whole than he'd expected to be.

Emotions raced through him, feeding a roiling cauldron of feelings. He couldn't tell which was strongest—triumph and jubilation, remembrance and sorrow for those who'd passed, a tingling, scintillating sense of expectation, satisfaction, content, soaring joy, and immense relief.

He felt them all, a giddy whirl where one rose high, then fell back to be supplanted by the next. Like a rudderless ship on a storm-tossed ocean, he pitched and swung.

Then he glanced at Loretta, seated alongside him, and his inner sea calmed.

She felt his gaze, turned to meet it. And smiled.

He returned the gesture, felt his heart swell. Beneath the table, he found her hand, closed his around it, felt the gentle pressure of her fingers on his.

And knew.

Love was the strongest emotion of them all.

Even as she turned to answer some query, he felt his smile grow silly, besotted.

Didn't care.

The Black Cobra was his past.

Loretta was his future.

And more—she was the reason he was there.

All the battles in his past, all the recent trials and tests, the hurdles of their adventure, he now saw with new eyes. He'd never previously viewed such events as having a higher purpose, not in terms of his life, but now he knew—they'd brought him there.

His past had brought him to the here and now, to this particular moment in time.

The moment when all became crystal clear, and his life took on a new direction, a deeper meaning.

Loretta held his hand, felt the strength of it enfolding hers, and rejoiced. She could barely contain her delight, her joy, her profound relief. She didn't want to think about that moment in the inn's parlor, a moment when fate had stared her in the face and asked her to choose. His life over another's.

She still felt stunned by her utter lack of hesitation.

Still felt stunned by what she knew it meant.

If it hadn't been for the ladies around her, for the way they, too, so transparently felt for their men, she'd be shaken, unsure, worried by herself.

Killing—even if she hadn't, she'd intended to and knew it—wasn't to be taken lightly.

But all she'd felt—the emotion that even now had her firmly in its grip—was so powerful it couldn't be denied. Not then.

Not now. Not ever again.

Sliding out of the conversation, she glanced at Rafe. Found his gaze on her, and met it.

Let her smile say all she couldn't yet say in words.

Then she briefly leaned his way, pressed her cheek to his shoulder. "Later," she murmured.

And returned to the world—to the celebration of success, the triumph of good and right that encompassed and embraced all about that long board.

Later proved to be hours away, but eventually the long and often harrowing day caught up with everyone.

Their carriages were called and the Cynsters and Chillingworths left, taking Del and Deliah with them. All the others remained and, Loretta had learned, everyone was expected to stay and celebrate Christmas, now only three days away. As anyone glancing at the heavy sky could tell, there was more snow on the way. As she climbed the stairs with the other ladies, she was composing a note to her family; she was perfectly sure they'd be satisfied knowing that she was safe, and that she was spending the festive season in such august company.

Smiling, still giddy, she, Emily Ensworth, Linnet Trevission, and Minerva parted from the others at the top of the stairs. The ducal apartments lay at the end of a long wing. Closer to the stairs lay the bedchambers assigned to the three of them who'd arrived unexpectedly with their respective men.

Loretta paused outside her door, smiled at Minerva. "I can't thank you enough for this gown." She spread the skirts of the magenta silk evening gown Minerva had lent her. "And all the other things, too."

"Nonsense." Minerva patted her arm. "It takes a certain fortitude to travel without luggage, and you've stood up to the rigors so wonderfully well the least I can do is assist you now."

Linnet laughed. "You should take her at her word," she advised Loretta, "if only to keep me company. I, too, own nothing I have on—only Emily and Deliah managed to arrive with gowns and actual luggage."

The sound of male voices on the stairs had Minerva glancing back over her shoulder. "Indeed, but now it's time we were all abed. Or," she amended, a decided twinkle in her eye, "at least in our rooms. We all, after all, have our private celebrations to attend to. Good night, ladies."

With a wave, she picked up her skirts and hurried down the corridor.

The three newcomers to the household watched the Duchess of Wolverstone reach her door and whisk through it.

"I've a suspicion we should take her advice to heart," Linnet said.

Emily nodded. "Indeed. She probably qualifies as an expert." She smiled brightly at Loretta. "Good night."

"I was about to say sleep well, but perhaps you can do that later." With a grin and a salute, Linnet headed after Emily.

Loretta opened her door, slowly stepped inside, and heard two doors down the corridor shut. Smiling, grinning, she shut her own door, and wondered.

Where, how—what should she do?

She'd barely formed the thought when the door opened again, and Rafe looked in. Seeing her standing dithering at the foot of the bed, he came in and shut the door.

A lamp had been left burning on a table between two windows and a fire was leaping in the grate. Between the two sources, there was light enough to see—to see that, as Rafe crossed the floor to her, his gaze, his attention, his entire being, was focused on her.

Her lungs seized even before he halted directly before her, before he raised his hands and framed her face.

Mouth dry, she moistened her lips, waited for him to bend his head and kiss her.

Instead, his gaze searched her face. Drank in every feature, then he looked deep into her eyes. "I need to tell you something—something I had absolutely no intention of telling you, not now, not ever. I never intended to let the words past my lips, not because I don't want you to hear them, to know them, but because of how they make me feel.

"But today everything changed." Rafe dragged in a breath, held her gaze, let it hold him. "Today . . . I thought, for one moment in that parlor, that I would die without telling you these words. Without letting you hear them, letting you know them. Without giving you the truth—that you are the most important thing in the world to me, and that I cannot live without you. That I would not want to live without you. If you had died in that parlor, I would have died, too—nothing is more certain. But even that . . . those aren't the words. The words I need to say.

"The words I can no longer not say. I can't hold them inside me any longer. They're too powerful. To me, they're too real, and too insistent. Too much now a defining part of me." He held her blue eyes, those lovely periwinkle blue eyes, and simply said, "I love you. I love you, Loretta Michelmarsh, and I want you to be my wife, to have and to hold, to defend and protect, from now until the end of my life. I want you by my side, now and forever. I want to spend my days near you, and my nights beside you. I do not want us ever to be apart."

"I want the same thing." Loretta raised one hand to cradle the back of his. "I didn't know, not until that same moment in the parlor, that I could feel like this—that I did feel like this. That the emotion that was already a part of me was so powerful, so complete. I didn't know it could wipe away fear, that it could bolster courage to such a degree—that it could make me do what I did, and leave me knowing I would do the same again, in an instant, if that was what was needed to keep you safe. To keep you with me. But even then I didn't know, not until we reached here, that this is how love is supposed to feel. That this, all we feel, you and me together, for never doubt that we're together in this, is the glory and the wonder that others speak of, that others strive for—and it's already ours."

His lips curved. "Ours if we wish to seize it." He bent his head.

"I do." She stated it fiercely, tugged him nearer.

"As do I."

Their lips met, and love rose up. Not simply passion, not mere desire, but something so much finer.

They knew the difference, felt it, tasted it, knew it in their hearts.

Sensed it in their souls.

This was joy, the ultimate pleasure, a delight that knew no bounds.

This was meant to be. Was how they were meant to be. Together in passion, in adventure, in joy. In reckless abandon and flagrant wonder.

In love.

Soft touches melded with murmurs, whispers of silk slid across heated skin.

Fingers touched, caressed, lingered.

Pleasure welled.

And love took them, joined them, raised them high on her passionate sea, and welded them anew, let desire and need and hunger collide and light the spark of her bounty.

Let ecstasy explode like a nova upon them, in them, over them.

Let bliss pour, at the last, through them. And fill the void.

Then love laid a gentle hand upon them, in benediction, in grace, and left them sleeping, tangled and slumped, sated and wracked, amid the billows of the bed.

At peace at last, truly home at last, together in each other's arms.

≈ Epilogue ≈

*O*n Christmas Eve, with the hint of snow in the air, all those involved in the capture of the Black Cobra gathered at Elveden Grange for a celebration, not of the end of the fiend's reign, but of life, love, and the future.

Of the passing of one year and the promise of the next.

The party was swelled not just by the Cynsters but by all those who'd joined them at Somersham Place for their customary Christmas Celebration. Minerva had ordered the rarely used ballroom opened; she and the small army of ladies staying at the Grange had spent the intervening two days flinging themselves with joyous abandon into the task of creating the perfect setting for their yuletide celebration.

Their children had helped, running here, running there, fetching and carrying, contributing in myriad ways both to the event and even more to the atmosphere. Even the infants had been brought down by their nurses to see and to be enthralled. To share in the event and be touched by the uplifting, invigorating spirit that seemed to flow and swirl like fairy dust through the house.

While the ladies had been engaged and their families absorbed, the men had taken care of business. Royce, backed by Devil and Christian, had notified the authorities in London of the known crimes and capture of the Black Cobra, of the involvement and subsequent murders in England of Roderick Ferrar and his half brother Daniel Thurgood, thus setting in motion the Black Cobra's trial.

On the day of her capture, Kilworth had remained outside the Laughing Trout Inn. He'd waited until Royce had come out and confirmed his half sister's involvement; from a distance he'd watched her led out and driven away. He'd taken on the duty of notifying his father of the fact, and of exactly who had been responsible for Shrewton's legitimate son's and his illegitimate son's murders.

After some discussion, Royce had written to Shrewton informing him of his illegitmate daughter's arrest as the Black Cobra, and of her pending trial. He'd included the information that she was being held in the Bury St. Edmunds jail in case Shrewton wished to visit her.

None of them imagined he would.

That done, the assembled gentlemen had wandered into the ballroom to view their ladies' efforts—and had promptly been conscripted and dispatched to the farther reaches of the surrounding woods to fetch boughs of fir and holly of the right size and conformation to garland the many doors, windows, and fireplaces in the house's reception rooms. They were also instructed to return with any mistletoe they might find, an order much more to their taste.

For two days a joyous bustle had filled the house. By the time Royce and Minerva quit the open double doors of the ballroom and turned to mingle with their assembled guests, all lingering vestiges of the Black Cobra's dark malice had been swept away.

Dodging a streaming line of laughing children—it was just after five o'clock; in view of the distance the Cynsters and their guests would have to travel home, and the light dusting of fresh snow that had appeared overnight and the everpresent promise of more to come, Minerva had decreed an early start to the festivities and had stipulated that all children, both at the Grange and at the Place, were also included in her invitation-cum-summons—Royce glanced at his wife, cynically if resignedly inquired, "Did you plan this from the start?" When she glanced his way, gray eyes widening in question, he clarified, "Is this why you invited all the Bastion Club wives plus their families to stay? So we could have"—he gestured about them—"this?"

Minerva blinked at him. "Well, of course." Her lips curved. Claiming his arm, she stepped close to avoid a throng of young Cynsters, Pevenseys and Gascoignes. "You're the one who's known for planning to the last degree. It was obvious that, if all went well, the adventure would end here, at this time, and that everyone involved would be in need of"—she mimicked his gesture—"this."

"Ah—I see." He did. While he had, indeed, planned to the last degree all that was physically, militarily, and politically possible to ensure the mission's success, he hadn't thought of, let alone planned for, the emotional requirements, although he now saw, understood, and acknowledged the need.

Glancing over the assembled throng, from the corner of his eye he saw Minerva's smile deepen. He turned to meet her eyes.

"Yes, I know." She held his gaze for a moment, then stretched up and fleetingly touched her lips to his. "But that's why I'm here—it's one of the many reasons you need me."

Stepping back, drawing her arm from his, she pressed his hand. "Now go and circulate, and I'll do the same."

Royce smiled and let her go.

She started into the crowd, but then glanced back and called, "I meant to warn you. Once we all sit and you finish welcoming everyone, there are a number of announcements—Devil will follow you and make them."

He arched his brows, but Minerva merely waved and headed into the melee. He hesitated, then made his own way into the chattering, constantly shifting sea of guests. He had a strong suspicion as to what Devil's announcements would be, but as he was bailed up, first by Lady Osbaldestone, then by Helena, Dowager Duchess of St. Ives, supported by Lady Horatia Cynster and Augusta, Marchioness of Huntly, all of whom demanded a full and complete accounting of all that had been going on—and expected him to provide it—he got no chance to speak to Devil or any of the four gentlemen he assumed were involved to verify his assumptions.

So when, half an hour later, he rose and, looking down the long tables filling the huge room, raised his glass and welcomed the assembled multitude to his home, when he asked them to raise their glasses in a toast to the season—to the success of the past year, especially of the past months, weeks, and days of their recently concluded endeavor, and to the promise of the year to come—and they all drank, he had no real notion, as he turned to Devil, seated beyond Minerva, whether it was appropriate to say, "And now I believe Devil has something to say regarding that promise of what is to come."

Devil's grin as he pushed back his chair told him he'd guessed right.

Rising as Royce resumed his seat, Devil considered his glass, then raised his head and looked out over the room, at the many eager, expectant faces. "We've come here today— been brought here today—by a confluence of events. Events that started many months ago in faraway Calcutta. Those events set in train a series of four journeys undertaken by four close friends, friends who, to accomplish their vital mission, reached out and tapped us"—with his glass he gestured to those seated around about—"many of us here, on our shoulders. We responded and banded together, and under Royce's direction, with the help of all involved our four friends have come into safe harbor, and have successfully completed their mission.

"So our four friends are with us again, hale and whole, but with one pertinent alteration. Through their journeys each met a lady, and each had to learn, was forced to learn as so many of us here already have"—smiling, Devil inclined his head to Minerva and Honoria, then swept his gaze over the other ladies seated nearby—"to trust, to value, appreciate, and venerate the talents and support of such ladies of like mind."

Devil paused to let the laughter, understanding and warm, roll through the room. As it quieted, he continued, "And just as those of us who have gone before them, our four friends and their four ladies have concluded that a successfully shared adventure is a sound basis from which to progress to a successfully shared life."

Devil raised his glass. "I would therefore ask you all to charge your glasses, to rise and hold them high, and to drink to the betrothals of Captain Derek Delborough and Miss Deliah Duncannon, Major Gareth Hamilton and Miss Emily Ensworth, Major Logan Monteith and Miss Linnet Trevission, and Captain Rafe Carstairs and Miss Loretta Michelmarsh."

With roars and cheers, clapping and laughter, to the sound of chairs scraping the company rose and as one raised their glasses and shouted after Devil, "To the promise of shared lives!"

All drank. Then under cover of the clapping, the laughter and smiles, eyes met, and couples who already knew the reality of the magic of a truly shared life shared glances, private smiles. To quirked brows, laughing eyes, and wordless vows, they sipped again, toasting each other.

Then the company sat, Minerva signaled her staff, and the banquet to end all banquets began.

Royce leaned back in his massive carver, looked out over the room, then reached out, caught Minerva's hand, drew her near. He met her widening eyes, raised her hand to his lips, kissed, then simply said, "Well planned."

January 5, 1823
City of London

Rafe met Gabriel on the pavement before the building in which Sir Charles Manning maintained a business office.

Rafe glanced back at the unmarked black carriage that stood waiting at the curb half a block away. Loretta had accepted that dealing with Manning would be best left to men, but had wanted to be near to hear the results immediately.

Gabriel blew on his hands and glanced about. It was early afternoon, yet even in this season the city pavements were bustling with clerks of all descriptions scurrying hither and yon. "Roscoe should be here soon."

Rafe nodded. Neville Roscoe's involvement in their plan had been a surprise to everyone. Christian had suggested asking Roscoe, who apparently knew a great deal about the shady side of London business dealings, for his opinion on Manning and how best to deal with him. Montague, the highly respected Cynsters' man of business, who also acted for Esme, had supported the suggestion; he, too, knew of Roscoe and patently valued the man's insight.

Royce and Minerva had come down to London as Royce had more yet to do with bringing the charges against the Black Cobra. Rafe was staying with the ducal couple at Wolverstone House while Loretta had returned to her brother's roof. But as soon as Manning was dealt with and Esme's release from captivity assured, Rafe and Loretta would head into the country, first for a visit with Margaret, Loretta's eldest sister, then to stay for a time with Rafe's family, who were, after all these years, eager, even ecstatically so, to embrace him and his betrothed to their collective bosom.

All those involved in dealing with Manning had met the previous evening at Wolverstone House. Royce, Rafe, Loretta, Christian, Gabriel, and Tristan had all been present, as had Montague, and, to everyone's surprise, Roscoe had sent word that he would attend, too.

When he'd arrived, Minerva had blinked, but then she'd smiled, welcomed him, then left them to their deliberations.

Roscoe had exchanged a look with Royce, but then had sat and told them what he'd learned of Manning's business affairs. Montague had confirmed some points, but had been intrigued to hear of others, his attitude leaving little doubt he considered Roscoe's intelligence sound.

Once all their information had been verbally laid on the table, they'd concocted a plan—a reasonably simple one they'd all felt would work.

However, while Roscoe had agreed that their plan would release Esme from any threat from Manning, he'd pointed out that the most likely result was that Manning would sell his shares to someone of similar ilk who would then take up where Manning had left off, and Esme and her fellow shareholders would once again be besieged.

Roscoe's proposal to eliminate that risk had made them all blink, but Montague had seconded the idea, and after a moment's consideration, Royce had given it his imprimatur as well. That had been enough for the rest of them.

Which was why Rafe and Gabriel were waiting for Roscoe to join them before confronting Manning in his lair.

The various bells of London had just started tolling two o'clock when the tall figure of Roscoe, impeccably groomed, turned the corner. He saw them and strode briskly up.

Roscoe exchanged nods, then tipped his head toward the door. "You lead. I'll play the part of silent and enigmatic supporter until we start explaining what will happen next."

Feeling very much like he was leading another charge, Rafe led the way up the narrow stair. They walked into Manning's outer office without knocking, awed the crafty-looking secretary and sent him scurrying into the inner office to announce their presence and convey their desire to speak with Manning on a matter of urgency regarding Argyle Investments.

Less than a minute later, they were shown into Manning's inner sanctum.

The man himself—a gentleman, well-dressed, elegantly turned out, of middle age and just a touch portly—rose from the chair behind a large desk. "Gentlemen." His gaze flicked from Gabriel to Rafe. "I take it you are the Mr. Carstairs who has recently become betrothed to Miss Michelmarsh?"

Their engagement had been announced in the *Gazette*

three days before. Rafe nodded. "Indeed." He gestured to Gabriel. "I assume you've heard of Mr. Cynster."

"Ah, yes." Manning's expression suggested he couldn't understand what Gabriel was doing there; the uncertainty took the edge off his arrogant assurance.

Especially when neither Rafe nor Gabriel made any move to offer their hands. Nor did Rafe introduce Roscoe, who had hung back by the wall just inside the door.

An awkward pause ensued, then, considerably more sober, Manning waved to the chairs before the desk. "Please be seated, gentlemen."

They all sat; Roscoe subsided into a straight-backed chair against the wall. Rafe hid a smile. Christian had warned that while Manning wouldn't recognize Roscoe by sight, learning his name would have a definite effect. Apparently Roscoe ran a number of questionable enterprises with an iron fist, but the code he adhered to was rigid, unbreakable; he was one of the few men in London guaranteed to put the wind up a slippery practitioner like Manning.

Like a jackal coming face-to-face with a full-grown lion.

"Now then, gentlemen." Manning clasped his hands on his blotter and looked from Gabriel to Rafe. "What can I do for you?"

"It's more a matter," Rafe informed him, "of what we can, or will, or might deign to, do for you." In an even tone, he related what he'd learned in Mainz, all the Prussian had told him, and described the sworn document, now in the keeping of a magistrate, that named Manning as the Prussian's employer in the attempted abduction and murder of Lady Congreve.

Manning rushed to open his eyes wide and spread his hands. "I had no notion of any of this. Clearly the Prussian was misinformed—it was not I who hired him."

Gabriel smiled, all teeth. "We thought you might say that. However, we've confirmed that you have acquired a position in Argyle Investments, a company with charitable aims, and are seeking to alter the company's direction against the wishes of the other, original shareholders. Of particular note, you borrowed heavily to purchase the shares, no doubt counting on a windfall should Argyle accept the offer made by Curtis Foundries."

"It's plain," Rafe said, reclaiming Manning's attention, "that were you to be pressed to repay the interest on those loans, let alone the loans themselves, prior to any windfall, you would be run aground—which leaves you with a very real motive to seek to remove Lady Congreve."

"Further to that," Gabriel continued, "we've confirmed that certain parties in the city"—he listed the names; as each was spoken, Manning's face paled a touch more—"now hold notes of hand from you. Each and every one is growing anxious for repayment. However, what you failed to mention when you borrowed from each was that you were simultaneously borrowing from the others." Gabriel shook his head. "Your creditors are not at all happy with you, Manning."

"Indeed," Rafe said, "you might say they're baying for your blood." He tilted his head, his gaze on Manning's now wide and fearful eyes. "Or they would be, except . . ."

To say that Manning was close to panic would be an understatement. He gripped the edge of his desk, in a strangled voice asked, "Except for what?"

"Except for me." The words, in Roscoe's deep voice, floated past Rafe's shoulder.

Manning focused on Roscoe. Frowned. "I don't believe I know you."

From the corner of his eye, Rafe watched Roscoe uncross his long legs and gracefully stand. Roscoe was over six feet tall and, like Wolverstone, exuded a pronounced predatory aura.

"No. You don't." Roscoe walked forward to stand between Gabriel's and Rafe's chairs. "All you need to know is that I now hold all your loans, all your notes of hand."

Manning's eyes grew round. His jaw went slack. "All?"

From beneath hooded lids, Roscoe watched him. "You, Manning, are a minnow swimming in a pool of sharks. You've been splashing in the pool, stirring up mud—the sort of mud that brings me looking, and the sharks don't like that. They'd much rather I stayed focused on my own concerns and didn't look too closely at theirs.

"So." Reaching into his coat pocket, Roscoe drew out a sheaf of papers. He fanned them out, showing Manning, who looked, and lost the last of his color. "I now hold these, but I haven't yet paid for them. If I hand them back to their present owners and tell them what I know of your finances, they'll tear you to shreds. As you know, given the nature of these gentlemen, I am not speaking figuratively."

Manning wasn't stupid. Terrified to his toes, but not stupid. He raised his eyes to Roscoe's. "What do I have to do?"

Roscoe smiled, a chilling sight. "To make this nightmare go away you need to do two things. One—make all your shares in Argyle Investments over to me. And two—retire from the city and never let me hear of you dabbling in investments again."

Manning paused. "If I make over the shares, you'll redeem the notes of hand, the loans?"

Roscoe nodded. "I will." He tipped his head at Gabriel and Rafe. "These two gentlemen can bear witness to my word."

Both nodded.

Manning noted their certainty, then looked up at Roscoe. "As for the second stipulation, I—"

"Let me be frank." Roscoe spoke over him. "I don't like having shady characters like you operating in the same market I do. You may be well born, but you give us all a bad name. Removing you permanently would be no great difficulty— many in the city expect me to effect your disappearance, one way or another, now that I know you've been muddying our waters. I can't be seen to be weak, after all—so one way or another, you will go." Roscoe's thin-lipped smile was the epitome of deadly. "I'm merely being kind enough to allow you to choose the manner in which you disappear."

The trick in uttering threats, Rafe knew, was to believe in them yourself. In Roscoe's case, there was absolutely no doubt that he meant every word.

Manning was outgunned, outclassed. Never taking his

eyes from Roscoe's hooded ones, he nodded. "I'll have my secretary draw up the necessary papers."

Roscoe smiled approvingly. "Excellent." He looked at Rafe, then Gabriel. "I believe I can handle matters from this point, gentlemen." He glanced at Manning as Rafe and Gabriel rose. "And I believe you may inform Lady Congreve that Manning here has lost all interest in her continuing health, in light of concerns over his own. Is that correct, Manning?"

"Yes. I mean . . ." Manning dragged in a breath. "I never had any interest in her ladyship's health, and I certainly have none now."

Rafe smiled. "Excellent. I'm sure she'll be delighted to hear that." With a nod to Roscoe, he headed for the door.

Gabriel followed him out of the room, down the stairs, and out of the front door. He halted on the pavement and held out his hand to Rafe. "An excellent outcome all around. I'd heard whispers that Roscoe dabbled in some non-profit-making enterprises, but for all his obvious presence, the man prizes his privacy. Still, you can tell Lady Congreve that Argyle Investments have a new shareholder and a very able protector."

Shaking his hand, Rafe nodded. "Thank you for your help."

Gabriel smiled. "That's what old friends are for."

They grinned, exchanged salutes, then Rafe headed for the carriage while Gabriel strode off in the opposite direction.

Loretta leaned forward as Rafe opened the carriage door and climbed in. "Well? How did it go? What happened?"

Still grinning, Rafe closed the door, dropped onto the seat beside her, pulled her to him and kissed her soundly.

Then he told her all that had happened, ending with the need to send an express letter to Esme in Bingen informing her that it was safe to come home.

"Thank goodness." Loretta leaned against his shoulder, comfortable within the circle of his arms. "She'll be home in a month or so, in good time for our wedding." She met Rafe's eyes. "I wouldn't have wanted to get married without her."

Rafe laughed. "I wouldn't dare."

The carriage turned into Mayfair. He glanced down, and saw a pensive expression on Loretta's face. "What is it?"

She looked up, then smiled. "I was just imagining—trying to imagine—the next meeting of the board of Argyle Investments. What do you think will happen when Esme and Roscoe meet?"

Rafe thought, then said, "I think they'll get on famously."

Loretta nodded. "Esme has little respect for rules. I rather think Roscoe's the same."

Rafe thought of Roscoe, of Esme, and of them both together. He grinned. "I suspect it's the other investors in Argyle who are in for a disconcerting time."

May 29, 1823
London

Alexandra Millicent Campbell, née Middleton, the lady who'd achieved notoriety as the Black Cobra, was hanged that afternoon.

None of the four officers who had played the crucial roles in her exposure and downfall attended.

They'd been far too busy attending their wives.

Deliberately. They'd discussed it, and had each decided that watching the hanging would do them no good. Their part in the Black Cobra's saga had ended on the twenty-second of December. Since then, all four had been actively building their new lives.

None of them saw any need to step back into their past.

That said, they hadn't been able to escape attention entirely.

The news of the arrest of a well-bred Englishwoman for unspeakable crimes committed both in India and more recently in England had broken in early January. The news sheets had fallen on the story with glee. The first reports had been so hysterical that the four couples had been seriously disturbed. Even distressed. By their very wildness the reports turned the Black Cobra into a fantastical figure, by contrast cheapening and lessening, certainly showing scant respect for, the many horrific deaths she'd caused.

That was when Loretta had confessed that she had the ability to write their history as they would have it told, and to have it published verbatim. They'd all been stunned, then delighted, and had accepted her offer gratefully. Thus the *True Story of the Black Cobra* came to be penned by that well-established columnist, *A Young Lady About London,* who had herself only recently returned from a trip through Europe, as witnessed by her *Window on Europe* vignettes. It was popularly supposed that the Young Lady had met the officer-couriers on her journey and had gained their confidence.

With no hope of finding any similar sources of such compelling and verifiable truth, the other news sheets regretfully dropped the story, leaving the *London Enquirer* to enjoy popular success beyond its publisher's wildest dreams.

The serialized *True Story of the Black Cobra* had concluded with a hair-raising account of the fiend's capture, that had been published six weeks before the commencement of Alexandra Campbell's trial.

With the public's focus switching to the Old Bailey, the four couples had been able to retire from the public eye—and attend to the matter of their weddings.

Through the early weeks of the season, they'd been very much the heros and heroines of the hour. Del, Gareth, Logan, and Rafe had been publicly lauded for their bravery, loaded with medals, pensions, and awards from the army and the East India Company—and unexpectedly created barons by a sovereign sincerely grateful to have the public distracted from his own shortcomings and thoroughly relieved not to have been personally mired in the scandal.

However, once loaded with said honors, and with the news that they were all as rich as nabobs somehow circulating through the ton, Del, Gareth, Logan, and Rafe had found it expedient to cling to their fianceés' arms, if not their skirts.

Rafe had declared he'd rather face a couple of cult assassins than the ton's matchmakers with him in their sights.

They'd married as soon as they'd been able to arrange it, and by chance the order of their weddings had matched the order in which they'd returned to England's shores. The other three couples had traveled first north across the Humber, to the tiny church at Middleton on the Wolds, where the men had stood as groomsmen and the ladies as bridesmaids and watched Del and Deliah exchange their vows.

The couple had left the church beneath an archway of sabers held by all the members of their old regiment who had attended, the Cynsters among them, with the ranks further swelled by the members of the Bastion Club. Del's aunts had been beyond delighted with the outcome of their matchmaking.

From there, the cavalcade had moved on to Oxfordshire, to the sleepy village where Emily had grown up and outside of which her parents still lived. Another happy ceremony had ensued, filled with the cheer of a larger, very welcoming family.

By then, the guests and the brides and grooms had become a tight-knit traveling party. They'd journeyed to Plymouth, and found the *Esperance* waiting. A brisk run to St. Peter Port had given too many of the ladies too many ideas, then a journey across the island in donkey-drawn carriages had delivered them to Mon Coeur for a magical week. The highlight had been Logan and Linnet's wedding in the tiny church on the cliffs above Rocquaine Bay. Will gave Linnet away, Jen and Gilly were flowergirls, with Brandon and Chester as pages. Muriel and Buttons had never stopped beaming.

Last to tie the knot had been Rafe and Loretta. They'd spoken their vows before the altar of the church in the small village midway between Loretta's sister Margaret's house and Rafe's family home—a village Rafe and Loretta had selected as their own, and outside of which they'd bought a sprawling manor house to make into their home.

There hadn't been a dry feminine eye in the church as, pronounced man and wife, the pair had kissed, then turned, and, radiant, the both of them, had started back up the aisle, the joy in their faces as they'd embarked on their new life a joy of its own to behold.

So now they were all married, and had gathered in Del and Deliah's London town house to see out the final chapter in the story that had brought them together.

The trial had been lengthy, but straightforward. Throughout the accused had uttered not one word. Regardless, the nature of the charges, coupled with her arrogant, contemptuously silent attitude and the details of her birth and connections, had ensured that the news sheets had never been short of fodder.

Once Alexandra Campbell's connection to the Earl of Shrewton had become public knowledge, the public as well as the ton had taken to labeling the trio who had created and governed the Black Cobra cult as "Shrewton's nest of vipers." The earl had had no choice but to retire from public life and go into social exile, leaving Kilworth—untouched by the scandal and supported by Wolverstone, St. Ives, and the grandes dames—to be the public face of the family.

As Royce had prophesied, Alexandra Campbell's hanging had drawn a record crowd.

"But now it's over." Deliah pushed back from her elegant dining table. "I suggest we all repair to the drawing room—bring the decanters, if you wish. It's a balmy night and the windows are open in there—it'll be much more pleasant."

Emily, Linnet, and Loretta rose and joined Deliah for the short stroll down the corridor to the lovely drawing room in which they'd congregated earlier; on the first floor, the room looked over Green Park, wide windows giving access to an iron-railed balcony.

Exchanging relaxed grins, the men rose, too. Falling in with Deliah's suggestion, each picked up a cut-crystal tumbler, Del picked up the decanter of port and Rafe the one of brandy, then they ambled in their ladies' wakes.

In the drawing room they discovered the ladies already disposed on the chaises chatting about ton affairs. Setting the decanters on the sideboard, they helped themselves to drinks, then, after one glance at the feminine conference taking place before the hearth, stepped out onto the balcony.

With all four of them on it, the balcony seemed small. Their backs to the windows, they stood shoulder to shoulder, and, as if drawn, looked up at the stars.

"The night sky, the stars, were very different there."

None of the others needed to ask which "there" Logan referred to.

Silence held them. Memories stirred, rose, then washed through them.

Then Del raised his glass. "To absent friends."

Gareth held his glass to the stars. "Gone, but not forgotten."

"Never that," Logan murmured, lifting his glass, too.

After a heartbeat's pause, Rafe raised his glass. "To James MacFarlane, the true hero without whom we wouldn't have reached today, without whose bravery we would not have seen the end of the Black Cobra." Eyes on the black velvet sky, he said, "Vale, James. Rest in peace."

He sipped, then drained his glass.

With soft hear-hears, the others did the same.

Silence fell—a silence filled with regrets released, with the simple knowledge of vengeance fulfilled, of promises kept, not broken. Of a man, a younger man than they, who would live forever in their memories.

Then a stir at their backs had them turning.

"What are you all doing out there?" From the other side of the windows, Deliah frowned at them as if she didn't know precisely where their thoughts had strayed. She beckoned imperiously, ignoring the sudden gravity that had infected them. "Come inside—we're discussing plans for later this summer. If you don't come and listen, and make your wishes known, you might just discover that our plans are set in stone."

The four men exchanged glances, then slow smiles broke across their faces, dispelling their solemnity. Dispelling the past.

One after another they stepped back across the sill, looking ahead caught their respective lady's eyes, and followed Deliah deeper into the room.

Back to what now mattered most.

Their wives, their homes, their prospective families—all solidly rooted in the green fields of England.

CAPTAIN JACK'S WOMAN

Bored by society's rules and strictures,
Kathryn 'Kit' Cranmer yearns for adventure – and
finds it on Britain's rugged eastern coast, dressed as a boy
at the head of a rag-tag band of smugglers. But there is
another who rules the night: the notorious Captain Jack,
ruthless leader of a rival gang . . . who stops Kit's breath
with his handsome features and powerful physique.

When Captain Jack sees through Kit's brazen
disguise, he tempts her with kisses that compel her to
surrender her cherished independence. But her lover is
much more than he seems – a man of secrets and dangerous
mystery – and becoming Captain Jack's woman will
carry Kit into a world of sensuous pleasures
and unparalleled perils . . .

978-0-7499-4018-8

THE LADY CHOSEN

Tristan Wemyss, Earl of Trentham,
never expected he'd need to wed within a year or
forfeit his inheritance. But he is not one to bow to the
matchmaking mamas of the ton. No, he will marry a lady
of his own choosing – the enchanting neighbour next door.
Miss Leonora Carling has beauty, spirit and passion;
unfortunately, matrimony is the last
thing on her mind . . .

Once bitten, forever shy – never again will
Leonora allow any man to capture her heart and break it.
But Tristan is a seasoned campaigner who will not accept
defeat, especially when a mysterious blackguard with
dark designs on Leonora's home gives him the excuse
to come to the lady's aid – as her protector,
confidant, seducer . . . and husband.

978-0-7499-4023-2

A GENTLEMAN'S HONOUR

The season has yet to begin, and Anthony Blake,
Viscount Torrington, is already a target for every
matchmaking mama in London. But there is only
one lady who sparks his interest . . .

Desperate and penniless, but determined,
Alicia plans to make an excellent match for her ravishing
younger sister. But one moonlit stroll may prove Alicia's
undoing when it leads to an accusation of murder.

Every instinct Tony Blake possesses tells
him that Alicia – the exquisite beauty he discovers
standing over a dead body – is innocent of serious
wrongdoing. His social prominence will certainly work
in her favour. But it is more than honour that compels
Tony to protect her – and he will do everything in his
seductive power to make Alicia his.

978-0-7499-4028-7

A LADY OF
HIS OWN

Impatient to find his bride-to-be yet
appalled by the damsels of the ton, Charles St Austell
seeks refuge in his castle and discovers Lady Penelope
Selborne walking the deserted corridors at midnight.
Years ago they'd consummated their youthful passion
one unforgettable afternoon. While the ardent
interlude still haunts Charles, Penny vowed never
again to be seduced by the dashing Earl.

But resisting a stronger, battle-hardened Charles
proves difficult, and when a traitorous intrigue threatens
them both, Penny discovers that her first love is her
fated champion and protector – and will not rest
until he has made her his own . . .

978-0-7499-4033-1